The Betting Shop

Keith Wild

Pen Press

First published in Great Britain by Pen Press

All paper used in the printing of this book has been made from wood grown in
managed, sustainable forests.

ISBN: 978-1-78003-379-2

Printed and bound in the UK
Pen Press is an imprint of
Indepenpress Publishing Limited
25 Eastern Place
Brighton
BN2 1GJ

A catalogue record of this book is available from
the British Library

Cover design by Jacqueline Abromeit

Author's Notes

Following the publishing of The Station in 2010, this book is number two of my promised trilogy. Again it is mostly based in Surrey and about a family torn apart by deceit and greed.

The book is deliberately aimed at confirming what life really is like and especially how blind ambition and get-rich schemes can be a quick route to disaster.

The feedback was amazing from book one, The Station, and although many people liked it, thank goodness some didn't! The reason is that negative comments have helped me plan The Betting Shop in just the same way, so sorry folks, if you don't like it, it's just tough.

I do, however, hope you enjoy it and again any comments are really welcome.

Keep up-to-date with comments this book on www.keithwild.com, or email me at boxbored@aol.com.

Keith Wild
May 2012

Preface

Throughout life we all intend to do things that we know we are most unlikely to get around to.

The dying person may still wish the extreme and the impossible, or maybe just wish that they had visited a faraway place, eaten in a restaurant with a Michelin star, met a famous person or even to have made love more often and possibly with more people.

This book describes the pain caused by double-crossing and deceit between so-called friends, resulting in a battle for one man to achieve everything he has promised himself after serving a short sentence in prison.

Initially he wanted to find out who grassed him up to the police, but as the search for the truth begins, to track down the person or persons unknown, a much more sinister set of circumstances occur. Mark Lavender makes it very clear to everyone what his intentions are.

The recession had hit hard in 2008 and many people suddenly found their investments, pensions and disposable income reduced dramatically in a matter of weeks.

The stability of the country was at risk, massive unsecured debt was revealed, the banks were panicking, and the USA started a financial run as property portfolios where discovered to be seriously overvalued. The wheel had again come a full financial circle and controls on lenders were shown to be totally inadequate.

In the UK the easy opportunity to obtain mortgages and loans was all but withdrawn and many youngsters were renting or living with their parents; some were sitting on whatever money they had saved, waiting for times to get better, if they ever did.

The chances to get easy money for Luke and Vince were slim; they sat in their local pub, The Plough in Sutton, as Luke worked out a plan. It spelt danger but it was quick money with a minimum of risk. Crime always carried some risk, but Luke had weighed it up and he had much less to lose than his friend. They had good information on their target and they expected little resistance.

The job would require a firearm and Luke had difficulty at first convincing Vince that he would only use it to frighten, and not to kill or wound. The possession of the weapon would classify them as armed robbers and it worried him. He knew that to be certain of success they needed to be tooled up; he just hoped they didn't have to use the weapon.

Alternatives to get money quick were few and far between; the more pints of lager the men drank, the easier the whole idea became. In reality it would soon have many more implications than they could ever have anticipated.

The subject of money was far from the minds of the 22 rain-sodden footballers kicking the hell out of each other on pitch number one a couple of miles away at Tudor Drive, Morden.

The match was crucial for Ronnie Smith; he paid for the team's shirts, ground, dressing rooms and then the unofficial bungs of fivers passed to his team in the pub after the game.

He was a wannabe big league soccer team owner, his technical knowledge of the game was very limited and as he stared through the driving rain he could just about pick out which players on the field were in his team.

Ronnie wanted recognition; sometimes he thought that all he was good for was shelling out money to his over-the-hill players. To his credit, he had stuck at it with them but now he was almost ready to quit and put his long-term plans into action.

His right-hand man and team coach was a long-retired Chelsea player called Steve Foy. Ronnie was convinced Foy would help him to achieve his ambition to win both the local Sunday League and the County Cup. Performances from his players did sometimes depend on how much, and what, they had consumed on a Saturday night but as long as Ronnie got the end result he didn't care. He would buy players for boot money and tell Steve to get rid of ones that let him down.

Achilles FC had lost only one game in a year and Ronnie was convinced that the referee had been got at in that fixture, he was sure he must have received money from the opposition to award the last-minute penalty against his team. That was all history now and although the league title was more or less a certainty for his team, the quarter final of the County Sunday League Cup was proving more difficult.

Steve Foy chaired the half-time discussion in the team dressing room, but Ronnie could not stay outside, his team were two goals to nil down and half of them had yellow cards. He was smouldering as he saw his big chance of being recognised as a winning football team owner in Sunday football going up in smoke; it was the cup that really mattered to him.

The final would be held this year at Selhurst Park, the home of Crystal Palace FC, in a month's time. Ronnie desperately wanted his team to be the winners, second best was not an option. He had bigger plans for later but this was his first step on the proud ownership ladder.

Steve tried to keep calm. He knew if he reacted aggressively to the team's first-half performance he could finish up with red cards in the second half and that would be a disaster. He needed to motivate them. Ronnie didn't share his soft approach but he had promised to keep quiet as his coach swung into action.

'They are quicker and fitter than us, that is why we continue to be so fucking late with our tackles, the long-ball plan needs to be put into action. Jake and Dean, you stay on the halfway line and wide, do not defend, leave that to the others.

'Alan, Len and Claude, when you get possession at the back, belt the ball down the channels, it's drier and faster in those wide areas and Jake and Dean then have a real chance to get one over on the fullbacks.'

Nobody said a word as the players filed out of the dressing room; they knew what they had to do. It was basically shit or bust; they were playing a better team so they had to change tactics.

Ronnie finished his hot tea and ate the last mint from the second packet he had brought to the game. He was hoping for miracles but then he had faith in Steve, his half-time team talks usually inspired the players to produce a goal, or even two.

The result in the coach's mind was three goals to two and that's exactly what did happen, the wingers suddenly found their feet with the long balls down the channels. The team were knackered and looking forward to the first pint and many more afterwards, they just held out in the final minutes for the key result. They had done what Steve Foy had asked and it had worked. Ronnie shook his hand and gave him some beer money for the lads, then left without congratulating his tired and derelict players.

Ronnie had urgent business to attend to. It concerned the first steps on his road to being a man that everyone in South East England, and perhaps even Europe, would look up to.

Achilles FC was a hobby but he was learning; he knew that to be successful he had to cut corners, upset a few people, buy occasional favours and maybe bloody some noses.

He was pissed off with England, by his own actions he had created a lot of interest from the police, and they were getting closer to pinning something on him. By his reckoning he had two or three years maximum wheeling and dealing, then he would sell his business interests if the price was right.

If not, he would find some *reliable* people to manage his business locally and he would run everything at arm's length from Spain or Portugal. The staff running his business would probably skim off some cash but provided they made decent profits he would turn a blind eye. He would pay a couple of bookkeepers to deal with any problem areas and Ronnie would keep well away from his home country.

His ambition was driving him to what seemed an impossible dream, but not a goal that Ronnie would just talk about; his dream would be reality and nothing would stand in his way.

Chapter one

The Family

Saturday November 23rd 2008 was a grey winter day as Mark Lavender collected the dirty red Ford Sierra from outside Luke Devine's garage. Luke had illegally rescued the car from a scrapping unit a few days before, and it was going to be used for a few final hours.

Mark parked the car a long way from the Lavender house and hid it behind some garages; he would not be seen in it until they did the job. He had his lunch at home but then he paced up and down, he was nervous and sweat was pouring off him, he kept watching the clock and drinking mugs of tea. His mother, Barbara, noticed his edgy behaviour, he looked very anxious and not at all like the confident young man he had become.

'What on earth's the matter with you, Mark? Sit down and tell me.'

'Mum, I really am OK, stop worrying. I'm just hoping my horse won at Haydock Park today in the big race. I put a lot of money on it.'

'Why not go to the bookies or check the results on TV. Please do something, Mark, you are making me nervous now. Is everything all right at the sports club? Are they asking about your results in the personal trainer exams?'

'Everything's fine, Mum, just stop asking me questions all the time, please. I'm off now but I'll see you later. I might go straight out and meet up with Vince. If I win we will be celebrating big time as he has backed the same horse; if we lose we will be drowning our sorrows in The Plough or somewhere like that, please don't wait up for me.'

Although Mark was 28 he was still living at home, he wanted to move in with his long-term girlfriend, Kate, but he did not earn enough for even 50% of the mortgage. Kate was an independent lady; she never told Mark what her job really involved, all he knew was that she was involved in money and deals. Kate played everything close to her sizeable chest; she frequently went abroad but she told Mark as little as she could get away with.

Mark was very envious of his elder brother, Vince. He was 32, had his own house and was married with a baby on the way. All his life he had looked up to his brother and Mark just wanted the same lifestyle and security that Vince appeared to be building.

His sister, Sharon, lived a couple of streets away from her parents' house, sharing with her friend, Liz. It was Sharon's house; everything was in her sole name. She had put every penny she had into it so she could get on the property ladder.

Her job at a major high street investment bank was well paid, she was a financial consultant and very astute at the tender age of 26. The rewards were good, her annual bonus and commission over the past five years had all been saved for a large deposit on her house.

She loved her independence and she was not sure if she was ready for a man to live in the house; several had found their way to her bed but none had been asked to stay on a permanent basis.

Her friend Liz Smith lived with her and she paid over a third of all the household costs, but she was on the look out for a place of her own. Her father, Ronnie Smith, was a rich man and would help her, but Liz also wanted her own property. Unlike Sharon she spent more than she earned, and the Bank of Dad frequently came to her rescue. Liz worked on the front reception desk in the same company as Sharon, she was good at her job and liked by the customers.

One day she hoped to follow Sharon into a higher position and she had an idea or two on how to move up the ladder quickly; not the normal route but with her looks she was planning a discreet career accelerator. Liz was very much her father's girl, always looking for an angle or an opportunity to make money and prove to her father that she could do it on her own.

Sharon and Liz had been close friends for a long time and they were comfortable sharing the house. Liz knew she needed her friend as she had few other options for accommodation; her parents had divorced and the deal with Sharon worked well for her. One day she would find the right guy and marry him but she had big ambitions and it might take a long time. She was used to money and she spent hours discussing both suitable and unsuitable men with her ever-patient friend, Sharon.

Liz's problem was that because of basic insecurity she could be promiscuous; she mostly thought that on the whole it was a nice problem to have until it got her in trouble; sometimes she would see two men in the same evening. She slept with most of her dates pretty soon after meeting them, nobody ever turned her down and Mark Lavender was no exception.

Sharon caught them in bed together one afternoon and her initial surprise turned to annoyance when she discovered that both should have been working, the result being a serious 'sister-to-brother' telling off.

Liz had nearly messed up when she came on to a guy in a pub that Sharon was dating, fortunately Sharon had not found out yet and she thought she had probably got away with it. She needed to stay with her, as to fall back onto her dad's mercy and move back home was out of the question.

She loved her well-known father, Ronnie Smith. He was a local bookmaker, scrap merchant, entrepreneur and wheeler-dealer. Liz knew that really she should be living at home with him but she couldn't stand the sight of his latest live-in lover; they all wanted his money and very little else.

Jean, the current live-in incumbent, was no different except she was cleverer than the average Ronnie girlfriend. She had warned her dad about her but he got very annoyed so Liz decided to take up Sharon's offer to share the house. She still phoned her dad daily and she hoped to get involved in one of his companies.

All three of the Lavender children had a good education. Vince and Sharon both went to university and got acceptable degrees. Vince had taken a job in engineering and he was involved with major bridge and road constructions. Sharon had a marketing degree and after gaining experience at the bank, she had ideas to eventually run her own financial business.

Vince Lavender was bored with his job and impatient, but to control his own destiny he needed money to finance his ideas. His mortgage was £1,500 a month and with his wife expecting a baby, everything would be very tight for some time once his wife stopped working.

His young brother, Mark, had tried a few jobs, he had average results from his education but he didn't do enough to qualify for university so the search was on for something he could make into a decent career.

His current job did not inspire him, he worked long hours at the leisure centre supervising in the gym, at the same time learning to be a personal trainer. The money could be good but he needed to be fully qualified and busy to make enough to buy his own place. The recession had hit fitness and leisure clubs hard and he doubted even if he was fully qualified he would have sufficient customers to make a decent living; he had to get money somehow to move out of his parents' house.

His girlfriend, Kate, was his dream partner but he had a nagging feeling that he was out of her league, he felt he was just hanging on to her knicker elastic. She loved his sexy, well-toned body and his mild nature, but unless he could improve his earning potential she would probably move on as soon as she found someone new.

The Lavender family all knew Kate Whitehead in different ways; Barbara Lavender knew her mother and when Mark and Kate were kids they played together at each other's houses. Sharon Lavender and Kate were close friends at senior school, Sharon was also certain that one day she would dump her brother but she did not care, she was certain Kate was a gold digger and too complicated a partner for Mark. In the long term she would be nothing but ambitious trouble for her brother.

Kate had been coming to the Lavender house for years before Mark became her steady boyfriend. Vince always had his eye on her before he married Donna and even after; Donna watched him when they were all together with the occasional warning that his punishment for any indiscretion would be very painful.

He ignored the warning and took Kate out for dinner just once, but they were not compatible. Vince got drunk before the food arrived and Kate went home early, as Vince became argumentative after she asked him why he kept watching the pub door; he was half expecting his wife to walk in.

They never spoke again.

Kate's big secret had been a short affair with Gerry Lavender, the father of the three children and husband to Barbara. The party organised by Vince and Donna for his 60th birthday went too well and the result was a short liaison between the unlikely couple.

The thrill of the chase for Kate was realised a couple of weeks later when Gerry arranged a working weekend in Brighton. No questions were asked by Mark and Barbara and the three days of fun ended with a kiss and a 'maybe we will do it again one day' comment.

No damage was done from the brief liaison. Kate asked Gerry about his business and how she could improve herself, Gerry gave her some commercial ideas and he promised to help her in the future.

They parted at Kate's house as her phone rang with an inquisitive Mark checking up on her, Gerry waved and blew a kiss as he departed. He had a strong feeling that one day they could meet again.

Gerry Lavender was semi-retired, he had owned an engineering company, and eight years previously he had sold his company to enjoy the benefits of his sizeable pension. He had hoped to move to the countryside but his new hobby might affect his plans; he told everyone that he was into antiques, buying, selling and restoring them, but few people had actually seen anything he had bought or sold or even believed his story.

Over the last two years he told his family that his 'hobby' had expanded, he never gave details of how but he boasted that he was making serious money from his business, leaving no clues as to the secret of his success.

Vince and Sharon's education was paid for from the large profits of his previous successful business. Mark had been promised a sum of money when he wanted to buy a house and leave the family home, he would be the last of the three to leave. His parents were not putting him under pressure but he knew they had plans to eventually move away from the town.

Barbara had kept working as a teacher during the years when Gerry was away; she had her own circle of friends, which did not include Gerry. This annoyed him but provided she was happy he did not complain.

The relationship between them had gone seriously downhill since he retired, they did not go on holiday together and rarely did they eat together. Gerry was always travelling or meeting so-called 'clients'. In the lonely evenings her mind began to wander, she was bored with her girlfriends but she didn't tell Gerry, she knew he would ignore her and carry on as normal.

She was very much looking forward to the arrival of Vince and Donna's baby. It would be her first grandchild and she wanted someone to spoil, she was secretly hoping that her daughter-in-law would return to work and then she could look after the baby every weekday.

Barbara had no knowledge or prior warning of the trauma and upset that would hit the family in the coming year, the result would be a complete change in her lifestyle and also to the people around her.

Chapter two

Robbery

When Luke and Vince had first put the idea to Mark he was excited and virtually fearless, he was sure he would not be caught, his brother and Luke had planned everything very carefully but his over confidence would soon be overtaken by reality.

Mark would repeatedly go over in his mind that day's events and what had happened after the robbery, he knew somebody had put his name in the frame; the CCTV pictures of the scene did not appear to conclusively confirm he was the driver, but a single fingerprint on the door handle matched his thumb.

The betting shop owned by Ronnie Smith was an easy target, the big race at Haydock Park was over and the outside winner meant that the shop should have more cash than normal. The favourite would have been heavily backed but finishing at the rear of the field would leave lots of disappointed punters and a lot of cash. The decision to rob Ronnie was based not just on the take from one race but from information that more cash than usual would be in the shop that day.

Apart from a guy staring at the evening dog racing programme on the wall, the shop was nearly empty as Vince and Luke Devine burst in. They looked like men from outer space dressed in yellow PVC safety jackets with black hooded coats underneath. The sawn-off double-barrelled shotgun in Devine's hand quickly identified to the shop staff the men's intentions.

Luke Devine was a retired footballer, he had been forced to leave a Championship Division football club early due to a bad knee injury, the compensation was a lot of money but he had managed to gamble most of it away in less than three years, plus money he had got when his wife divorced him and they split up, selling the house.

He was a bitter man, his mates were now earning £20,000 a week and more since he had left the game, he wanted just a few hundred thousand and then he would disappear to Spain.

Vince was the brains behind the robbery; he knew the procedures in the shop. The minute the three entered was the exact time Billy Bootle, the manager, had the large office safe open to deposit all the takings for banking on the following Monday.

'You can keep that safe door open now, mate, otherwise I'll blow your head off,' said Luke, loving every minute of his Billy the Kid cameo role.

Vince told the single customer to stay still and study the dog runners as Luke pointed the 12-bore shotgun at his face; the man went white and turned to the wall shaking with fear.

'Put all the money in these two bags quickly, mate, and you'll be OK, and I mean all of the money.'

'You won't get away with this, you bastards,' replied Billy.

'Like fuck we will. Your CCTV is not working, we can see the wire hanging down, and I know where you live, so I suggest you have a bad memory day, Mr Manager.'

Angela Tate started to cry and Vince went towards her with one eye on the other man in the shop.

'Stop crying, you will be OK provided you belt up!' Luke shouted in her face.

The noise of his gun deafened the two employees; he had fired into the ceiling as Billy started to reach below the counter. He didn't reach whatever he was looking for; if he had Luke may have given him the other barrel in his legs.

Angela crumpled behind her space under the desk, Vince saw a small puddle gather beneath her as she wet herself, yellow liquid running down her leg. He felt sorry for her but only for a couple of seconds.

Luke waved the gun over his head as Vince put the contents of the safe into two large holdalls.

'Come on, mate, let's go. Someone will have heard that bang,' said Luke as he walked quickly to the door.

'OK I'm ready, I've got all the money. I'm just going to lock this bloke in the bog with this big chair so we get a start. Look, lady, don't let him out for at least five minutes otherwise I'll come back another day.'

He grabbed Billy by his collar and pushed him into the small toilet then jammed the chair under the lock, the girl would be able to move it but they would have more than enough time to get away. The bang of the shotgun had been heard in both the adjoining shops but both were closing; they would probably ignore the noise assuming that it was a car backfiring in the road.

The two men walked quickly from the shop complete with the office phone and the mobiles of the two employees, Vince put them in the lamp post rubbish bin as Luke threw the bags onto the back seat.

'Go, for fuck sake go, Mark.'

The car engine was already running and was in first gear.

Mark carefully pulled out into the main road traffic as Vince and Luke removed their hood jackets and yellow coats. The journey was no more than two minutes to the incinerator positioned just next to the local rubbish dump; Luke had been working part-time at the site and knew the procedures for burning rubbish.

The three men jumped out of the Sierra and ran to a parked Vauxhall estate car; they opened the boot and threw the moneybags in and then stripped off all their clothing just leaving their pants, socks and trainers. They grabbed three tracksuits from the boot and put them on. Luke went to the chutes which lead straight into the incinerator and opened the lid wide so Mark and Vince could throw everything into it, including the dismantled gun.

'Will that work, Luke?' said Mark looking anxiously at the chute.

'Yes, the temperature is so high that everything will be burnt to a cinder. The police lab blokes could possibly work out what the metal bits are but any connection to us would be impossible.'

'I hope you're right, Luke, that bang scared the shit out of me and I was across the road in the car.'

'Yes, sorry about that but I'd little time to move as he went to press something under the counter; it may have been a lock for the front door or the focus and position of a camera on us. We couldn't risk being stuck inside or being on film so I had to make our position clear to that bloke.'

All three laughed at the thought of the manager locked in the shit house. The girl had left him and ran to the pub to use the phone, in fact, she forgot about him until the police turned up 30 minutes later. Billy Bootle had certainly learnt how to use a toilet during the delay.

Vince tapped Mark on the shoulder as he drove down the dual carriageway back towards his parents' Sutton house.

'Mark, don't forget we're taking the Vauxhall to Dad's old garage as planned, I've got the electric opener here and I'll see to the roller shutter door, don't either of you get out until we're all inside.'

The door opened and Mark slowly drove into the narrow space but his driving skills let him down and he scraped the car on the wall making a loud noise.

'Shut the door, Vince. I'm sorry about that, mate, I misjudged it. You've got a nasty mark on the door,'

'No problem, Mark, it's just that I know the house across the road is owned by a copper and I didn't want any nosey parker to see us just in case. We can unload the money now, put it all on the bonnet so we can count it.'

The money was a mixture of bundled notes and loose ones. Luke took control and did the counting as the others emptied the bags.

'Fuck me, by my reckoning we have got nearly £300,000 here. I can't believe there's so much but who's complaining, it's just like we were told it would be. I think Ronnie Smith must have been up to some type of scam. So lads, it sounds like we have exactly £100,000 each less a small pay-off for our friend and a good piss-up in a few weeks' time when things have died down.'

'Yes, that sounds good but best to have separate piss-ups to start with, we don't want to be seen together for some time. We know what we're doing with our cut, don't we, Luke? We suggest, Mark, that you keep yours in a very safe place and later you can come in with Luke and I in a small investment.'

'Ronnie Smith is going to go fucking mad over this. We'd better not use his shop for a few weeks. I couldn't look the bloke in the face.'

'Listen, Mark, if you don't go in he'll notice so don't change your routine or he could get suspicious.'

'OK, Luke, but ending up with around £100,000 cash was not what you said to me. It's much more than expected, I'm really nervous.'

Luke and Vince stayed in the car as Mark left the garage by the back door and went into the alley that led to the main road. Mark turned towards his parents' home, in the corner of his eye he felt sure he saw a curtain move in the house across the road but he could not be certain and he speeded up until he got to the big family house.

He threw the bag of money into the boot of his Mini parked on the drive then went into the house, he wondered what else he could do with it but then he couldn't take it in the house in case his parents questioned him. He had not considered what he was going to do with the money but he thought that his new problem was a nice one; the Mini boot had to be just short-term storage.

'You look a bit happier, did your horse win?'

'Yes, Mum, but I'm going to save the money this time.'

'Was it a lot, Mark?'

'Yes, Mum, a few grand.'

'Mark, have you seen your dad? He went out earlier and I'm worried.'

'No, I haven't seen him.'

'Didn't he tell you anything about what he was doing?'

'No, he was a bit jumpy all last night. He took a late call on his mobile, which he just said was as friend, it didn't sound very friendly to me.'

'He will be OK, Mum, probably an antique deal gone wrong. He'll call us or just appear. You know Dad is Mr Reliable.'

Mark went to his room to undress for a shower; his phone rang as he undressed.

'Hi, Kate, what've you been up to?'

'Not a lot just looking for a man to take me out tonight, are you interested?'

'You bet, see you in an hour. I had a bet on the big race and it won so we can have a drink and a curry.'

'Brilliant, I'll have champagne, chicken curry and double fried rice, please.'

'Certainly I know how to please a lady. Could I have hold-up stockings, black suspenders a lace bra and underneath a red silk thong?'

'Sounds like we could be having a takeaway instead. See you later.'

'Yes, did you have any trouble at the bookies today?'

Mark gulped and replied without thinking.

'No, Kate, I didn't use Ronnie Smith but the new shop in the High Street.'

'Who said you used Ronnie? It was just that Angela, my friend, called and said they'd been robbed, she just left the police station and wanted to go for a drink to calm her nerves. Could we have a quick one with her on the way out?'

Mark had to think quickly as he didn't want Kate to get any idea that he was avoiding Angela, but then why should he worry, unless she got a glimpse of him in the car?

'Yes, fine, but just a couple. I'll pick you up and then we can collect Angela and leave the car at her place and take a cab if we're celebrating.'

Chapter three

Departing

Vince started the Vauxhall and opened the shutter door. This time they got it out of the garage without damage or attracting any attention, they headed back to Luke's flat in the next road.

'A good day's work, Vince, my old mate. It's so much more fucking money than we thought. I suggest we buy the new Spanish place outright rather than a rental share on one.'

'I can probably get the place in Marbella for cash, it doesn't leave us much but I'm told we can start renting it out next year when it's finished and get a nice little income, which we can keep in Spain.'

Luke had other ideas but he had to convince Vince for a few more minutes that they could be equal partners and they would buy the place together. He knew he had to leave the UK and possibly permanently, but one day he would square it with his mate.

'Yes, fine by me, Luke, I'll leave it to you. Get rid of the cash tomorrow, take it to Spain and see that lawyer to put the wheels in motion to buy the place straight away. I just spoke to Matt Jones in Brighton Marina, he'll charge you a grand to take you to France by boat with the loot, it's expensive but you can't risk being pulled by customs with that amount of cash in your bag. Remember the other pay-off too, Luke, I know he's an idiot but we've got to keep him sweet.

'Take this map. I've written the train route from Calais to Spain, it'll take you a day or so. You won't see many police on this route provided you don't start spending a lot of money and flashing it around. Change what you need in France not here and no more than a few hundred quid at a time.'

'Yes, great, but don't you trust me, Vince? You look bloody worried, mate?'

'I've got to trust you, Luke, if this is how we are going to set up in Spain. I have no choice, but it's a long life if you screw my brother or me.'

'I get the message, keep your hair on, Vince. We're a good team, just keep a hand on your brother as once I'm gone he may get nervous. I'll stay in

Spain near my mum for a few months with an old pal, he plays for the local mob in the Spanish Primera BBV, or in other words what we know here as La Liga, he's got more money than sense so I'll be OK.'

'What about your place here?'

'I've sold it already as it looks like I may be bankrupt so it was a very quick sale. I need to do a bunk and leave a few things behind. I managed to get some money sent to my mum in Spain and I was leaving anyway next week, after today's result the sooner I leave the better.'

'OK, Luke, but my nest is here, Donna and I will come over for a holiday in a few months when the baby is born, so watch your back.'

'Remember, mate, keep a close eye on Mark he looked very nervous, he needs to keep cool. Talk to him now, Vince.'

'Sure, of course, he listens to me. You forget he's my kid brother. I'll sort him, I'm pretty sure that it's the amount of stolen cash that's worrying him. I'll help him so don't worry, just get on your bike to Spain, text me when you arrive. I may just get a cheap flight in a couple of weeks so we can review our plans.'

The two men shook hands, Vince was nervous about Luke leaving but he had always wanted a property nest egg in Spain and this maybe was a good solution; it would give him the extra income he needed once Donna had stopped working. Vince thought they would get no more than £30,000 each from the robbery, Luke somehow knew more money than usual would be in the shop that day but he never imagined it would be as much as £300,000.

Vince was suspicious of Luke's story about his pending bankruptcy but he had no choice but to trust him to launder the money. His own plan for an early visit to Spain was definitely a priority, to meet him and check out he had started on the purchase of the place as agreed.

As he took the back route to his house he couldn't help thinking about the betting shop. What was Ronnie Smith up to with all that money in the shop? Maybe he should find out when things had quietened down. It was all far too easy. He was brought back down to earth by an approaching figure.

Vince had not seen his wife all day and was surprised to see her walking towards him as he approached the house.

'You look ill, Donna, is the baby all right?'

'I was just walking to your parents' house, it seems your dad has gone missing. He went out in the car very early this morning saying he was going to look at some antiques but he hasn't been seen since. Your mum is panicking, Sharon is away and Mark is out so I said I'd go round, it's too early for the police so we need to try and find him ourselves.'

'She's a bit quick off the mark. I suspect they had a row last night and he's gone to see that bird he told me he had an affair with a few years ago.'

The relationship between Vince and his father was sometimes a difficult one; Gerry Lavender wanted Vince to work with him but his son had other plans. Gerry sold his first business at the right time but now his so-called antique sales kept him occupied. He wanted Vince to be a partner but his eldest son didn't want to work with him, Mark was not bright enough and Sharon had her own career.

The two quarrelled a lot but they had mutual respect. Vince was one of the lads locally, he had lots of contacts and he had been introduced by a mate to ex-footballer Luke Devine, a man with a lot of history on the field but nothing else.

Gerry could see trouble on the horizon with this bloke and he wanted Vince to settle down, especially now as his wife was pregnant.

Donna stared at her husband, hands on hips.

'Anyway, where the hell have you been, Vince, you didn't answer your phone?'

'I was out with Luke, my darling; we had a small result on the big race so when Dad does turn up we can have a bottle or two with him as well.'

'Have we got money to gamble with then, Vince? Everything is bloody tight you know that, why don't we save something?'

'Yes, I've done it, I'll explain later but first we've got to find my dad.'

Vince just wanted his inquisitive wife off the subject, when she verbally attacked him he went on the defensive, he was a bad liar and he knew he could sound very unconvincing. He sniffed around bar girls and the occasional prostitute but the difficult bit for him was getting his alibi right.

The robbery had made him hyper and Donna noticed it, she was sharp and she smelt a rat so he quickly excused himself, almost running to his car, she would be asleep when he got back and by the next day he would have calmed down.

Chapter four

Ronnie Smith

Detective Inspector Derek Lawson had been on the local patch for nearly ten years, to his constant annoyance he had seen Ronnie Smith grow in apparent wealth. He was known among the locals as a shrewd self-made tycoon from a very modest South London upbringing.

He didn't have a criminal record but Lawson started to wonder more about him and what he was up to. He had noticed earlier in the year a new AMG Mercedes, following his move the previous year from Lewisham to a very big house on the St George's Hill Estate in Weybridge.

This alone did not directly indicate he was getting money illegally but Lawson was suspicious of everyone and Ronnie was definitely no exception.

The policeman pulled up outside the shop; his sergeant, John Hampton, had taken the call. In just 40 minutes they caught up with the local response team, who once they knew a gun had been fired had surrounded the place a few minutes earlier, then left once they realised they were too late. Ronnie Smith was on the front step waiting for the detective and his sergeant.

'Hello, Ronnie. I hear you had a noisy visitor?'

'Don't fuck about, Inspector, I've been done over good and proper.'

'Show me then, Ronnie.'

'The two blokes came in wearing yellow jackets and hoods, a sawn-off shotgun blasted the ceiling and they took everything from the safe. Billy Bootle the manager had the shit scared out of him and Angela the shop girl was bloody frightened to death. She pissed her pants and will probably take a month off sick with stress.

'They locked Bootle in the toilet, serves him right for not keeping it clean, he looked pretty bad when we let him out.'

'Who told you about the robbery Ronnie? You got here bloody quick, just a few minutes after the robbers left according to the armed response team.'

Ronnie looked down at the floor and replied.

'Don't laugh but I had a tip-off my shop was being robbed, then the geezer put the phone down. I rang the number back but, of course, it wasn't available.'

Ronnie didn't look at the policeman he was uncomfortable and wanted to get away.

'We can check that. Give us your phone, Ronnie.'

'No way, I need it, especially now.'

'OK, bring it to the station tomorrow and we can check your phone in 30 minutes by talking to your provider. Now how much did they steal, Ronnie? Show us a copy of your till record.'

'We hadn't finished cashing up; probably the week's takings including the float about £50,000, the computer was playing up so I can't be sure. They also took some papers relating to my accounts but hopefully my accountant can reproduce those for me.'

'It sounds to me like a small-time job, probably local lads after beer money but I'm surprised about them firing a gun. We need to speak to Bootle, Angela and the customer who was in the shop. Sergeant, get all the details.'

'The insurance people will be here on Monday and they'll want a look at the CCTV tapes that Bootle has left here for you. Can you let us have them back? I'll make my own enquiries.'

'Don't do anything silly, Ronnie, especially just for £50,000.'

The policeman laughed as he left the shop and Ronnie spun on his heels in the direction of his manager.

'I don't like it already, John.'

'What do you mean, sir?'

'I smell a rat; his story doesn't work but I don't know why. Ronnie seems to be pretty angry, but then wanting to sort it out himself.'

'Do you think it's an inside job, then?'

'It could be but we need to dig a bit further and look at that CCTV tape.'

The Detective Inspector's mobile rang and he sprang into life.

'Yes, that's good, we'll be with you in a few minutes. That was the local area policeman, he's found a beat-up Ford Sierra untaxed near the incinerator in Garth Road. Don't you remember Angela Tate, the bird with the wet knickers, said she saw a Ford accelerate away through the side window of the shop?'

The two policemen needed some early clues and they got to the dumped car in five minutes. A fingerprint man was brought in, as they were pretty certain it was the getaway car.

'My hunch, sir, is everything they used in the robbery, except the money, was put into another car. Their clothes and probably the gun went straight in the chutes to the incinerator. I don't see any point in getting them to check inside it tonight, it'll be too hot, but tomorrow we can see what the refuse men can do to help us. It's probably all just ash by now.'

'We'll leave Angela and Bootle until the morning. Come on, let's go and have a chat with a Mr Alan Goody, who I'm told was the sole customer in the shop.'

Alan Goody lived in a caravan park near the Wandle River about 30 minutes from the betting shop. He was not surprised when the police knocked on his door in the middle of his beans on toast and can of lager.

'Come in and sit down. Not much I can offer you I'm afraid, but do you fancy a beer?'

'No thanks, Mr Goody, it's a bit early for us, just tell us what happened today and then we'll leave you to your beans.'

'Simple really these two guys, both about six feet tall, dressed in dark clothes with hoods, yellow jackets and looking like workmen, burst into the shop. They told Billy the manager they wanted the money, for some unknown reason one of them fired a shot into the ceiling. They grabbed the money from the safe, put it in zipper bags and left. It all happened very quickly. I waited a couple of minutes before going outside in case they opened fire on me but they jumped in the car and drove away.'

'Did you see anything unusual, Mr Goody?'

'No, not really. I was scared as hell but in a funny way it was almost as if Billy knew something was going to happen but it could have been a coincidence.'

'Why did you think that?'

'The second man didn't know the gun was going to be fired, he was as surprised as anyone. Billy reached under the counter and the geezer fired. Before the robbery, Billy cashed up quickly then fiddled with a machine, which I think was to the shop CCTV. I went to put a bet on the dogs but Angela said they were closed, which was unusual as Ronnie always takes my bets, even when the till is closed.'

'OK, thanks. We'll need you to make a statement tomorrow. Please come to the station. Were there any other punters in the shop, Mr Goody.'

'No, not on the shop side. As far as I could tell only Angela and the manager were on the other side. Yes, sure, I'll come down to the nick tomorrow. Do you think you'll get the men?'

'Hopefully, Mr Goody. We have a few things to go on. Just one question though, why do you drive for 30 minutes to the betting shop when there's one across the road?'

'Don't drive actually, I get the bus. I need a ride on a Saturday as I live in this dump most of the year as I can park my van for nothing but I don't like the people.'

Lawson nodded and pointed his sergeant to the door of the filthy caravan, he'd had enough of the revolting smell and needed fresh air. They were not convinced with his story but it would be on the agenda again for the next meeting.

'I'm off home, John, see you early tomorrow. I have a feeling this robbery could be just a one-off so let's see if we can get a name or two on it before the weekend is over.'

'I agree, something doesn't fit. We've got to do some digging around and maybe even have an early trip to St George's Hill.'

Chapter five

A Night Out

Mark had already left his parents' house before his mother, Barbara, phoned Donna. She hadn't heard from her husband all day and his mobile phone was switched off.

She had no idea where he had gone, he left early and the only words spoken were, 'here's your tea, darling', which Gerry religiously brought to his wife in bed; that day he had left before she could reply.

Donna and Barbara had decided to wait before sending someone to find Mark; now Vince was on the case as well, surely they could find Gerry. The prospects on the wet November night were slim, where should he start? Vince had no real ideas so he decided to first check a couple of local pubs his dad used in the past.

Mark turned up at Kate's flat just as Angela Tate got out of Billy Bootle's car, Mark at first hung back then he realised that was silly; he had to go inside as she would be there anyway.

Angela saw him and smiled.

'Hi, Mark.'

'Angela, have you been crying?'

'Come inside, it's a long story.'

Mark and Kate sat together on the settee and listened to Angela tell her story of the robbery, it was an adventure of a lifetime for Angela and she had no trouble in embellishing the facts, she described the robbers as nasty, aggressive men, swearing as they grabbed the money and threatening poor Billy with death.

'It all sounds pretty horrible, Angela. Are you OK?'

'Yes, Kate, I'll be better after a drink. I was so frightened I pissed myself, when I got home I just soaked in the bath for 20 minutes and threw away my clothes but it's good to still be alive. I thought I'd been shot when the gun went off.'

Mark could not resist a comment as he listened to the girl's dramatic story, the only truthful thing was that she had wet herself but that didn't bother Vince or Luke, they had no intention of hurting her.

Kate went to order the taxi for later and book the Curry Palace, Mark saw his opportunity to give Angela some advice.

'Angela, you must make sure your story is really dead right when the police interview you again, they'll have spoken with Billy and Ronnie already so try to keep to the truth and don't confuse them.'

'I won't confuse them, Mark, but why should you worry, you didn't rob the shop, did you?'

She smiled as she said it; did she know more? Had she recognised him?

Her straight look into his face almost said, 'I know something'.

'No, of course not. I'm sorry, Angela, I didn't mean to sound patronising but it's just that the police sometimes get the wrong impression if they have different witness stories.'

Kate came back into the room catching Mark's words and she laughed out loud.

'Mark, who the hell are you, Sherlock Holmes or Inspector Morse?'

He knew he had to get the girls off the subject. Kate went to get her coat and Mark put his arm around a shaking Angela.

'Come on, get your make-up and we'll all go to The Plough. Are you seeing anyone else tonight, Angela?'

'No, Mark, I split with my boyfriend a few weeks ago, we tried to patch it up but then I heard he'd someone else so it's all over. I'm on the lookout for a new man with money.'

'How much would he need to have, Angela?'

'For tonight I'd settle for one with enough for half a dozen vodkas, a hot chicken curry and packet of condoms, for the future, loads and loads.'

'Well, I think I can help with items one and two but Kate might complain about number three.'

'Mark, I do fancy you, have a night off from Kate and we could have a good time?'

'I love Kate and although you are a nice girl, Angela, I don't mess around.'

'Good job you said that, Mark, I was only testing you.'

Mark frowned then smiled, he knew she wanted him but maybe another day. Angela had been around the block and had been out with most local guys in her younger days but now she wanted to settle down. She was selfish and wanted a man with money so she could have kids and never work again.

Kate came back into the room and almost guessed what had been said when she saw the two red faces, strangely the new competition from Angela didn't seem to worry her, she had her own new plans in mind and they didn't include Mark Lavender.

The trio had downed the third drink in the pub and were almost ready to leave for the curry restaurant when Mark's mobile phone rang. Once he saw his mum's name on the screen he stepped outside the pub; she only phoned if she had a problem.

'Mark, we can't find your father. He went out early this morning and we haven't had a word from him since. His mobile phone is switched off and even the answer machine isn't set up to take a message. I know he probably has a good reason for not contacting me but that's not like him.'

'I'm sure he's OK, Mum, he's probably been looking at antiques and his phone is just playing up, he's always having trouble with it. Give him some time he'll surely turn up later but d'you want me to come home?'

'No, stay with Kate and if nothing happens overnight I'll call you first thing in the morning. I expect he'll turn up, I've spoken to the police and they will check if any road accidents have been reported with unidentified people. I'm worried, Mark, but Donna's here with me so I'll be OK.'

'Yes, Mum, I'm sure it'll be all right. See you in the morning.'

Kate wanted to know what was going on and shouted at her boyfriend.

'What's the problem, Mark?'

'My dad has gone missing or really it's just that he hasn't come home after leaving the house early without telling Mum where he was going. It may be nothing but she's very worried about him, he's so reliable, normally he would tell her exactly what he's doing, it seems he told her nothing about his plans for today.'

'Are you going home?'

'No, I want to stay with you two but I'll keep my phone on in case I'm needed.'

Mark was deep in thought and he was not much company for the two girls as he tried to think back if his dad had said anything to him that week, but nothing stuck in his mind.

Gerry Lavender was a private man, much more wealthy than his wife knew. He had sold his main business and nobody really knew how he was now making his money. Antiques did not fit with him and Barbara could not see why he bothered with them. He had transferred the invested profits from his old business into various properties for rental and this gave the Lavenders a comfortable living.

Kate jumped as her mobile burst into life; she turned her back and left the others, motioning she was going to get her coat, but also making sure her boyfriend and Angela did not hear her conversation.

Angela grabbed her opportunity and put her hands around Mark and squeezed him tight.

'I was so frightened, Mark, I really do need a man tonight.'

'Yes, I can see that, but first help us find my dad and then maybe I can introduce you to a mate who can help.'

Angela frowned, she knew her pass on Mark had been badly timed but she was in need of comfort and he was the nearest man she could get her hands on.

'Kate, I'm going home to get my car.'

'Why, Mark? If we hear anything about your dad we can get a cab over to your house?'

'No, Kate, I want to be flexible and I'm not drinking tonight.'

'OK, I'll take you. Come on, Angela, get lively and take your eyes off my boyfriend or I'll put you over my knee and give you a good spanking.'

He laughed out loud as she said it; nobody argued with Kate.

Mark jumped out of the car and followed Kate to the pub; he parked the car near the door so he could see it easily. His mind was on fire; he had £100,000 in the boot, what should he do with it? One thing for certain, he couldn't leave it in the car overnight, it had been stolen once before and he could not take the risk of losing his cash.

He was nervous and Kate assumed it was because of his dad. The girls all but left him in the pub and went to talk to an older group of girls on a hen night; Mark decided to play the poker machine and try to think.

The tap on his shoulder made him jump; Sergeant John Hampton just pointed to the table, ordered a pint and sat down. Mark started to shake as he placed his coke on the table.

'Is it my dad, John?'

'No, but why are you asking that, Mark?'

'Oh, it's nothing, my mum has just lost him, he's probably on a bender somewhere.'

The two men knew each other, they had been to the same school but John Hampton was two years older, he had a promising career ahead of him and had already applied for promotion even though he had been a sergeant for less than three years.

'Mark, actually we just got an anonymous phone call with some odd information and I need to check out your car, please come with me and open it up, we can then have a pint and catch up.'

He wanted to be sick, he had no escape from the policeman. They went to the car and he opened it; John Hampton went straight to the boot and looked inside, he pulled out the bag.

He turned and looked at Mark who already had a face with guilty written all over it.

'Did you win on the horses today, Mark?'

'Yes, how did you know that?'

'Well, it looks like about £1,000 in that bundle and that's a lot of money.'

Mark was sick all down the wheel arch but it helped his situation as the policeman was distracted.

'Are you OK, mate, have you been drinking?'

'That could be the problem, John, just coke as I'm driving tonight and the girls are drinking.'

'Mark, we go back a long way, clean yourself up and pop into the station on Monday after work for a chat. I'll explain then what this is about and you can give me more details of the bet as well. I'm off now, take some water or better still have a few pints and leave the car here.'

Mark went back into the pub; his mind was racing, what should he tell Kate? The minute he got to the bar she put her arm around him and pulled him against her breasts. She fortunately had not seen him talk to the policeman; she was listening to the intimate details of the 'strippergram' planned for the hen party.

'Kate, I've got to have a beer, I'll leave the Mini here until the morning. I'm playing football so I'll pick it up afterwards.'

'What's the matter, big boy?'

Kate was hot, the talk of the male stripper and sex between the girls had got her heart pumping and Angela had helped with some suggestions about a threesome on a stag night.

'I'm OK, Kate, just worried about my dad.'

'Bloody hell, Mark, he's only been missing for 14 hours, he'll turn up soon.'

Mark knew more, recently his father had told him about a deal with a foreign guy that was proving difficult to close. He was a worried man, and he could see it in his father's face; normally nothing bothered him but he told his son that it involved big money.

Gerry didn't know why it had gone wrong other than he had lost control of the deal. He had confided in Mark for no other reason than he needed someone to tell. Vince would have just laughed at him, Barbara and Donna would just tell him to retire and stop messing about with something he did not fully understand.

The advice from Mark was that he should just give the money back and ditch the furniture to the Red Cross. Unfortunately, Gerry's problem was much bigger than antiques or furniture; he was in the land of big money and he feared for his life.

It all seemed like a simple problem to Mark but he did not know the full story, his mother also seemed visibly very worried. Gerry had been acting odd; Barbara had noticed him making quick phone calls from the car and garage. He denied it when she asked about them, saying he was just checking text messages.

Mark knew his mum and dad were very wealthy. He also knew that in his working life Gerry Lavender had upset a few people, those people knew he had money and maybe it was payback time.

After a few drinks the three of them went to the Curry Palace and ordered a takeaway. Mark decided to drive; sometimes three pints would put him over the limit to drive but at other times if he made the beer last a few hours he felt nothing as he drove back from the pub. His theory had never been put to the test and that night he had taken his time and drunk the beer slowly as he tried to put the meeting with the policeman out of his mind.

He grabbed his mobile from his coat as they waited for the food and dialled the number of his brother, Vince.

'Vince, did you move the money out of my car? I just had a fucking policeman search it after a tip-off and I only have about £1,000 left in the bag.'

'No, mate, I've been with Mum all night. Are you sure it was only a grand?'

'Yes, even the copper looked a bit puzzled. I've to go down the station on Monday to have a chat with them. I protested, but throwing up in front of him didn't help. He said they had a tip-off this evening that I was carrying a lot of stolen money.'

'None of this adds up, Mark, only three of us knew where the money was and Luke has gone to Spain. I saw him go in the station to catch the train to Brighton and he was with me all the time before then.'

'Has he got your money as well, Vince?'

'Yes. Look, I sort of trust him, we had to move the money fast, it's difficult enough to move cash and as it was so much more than we thought, I decided to buy the property outright with Luke and then we own it between us. We can all use the place, the original idea to just buy a share in this place in Marbella was based on getting about £15,000 each, this way with the extra money we can buy and let the apartment and get an income when Donna has the baby. She won't be working at first and we may be short of money, this'll be just what we need to fill the gap.'

'OK, sounds good but what about my missing money? Who the hell has got it, Vince?'

'Did the copper take the £1,000 from your car?'

'No, as I just said he was as surprised as me and when I said I won it on the horses he sort of accepted it. Maybe he didn't trust the tip-off. I just don't get it, Vince.'

The phone call was cut short as Kate thrust the wrapped meal into Mark's hands.

'Must go now, Vince, I'll see you later.'

Vince closed his phone and went into the lounge of his parents' house.

'Who was that, Vince?'

'Just Mark, he was asking about Dad.'

'Donna, you stay here with Mum, I need to go out and see a couple of people. I'll get back as quick as I can.'

'Don't be long and keep your mobile on.'

Vince had to get away to call Luke and check on Mark's money but then he thought otherwise, he knew where he was going and he intended to fly to Spain soon to check everything out. But then he knew he wouldn't do it, how would he ever get that past Donna? He could talk his way out of a quick short-term fling but not a trip to a foreign country.

He called a contact who he knew was handling the properties in Spain; he came on a recommendation from his father but Vince had not met him. All he got at first was an answer machine in Spanish then it diverted to one of his partners. Señora Rosa introduced herself and at first she was annoyed at the call late on a Saturday evening.

She calmed down when Vince mentioned his father and she would expect the call from Luke soon, all the papers were ready for the property deal. With the extra cash coming she would put the deal on hold until she heard from Luke.

Luke Devine had told Vince that he planned to live near his mum in Valencia; the idea was to stay with his mate so he could quietly disappear until the new property was ready for occupation. He hadn't told Vince that he would live in the place permanently and somehow he had to get that over to him when he came to Spain to view it.

The Marbella law practice had a good record among English ex-pats; the main partner spoke good English and he knew the Spanish systems well. He was an expert at being unhelpful should people other than the Spanish authorities ask about ownership. It was not surprising that the local authorities never asked him anything other than what time and date they should meet him for the next football match.

Mrs Devine had been in Spain for ten years, she was recovering from a serious illness and her son would be good company for her in her convalescence. He was not sure about the move to the sun but as his bankruptcy was looming and his ex-wife was being a real pain in the arse, he decided that he had no choice but to leave the UK.

Spain had been a popular choice for British tourists to take up residence for many years, it was sometimes a country where criminals from the UK also made their home; it was not a safe sanctuary as Spain was very much in the EU but it was still difficult to track people down.

Luke thought he had a much better chance of keeping out of trouble away from London and he would be close to his mother. Ambition was on hold for him. Once he had a place to live he could then check out a few mates who had moved to the sun for one reason or another.

In Luke Devine's case he technically had a clean record, but if the UK police put his name in the frame for the betting shop job and they couldn't find him, they would certainly ask the Spanish police to help. He knew he was not safe from extradition if the police had good evidence on him but that was the risk he had to take.

Chapter six

Baby

Mark was pleased to be in his own bed, he had foolishly driven the Mini after drinking but he made it back to his parents' house without incident following a big bust up with Kate. He could not explain to her the reason for his odd behaviour other than what she knew about his missing dad, she accepted that as an excuse but she was not happy.

His mother and sister were in bed but probably not asleep when he got to his parents' home. He took the opportunity to bring the bag of money into the house, he counted the notes over and over again, it still came to exactly £1,000, which would have been the amount he would have won if he had placed the bet. Who knew he was going to bet? Not many people, just his brother and maybe some mates he talked to in the pub.

Mark was puzzled more than angry, he worked out the bet several times and the amount was dead right, he threw the bag on the floor and went to kick it under the bed; the police had seen it and let him go, what had he to fear?

In the corner of the bag was a small screwed up piece of yellow paper, which had been hidden from sight by the folds in the bag.

The paper was a carbon copy of the bet timed at 14.05 headed 'Ronnie Smith Bookmakers'. He shuddered and put his head in his hands, someone was helping him but in doing so had relieved him of nearly £99,000 – was it his brother or Luke Devine? They were the only people who knew about it.

Who placed the bet? It had 'AT' on the bottom line so whoever did it placed it with Angela Tate or used her till. He would ask her but she was silly and he doubted that she would tell him, but surely she could remember if she paid out the £1,000, and to whom she gave the money.

Then there was the question of his dad. He lay awake trying to make some sense of the day's events, the alcohol and the curry had long gone into his guts and he wished he had stayed with Kate, he would ring her early in the morning and arrange to see her.

Angela stayed the night with Kate, she had suddenly become frightened and wondered if the men who robbed the shop would find and attack her. Kate calmed her down and they finished the remains of the curry with a bottle of wine.

'Were you frightened they would shoot you, Angela?'

'No, Kate, it was just the bang of the gun that gave me the wee problem. It had been a funny day. We had a lot of customers but we seemed to be winning on most races, that happens sometimes and it just gives me more work as the till gets full, I've to count the money and then move it to the safe. Every time I went to do it Billy stopped me until just before the robbery when he moved almost everything from the till.'

The noise of the house phone broke the Sunday morning silence in the Lavender house; Barbara picked up the bedroom extension and gasped as she heard her husband's voice.

'Barbara, just listen. I'm safe and I'll contact you again soon when I've got my head around things.'

'Yes, Gerry, but what is it and who are you with? When will you be back?'

'No answers at the moment, Barbara, please try not to worry. I'll contact you again soon—'

Barbara could hear other voices in the background and they sounded foreign, she was just about to speak again when the line went dead, he had put the phone down or someone had cut Gerry off.

Barbara tried to redial the number but it was not available, Gerry had not used his mobile and his phone call had lasted a few seconds; she didn't know what to think. Who should she confide in? Should she tell the police? Her mind was racing.

Donna and Mark were still asleep as she went downstairs to make a cup of tea; it would help her clear her head before she made a decision about what to do.

Her thoughts were confused and she needed help but the loud noise from Donna's room was to change her priorities very quickly.

'Mum, I need you!'

Barbara ran upstairs nearly tripping over Mark's shoes, which he had taken off and left in the middle of the hall.

'What is it?'

'I think my waters have broken. I feel different and look at the bed, it's about two weeks early.'

'OK, Donna, I'll ring Vince to take us to the hospital, you'll be fine.'

She shouted down the corridor in the direction of Mark's room but he was already up.

'What's the noise about, Mum?'

'It's Donna, she's having the baby.'

'Shit! What, here?'

'No, we've time to get her to hospital but we can't hang about. Phone Vince for me and he can take her, she's too big for the Mini. We can all go, I've something to tell you.'

Vince was on the doorstep in ten minutes and they helped Donna into the front seat, complete with the overnight bag she had packed a few days before.

'You must have known something was happening, Donna.'

'Yes, Vince, I just had a feeling he'd be early.'

'What do you mean, is he a boy?'

'Not sure, but I think so. Don't buy the Chelsea football shirt yet. Slow down, Vince, we've plenty of time.'

'I need to tell you all something about Dad,' said Barbara quietly.

'Was that him on the phone? It was a short call.'

'Yes, he just said he was OK and I shouldn't worry and he'd ring again soon. He sounded all right but he got off the phone quick or someone cut him off, the number wasn't available to redial.'

'Well, that's it then, we can all stop worrying,' said Vince coldly.

'I'm glad he phoned but now I'm more worried than before. What's he really involved in and is it legal, should I tell the police?'

'I hope it's not dodgy rip-off antiques. Why did he ever get involved in selling them? He really doesn't know what he's doing.'

'Your dad usually knows what he's doing, Vince, but this time I've no idea at all what it is. He said we'll hear from him again soon so we should keep quiet, don't tell anyone about his call and that includes the police and Kate – do you understand that, Mark?'

'Yes, Mum, but—'

'No buts, we just keep quiet until we get another call and hopefully it'll be soon.'

The journey to the hospital was easy on a Sunday morning without traffic. They all went into the maternity unit as Donna was admitted immediately; her contractions had slowed down so Vince did a round trip and dropped Mark and his mum back home. He grabbed a sandwich to eat en route back to the hospital and nearly crashed the car eating it.

Mark was still shaking from the previous day, he could not believe everything that had happened in a short space of time. Was he going mad? The missing money was driving him to despair. He had to speak to Vince on his own. He sent him a text message and asked him to phone him when he left the hospital.

It was five hours before Vince rang him.

'It's a boy, Mark, tell Mum the weight is 7lbs 2oz and he's called Shane, she can visit tonight. Donna is fine and fast asleep, he definitely has footballers' legs.'

'Brilliant! I need to see you, mate, I'm screwed up about this money.'

'OK, I'll go home and shower and meet you in The Plough about five o'clock.'

'Thanks, see you then.'

Vince had only one thought and that was about his new baby boy, the events of Saturday were a blur and as far as he was concerned the robbery was history already.

He'd get some time off work when Donna came home, the trip to Spain wouldn't happen now, he would leave everything to Luke and the local lawyer.

Mark was just about to enter the shower when the house phone rang. The brief call from Gerry had made everybody nervous so Mark decided he would take the call.

'Mark, it's me, Sharon. I got a text message to ring home. What's up?'

Sharon was away on a short holiday with her housemate, Liz, and she had just seen the text from earlier in the day.

Barbara had decided to tell her about her father going missing, but as Gerry had now phoned her, she would wait until her daughter got back home. By then she hoped Gerry would have appeared.

The text message was just to tell her about the arrival of the baby.

'Nothing up, Sharon, just some good news, Donna's had a baby boy and Vince is on cloud nine. I forgot the weight but he's OK, they're calling him Shane.'

'Fantastic. Can you ask Vince to take a picture on his phone and send it to me, please?'

'Yes, OK. When are you back home, I need to bounce something off you maybe?'

'Why just maybe, Mark? What have you done?'

'Nothing, Sharon, that's the problem. I need a new life, any ideas?'

'You sound depressed, Mark, is everything OK with Kate?'

'Enough, Sharon, enjoy the rest of your holiday. I'll pick you up from Gatwick on Tuesday, we can lose Kate then have a chat.'

'OK, I'm pissed off here. Liz had to go home early so I can't wait to get back. Don't worry, there's nothing we can't sort out, Mark.'

He put the phone down and went into the shower.

'Who was that, Mark?'

'Just Sharon. She got your message and I told her about the baby but not about Dad.'

'OK, thanks. I hope he turns up before she's back. Maybe we'll get another call, your dad sounded a bit stressed but strangely enough not desperate. It isn't like him but there again sometimes I feel I don't know him as well as I did. It all started once he got involved in those bloody antiques.'

Mark sat naked on the bed. He had finished his shower and the water from his hair dripped onto his mother's bedroom floor.

'Mark for goodness sake grab something and cover yourself up. It's like the start of a porn film.'

Mark laughed at his prudish mother and grabbed a dressing gown.

He sometimes wondered if she still had a sex life. Could she have a lover? The marriage between his mum and dad was not a loving one but then maybe his dad was the one to have a ladyfriend. Could that be the reason for his sudden disappearance?

He snapped out of his daydream and put his arms around his mum.

'Mum, did you actually see any of the antiques Dad is selling?'

'No, come to think of it I haven't, but then he does everything through his friend Dick Cohen in Wallington. He keeps most of his financial books and I think your dad always sells for cash, he told me he always had cash in the safe. He also has another account somewhere and he'd never tell me where it was. He said one night after a few too many beers that if he told me then I might get kidnapped for the information. I thought he was joking but I'm not sure now.'

'Shall we have a look in the safe, Mum? We can see if he's done any recent deals, it may give us a clue.'

'I'm not sure, Mark, that's going behind his back.'

'Mum, he's not here and something isn't right, we need some clues as to what he's doing. Please get the key and we can have a quick look inside.'

Barbara Lavender had her own bank account; Gerry always insisted she had her own money and assets separate to his. If he was to go bankrupt or got in serious debt she would be excluded, so as a couple they had a fall back.

Only Vince knew where the keys to the safe were kept other than his parents. Mark waited by the kitchen door as his mother produced two long, expensive-looking brass keys.

The safe was in the floor of the toilet. Gerry's brother was a locksmith but also a plumber. A few years before he had put a new downstairs toilet in the house, at the same time Gerry had got him to cement a safe into the floor.

A switch behind the toilet itself opened a trap door and two keyholes appeared. Once the outer door was open the safe automatically raised up from the floor on an electric scissor lift.

Mark left his mother as she opened the safe; he had nothing to learn from watching her. It was the keys he needed to start with and he had seen where they were being kept. His mother entered the home phone number as the combination.

The lock clicked open after the ten-digit number was entered, the safe contained just three wrapped parcels, and the first parcel contained passports, premium bonds, deeds and share certificates.

The second parcel was very heavy; Barbara had not seen it before and she tried to lift it without success. Mark took over and pulled the parcel to one side then lifted it onto the safe lid.

'Bloody hell, Mum, this is a lump of lead. What's it doing in here?'

'Not lead, Mark, look at the end of the parcel, it's a gold bar.'

They looked at each other open mouthed. They had no idea of its value, all they knew was that it was worth a lot of money, but why was it in the safe?

Their attention was then drawn to the third parcel.

'That, I know, is emergency money.'

The parcel was also heavy and much larger than the gold bar. They could see through the polythene wrapping that it contained mostly foreign currency and some sterling.

She opened the end of the parcel and immediately knew she was wrong about the amounts, a small envelope contained the sterling money she knew about but the rest of the parcel contained fresh and clean euro notes. She quickly counted the pile.

'Mark, look at the slip on the top, there is 1,000 x 100 euro notes here, that's a million, in today's money about £850,000.'

'I like Dad's antiques, Mum, can I have a loan?'

'Mark, I know nothing about the gold or the euros, I did expect some emergency money but it's much more than I thought.'

She quickly put everything back and locked the safe, which once secure disappeared again into the floor totally out of sight and almost impossible to find.

'Actually, Mark, that exercise told us nothing other than your dad has some explaining to do when he surfaces.'

Barbara was angry. She had no idea what the contents of the safe would be, but then Gerry knew she had access to the keys and she knew the combination, maybe he wanted her to find it if he didn't come home.

The knock on the front door startled them both.

'Who is that? Maybe Vince has forgotten his key.'

'No, Mum, we're meeting in the pub, it's not him. Stand away from the door until I see who it is.'

Mark opened the door.

A medium-built man dressed in an overcoat with a suit underneath stood on the doorstep. He was of a suave, Mediterranean appearance and Mark thought he was probably a professional man, accountant, lawyer or similar.

In a quiet voice with a strong Spanish or Portuguese accent, he looked straight at Mark and quickly said, 'Mr Gerry Lavender is he here?'

'Who are you and why do you want him?'

'My name is Juan Villa, I am from Spain and you have nothing to fear, I just need to speak with Mr Lavender, please.'

Mark looked at his mother and she nodded, it was the please that got him inside the house.

'Come in.'

'Thank you. Is Mr Lavender here?'

Barbara decided to take over and she asked the man to sit down.

'Mr Villa, it is Sunday evening and we are obviously suspicious of you. My husband is away on business but you can give me a message for him, he'll call us soon.'

'I can only tell you, Mrs Lavender, what I have been asked to do by clients in Spain. I speak the best English in our small company. We are attorneys, notaries or lawyers, whatever you want to call us. Our speciality is residential and commercial property. In our country we have many foreigners buying and selling property and no doubt you have the same in the UK, the difference is some of these people are criminals past and present, so we have to be very careful.

'We have for sale a very big new building project in Marbella and it will be complete hopefully next year. The complex has many apartments, houses and a leisure centre with a new golf course designed by a famous golfer. The documents for many sales are all ready to be signed and we have received them back from the solicitors for the seller, or I think you call them developers, one man has to sign for several properties so we can complete but he cannot be found. Yes, I think you guess, the buyer is your husband, Gerry Lavender.'

'Are you sure it's my father, Mr Villa?'

'Yes. I thought I knew Mr Lavender very well and when he did not turn up to sign, we asked a detective agency to check him out. Everything is fine with his identity but he is nowhere to be found and he does not answer his phone. Please tell me, is this your husband in the picture, Mrs Lavender?'

The picture was recent, it certainly was the missing Gerry Lavender, his clothes were the ones in the wash and Barbara guessed the photo was taken only a few weeks before and from the background it looked like an airport.

'Did you take the photograph, Mr Villa?'

'No, Mark, it is from the detective agency. I think it is here in London Heathrow Airport.'

'You know my name as well?'

'Yes, we have a good background on you and your family from your father. I have also had an enquiry from your son, Vincent, a few months ago but it's Gerry we want now. We need him to come and see us urgently as we have everything ready to complete the deal but he is the only one that can sign.'

'What does the lawyer or attorney for the seller or developer say about it, then?'

'That is the problem. I am afraid one of the people involved in the transaction was found dead three days ago in his apartment in Malaga. The police are not saying anything but we hear that possibly it was not a natural death or suicide. So that is why I am here, people in Spain are nervous and we need to complete.'

'Mr Villa, this is all too much for my mother, please can you go now. Leave your card and we'll contact you when my dad turns up. Will you stay in London?'

'For a few days. Please don't contact the police otherwise they will contact Spain and then I could have problems.'

'This is our phone number, ring us in a couple of days. We'll contact you if he arrives back here, if he does phone we'll tell him you called. My husband is not a criminal but he may be into something he can't handle, we have no idea were he's gone or if someone is keeping him prisoner.'

The Spaniard picked up his coat and shook their hands, he had a minicab waiting for him at the end of the street and he disappeared as quickly as he had arrived.

'Go now, Mark. Get dressed and meet Vince, tell him what has happened and bring him back for coffee. He'll be on his own for a few days and on holiday, so apart from seeing Donna he'll be free to help us. Somehow we have to work out where your dad can be. I want Vince to tell me more about Mr Villa and his business, your father must have told him some things about Spain and he hasn't said anything to me.'

'Yes, Mum, but you know what Dad and Vince are like, they never tell the rest of us anything about a deal unless they need help. It's an old way of doing things, you don't tell people you love about danger or problems until you've sorted them, the less people that know about a scheme the better.'

'I don't like it, Mark, and Vince needs to do some talking.'

Mark saw his mother's face going red and he knew that was the sign for him to go and he quickly left the house.

Chapter seven

Instant Credit

The National World Bank in Lewisham was easy prey for a robbery, especially when the bank manager had gambling debts and was desperate for cash. The bank had just two UK branches, Lewisham and Manchester, the head office. Ahmed was the Lewisham boss, his father was the major shareholder and Ahmed owed a lot of money to local bookmakers.

Ronnie Smith met with two acquaintances in the Crown at Morden, the perfect venue to plan a robbery as nobody but criminals went there since the recent murder. It was due to be closed soon for refurbishment, or more likely total demolition.

He bought them just one beer each – he had to keep them sober as they had very little brainpower – if they had more they would totally forget what to do. They were men who needed money urgently, all of them for a different reason.

'Oscar, this isn't a difficult job, in fact it's a piece of cake, even for you and John boy, so make sure you don't fuck it up.'

'Yes, boss, but go through it one more time then we'll do a runner and check the car out.'

'Right, listen carefully this time.'

'You collect the Vauxhall Astra from the address I gave you, the owner is having it serviced and the garage has parked the car for his collection tomorrow. A friend in the garage got this key for you, it's a maintenance key and it just opens the car and starts it, you won't be able to use the boot so keep the parcels you collect under the seat. Drive to the High Street and park it carefully in the multi-storey car park, the pay and display one opposite the cinema, the other car parks in the town are no good as you have to get a ticket and stop at the barrier. The first half an hour is free in the cinema one but you have to get a ticket from the machine and leave it on the dashboard, so no barrier, no nothing, it's dead easy.

'The whole place has CCTV coverage so you'll be seen on film but provided you do as I say they won't be able to recognise your faces. Take these two pairs of blue overalls and caps, they are marked with the name of the security company, put the caps on and pull them down over your foreheads. It helps that you're black as it's dark in the car park and the CCTV will be lousy.'

'That's a bit racist, boss!'

'No it fucking well isn't, it's just a fact of life in Lewisham, son. Go to the bank, it's just a couple of minutes from the car, it's on the other side of the road from the car park, use the crossing otherwise you will have to run through the traffic to get there and that will attract attention. The place has a big blue sign with "NW" on it and that's not the Nat West one, which is a few shops down, make sure you go to the right bank. Find the side door and ring the bell then ask on the intercom for Mr Ahmed, give him the name of the security company, he'll be expecting you and he'll let you in.'

'What'll he do, boss?'

'He'll bring two big parcels wrapped in a heavy-duty bank security cover, don't worry you aren't blowing anything up and robbing the safe, just collecting the parcels. Sign the paper he gives you with a scribble then leave, don't say a word. As you come out to the high street, just walk don't run and when you get to the car, hide the parcels under the seat and slowly drive out. Go straight back to Ladywell Railway Station and park the car, it's at the other end of the street from where you nicked the car. Leroy, the owner, will just think the garage parked it in the wrong place.

'That bastard will regret fixing me up. He'll see his car outside the station as he comes out, he must do as it's that terrible bright blue colour, the old bill will put him in the frame from the car park CCTV, and I'll make sure they're tipped off. Then I'm even with him. Make sure you leave the overalls and caps hidden under the seats'

'What did he do, boss?'

'He robbed my daughter of her handbag in Lewisham shopping centre and she recognised him, he didn't remember her but she told me it was definitely him and she doesn't get men wrong. I'll be on the other side of the station in the white Mercedes. Jump in the back seat and put the parcels on the floor, we'll drive back here. When we arrive I'll give you £5,000 each in cash. Don't start throwing the money around, just take your time with it, maybe save it, buy an ISA or something.'

'Is an ISA a Lexus, boss?'

'No, Oscar, it's a tax-free savings account.'

'But we don't pay tax, we're self-employed.'

'Good point but don't shout it around otherwise someone will be coming round and start looking under your bed. It's easy, boys. Any questions?'

'Just one, boss. This Ahmed bloke we see at the bank, who's he?'

'His dad owns the bank but Ahmed owes the bookies shitloads of money, including me, and he's faking this robbery to clear his debts. He uses a security firm with the name on your overalls so it's just a normal pick up.

When the real guys turn up later he will call the police. Clever if it all works, it should do.'

'It must be a lot of money, then.'

'Yes, Oscar, it's enough for me to follow you for the rest of your life if you double-cross me.'

'No, boss, we won't do that, promise. We still want to play in your football team.'

Ronnie just looked at them, they smiled at each other and shook hands. He knew they would deliver – football meant everything to them.

The robbery went like clockwork, the police pulled in Leroy, the owner of the car, and he had a night in the cells but the police had no real evidence. He had already found the overalls and thrown them away. As the car had moved from where he had parked it he guessed that someone had borrowed his car, maybe mechanics or someone like them, but really he had no idea who it was other than they were black, the police had told him.

Ahmed was a bad liar and his father didn't believe his story, he was sent back to the Middle East never to return to the UK.

Ronnie had a lot of cash hanging about and he had to get it to Spain, he was already working out how to do it, he had several plans but he needed to get on with them soon. The dream deal would be ready one day and he had to be ready to move quickly.

Chapter eight

A Toast to the New Arrival

Vince was already at The Plough when Mark arrived, he was halfway through his first pint as he had lots to celebrate, a baby boy and a share in a property in Spain.

'What you drinking, Mark?'

'Pint of lager, Vince. It'd be good if we could celebrate. So what do you reckon happened to my money? I've been wondering if it relates to Dad in any way, what do you think?'

Vince was not concerned about anything other than his baby son, at least until Mark told him about the mystery visitor.

'You say he was Spanish, did he give you his name?'

'Yes, he said he was called Juan Villa and he told us that he knew you, he was an attorney or lawyer dealing with the buying and selling of property for foreigners in Spain.'

Vince went pale and gulped the remainder of his pint down in one mouthful.

'You all right, mate? You look like you've seen a ghost.'

The news about the Spanish visitor had rattled Vince Lavender, he knew the guy from his dad but he had never met him; Mark knew Luke Devine was already on his way to Spain but he didn't know that he was going to buy some property and meet the lawyer that his dad knew.

Vince knew his father was into something in Spain but if the lawyer was in the UK it had to be serious. He didn't know why he had gone missing but he guessed now that it involved a deal. What a time to disappear, he thought, as Mark stared at him for an answer.

'Yes, I know him. Mark, listen, I'm only going to tell you this once and you have to listen carefully. Come away from the bar and sit at the small table. Get two more pints in, I've to make a quick phone call.'

Mark did as instructed but as he bought the drinks he saw Angela Tate at the other end of the bar with a girl that he didn't know. There was no sign of

Kate, which was a relief to him as the business with Vince was serious stuff and he didn't want his girlfriend eavesdropping on the conversation.

'Hi, Angela, I'm a bit busy for a few minutes, I'll buy you a drink when I've finished.'

'Great, come over when you're ready.'

Mark felt a bulge in his trousers, what the hell was he thinking, this girl was dangerous and it could mess up his friendship with Kate. He didn't think about the downsides for long as he returned to the corner table to hear his brother's revelations.

Mark pushed the pint in front of his older brother; he grabbed it and drank half of it before starting his speech.

'Luke and I are buying a property in Spain. He has both his own share of the robbery money and mine. He left by train for Spain immediately after the robbery and we got him secretly across the channel. The property was a dream Donna had and I hope Luke won't double-cross me. At first is was just a timeshare but now, with this extra cash, we should be able to buy a place outright. The guy, Juan Villa who came to our house, is our lawyer and yes, he's working for Dad on something as well and it was Dad who recommended him. I have no idea though where he is but you said that Juan mentioned that one of his clients had been found dead. That's not our business. I've left a text message for Luke to ring me tomorrow.

'Now about your money, I have no idea what happened to it, Mark, other than I am suspicious about Luke. What did the copper say last night?'

'Not a lot, he seemed bored with the whole thing. It was John Hampton from my old school, he is now a sergeant. I've to go to the police station tomorrow after work and I hope I can keep my nerve. I wonder who tipped him off to look in my car, Vince.'

'No idea on that one, Mark, but you've got to play it cool, they don't have any evidence on us. Just answer their questions and get out as soon as you can. The notes looked like they were all old ones so they can't easily be traced and no way would Ronnie have got the numbers written down. After all, you still have some of them and if you say it's only a grand, spend it, don't keep the notes hanging around. What did you say about the betting slip?'

'That's what's giving me the creeps, Vince, the slip is for a bet placed at the bookmakers, handwritten and timed at 14.05. It had Angela Tate's initials on it, the amount was £1,000, exactly the amount in the bag. I didn't put the bet on but I did talk about doing it to people, even in here.'

'Yes, I see what you mean, it's as if someone was taking the piss out of you and the police. They get a tip-off but then someone lifts the bulk of the money before they check your car.'

'Vince, I've tried hard to think back about everything that we did after leaving the bookmakers and up to the time when the policeman came to the pub. The lock on the Mini boot can be opened with a screwdriver so whoever took the money could have done it in a minute, just leaving £1,000 and the betting slip in the bag.'

'I better tell you something, Mark, that you don't know about Dad. He knew about the robbery and he also told Luke and I how to know that a lot of money would be in the till. I just wonder if he got someone to take the money from your boot and at the same time give you a reason for the remainder confirmed by the betting slip. Possibly he knew something was going to go wrong and it was his way of helping you, but then that's not like Dad.'

'I don't understand, Vince?'

'Dad has a sort of love and hate relationship with Ronnie Smith. He cheated him out of a lot of money a few years ago and he gave Luke and I the idea to rob the betting shop. He seemed to know it was virtually minimum risk for a lot of money. Somehow he knew that he could get us the time that Ronnie would have much more cash than normal in the safe. I don't know who took the money from your car but I suspect it could've been Luke on his way to the port. If I can get hold of him I'll check it out.'

'Yes, but Vince, the police somehow know about my bet, which as we both know didn't happen.'

'We know someone tipped them off and if you think about it the £1,000 could help put you in the clear as it matches the payment you were due. You're right what you just said, Mark, you mentioned to us all last week in here about the bet you might put on but then probably due to the robbery you forgot it. You were throwing money around when you were a bit pissed. Somebody else must have put the bet on for you. Think back, who was in the pub that night?'

'I don't remember a thing, mate. So what do you think has happened to Dad? I really need his help now, Vince.'

'As I said already, mate, I'm sure he's OK but is in deep with something or someone. I don't expect to see him until it's sorted. My feeling is we could have some surprises to come, I can possibly tell you more tomorrow after I've made some phone calls but I tried earlier and got no replies.'

'You're right, Vince, as come to think of it, Dad told me to take care the last time I saw him and he never ever said that to me before. He obviously knew something was going to happen. As Luke and you planned the robbery, I was happy it would be a piece of cake.'

'It was easy, Mark, until someone tipped off the police and maybe Ronnie as well. I'll try to find out who it was but we have to be careful, the police will be asking similar questions, maybe they'll find out first then we'll see what we're up against.'

'Where do you think my money is, Vince, you must know?'

'I think we'll ask Luke that one, or Dad when we find him. Don't worry, little brother, I'm on the case.'

'Vince, sorry, one last question – why did Luke fire the fucking gun into the shop roof?'

'Easy, it wasn't just at the ceiling but at the CCTV camera, he had to do it because Billy Bootle went to move a switch under the counter, it looked like a panic button but it must have been a device to change the camera angle so it would get us all on film. Luke saw the CCTV camera, he hit it and it fell down with three or four ceiling tiles but then we saw it had no wires, they must have had another one, hopefully with our hoods up they couldn't identify us. I didn't think Luke would do it, but that's him sometimes and it certainly got Billy Bootle moving, before then he looked as if he didn't care.'

'Yes, if there was another camera it might have pointed out the front and in the excitement I forgot to put my fucking hood up in the car.'

'Let's hope it was just pointing inside like they usually do.'

Mark smiled but he was worried. If the CCTV was focused on the outside, or maybe there were two cameras, someone inside may have recognised him. He had so much going through his mind he just nodded and turned to his brother and shook his hand.

'Thanks, mate, let's stick together, we'll celebrate later.'

'Agreed, Mark, try not to worry, go and get a drink. I'm off now.'

'Angela Tate is in the bar and she seems very anxious to get to know me so I'm going to buy her a drink in a minute. I won't mention anything about the robbery but it might be interesting to hear what she comes out with after a few vodkas, she's not the brain of Britain so I'm expecting some stories.'

'Be careful, Mark, you know Kate would chop your balls off if she knew.'

Vince drank his pint up quickly; he grabbed his coat and jumped into a taxi waiting at the rank.

'Where are we going, sir?' Vince passed a card to the driver.

'As far away as possible but we'll start with the champagne bar at The Mandarin Oriental. I've got a new baby and I'm going to celebrate.'

The driver knew what his customer wanted.

'Hope you've got lots of money, mate.'

'I've got plastic and that'll buy me anything I want.'

Chapter nine

Spain for Safety?

Luke Devine's journey through France and Spain was long and uneventful. He was careful not to use his mobile and as he stopped in Southern France then Barcelona, he found cafés with internet access and checked his email. People were looking for him but for unpaid debts and definitely not the police.

He read a brief report in a day-old copy of the Daily Mail about the robbery, but he smiled as the message it gave was loud and clear, the police were not saying anything. They had not given the paper any descriptions or requests for information, but that was usual; it was early days. His main worry was not his mate Vince, but his brother, Mark. The loss of the money from the Mini was not in the plan but Luke had decided to take it, maybe he would square it later with Mark, but in his situation, maybe not.

If Mark still had the money, Luke would have been more concerned that he would have been flashing it around but that was not his reason for taking it.

Once he arrived in Valencia he had planned to make a phonebox call to Vince, the money was burning a hole in his mind. He would tell Vince he had Mark's money and he was going to invest it. For a time he thought about double-crossing his friends but that was one move too many for him, the plans would stay the same but with Mark's money being used as well.

Luke was known to change his mind and he thought again that perhaps a call to Vince was a bad idea, he needed to keep all his options open and he would watch his email for messages good and bad before deciding the fate of the money.

He slept with the bag under his pillow, not leaving it unattended at any time during the journey, especially on the InterCity trains, which had a reputation for petty crime.

On the final leg, the train slowed down for its arrival into Valencia, Luke breathed a sigh of relief as he saw his mother, Diana Devine, and his old friend, Mario Ramos, waiting on the platform.

Diana Devine had been a stunning woman in her younger years and was still very desirable to the lecherous Spaniards as a single woman in her late 50s. She had been very sick after receiving intensive treatment for breast cancer.

Her progress was slow but effective and the hospital had told her she was doing well and would likely make a full recovery. The arrival of her only son Luke was a wonderful bonus as her husband had died three years before, and apart from some casual friends of both sexes, she had mainly been on her own.

The move to Spain was originally all linked to their retirement; she had considered moving back to London many times before Luke told her his plans, now she was rethinking everything. If Luke did go through with a property purchase she might stay in Spain. She had friends in other areas of Spain and her idea was to help Luke settle in to his new life and maybe live with or near him.

'Mum, you look great. How do you feel now, are you all right?'

'One question at a time, Luke. Actually I'm much better, I've even started looking at men again.'

She placed her hand on Mario Ramos's perfect bum and squeezed it, he made an imitation squeal and they all laughed.

Mario embraced Luke then the Englishman put the Spaniard's head in a friendly headlock but released him almost straight away.

'Leave my mum alone, she doesn't have footballers as lovers.'

'Luke, welcome to Valencia you know Mrs Devine is safe with me. Now did you have a good journey from England?'

Changing the subject quickly indicated to Luke that Mario might have had something to hide but on this occasion Luke gave him the benefit of the doubt. He made a mental note to keep an eye on his Spanish friend and if he got the chance he would check his phone.

'Yes, OK thanks, but I've had enough of trains for ever, Mario. I'm now looking forward to a cold beer, a shower and a soft bed, in that order. Am I still OK at your place until Mum is totally better?'

'Yes, of course, Luke. I'm playing tomorrow night and Sunday, both games are away matches. We're doing well in the cup but that means I'm on busy schedules so you will have to look after yourself.'

'My place is too small for you, Luke, as I've my lodger Anna with me. She helps with the cooking and housework so I don't want her to leave yet and there isn't room for three people. What is the news on your place in Marbella?'

'A few things have happened. We have more money to spend than we first thought. I'll probably become a permanent resident in Spain, but one day I may spend some time in the UK and also time here. I've a partner who's investing in Spain big time and the property will have lots of facilities – apartments, houses, a golf course and leisure centre. My interest is just somewhere to live and probably in a house big enough for guests and maybe you, if you want.'

'Sounds very complicated, son, tell me more later. Let's get out of this smelly station. Have a wash at Mario's place then come around for dinner. Anna is cooking paella.'

Mario drove his Mercedes fast through the streets of Valencia; at 28 he was already a multi-millionaire. His career had included two seasons each with Barcelona, West Ham United and Bayern Munich. He had returned to his homeland for a four-year deal with FC Lecont, a newly promoted side in La Liga and a club with lots of ambition.

Mario had met Luke for the first time during a European Cup match five years before; after a few crunching tackles each, they shook hands and exchanged shirts at the end of the game. Barcelona had beaten the London side by two goals to nil in Spain after a draw in England.

A trip to Spain followed a few months after the game. Luke had the same interests as Mario: money, football, women and the good life, in that order. The Spaniard showed Luke the delights of Spain and the Englishman was hooked. At first he wanted a move to Spanish football but his agent found no takers, plus his wife did not want to move out of London.

The big difference between the men was that Luke had married his childhood sweetheart, Susan, and once his standard of living improved so did his attraction to women. He then messed up big time; gambling, then the daily revelations in the newspapers about his none-too-private life, bought him an expensive divorce.

Luke's bad luck did not end there, he got a serious knee injury and he started to gamble more and drink heavily in his newly found spare time. With no wife to bring him into line, he got into financial problems and soon his creditors were forcing him in the direction of bankruptcy.

His football-playing days were over and finding work was difficult. He had a few short-term jobs with lower league sides but the money was poor and his frustrations showed very quickly.

He turned to his so-called friends, and the idea of the betting shop raid came out of the blue; the suggestion of the robbery by his friend's father was very interesting. He also knew that his mate, Vince, wanted to get a place in Spain and if the pay-out was likely to be as large as he had been told, the crime was worth the risks.

They needed a wheelman and the only person they could really trust was Vince's younger brother, Mark. He didn't need much persuasion and the three young men shook hands on a deal that would make them all criminals.

Luke was in a daydream as Mario opened the door to his new four-bedroom apartment. The main view was over a sleepy green park and the bedrooms almost touched the olive grove, a tranquil place were the footballer could hide from his supporters.

'This is brilliant, mate, is it yours?'

'No, actually the club owns it. I have a house in the country but this place is just 50 kilometres by autoroute to the training ground and 60 kilometres to the ground. The fans don't know about here, or at least not yet, when they do I move.'

'We used the only entrance – it's via the underground car park so few people see me arrive and go out again.'

Diana Devine sat down and listened to Mario, she didn't need a tour she had already had one or two or three already.

'I'm off now, Luke, you know the route to my place for dinner, say nine o'clock?'

'That's late, Mum.'

'Luke, this is Spain, we eat late. You'll have to get used to it if you stay here.'

'I have to stay here, my finances are actually a bloody mess and Susan is still after more cash from me, the bitch.'

'Luke, you messed up, not her. Have you money to live here?'

An embarrassed Mario interrupted the inquisition.

'This talk is not for me, Diana. I'm going to pack my bags for tomorrow. I'm away early so I'll skip the paella today.'

'OK, Mario, all the more for us.'

'Let's talk later, Mum, but yes, I reckon I've enough money for a place and cash for a few years if I'm careful here, but I need to find a job of some sort, anything really. I know I said about going back to England sometime but that's unlikely. Mario, have you any ideas?'

'Don't know, Luke, but I'll ask around.'

The Spaniard did not want a permanent lodger so he was less than helpful to his friend but Diana had contacts in the restaurant business and Luke had already told her to sound out a couple of her suggestions.

'If I don't see you tomorrow, Luke, here's a key. If you need me this is my phone number, just send me a text and I'll get back to you. I'm back here in three days. How long will you stay?'

Already Mario was worried that Luke could be a long-term visitor. He gave him the ground rules and one was that he just had a few weeks to sort out his own place; he blamed the club, saying they didn't allow visitors.

Luke grabbed a beer and used the shower, as he was drying himself his phone rang with no number showing on the screen. He was unsure whether he should answer it or not. Susan hadn't got his number so he decided to risk it. The voice was familiar.

'How are you?' said the voice.

'You didn't tell me it was so much money, including the chunk I got back from Mark. I think I've got around £290,000 left. I'll check it all later but then I need to offload it.'

'Yes, OK, you are right. A Spanish man will call you tomorrow and the code is the name of the city, Valencia, take a further £2,000 for your expenses and arrange to meet him, he'll come to you. Give him the rest of the money, but count it in front of him and bundle the notes, he'll complete two forms and sign them, you sign them and keep one safe, he'll then disappear. The investment is safe and I'll give you full details soon.'

'What are the police saying?'

'Nothing, it's early days, just a few lines in the paper. I think you guys are in the clear. I'll see Vince and Mark right. If Vince calls you, don't mention me.'

'How is Mark? He was the one that worries me. I heard the police bent his ear. I bet he was pretty shocked when he found the money had gone from his car boot, but he'll get over it. That stupid guy Bootle sent me a text to say he was waiting in a pub on the Brighton road expecting one of you to turn up. I phoned him from a public call box. I knew you had taken the money from Mark's car and were on the way to Spain. He wasn't a happy chap. I said we were investing it for him, he got a bit aggressive so I arranged for him to get some money, actually £3,000 just to shut him up. He had no idea how much you'd taken. After a few swear words he went and said he'd see you in Spain.'

'Yes, he has problems. You'd better watch out for him.'

'He doesn't frighten me, but warn Vince that he's on the warpath.'

'Yes, I'll get a message to him. It may be we have to give him a few grand when the dust settles but that will be his lot. If I don't hear from you I'll assume everything is done with the courier. If you get any difficulties, phone me from a public box.'

'OK, but when will I see someone about our place in Marbella?'

'You'll be contacted soon by a lawyer once all the money is banked, he'll help you. Stay in Valencia and keep a low profile, don't tell that footballer or your mother too much.'

Luke switched the phone off completely, he had hardly any battery. He knew his contact would not phone until the next day so he would have an evening of peace and quiet with his mum, something he had not done for ten years.

Diana Devine's apartment was as tiny as she had described. When her husband died, she downsized to make sure that long term she had enough money to stay in Spain.

'This place is OK, Mum, but I see what you mean, it's for one and a half persons, not a family.'

Before she could answer, Anna the lodger entered the one main room from the kitchen, she shyly held out her hand and in perfect English but with a strong accent she spoke to Luke.

'Hello, you are Luke, I am Anna and I come from Marbella. I am the half person here.'

Luke laughed at her cheeky joke.

'Pleased to meet you, Anna. I hear from my mother you're a good cook.'

'Wait and see, Luke. You like paella?'

'Never had it but I'll try anything once.'

Luke gave the 23-year-old girl the once over and his mother caught him staring at her.

She was small and slim with a dark complexion and long black hair pulled together in a ponytail. Her body was in perfect proportion and the white kitchen overall reminded Luke more of a nurse than a cook, he was in love with her already but she was far too young for him.

'I can see your eyes talking, my dear, take care to keep your trousers on. You need to settle before you jump into a relationship. She's intelligent and sexy but very young and there are many more where she comes from.'

'Mum, you make me laugh. How many lovers have you had then since Dad died?'

'Mind your own business, remember I have been ill. But to answer your question, just a couple. There's no rush at 56 years old, my health is my number one priority.'

The meal was served and the speed Luke ate it showed his hunger and enjoyment for the traditional dish. He finished his plate and after chatting at the table for nearly an hour, Diana suddenly stood up.

'I'll wash up, we don't use a dishwasher here, then I'm off to bed. My tablets will knock me out, so Luke come around tomorrow and we can catch up with all your news from England.'

'That'll take me five minutes, but yes, I'll see you about eleven o'clock.'

'Luke, how is my English?' said Anna shyly.

'Good, Anna, but how is your practical?'

'Sorry, don't understand, I think.'

He explained his comment and she blushed, it was almost too provocative a question for a first meeting. The girl had never spoken to an English man for any length of time. Diana was her main help in getting her sentences, verbs and adjectives in the right order.

Luke waited for his mother's bedroom door to close then moved alongside the girl on the couch, she smiled and made no attempt to move away.

The only subject that Luke really knew anything about was football and he told Anna all about his career, his injury and how important the game had been in his life. The reality was that at 38 he had no job and expensive habits that would have to end. The girl asked many questions so he told her about his wife, the divorce and the idea that he should live in Spain.

He caught her looking at him and he reacted by placing a small kiss on her cheek, she gave another big smile and kissed him, also on his cheek.

Luke pulled her towards him and the small girl all but disappeared inside his large body as he hugged her. She pulled away from him and stood up.

'Where do you come from, Anna?'

'I told you already, Luke, I am from Marbella. My father wants me to finish my studies here as an accountant. I will return home once the exams are finished in a few months and then I start working with my family when I am qualified.'

She stood up and grabbed the empty plates.

'I am going to bed now, see you again, goodnight.'

Luke was disappointed she was leaving, as any ideas he had about her were soon lost as she left the kitchen and opened the door to her room.

The girl had suddenly remembered the age difference between them and she almost regretted kissing him; as she left Luke stood up.

'Wait, Anna, don't rush, sorry if I upset you.'

The girl stopped and looked at him, releasing her hair from its band.

'I know what you want, Luke, and I am flattered if that's the right word. I am only 23, find me a young man.'

She laughed as she said it. Her English was better than Luke knew, her mother was from London and her father was Fernando Lopez from Marbella.

'Goodnight, Anna, sleep well.'

He waved as she closed her bedroom door. He left the small apartment and walked to his friend's place; the evening was warm and the wind had left the downtown streets of Valencia. He saw the lights from the harbour as he climbed the steps to the apartment door and hesitated, taking in the quiet beauty of the city. In his mind he was relaxed but he knew that he must watch his back, as his creditors would be looking for him.

He failed to notice the shadow of the tall man across the road; someone was watching him.

Chapter ten

A Brief Liaison

Mark was sorry to see his brother leave the pub but he felt more comfortable now they had discussed the events of the weekend. He looked across the bar to see if he could see Angela; she was already looking in his direction. Her friend was in a deep conversation with a barfly, the girl was hoping that Angela would move away so she had the boy to herself.

'Hi, Angela, are you feeling better now after yesterday?'

She moved away from the bar to the first table and sat down.

'Yes, I'm fresh as a daisy and looking for fun. Ronnie has given me two days off, not a big deal but he also gave me £50, he must have felt guilty about what happened.'

She leaned on Mark and kissed him on the cheek then pushed her glass into his hand.

'Vodka and tonic, please. Large one, Mark.'

The evening passed quickly, Mark answered a text message from Kate.

'Gone to see Donna and the baby call me tomorrow x'

That's odd, he thought, Kate never usually sends text messages, she just likes to talk, maybe she couldn't use the phone in the hospital. He decided to call her when he had finished with Angela; he was not looking for an all-night session with the shop girl.

Angela looked at the pub clock and realised she had to make her move.

'Mark, I'm feeling a bit drunk and tired. Why don't you come back to my flat and we can have a special night cap?'

'Yes, come on, let's go,' said Mark as he jumped to his feet.

She grabbed his arm and they took the first taxi in the rank.

Little was said between them en route to her flat; Angela had a lot to say but not when a nosey cab driver was listening.

Already he was watching them through his rear-view mirror as Mark put his hand on her knee and she put hers on top of his, pushing her fingers between his own long, beefy specimens.

Mark knew Angela had been around the block with a few men, but what the hell, she seemed to have no regrets. She had regular checks at the clinic when she collected her pills. She felt like a prostitute sometimes but her simple view was that as she couldn't change her lifestyle, she should make sure she was always checked regularly.

Unfortunately, drink did get the better of her and sometimes she liked the girls as well. For more than one reason she wanted Mark and her instructions to him would be clear and precise.

The flat was in darkness as Angela put the lamp on; Mark could see that it was little more than a bed-sitting room with a separate kitchen and bathroom.

In spite of its size, the place was immaculate and the settee had already been made up for the night, it was covered with a large red duvet and two pillows, Angela had been expecting company.

'I've whisky or beer, Mark, or both, what would you like?'

'A whisky, Angela. What are you having?'

She waved a very large vodka and tonic in front of his face and passed him his whisky as he lay back on her bed settee.

'It's my usual drink, Mark. I just get to a level then I don't get any drunker as long as I don't change the drink.'

'Yes, I can see you look pretty sober and that's amazing after what you have put down your throat, it must be expensive to get really pissed?'

Angela didn't answer, she took Mark's drink untouched from his hand and put her own drink next to it.

'We'll finish those drinks later.'

Before he could answer she pushed her lips against his and she skilfully locked her arms around his neck. Mark was a big man and she felt good as she started to explore his body.

Mark did not protest, this girl knew what she wanted; he switched one of the bedside lights off which gave the room a soft and seductive atmosphere.

Angela was on fire but not noisy, the alcohol was in control.

The whole event took less than ten minutes and he realised that for Angela it was just another man, no feelings except for the story she had to tell him.

'Mark, that was good. Now listen.'

He sat up in the bed but kept undressed, he was already thinking about another go with this hot lady when she had finished her speech.

'Mark, you know Kate is one of my friends and although I like you, I would not step between you two. My reason for inviting you here was firstly to have sex with you, which was very nice, but the main reason was about the robbery on Saturday.'

'What do you mean, Angela, what's going on?'

'As we both know, you and your friends robbed the betting office. That same afternoon I was told by Billy Bootle, the manager, to write a betting slip without a horse on it in the big race but with your name on the top. After the race I put it through the computer with the winner written on it, he altered the time by hand and put just £1,000 in a bag, the money almost matching the stake and the winning odds with only a few pence difference. He gave me the original to file away but the copy of the slip he left with the money. I never saw it again. When your friends burst in, I think he was sort of expecting them, the only person frightened was me. I told you what happened, I pissed myself, which was a bit messy but at least I was alive.'

Angela looked at Mark and handed him his whisky.

'Why did you say it was me in the shop during the robbery?'

'I didn't say in the shop, Mark, it was you in the car. I have a TV under the counter and I could see you clear as day from the other CCTV camera. There are two and one views outside. I saw Billy Bootle set it up and when I asked why it was pointing outside he just laughed and said it was in case we saw someone we didn't like.'

'Bloody hell, are you sure it got me, Angela, was it a good picture?'

'Yes, sorry Mark, it was a very clear picture of you and the police may have the tape already.'

'Fucking hell, Angela, I've been fitted up good and proper. But why did he set the CCTV on me? I didn't think he hated me that much. I better go home now and do a runner before the police play the tape. What the hell am I going to do, where can I go?'

'Look, Mark, once I thought about it I knew the raid looked dodgy and not real I started to think why, somebody knew that there was more money than usual in the safe. Stay with me tonight, nobody knows you're here, perhaps I'll get some ideas.'

'Thanks, Angela, you're right, I've got to think this through carefully. Maybe in the morning it'll have been just a bad dream.'

She smiled at him as they fell asleep together. In the months and years to follow, she would remember this night as a lot more than a bad dream, the consequences of the conversation for Mark, his family and his friends were devastating.

The robbery was carried out by amateurs, none of the boys had form but they all had one thing in common – they needed money and for different reasons. Luke Devine had big survival reasons; Mark wanted a better career and he needed to take time out and think about his future, money would give him some security. Vince wanted a place in the sun. He talked big to his mates in the pub, a few had places or rented them in Spain in the summer, he wanted some of it and now was the time.

Chapter eleven

Sharon and Liz

The five-day break to the Costa Brava sunshine was a last-minute idea; Sharon had found some cheap air tickets and the hotel was one of the few open in the early season.

In many respects Sharon was uncertain about a week with Liz and it was not long before her fears were realised in more ways than one. On the third night, after far too many tequila sunrise cocktails, the girls found two local men – actually boys – who did not look a day over 18 but swore they were 21.

Sharon managed to shake off her groping, bad-breathed Spaniard, but Liz was determined to hang on to Pepe. He seemed a nice boy even to Sharon and without too much protest he was taken back to the hotel and then into the girls' room.

The fight for the bedroom was soon lost, Sharon could see the plan and she grabbed her sheets and pillow for a quick exit to the lounge area; it was small and had just a mini settee a safe distance from her friend and partner.

The sunshine broke through the curtains as the day began to hot up; Sharon washed and dressed with the intention of a late breakfast leaving the one-night lovers in peace.

Her plan was halted by the ridiculous sonic noise of Liz's mobile. At first Sharon ignored it but when it rang again she guessed it might be important.

'Hello, Liz's phone.'

'I see, a talking phone now. Is that you, Sharon?'

'Yes, Mr Smith, it's me. Do you want Liz?'

'Please, Sharon, I need her urgently, is she there?'

'I think so, wait a minute and I'll check.'

'Liz, are you awake? Your dad's on the phone.' Sharon shouted twice before the reply came.

'Yes, yes, Sharon, I'm coming.'

The bedroom door finally opened and Pepe made a run for the front door, dressing as he passed Sharon.

'Not stopping then, Pepe? I hope you paid her.'

Sharon's comments were ignored as the boy had one idea only and that was to get out and away from the two English girls as soon as possible.

'Yes, Dad, what do you want?'

'That sounds a bit unfriendly, Liz; I need you back home, now, something is very wrong.'

'What do you mean, now? I'm on holiday!'

'Listen, this is serious stuff. I want you on the next flight to Gatwick. Give Sharon a couple of hundred euros for her booze for the next few days and also give her your apologies, blame it all on a family matter.'

'I get the message, Dad, but is someone dead?'

'Yes, I'm afraid so, but not someone close. The details will wait. I'm after some information and then someone else could be very ill as soon as I get my hands on them.'

'Calm down, Dad, I'll sort out a plane and text you my flight number. Can you pick me up?'

'Yes, then I can tell you what's happening.'

'All right, see you tonight or tomorrow, bye.'

'Sharon, I'm really sorry but I've to go back home tonight or tomorrow morning, my dad has some big problems and he wants me to help. I've got to do it, I love him and he needs me.'

'I see you've made your mind up already. I'm OK here, everything is paid up and I'll just chill out by the pool for the remaining days. You never know, I may find a millionaire who'll sweep me off my feet.'

'Yes, but don't start with Pepe.'

'It sounded OK to me.'

Ronnie was relieved to see his daughter and managed a weak smile.

'You look very healthy, my dear, your tan makes you look like a little girl.'

'Stop the flattery, Dad, and get to the point on why I'm back here when I could be drinking and shagging in Spain.'

'Jump in the Merc and I'll explain.'

The cold night air hit Liz between the eyes, she would do almost anything for her dad; he was very close to her since her mother left him. He stopped and opened the car door for her, something he had never done before.

'On Saturday my Cheam betting shop was robbed and I was cleaned out but I'll explain more about that in a minute. The big problem is that some bastard killed Alan Goody the next day.'

'You mean my Uncle John Smith don't you, Dad?'

'Yes, of course, Liz, but you know he changed his name after he had the breakdown, his wife dying then his son being killed in Northern Ireland. It all just about did him in. He's spent every day in the Cheam shop since last December; the betting kept him alive. He just needed company and he talked all day to Angela Tate and Billy Bootle, who probably wished he'd leave,

Billy was always arguing with him. That Bootle really is a miserable bastard.'

'So who the hell killed him, Dad?'

'I've no idea, Liz. The police don't know but someone must fucking well know, I want the murderer found, Liz, I want to get my hands on him before the police get hold of him.'

'Dad, please don't do an Al Capone act on me, why do you really want the killer found other than to bring him to justice?'

'OK, Liz, this basically is the story—'

Liz Smith listened in amazement to her father's revelations about some of his past financial dealings. He was in a secret and complex business deal that the killer had got to know about, and that included Ronnie's own eventual retirement.

In the dead man's pocket was a betting slip with scribble on it, the slip was headed 'Ronnie Smith Bookmakers'. It had to be from the murderer, which was a perverse way of sending a message to Ronnie.

Ronnie was determined to find the killer, Liz would help gather in all the information from the betting shop on her dead uncle; Angela and Billy would be more relaxed with her and Ronnie knew it. She would ask around in the newspaper shop and the pub next door and try to speak to the very few friends Alan Goody had and pass their names on to her dad.

Ronnie knew that if he jumped in himself and asked lots of questions he would be unlikely to find anyone that was willing to help, including any of his staff. The police were definitely no help at the moment, the local constabulary and Ronnie had a mutual dislike for each other; they would be around to the shop soon anyway.

'What did the note say, Dad?'

'Thanks for the money – but it may not have been intended for me, it could be a coincidence. It could be someone was trying to tell me something about the robbery, or money that my brother owed. I haven't shown it to the police, if I can't work it out they won't either.'

'Right, Dad, I'll do my best, but I only have a couple of days, I'll sniff around best I can but I need to get back to work sometime next week.'

'Yes, I understand, Liz. Would you consider coming back home?'

'No, Dad. As long as that bitch lives with you the answer is definitely no. You know she will fleece you and then piss off. Did she know Uncle John or Alan, whatever he was called?'

'She never met him, Liz. I'm sorry you feel the way you do but I need someone, if it's any consolation I don't love her but she does the business and looks good.'

'Charming, Dad, but I sort of know what you mean.'

'This is the list I've put together for you, Liz, and what I know about each person. Be careful, start with John's friends if you can find them. There are only three or four. If not, make friends with Angela Tate, she's a mouthy bird and I'm sure she will blab anything she knows. One last thing, Liz, have you been seeing that creep Billy Bootle?'

Liz had to be convincing on this one; her dad looked straight at her.

'No, why?'

'Just that I caught him talking about you almost as if he wanted me to hear, but then he shut up. Watch him, Liz, if he plays up I'll chuck him out.'

Liz didn't reply she just shook all over and her stomach turned, she knew that she could never tell her dad the truth.

Ronnie delivered his daughter to Sharon's house and went in with her as the place was in darkness. In the house the cold and dampness in the stale air made Liz sad. Why had she come back? she thought to herself.

She knew her dad needed her but she needed a new life; a man and some money was the answer. She hoped her dad might help her if she helped him get information on her uncle's death.

Liz made a coffee and phoned Sharon, it was only nine o'clock but she was already in bed, blaming her friend for keeping her awake the previous night.

'Sorry, Sharon, but Dad really needed me here. I'll tell you all about it when you're back. Just one question, do you remember my Uncle John, we met him one night in the pub, he looked like a tramp and we had to buy him a drink?'

'Yes, vaguely, Liz, all he talked about was horses and dogs.'

'He was sick, mentally sick, but worse still he's been found dead and badly beaten by some maniac. Dad was also robbed the other day in the Cheam shop so everything is happening here. I've suddenly become a private detective but only until next week. My dad seems to think I might get a clue about the killer easier than the police or him.'

'Bloody hell be careful, Liz, I don't like the sound of it all. If you arrange to meet anyone, don't go on your own, wait until I'm back. Understand that, Liz? I'm not joking.'

'Yes, thanks, Sharon. By the way, are you shagging Pepe yet?'

'No, but I've got my eye on his dad, looks strong and healthy with nice grey hair, big smile, but a big dodgy beer gut with his belt underneath. See you soon I need some sleep.'

'Lucky you but by the way, we got a message on the answerphone that your Donna is in hospital having the baby. Barbara must have forgotten we're away.'

'I've just spoken to Mark and they're going to the hospital now, it's a boy called Shane.'

'Yes, sorry, I should have told you but I forgot.'

'Keep clear of him, Liz, stick to one of your regulars, you are too dangerous for my brother.'

'OK, see you trust me again, Sharon. I will start cleaning the house. See you soon.'

Both girls knew that Liz wouldn't clean the house; her mind was set on helping her father. Being an amateur detective didn't appeal to her, but if it got her in his good books she would do anything once.

First she would go and see the new baby; maybe she would see Mark as well, ignoring her friend's advice.

Chapter twelve

Vince and Donna

'How are you feeling this morning, Mrs Lavender?'

'A bit sore, Sister, but when I look at this little man I know it was all worth it, I fed him and he slept like a baby.'

'Actually, if you haven't noticed, he is a baby and he'll be crying a lot for you very soon so I suggest you try and get some more sleep. By the way, you are very popular look at all the flowers that have arrived and it's only twelve o'clock.'

'Are they all for me?'

'You bet they are and this one had no name on it.'

'Oh dear, please take them away. I better not keep them as when my husband arrives he'll be checking the labels to see who sent them all.'

In her doze she was wondering who it could be, she didn't have to think for long, it could only be one person and all she wanted now was to get him out of her life. The brief fling with Luke Devine was the result of a chance meeting. He must have found a computer and looked on her Facebook page with all the congratulations from family and friends.

Vince had brought Luke home just over a year before and within weeks they were exchanging texts and clandestine phone calls. She desperately wanted a baby and she had temporarily gone off the rails as Vince spent most of his time out with his mates, and she had no doubt that he was also putting it about a bit with various ladies.

The question in her mind was whether it was Luke's baby or was Vince the father? She studied baby Shane in the adjacent cot and she had no way of telling. Donna convinced herself it was her husband's child; she had to bury her dark secret in the back of her mind.

Donna woke up with a start from her confused sleep to the sound of Vince's voice.

'Hello, my sweet, how're you feeling?'

'I'm a bit sore. You'll have to give me a bit of time before we try to make Shane a brother or sister.'

'That's OK, Donna, just try to get some sleep, the sister said that with a bit of luck we can get you out of here in a couple of days.'

'Are you behaving yourself, Vince? What's Luke up to?'

'Why ask about Luke?'

'Just you always get drunk when you're with him and that worries me.'

'He's gone to Spain and I gave him some money for our apartment. I told you I won on the horses on Saturday.'

'Yes, I remember that. How much was it, then?'

'A few grand.'

'Vince, tell me how much, don't mess about.'

Before he could reply he felt a tap on his shoulder and stood behind him were his mother, brother and Liz Smith.

'Hi, Donna. Blimey he looks just like his dad, is he a good baby?'

'It's only been one day and a night but so far he's the perfect baby, Liz.'

'Anyway, I thought you were on holiday with Sharon.'

'I was but I had a small problem to deal with for my dad so it was cut short, it was one of those things that couldn't wait.'

'Must have been important, Liz, to leave our Sharon on her own?'

'Yes, sorry, Mrs Lavender, but Sharon is OK. I just spoke to her. She may hate me when she gets the bar bill as we had a night apart with different "friends" and I ran up a lot of money on champagne.'

'Don't tell me anymore, Liz.' Barbara scowled at the thought of her daughter looking for a man and probably not just for a drink or two.

Vince decided to get away from the overcrowded bedside. He kissed his wife and smiled at the baby.

'Mum, I'm off home. See you later, Donna, anything you need?'

'Just a newspaper and of course an answer to my question about the bet, when you get back here, you know what I mean, Vince.'

'Is there any news on my father-in-law, Barbara?'

Vince turned away and went bright red as he slowly crept out, the ladies looked puzzled, he waved behind him and almost ran out of the hospital. The amount of money was not something he could tell his wife about, Donna was sharp and would know if he was lying to her. He had time though to think what to do.

Barbara saw the look on her son's face as he left and changed the subject to her missing husband.

'No, Donna, we just had that one call from Gerry, I'm expecting him to turn up anytime. If I told him about the baby it might help but I don't know. Someone could be holding him, but I really can't believe that.'

As Barbara and Liz left the hospital they said their goodbyes and went separately to their own cars. The car park at St Helier Hospital was a massive area, dark, confusing and totally full of cars belonging to staff and visitors. Liz had just squeezed her Mini into a space a long way from Barbara's car.

As she approached her car she could see someone leaning on it, at first she didn't recognise the figure as he was dressed casually and not in his normal shirt and tie.

'What the hell are you doing, are you following me?'

'You bet I am, you tart. I've got your dad and the old bill bloody well crawling all over me and also the shop. You seem to forget that I was in your bed a month ago fucking you.'

'Billy, you are the biggest pile of shit ever born on this earth, sleeping with you was a massive mistake and if my dad knew he would rearrange your face.'

'Yes, but what'd he do to you, Liz?'

She didn't reply as she knew her father would never forgive her for allowing Billy anywhere near her naked body.

'I want you, Liz, I love you. I've got a decent amount of money saved to buy a place one day and I can take you with me to live permanently away from this bloody country. I know you won't tell your old man because if you do I'll tell him how many blokes you've slept with and who they are. I'm sure to know every one of them. I would start with the lads serving in the pub, probably all four of them, plus Mark Lavender and probably the old man Lavender as well. Ronnie would arrange to get them all a good kicking and it's bloody certain you'd never get a penny from him.'

'It's my risk, Billy, and your worry. I'm coming to the shop soon to do a job for my dad so don't get in my way. I'll be checking a few things. Piss off, I'm driving home.'

Billy knew he was losing the argument; he turned to his car and gave Liz a further combination of filthy threats and abuse as he angrily blasted his modified Skoda out of the tight car park and into the busy main road.

Liz just stood and shook; she just wanted to be loved but definitely not by that creep.

Her dad had asked her to help him, so this time she would do as he asked, she was tough and it was just possible she could find a lead on her uncle's death.

She would spend only a few hours in the shop but somehow at the same time she would have to try to keep away from Billy as much as possible, and she knew that would be difficult in the confined space of the betting shop.

The sudden meeting with Billy had shaken her up and she was starting to doubt if she could do the work for her dad. She had nobody to discuss it with other than one old friend; she knew where he would be as his wife was in hospital; she went straight to his house and used the back entrance.

Chapter thirteen

Weybridge

The eight-bedroom mansion on the St George's Hill Estate in Weybridge was a far cry from Ronnie Smith's roots.

His family originated from Lewisham in South London. Straight from school, and even before, Ronnie was a wheeler and dealer. Over the years he'd had a few failures but generally his business ventures had produced decent profits. He moved from London, investing wisely in a Georgian villa, which he had turned into a showpiece home. It impressed all his family and friends; especially the no-expense-spared garden parties held during Royal Ascot week.

His wife did not like the house or Weybridge; they had a messy divorce and she moved back to London with a large chunk of his money. His son, Jack, rarely spent time at home, he decided that his father's business was not for him and he trained hard to be an engineer. As soon as he qualified he moved to the USA and he had no intention of returning.

Ronnie lived on nervous energy; he always seemed to be in the middle of a deal or looking to do one. He had connections in scrap metal recycling, waste paper, the clearance of industrial waste and sometimes property. Football was his passion and he had big ambitions in the game for the future, but technically he didn't understand too much about what he was watching other than counting the goals. His interest was in ownership, and not just a park team. He had a plan.

His sentimental decision to still operate his dead father's betting shops was one of his worst mistakes; most of the time in business he got things right, but the five shops made hardly any money and all he got was aggravation and thieving from his staff.

As his father had been dead many years he decided that he had to do something with them when the leases expired; but then he had a use for the shops short-term and maybe at least for a year or two he could use them to launder money for his future investments.

Ronnie liked cash and his turnover and costs from the betting shops just didn't add up. His accountant somehow kept a track of things but he had advised Ronnie that he should not keep the cash in boxes under the bed or even worse, keep going abroad with it stuffed in suitcases.

He had recently been on a trip to Spain to pay a deposit on a contract with money he had collected from a big waste paper deal. His mistake was that he foolishly tried to change £200,000 to euros in Marbella. He thought he had done it carefully, opening an account in three different banks a few months before, then depositing a third of the money in each one on different days naively hoping to avoid suspicion.

He was wrong, the banks reported the transaction to the financial authorities but someone must have been paid off as nothing ever got back to the UK. The bad news for Ronnie was that he had dealt with a bank employee with a loose tongue and soon he had a shadow watching him to see if he made any more deposits.

On his way to the third bank to make the final deposit, he was followed from his hotel and as he left the taxi a few metres from the bank a large man dressed in a tracksuit and baseball cap grabbed him and knocked him to the ground. He grabbed Ronnie's briefcase containing the cash and left him face down in the street, bleeding from his head but conscious.

Most people would have run back home immediately but not him, he made a few phone calls to local mates and he eventually found someone who said they might be able to help him. The subsequent meeting in the pub on a beach near Estepona led to his introduction to Fernando Lopez, a man who would help change Ronnie's business direction in a way that could satisfy his plans.

Fernando was aware that men existed in the city who watched the Bureau de Change areas at the banks. If they spotted a regular customer like Ronnie they would follow him and when the time was right, take his money. The police were never involved as most of the cash had been obtained illegally and this seemed to be just small-time money laundering.

As Ronnie arrived at the pub heads turned in his direction, he spotted many English-looking customers like the types he dealt with in the South East London snooker clubs. He was relieved when a tall and very wide bearded Spaniard spotted him and walked over to the taxi.

The driver looked annoyed and left without waiting to be paid.

'Senor Lopez I presume, did you know that driver?'

'No, but he knows me and I don't pay for taxis. Anyway, Mr Smith, I'm pleased to meet you and sorry to hear from one of my employees that you were robbed of a very large amount of money and you want it back.'

'Yes, spot on. Some bloke was waiting for me near my hotel and jumped me from behind. He knocked me over into the road and took my briefcase. I have a fucking great lump on my head and the bastard took all my money and then just threw the briefcase over a wall.'

'It wasn't one of my men, Mr Smith, but we probably know who did it and we'll get your money back tonight, less a small handling fee.'

'How do you know who did it, are you sure the guy doesn't work for you?'

'Don't worry about that. I have something else to show you. My car is outside.'

Ronnie had no choice but to follow his new acquaintance. He climbed into the back of the large BMW four-by-four and sat next to the Spaniard. They drove for about 30 minutes to an area of open ground near the far end of a beach. Lopez spun the car around to face the sea and a derelict dock for small boats.

'What do you think, Mr Ronnie Smith?'

Lopez spread his arms wide – he was a big man with his stomach bursting from his shirt – as he turned in a semi-circle pointing at the sand and waste ground.

'What the hell am I looking at, mate, a beach and a broken wooden pier?'

'I'm buying this and I need partners like you maybe. We have full permission from the local authorities to build apartments and houses, a leisure complex, and a championship golf course, maybe later a marina, bars and a hotel. The plans are done and we start as soon as we have money. Already some old acquaintances from the north of Spain are promising me they will join the project but we still have some options for other new investors.'

'Why do you want me, is it just my money, what's the deal?'

'Not tonight, Ronnie. I'll call you. By the way, I'm just Lopez, everyone knows me here in this area. I only normally do business with people outside my circle of friends just in case someone tries to double-cross me and I have to deal with them.'

Ronnie frowned at the manner in which Lopez spoke.

'Charming, I think I'd prefer to be your friend.'

'Don't look so worried, I'm joking of course. I want new investors for sure and we all need friends as well.'

The Spaniard picked up his phone and made a call in his own language shouting instructions to someone; within seconds he was phoned back.

'That's simple, the money that was stolen from you will shortly be back on your bed in your hotel room, less 3,000 euro collection fee. Please keep it safe this time. I have an idea you will be giving it to me, and more, when I tell you about this little venture of mine.'

'Thanks, but can I really trust you, Lopez? I know you come highly recommended by my friends here so keep talking to me. I'm naturally cautious, if you tell me more I may be interested in a deal, but it's dependent on what guarantees you can give. I suggest we meet up again tomorrow when hopefully my head doesn't hurt as much, you can tell me then the details of what you are proposing.'

'I agree, say 5.00 pm at this address. I don't work until late afternoon, it's too hot in this part of Spain unless you are on the beach or by a pool. You can spot the English, they are playing football in the sun or leaning against the bar. See you tomorrow and put that money away immediately in the safe at the hotel, not even the room safe, put it in an envelope and seal it then ask reception to keep it. Watch them put it away in the deposit room, they will give you the key and sign for the parcel.'

Lopez stopped on the main road and called a taxi, immediately a car arrived from nowhere. When he saw Lopez, the driver got out and opened the door for Ronnie.

'I have to go in the other direction, the taxi will take you back to town. Remember, don't give him any money.'

'Not again, Lopez.'

The big man just laughed and waved as he drove away.

The hotel room was just as Ronnie had left it with a parcel on the bed as Lopez had promised. As Lopez had sorted it so quickly he was suspicious that one of his men had taken it from him or was it really just someone that they knew? It didn't matter as in a funny way he felt safe with the big Spaniard but he wasn't sure he wanted to get deeply involved with him; but then if he did, what level of investment could he be trusted with?

Getting his money back had been his priority, now he would wait and see what the man had to offer.

Ronnie's ambition was bigger than a development in the sand; he liked Spain but his focus was on one thing and one thing alone. Maybe now with this introduction, Fernando Lopez could move his idea forward but he needed more money.

He had approximately ten million euros in Spain, some in a safe deposit box at a national bank and a large amount in a floor safe at a friend's house; Ronnie's bank accounts were controlled by his accountant. The man was an ex-pat of dubious background who needed Ronnie to continue to help fund his stay in Spain. He was also a man who knew what would happen if he double-crossed his best customer.

The safe deposit box was in a lawyer's name, he checked it regularly and it cost him a hefty fee to keep its contents a secret.

It was incredible that he had managed to get large amounts of sterling out of the UK in the past nine years, especially as most of the time he just put the money in his suitcase and kept his head down, or hid it in the car and drove to Spain.

Only once had he been stopped but that was on his way back into Gatwick Airport, after a long weekend trip. The customs officer made him open all his bags and then pulled everything out; they found nothing other than a fake Rolex, he was clean.

He left the watch with the customs staff at Gatwick for them to destroy it; he didn't notice the camera taking routine pictures of him from the false ceiling, someone wanted him checked out and he would be watched in future.

His name was tagged in the computer and as soon as he appeared on a passenger list at passport control, the officials would be alerted.

Ronnie was no fool and already he had to set up other methods of moving money. He needed reliable couriers now as after the Lewisham bank job he had a lot of money to move from the UK.

After a few glasses of whisky, Ronnie bolted himself in the small room and pulled the blinds closed, he noticed a large dark car parked across the road with a man smoking a cigarette inside, blowing the smoke out of the window. He thought he looked like the man who hit him, but he didn't see his face properly when he was knocked over, it all happened so quickly. He looked at him again, thinking he must be working for Lopez, then maybe now for some reason he was protecting him. He remembered what he said, that he didn't mix business and friends, he made a joke of it but Ronnie suspected their meeting wasn't a coincidence.

He rolled into bed and as his head hit the pillow, exactly on the large red lump, he shouted out loud, 'I'll kill the bloke who did this!'

He rubbed the sore area above his right ear making it even redder, he dragged himself out of bed and put a cold flannel on the lump, he would soon feel nothing as the booze spread around his bloodstream like an anaesthetic.

The alcohol was working in his mind also, Ronnie could fight but he had no intention of chasing the guy who hit him, he would get someone else to do that. He had got his money back thanks to Lopez but he had caught a glimpse of the guy who hit him and one day he felt sure he would see him again. He would get even with him unless Lopez had already planned the man's fate.

Chapter fourteen

The Monday After

The police station car park was already full and DI Derek Lawson cursed and decided to risk an ear bending from the pedantic superintendent by parking in a disabled bay.

John Hampton, his detective sergeant, had arrived early to brief colleagues about the armed robbery at the betting shop.

'All a bit strange, John,' said the inquisitive duty sergeant.

Hampton had no time to reply as his boss walked into the room and answered for him.

'Yes, I thought that as well, shall we just see what we've got, just the facts for now please, John.'

'On the sheet in front of you is the first summary of what happened. The betting shop was not busy so we don't think they took much but we only have the manager's word on that, the takings are being checked and you can bet it was peanuts. Two men entered the betting shop in Tudor Drive, Cheam, at approximately 16.45, the shop is owned by Ronnie Smith. The men were dressed in fluorescent jackets, their faces hidden by a hooded garment worn underneath their jackets. One was around six feet tall and on the heavy side, the other was slightly smaller and medium build, he was carrying a sawn-off shotgun, both men wore sunglasses. The shop girl said they were white, she saw a bit of their cheeks. They had South London/Surrey accents.

'They demanded that the manager, Billy Bootle, open the safe but interestingly it was already open. He moved to one side as one of the men put the contents into two large brown zipper holdalls thrown at him by the first man. The second man fired the sawn-off 12-bore shotgun into the ceiling, three ceiling tiles fell down with a cloud of dust, some wires were found in the debris and an old CCTV camera. The shop girl wet her knickers. There was one punter in the shop. In the confined space the staff would have been deaf for several minutes and so would the robbers if they hadn't got ear plugs.

'The CCTV film from the main camera is being analysed again but it's mostly blank apart from one view outside, in fact we think someone switched the cassette over with a new one or edited it as there's nothing on it other than a single picture and just two seconds of it. We should be able to identify that guy. I have a feeling I may know him but we need to be sure so we're getting the lab to blow the picture up.

'The shop girl Angela Tate said there was only one punter in the shop and he had just had a big argument with the manager. It seems this bloke was a regular and so were the arguments, the girl said that she regularly saw Bootle give him money from his own wallet. The guy is called Alan Goody, we interviewed him on Saturday night, he didn't have much to add to the events. We found a car that we think they used and the incinerator on Garth Road is being checked out.'

'So where do we go from here, John? Have we got anything from forensics yet, did anyone check if any clothes were left behind? My hunch would be that the robbers changed and dumped all their clothes into the incinerator chute. On a scale of urgent cases this has to be five out of ten. I think it'll solve itself eventually. Our priority now is to sort out that murder in Sutton but I don't like local mysteries so we need to give the robbery our best shot at the same time. When do we meet the players in this stage show, John?'

'Ronnie Smith was reluctant to come to the station but as he's just been nicked for drink driving, he decided that it might work in his favour to cooperate with us.'

'Cheeky sod, definitely no chance of any help from me, the guy is a crook and one day we'll get him. Maybe this is an inside job but for what reason would he have set it up?'

'Then we have Alan Goody who seemed in the mood to help us, he lives in a derelict camper van so we have to see him today otherwise I have a feeling he may do a runner. Angela Tate and Billy Bootle are due in about half an hour, he is a piss artist and she is on the next step from a hooker, although I wouldn't mind giving her one myself.'

'John, please can you remember that you are a policeman not a social worker. Screwing the witness is not allowed under any circumstances.'

The policemen laughed together, John Hampton was a straight copper but he did like his women and that could be his downfall. His boss, DI Lawson, gave him the 'watch it' look and he changed the subject.

'What about that call we had about Mark Lavender and the money in his car? Did you meet him, John?'

'I checked it out quickly on Saturday night, boss, and although Mark was a bit nervous when he saw me it was all kosher money he'd won on a bet with Ronnie.'

'It sounds like someone was jealous and hoping you would catch him for drink driving.'

'Yes, that's a possibility but I think it was telling us something else and I'm not sure what. It's a coincidence that Mark got the money from the shop the same day it was robbed and then we get the dodgy phone call. That CCTV film may tell me more as I don't like coincidences.'

'Why what do you mean, John?'

'When you get a minute, sir, look at that five seconds of CCTV. I think it could possibly be Mark Lavender or someone very like him. This is a picture of him in the gym brochure. Once the lads have blown up and compared the pictures we'll have a better idea.'

The noise of the internal phone was a relief from a conversation that was going in circles between the policemen. Together they were very experienced and in cases like this, which in their view was a simple robbery, they would expect to find definite leads soon. The amount of cash stolen was small according to the manager, this had made the policemen very suspicious and the only man to answer the questions was Ronnie Smith himself.

'Yes, we do know that guy, we'll send someone down to the mortuary straight away to get the information. Is the pathologist on-site?'

The duty sergeant put the phone down and looked at his colleagues.

'The bloke knifed to death outside the pub in Sutton was your happy camper man, Alan Goody. His face was bashed in so badly the pathologist has only just established from his photo driving licence found in his wallet that it was him. The dental card in his pocket helped us to find his dentist and his records. I didn't believe it was possible to find things out so quickly, but sometimes we do have a bit of luck.'

'It's not luck, sergeant, we have a man lying dead, brutally murdered, after being briefly interviewed by us a few hours before. He knew something and we have to find out what it was. That old campervan may tell us more about him. Find the registration number, John, and put out a search for it.'

The policemen now had two cases and they were already working on a connection between them, the drifter in the campervan and his visit to the betting shop could provide an early lead on why he was killed. The robbery was second in priority but if the connection between the two could be established the investigation might move forward quicker.

DI Lawson saw some signs of a quick solution and pointed Sergeant Hampton into his office but before the two detectives could prepare their next move they were interrupted.

The duty sergeant knocked on the DI's door and entered the office.

'Angela Tate and Billy Bootle are both here.'

'Thanks, put Billy in room six and Angela in room seven, and can you get WPC Linda Dredge to join me in room seven? John, I will speak with Angela and you give Billy a going over, I've met him before, don't take any shit if he gives you silly answers. The key questions you know, but ask him if he knew Alan Goody as well, don't tell him we found him dead, I doubt he would know that already.'

Angela was dressed for action, her porn-star tendencies used to the full. Every male PC leaving the station gave her the eye as she sat calmly with arms folded and legs crossed.

Her short black skirt was a bad choice for the cold November day but her black hold-up stockings and tight red sweater would keep her warm in the cold and drab interview room.

The duty sergeant showed her into room seven and WPC Dredge sat across the room from her but as instructed by her boss, apart from saying hello, she remained silent. The policewoman got up from her chair as DI Lawson opened the door. Angela didn't move, she just looked up at the tall man and scowled.

'Thanks for coming to the station, Miss Tate. We're investigating the armed robbery at the betting shop on Saturday and we hope you'll be able to give us information which will help us find the criminals quickly. Firstly the formalities, can you just confirm to us your full name, address and date of birth, followed by a brief description of your job at the betting shop? This lady here is WPC Dredge and she will sit with us during the interview.'

Angela shuffled on her seat, her modesty was just covered by her black skirt as she frequently continued to keep crossing and uncrossing her legs. Derek Lawson, a married man with four young children, had seen it all before and he remained deadpan as she gave her details.

'I am Angela Josephine Tate, I live at Flat 2, South Garden View, Sutton, Surrey, with my cat. I was born 1st June 1984. My job at the betting shop is a bit of everything, taking the bets, paying out, checking the till money and sometimes making the tea, depending on how busy we are.'

'Thank you. On Saturday, Angela, at the time of the robbery, was the shop busy or quiet?'

'It was really quiet. We had been busy earlier but apart from a few punters collecting their winnings, only one guy was in the front of the shop with me.'

'Did you know him?'

'Yes, I've seen him before, he's a regular.' Angela was already bored and looking at the time on the wall clock.

'Do you know his name?'

'We call him Alan, I think it's his name.'

'Are you sure there was only one man in the shop?

Angela hesitated and frowned.

'Yes, I already told you, just one other person on my side, but then I couldn't see behind me in the office. There could have been people with Billy.'

'You said on Saturday that the shop manager had an argument with the man in the shop. Is that correct?'

'Yes, they were always arguing about something, usually about his bets, Saturday was nothing different to normal.'

Lawson frowned at the girl and stood up.

'That's a bit odd to be arguing all the time. Do you know why?'

'Money, always money.'

'Are you sure? How much money?'

'Yes, course I'm bloody sure. I'm no liar. No idea how much.'

'Did you ask Billy what it was about?'

'Yes, and he told me to mind my own business. Will I be long here, mate, I've a job to do?'

Angela definitely wanted to get off the subject of Alan Goody quickly, as she felt the atmosphere in the room change, she was deliberately trying to get away, she knew more but she didn't want to tell the police. She needed her job and this bloke was not her problem.

'Miss Tate you would normally be free to go very soon, but if we feel you are obstructing us, this interview will only end once you tell me everything you can about the robbery and not before. Please let me ask you some more questions.'

She frowned at the policeman but she knew that she was stuck with him until he ran out of questions or he got bored with her.

'Did you see any of the robbers' faces?'

'No, they all had hoods and they kept their heads down but I could see some white skin.'

'What did they actually say?'

'They asked Billy to open the safe door. It's between the shop and the back office. One of them emptied everything into two brown bags. It was the worst time for a raid on the shop as the door of the safe was wide open and it was all done really quickly.'

'Is the safe usually open all the time?'

'No, only when I empty my till, about twice a day. It had just been emptied a few minutes before and they even took the few quid left in it.'

'What did Billy do?'

'He made a move to press the button that alters the outside CCTV, I don't know why as it looked straight outside. They spotted him and locked him in the toilet. Serves him right, he could never piss straight and the toilet always stinks. I had to clean up after him so it's justice for him to have ten minutes inside the shit house on his own.'

'Charming. Are you really sure that nobody else was in the shop apart from the one guy? Think carefully before you answer.'

'No, I don't think so, I'd have seen them.'

'Had Ronnie Smith been in that day?'

'Yes, as usual. He comes in about once a day and puts things in the safe then leaves, he parks on the double yellow line outside so he doesn't hang about.'

Angela was starting to sweat and the WPC handed her a tissue.

'What are you nervous about, Miss Tate? All we want is for you to tell us the truth, we'll ask Mr Bootle the same questions and then we'll see if he's telling the same story as you. We think you have some more to add to what you have said. Did the CCTV camera work?'

'Yes, I think so.'

'Just a few last questions, then. I can see you are uncomfortable, but unless you are involved in some way you have nothing to worry about. You aren't involved, are you?'

The question caught her by surprise. Her red blouse was slowly changing colour under her armpits and sweat was rolling down her back.

'Can I have some water, please?'

'Sure. Sorry, this is a hot room and you're not the first person to feel hot here.'

Angela found a smile for the policeman, she liked the double meaning but he was too old for her and in the wrong career.

The WPC handed her a paper cup of water, she drank it in one gulp.

'I ask you again, were you involved in this robbery, Miss Tate?'

'No, course not, I just work in the shop.'

'Who fired the gun?'

'The smaller bloke fired it when Billy reached under the counter, it was just the old camera sticking out of the ceiling, it wasn't connected to anything. We have another new one mounted next to the window, it points outside but we can rotate it and watch it under the counter on a little TV, it covers the road and the counter as well, it was only put in recently. As I said a minute ago, that switch under the desk altered it.'

'Who would take the daily film from that machine?'

'I would some days but Billy did it on Saturday.'

'Is Billy a good boss?'

'Funny question, but yes as far as it goes, but really Mr Smith is the boss and if we have any problems he sorts them out.'

'Do you know how much money was in the till and safe?'

'No idea what was in the safe but the till tray had about £5,000 in it. I had just cashed up when the blokes burst in.'

'They took all of it, then?'

'Yes, they took everything in the till and the safe, it was thrown into the bags by Billy with some parcels as well. They were out of the shop pretty quick.'

'Could the parcels have contained money?'

'Don't know, never saw what was in them.'

'What about the gun? Once again, Miss Tate, which one of them fired it?'

'I told you all this already, it was the smaller bloke. I thought at first it was just to stop Billy pressing the lever under the counter, which might have been right, but then the bullets hit the old CCTV in the ceiling and the lot came down, it was a bloody big bang and I wet my pants.'

'It was a shotgun, Miss Tate, probably a 12-bore so it didn't have bullets just lead shot and he probably fired the gun to frighten you and Mr Bootle.'

The DI smiled for only the second time in the lengthy interview.

'Yes, you bloody well would smile wouldn't you, but as well as wetting myself, I was deaf for nearly half an hour.'

The DI knew that Angela had wet herself, it was in the preliminary report but he was not convinced that the robber fired the gun to frighten anybody. He had to stop Billy operating the camera lever and he thought it was probably just a coincidence the shot hit the old camera.

'I have one very last question for today. Did you pay Mark Lavender out for a winning bet on Saturday afternoon and if you did, what time was it?'

She hesitated and blushed.

'No, Billy asked me to do a slip for Mark as he phoned in a bet. I left the money out for Billy with the slip behind the grill, usually he rushes in to collect his winnings when he's lucky, but on Saturday it just disappeared. I think he must have collected it from Billy sometime late in the afternoon when I was in the toilet. It was definitely taken.'

DI Derek Lawson scowled. He had a strong feeling she had more to say but for now she had told him enough.

'Thanks, Angela, you can leave and go back to work. Mr Bootle will be with you in a few minutes. Please give us your mobile number, we have the shop number, if we have any further questions we will call you. Please just wait here a moment and I'll see if Sergeant Hampton is finished.'

The two men met in the corridor and went to the DI's office.

'She's lying and she was hesitant. Iit was probably about paying out Mark Lavender his winnings, possibly the rest was more or less feasible but she didn't want to drop Billy in it. What did he say?'

'He said much the same, just the punter, Angela and himself. He was very nervous all through the interview. He has more to tell for sure. He said Angela paid Mark out, so one of them is telling lies but now I suggest we meet our old friend Ronnie Smith again.'

'I agree but let me go to the morgue first. Mark Lavender should be here soon. I need to see what the pathologist is saying about Alan Goody. It is too much of a coincidence that he should die just after we interviewed him.'

'OK, but don't be long. I've sent a PC for Ronnie and he's sure to be troublesome.'

The duty sergeant shouted across the room, 'Mark Lavender is here to see you, John, what shall I do with him?'

'Throw Angela Tate out then show Mark into the room, make sure they see each other and let me know if there is any body language between them.'

The duty sergeant looked puzzled but nodded and went back to the front desk.

'Mr Lavender, come this way, please.'

The policeman opened the interview room door at the moment Angela Tate got up to leave, Mark knew she was going to the police station and he would call her later to find out what happened, as they passed he winked at her and she smiled back.

'Please sit down, Sergeant Hampton will be here in a minute.'

As Angela left the police station, John Hampton put his head across the reception desk and looked at his sergeant.

'What do you reckon? Did they say anything?'

'John, I saw it in his eyes, he has definitely given her one and probably recently.'

'You are guessing, aren't you?'

'Yes, John, sure I am. What's the bet?'

'No bet. I wouldn't be surprised on you being dead right but I'm not sure if it's relevant in this case but you never know in this job.'

John Hampton opened the interview door and caught Mark staring into space.

'You look guilty already, Mark, what've you been up to?'

'Nothing, John, and why did you want to see me?'

'At this stage it's just a chat. Let's say I'll tell you what I know and as old schoolmates, I expect you to do the same.'

'OK, fire away. I can't be long, I'm working tonight.'

'Are you still at the leisure centre?'

'Yes, it's OK but the money is lousy. I need a new job and I'm working on it.'

'Are you working on Angela Tate as well?'

The question came out of the blue and was too quick for Mark to think about, he hesitated and John Hampton smiled.

'I have a girlfriend, John.'

'That wasn't the question but your face answered for you.'

'We had a brief fling but nothing in it really. Kate would go mental if she knew and probably try to cut my bits off.'

'Painful, Mark, maybe we will talk more about that another time. She's helping us on the robbery at the betting shop, do you know anything about it?'

'No, nothing.'

'When did you collect the winnings, Mark?'

Mark gasped, he did not know what to say, and he had to lie.

'I can't remember the time.'

'On the copy slip from the shop, Angela Tate had put your name on it. Did she pay you out?'

'Yes, that's right.' Mark did not sound convincing but John Hampton let it pass without comment.

'Why did you come to the pub and look in the boot of my car?'

'I told you, if you remember, we had a tip-off after the robbery that some loot from the robbery was in your car, so I was just checking it out. We only found the money you had won, but you looked surprised. Why, Mark? Tell me the truth.'

Mark had to think quickly.

'I thought I'd dropped the bag off at home but I must have left it in the car by mistake.'

'Yes, Mark, and pigs fly. You knew the money was there, did you expect it to be more?'

'No, that's what I won.'

'Angela said she left the money on the counter but didn't see you, is that right?'

The hesitation didn't help but Hampton ignored it. Did it matter that much anyway?

'Yes, right.'

'Are you still living at home? I have the address after that party you had about four years ago?'

'Yes, still at home.'

Now Mark was sweating, the interview room was deliberately like a sauna, his whole body felt uncomfortable. John knew something was wrong but two text messages on his mobile distracted him and he decided that he would speak to Mark again, maybe in the pub were he could relax him.

'Off you go, Mark. We're done for today.'

Mark almost ran from the police station but composed himself enough to nod at the duty sergeant then stride out to his Mini.

He was very confused and his mind was racing away as he tried to work out who could have grassed him up to the police. Was it the same person that took the bulk of the money from his car? He had to find out and quick.

As he drove to work he had a feeling someone close to him knew a lot more than he did. That included Vince, Luke and even Angela, but then it hit him, could all this be connected to his missing dad?

Someone must be holding him captive and the tip-off to the police about the money was probably just a warning, he thought that unless his dad gave his captors what they wanted, more information would be passed to the police about him.

Mark knew his dad would not be blackmailed, even if it put any member of his family at risk; he was a tough nut and whatever he was involved in could be much bigger than the robbery at the betting shop.

He then did a double-take, Vince told him Dad had given them the idea, but how did Vince and Luke know that the safe would contain the large amount of cash on that afternoon?

He immediately doubted that his dad was being held by someone, more that he had gone away to escape from something and he must be abroad. His mind was spinning out of control, he needed a drink and a woman, in that order.

Chapter fifteen

Violent Death

Sergeant John Hampton had a good clear-up record and he was determined that in this case, as in many others, he would stay ahead of his boss.

He was pretty certain Mark was involved in the robbery and he had a feeling that he was the driver. The PC who checked the shop CCTV film told him for sure it was Mark in the driving seat of the car, he was just waiting for that to be confirmed. The police station CCTV picked him up as he arrived and left and forensics were comparing the pictures.

If it was Mark Lavender, he guessed that the other two were mates and he would ask around to see who his pals were.

The Sutton mortuary depressed him; the smell of the bodies made him retch. In the early days he was frequently sick as the corpses were dissected now he could just about control his stomach. The waste of life and the sadness of an unnecessary, violent death slowed down his enthusiasm for his job; his anger revived him. Hampton was a professional and he pushed away any negative thoughts for another day.

Oliver Hill was an old-school pathologist; he never stated to third parties the cause of death until he was certain what it was. In his 25 years in the job he had seen most things and the body of Alan Goody was nothing special, just another dead man, but in this case a badly mutilated one.

'Come in, Sergeant, don't just stand at the door.'

'Thanks, Mr Hill. What can you tell me about him? Have you any ideas on what may have happened?'

'As I've told you, Sergeant, many times and just like the TV programmes, we do not jump to conclusions in this job. I'll give you my usual non-committal summary and by the middle of the week, we should be able to give you a full picture. So here's my first shot. The man was identified as a Mr Alan Goody of no fixed abode. The wallet you see on the desk in front of you had the dental appointment card inside. This helped my assistant confirm his name with one phone call. The dental work seemed to match what the dentist told him so we have asked for the records to confirm this.

'We've checked everything else in the wallet and your forensic guys can have a look now and see if we've missed anything. The contents were limited to the dental card, £50.25 cash in five £10 notes and some change, a picture of a woman, a betting slip and a small key with a phone number written on a card in the zipped-up pouch. The dentist also gave us an address which my assistant looked up. I think you'll find as we did that it doesn't exist.'

Oliver Hill handed him the betting slip and wallet in a polythene bag.

'I want that back tomorrow, Sergeant, but take it for your fingerprint test, it has the name of the Ronnie Smith Betting Shop on it and a message thanking Mr Smith.'

'Did it indeed? Was there anything else on him, Mr Hill?'

'Nothing at all. His clothes smelled of cigarette smoke and his body was filthy dirty, he was in urgent need of a good bath. The PC at the scene should have given you any other details by now, Sergeant.'

'Yes, yes, I know that, but he left his report on his computer and I've not been in the station for very long yet, so please tell me everything, even things I should know.'

John Hampton was agitated, he wanted more information from the laid-back pathologist but the man could not be rushed, everyone had to work at his speed.

As an experienced medical man he had his own unique methods and the young policeman would have to wait until he was ready, as wrong information could result in delays to the investigation. In particular, relating to the exact cause of death, and more importantly who was responsible for it.

'I understand you interviewed him before his death, Sergeant.'

'Yes, he witnessed an armed robbery, we interviewed him at the weekend. He seemed fine on Saturday and was very willing to help us but he never got the chance.'

'Was it the betting shop robbery?'

'Yes, Mr Hill, but it is not for discussion yet, I just feel we may have a connection between the two incidents.'

'You are right, Sergeant, we must not jump to conclusions, it was just that I read about the robbery in the newspaper and the slip I just gave you was familiar, it reminded me about a guy we had on the slab last year who was also beaten up, he also had a Ronnie Smith betting slip on his body. In fact, it was covered in blood.'

'I remember the death. Didn't it turn out to be suicide, as the bloke jumped off a railway bridge? Are you sure about the betting slip?'

Oliver didn't reply, he just frowned; his answer was in his face before he spoke.

'The coroner pronounced a verdict of suicide while the balance of the mind was disturbed. He had recently lost his wife to cancer and then lost most of his money to horses and dogs, a sad case. The coroner and the jury seemed to ignore the fact he had been bashed around the face, as a witness said the man just walked to the railway bridge and fell in front of a train. We found alcohol in his body but the corpse was so badly mutilated that we couldn't say if he was inebriated.'

'When we saw Alan Goody in his mobile home he seemed fine. We'll need to piece together what he did after we left him, it was only a few hours before he died.'

'Come on, Sergeant, there has to be a connection. Think about it, son.'

'Don't patronise me, Mr Hill. Like you, I don't jump to conclusions either, but you've made your point pretty clear.'

'Did you read the Mail on Sunday? I think it's on about page six or seven. Printed at the bottom of the page was a report of the robbery, it's a section where they put late news.'

'Bloody hell, I don't like the smell of this. So what you're saying, Mr Hill, is that the robbery was in the paper in full detail on Sunday, then hours later one of the main witnesses was found dead.'

'No, not full details, just a few lines but otherwise you have it, Sergeant, other than it didn't mention the murder, as that was probably too late for the paper. It's an unusual death so in case you can link it to that old case and have a serial killer on the rampage, listen carefully, this is how I believe he probably died, but as I said before, it isn't official yet.

'My preliminary report will be in the usual format. The ambulance picked Mr Goody up from the King's Arms on the Downs Road. According to the police at the scene, the emergency call had been received at 21.30 and the ambulance arrived at 21.45 when the man was pronounced dead. Your people were already on-site. You need to check that, as your station should have the same information. My colleague, Harriet White, was called to the scene. She took all the details of the dead man. It was a bad one, Sergeant, lots of blood. The killer was very violent, he must've been in a real rage.

'He was found originally face down and his attacker had beaten him in the face, he must have put up a hell of a struggle and traces of hair and skin were found under his finger nails. He died from multiple stab wounds to the neck from a short, double-edged, sharp, serrated knife, an unusual instrument, probably a kitchen implement. I've never seen one like it, the weapon wasn't left at the scene.

'Death would not have been instant, but he must have been in deep shock from his beating so it would not have taken long after the attack. Looking at his injuries overall my comments would be that this was not just a brutal murder but a terrible malicious beating as well. It went much further than making sure his unfortunate victim was dead. From the position of the body and bloodstains found at the scene, his attacker beat him against a garden wall, stabbed him and then pushed him into the road. He was 30 yards from the pub and the lighting was poor, but from what we have found in his body, I anticipate death was around 21.10.

'The contents of his stomach revealed a recent meal of burger and fries, beer and tea. He had some beer in his system but was not drunk, he was a healthy man for his age, and from his dental records we're told he was 64 years old. The full details and cause of death are probably obvious but don't quote me yet, we need to open him up properly and have a good look first. That's it for the moment, Sergeant Hampton, any questions?'

'Can you get the attacker's DNA from under his nails?'

'Of course, we're working on it. Also, we found another type of blood on his hand, maybe he got a punch or a scratch on his attacker. We'll test the blood found on the slip of paper on the man that committed suicide to see if we have a possible match, unlikely but you never know. We'll send the results as soon as possible. That phone number on the card in the pouch may be an emergency number. I've written it down for you, it looks like a mobile to me.'

The ringing of the policeman's phone stopped the meeting. Hampton left the mortuary building whispering his thanks to the pathologist, who had already moved to a new body being undressed in the next room.

'John, please can you get back to the station double quick, we have Ronnie Smith here and he's not being very cooperative. If he continues to play up I'll put him in a cell.'

'OK, I'll be with you in 20 minutes, keep your hair on, boss.'

Ronnie was not a patient man, he paced up and down the police station and when John Hampton arrived he was studying the wanted posters next to the desk in the police station entrance.

'No, Ronnie, not one of you there yet, but we're working on it.'

'You cheeky sod, Sergeant Hampton. Let's talk now then I can get out of this fucking place as soon as possible.'

With nothing further said from either man they went to the first interview room and DI Derek Lawson took over.

'Ronnie, we have your comments about the robbery to the PC who answered the 999 call on Saturday. First thing I noticed is that you got to the shop very quickly after the robbery. How did you know something was going on?'

'I was going to the shop anyway when I got an anonymous call in the car, if I'd been a few minutes earlier maybe I'd have got my hands on those thieving bastards. I always go to the shop late on Saturdays but I vary my time depending on if I watch a local football match.'

'You said on Saturday you thought the total amount of money stolen was around £5,000 pounds, was anything else stolen other than the papers in the safe you mentioned?'

'No, they just cleared the safe and a few quid from the till, nothing else was taken.'

Hampton interrupted.

'Did you visit the shop earlier that day?'

'Yes, first thing, I needed some papers from the safe urgently, but I didn't stay long.'

Ronnie was fuming inside, he knew Billy must have told them he'd been at the shop in the morning; why couldn't he have just kept his big mouth shut.

'Odd, twice in one day, all the way from Weybridge and back. Are you sure you didn't leave any more money in the safe than was stolen?'

'No, I just bloody told you that.'

He stood up and started walking round the room.

'Sit down, Ronnie, please. We had a tip-off as well that it was a very large amount of money that had been stolen from you and the informer told us that it was in the back of a car.'

'Who told you that crap? It's not true, it was just a few grand.'

'Did you talk to the newspapers late on Saturday afternoon?'

Ronnie was on the spot, he told them that his younger brother worked in a news agency and needed stories; the robbery with someone shooting a gun was good copy and publicity for Ronnie.

DI Lawson was suspicious but accepted his explanation for the time being.

Hampton still had a theory that Ronnie was making sure someone knew the robbery had happened and that he was on the case to find out who did it.

'Do you know a man called Alan Goody and does he go in your shop?'

Ronnie was nervous; he started to look uncomfortable and his complexion changed to a bright red.

'What's the matter, Ronnie, you look ill?'

'Yes, I know him.'

'You didn't answer my question, Ronnie, does he go in your shop?'

'Yes, of course he fucking well does, he's a regular.'

'Do you want a drink, Ronnie, tea or water or something?'

'No, I've things to do. I don't want any of your rotten tea.'

Hampton sat back on his chair and stared directly at an uncomfortable looking Ronnie. He made eye contact; either Ronnie knew that Goody was dead or he just wanted to get away as quickly as possible from the station and speak to his shop manager, Bootle, about the robbery.

'I'm afraid, Ronnie, that Mr Goody won't be helping us with our enquiries. He was found dead last night outside a pub in Sutton. Can you tell us what you were doing between seven and ten o'clock yesterday?'

Ronnie put his head in his hands and went white as a sheet.

'Look, Ronnie, we have two new cases now, an armed robbery and a death, which will most likely turn out to be cold-blooded murder. If we find a connection between the two we'll be talking to you again very soon.'

'I don't kill my customers, I need every one of them.'

He looked at his watch and stood up.

'I'm done here, things to do, mate, I've got another meeting.'

Lawson wagged his finger at him.

'Ronnie this has been an informal chat today, please don't leave the UK for the moment. We know you keep pissing off to Spain so if you're planning anything give Sergeant Hampton a ring. Off you go.'

Ronnie wasted no time. He grabbed his coat and was roaring away down the bypass in his S-Class Mercedes before the police changed their minds and asked him some more awkward questions.

'What do you make of that, John? The news of Goody's death certainly rattled him.'

'I agree, sir, he obviously didn't know about it and I'm pretty sure he's off to his shop to find out what's going on. We'll need him back here soon. Have a look at this new report on the robbery just in from forensics.'

The DI skipped the jargon in the brief report and just concentrated on the summary of the work done by the experts, Hampton knew he had to wait for his boss to empty his brain before he would get the chance to speak.

'One fingerprint on the car door, several black strands of greasy hair on the front passenger seat and a three-inch 12-bore cartridge case is not a lot to go on. The cartridge case is unusual and it's very old and rusty. I don't think they still make that size or type any longer. It's a brand called Alphamax made by Eley, an English company. It's a very powerful load, almost too powerful for general use. The gun and cartridges must have been from someone using it in the 1960s, maybe even one of our Old Kent Road friends. The cartridge case was found at the incinerator, the robbers must have ejected both the used and unused one, the unused one was probably thrown in the fire with the other bits.

'From the girl's description it must have been a cut-down double-barrelled 12-bore, Bootle said it even had hammers on the breech. It's worth having another look around near the incinerator to see if the live cartridge is still around. This information tells us that probably the gun was unlicensed and whoever used it may have sawn off the barrel very recently, obviously we would have grabbed it on a licence inspection if the barrel had been shortened. If, as the girl said, the barrels were in fact very short, the gun would be light and easy to conceal in a coat. When it was fired the man grabbed his right wrist in pain. I bet he did, he was lucky that he didn't break it.

'My theory is that the villains bought the gun and the cartridges together. Get a check done today to see if a double-barrel 12-bore has been reported stolen recently. It's probably a waste of time but worth a go, more likely it's a black market job. The bloke who fired the gun either got nervous, or wanted to speed the robbery up, or he really was shooting at something in the ceiling. The noise alone was enough to frighten the shit out of the betting shop staff and the customer.

'I've no doubt that Ronnie was robbed, it definitely did happen. My gut feeling is that it was a lot more money than he's making out. He probably had a separate stash in the safe. Bootle would not have opened any sealed parcels, in his mind they were just Ronnie's papers. The shot in the ceiling will go down well with the insurance company as it adds authenticity to the robbery but then Ronnie is only claiming a few grand was stolen. I'm puzzled, we need to have another thread, John. By the way, did you check Ronnie Smith's phone? Remember he said twice that he'd had an anonymous phone call when he was driving to the shop, that it was being robbed?'

'Yes, we got the phone company to check it out and they said they'll send us a list of his calls later today.'

'Why the bloody delay, John?'

'They had problems with the network on Saturday and they're going to run a back-up for us.'

'OK, when they do come back get those guys to check your phone as well on the call you got about Mark Lavender on Saturday evening.'

'I did that already, boss, it was a payphone. I've been thinking more about the call and Mark's reaction when we opened up the boot lid. I really don't think that Mark placed the bet in person, he may have phoned it in but either way that girl Angela is lying through her teeth.'

'Have we got the telephone contact details he wrote down for us when he was in here this morning, and the ballpoint pen?'

'Check with the desk they should have it in the file.'

John Hampton returned smiling with the piece of A4 paper and a pen inside a polythene bag sealed at the top by the duty sergeant.

'Good, get that down to the lab now and also check the interview room. I saw him put his hands through his hair, maybe he left some behind.'

'See if we can get a fingerprint from the pen and a match. We'll still need another from Mr Lavender to be totally sure, a strand of hair could be conclusive. Get a couple of people in there to have a good look on the desk and floor, again we'll need another sample to be sure before we give him the third degree.'

When the sergeant returned from forensic he found his DI studying a photograph of the dead man, he picked it up and pushed it in front of his sergeant.

'Look at it, John, what do you see, who does it look like?'

'A dead man, boss.'

'No, no, look closer, please.'

'Bloody hell, he looks just like Ronnie Smith but older.'

'Yes, he does. Right, John, check it out, see if he has a brother, cousin or anybody in his family that fits Alan Goody's description. If he has, find out if we know anything about any of them. The name Goody could probably be just a joke. This may be our first lead into his murder. I wonder what Ronnie is up to, put a watch on him for a couple of days, that nice WPC Dredge could do with some leg work.'

The policemen laughed at the double meaning, the WPC was one of brightest girls in the station and DI Lawson had ideas for her in his team; keeping tabs on the elusive Ronnie Smith would be an interesting challenge.

In the briefing John Hampton had to make it very clear to her the dangers that could surround this man.

He told her she should just watch who he met and where he went and under no account get too close to him. If he knew he was being watched he would just disappear into his St George's Palace.

Chapter sixteen

Dick Cohen

Dick Cohen was in turmoil. He just sat at his office desk, spending too much of the day staring at the ceiling. His mind was going around and around, his best customer and friend, Gerry Lavender, had gone missing and he needed money to complete two transactions on his behalf.

He had known Gerry since school, he had been his personal accountant for over 30 years, and he knew almost everything about his previous business and thought he knew everything about his current ventures, but now he was not so sure.

The papers sat on his desk; he needed £750,000 within three days or Gerry would be defaulting on the deals. He would normally pay the money for him but in the current property climate he simply didn't have the cash readily available, unless he sold some assets. He knew that the only way the banks would help him would be with cast-iron security.

The phone rang and Dick feared the worst when he saw the number on the screen, he had not told the police about Gerry's disappearance and every call he had received in the last few days had put him into panic mode.

'Dick, it's Barbara. Have you heard anything?'

'No, nothing at all, how about you?'

'That Spanish lawyer man phoned again, he's as desperate as we are on Gerry's whereabouts and frankly, Dick, I'm getting angry. When Gerry phoned me he didn't sound like he was being held by someone, but then he was always good at covering things up, I also heard voices in the background and they sounded foreign. I just don't know what to think.'

'Give me the number of the Spanish bloke and I'll talk to him, Barbara.'

Barbara gave him the phone number; it was a Spanish mobile and Dick scribbled Juan Villa next to it on his pad.

'I'll call you later, Barbara. We've got to find Gerry and quickly.'

Dick wasted no time and dialled the number immediately. After several continental rings the phone was answered.

'Is that Mr Juan Villa?'

'Who wants to know?' was the guarded reply.

'My name is Dick Cohen and let's just say I have a client called Gerry Lavender who I think you are looking for, is that right?'

'Yes, that is correct, but firstly give me your phone number in case it does not record in my mobile phone.'

Dick gave him the number and before he could speak the Spaniard took over the conversation.

'I've been trying to find you, Mr Cohen. I've seen papers from you before but they all came from Mr Lavender and without a contact number for you.'

'Yes, that was deliberate and for my safety.'

The Spaniard laughed at the cloak and dagger approach of Dick Cohen.

'It's simple, Mr Cohen, we both need to see Gerry Lavender and every day that passes tells me that we could have an ongoing problem in locating him. One day I did think he may still be here in the UK but nobody has seen him, not even his wife, so possibly he is now abroad. I had an appointment with him here in London and he didn't turn up, from what I know about Gerry Lavender, that's not like him. The last contact I'm told was a phone call two days ago to Mrs Lavender but since then nothing. Have you informed the police that he's missing?'

'Yes, I know about the call, I spoke with her on the phone today and she told me. It's far too soon to involve the police, if we did involve them the actual call should be from Barbara Lavender or one of his family. I'm still hoping he turns up then we can finalise the deal. From our end everything is in place, I just need Power of Attorney.'

'Yes, it's the same with us at the moment, but one of the men working for the sellers on the deal was found dead last week which gives us a problem. The other parties in the group want to complete but if the bank gets "cold feet", I think you call it, Mr Cohen, all of us will have lots of costs, probably your client as well.'

'I think we should meet tomorrow, please give me your hotel details.'

'Good idea but we should meet at a neutral place, I suggest the Imperial War Museum in South London. I'll be wearing a white raincoat and will carry a newspaper under my arm. I suggest we have a coffee and discuss our mutual problem.'

'OK, I'll meet you at 11.00 am, come alone.'

'Of course, same for you.'

The phone line went dead and Dick Cohen replayed the conversation on his answering machine but he learnt nothing new. He would meet the Spaniard as they both had an urgent need to find Gerry Lavender but Dick was uncomfortable with the meeting. He decided to have a friend follow him and take some pictures of Mr Juan Villa just in case anything went wrong.

On his journey to London he stopped at the Lavender house just as Mark pulled up with his sister, Sharon, recently arrived back from a week in Spain.

'Hello, Mark. Is that you, Sharon, I didn't recognise you with the tan. Did you have a good holiday?'

'No, not really, Mr Cohen, I went with Liz Smith my flatmate and she got called back home last Friday on a family matter, so I've had four days fighting off lecherous waiters and tour guides.'

'That sounds terrible, Sharon, but you seem to have survived.'

'Yes, of course I did. It was brilliant, I didn't pay for a single drink apart from Liz's bar bill. I had a different guy every night, but I always out drank them and they fell asleep well before they started getting amorous.'

'Has Mark told you about your dad going missing?'

'Yes, Mum, already told me last night, she said it's not like Dad at all. I disagree, I know Dad is always up to something and probably this time he may have a bigger problem than we realise. Please try and find him, Dick.'

'I will, Sharon, but you lot can help by letting me know if anything happens around you or your family in the next few days. Also, think back about anything your father may have said in the past few weeks.'

'Did you see him, Dick?' asked Mark, who looked like he hadn't slept.

'Yes, Mark, briefly about a week ago, he called in the office for his financial summary, which is the record I keep of how all his investments are at a moment in time, or at least the ones he's told me about.'

'Did he do that often, Dick?'

'No, not more than twice a year but he was overdue for a review tax wise so maybe that's what he had in mind. If he had other assets and money it would definitely be abroad and I didn't declare anything. He left me quite happy and the only thing he did that I know about was that he recently renewed his passport. He also bought a lot of clothes, I even paid for them as his Amex card was out of date, he had forgotten the new one, he was in a shop in Croydon when he phoned me to go to the shop and meet him with cash. We laughed about it later, but it was the last time I saw him.'

Sharon bowed her head.

'Oops, some of that was my fault. I made him throw lots of clothes away a few weeks ago. He was in the process of replacing everything and it sounds like he was doing well.'

'I'm meeting this Spanish lawyer in a few hours and I've just come around to check with your mother to see if she's heard anything new.'

'Yes OK, Dick, we're going for a few beers and catching up, let us know how you get on.'

Mark and Sharon dropped the suitcases indoors, waved at Barbara Lavender and immediately jumped back in the Mini.

Mark could tell from the look on his pretty sister's face that he was in trouble with her.

'OK, now, Mark, tell me everything that has happened, and I mean everything, that includes you and Vince. I know you were up to something and from your face I think whatever it is you need to tell someone, so try me over a glass of wine.'

Mark looked her straight in the face.

'One day I will, Sharon, but not everything right away. Anyway, let's go and have that drink.'

He spun the car around and accelerated past Dick Cohen and down the drive to the main road.

Barbara came to the front door to meet her visitor, she moved towards him as he removed his overcoat and glasses and without saying a word she put her arms around him and they kissed passionately in the hall.

'I gather you're on your own, Barbara?'

'Yes, Dick, I've just said goodbye to the milkman so please come in, you look much more handsome.'

'That's an invitation I can't refuse. Shall we go upstairs?'

Barbara smiled and didn't wait for him to ask twice, she almost ran up the stairs and shouted to him over her shoulder.

'Yes, Dick, we don't have that much time, Mark and Sharon said they'd be back in an hour.'

'We better be quick then, afterwards we can talk about Gerry and my meeting later with our Spanish friend, Señor Juan Villa.'

Without ceremony Dick and Barbara undressed and climbed into the double bed in the spare room. She could not use her matrimonial bed for her lovemaking, it just didn't seem right.

'Slowdown, Dick, we do have some time.'

Dick didn't answer as he pushed inside her, Barbara gasped as she reached a massive orgasm, every nerve in her body seemed to react and she screamed out loud.

Dick was not an expert but good enough for her. She took her turn and relieved him as he lay on his back breathing heavily with his eyes closed, his small body stretched across the comfortable, large cotton duvet.

'I'm going to have a quick shower, go and make a pot of tea and I'll be with you soon.'

She kissed him softly on his chest and pushed her hands through his hair.

'You haven't lost your touch, Dick. I've missed you, it must be over a year now since we were together, and believe me, I haven't had sex since that day.'

'Same here, of course. Helen died 11 months ago and frankly that killed my desire for you or anybody, but times move on and I really like being with you. I did feel guilty having sex with you when she was ill, but in a funny way it kept me going and obviously my friend Gerry was not servicing you.'

'You make it sound like I'm a car, but no, he didn't come near me. Maybe he has someone else or he has totally lost interest. I'm told it happens more times than we think. Anyway see you downstairs. I'll be with you in ten minutes,' she shouted as she ran to the bathroom and turned on the shower.

Dick dressed and obeyed orders, he made the tea and poured it just as Barbara came into the kitchen, she had put on a modern black dress and she was flushed red from the combination of sex and a hot shower.

'Crikey you look nice, Barbara.'

'Thanks Dick I try to look my best, but since he went missing I feel really bad if I'm not thinking about him all the time.'

'It's your brain preparing you for the worst, Barbara, we both know he could be in great danger or he has a completely different agenda. To be cold and truthful about it, he could be ill or lost but somehow I don't think so. I really don't know what to say other than I'll keep his letting business going, but I suggest we meet every few days to review the position. Perhaps you can come to me?'

Barbara deliberately ignored his invitation, it was too soon but she would not forget his offer. She felt disloyal to Gerry even though nobody knew where he was.

'Yes, I suppose I should fear the worst but on the other hand he's a clever man and a survivor. I just hope that we hear some news soon. It's the waiting that's the worst thing.'

Dick left before Mark and Sharon returned. He parked at the station and picked up the underground to Lambeth for his meeting with Juan Villa.

The two men were on a similar wavelength and Villa told him what he would need to complete the deal that Gerry had started.

Dick was very cautious; he was fundamentally against any rescue attempt fronted by him and he told the disappointed Spaniard his view. They left with an agreement that Dick would contact him within a week to give him a yes or no on completing the deal.

Time was not on Juan Villa's side but he had managed to obtain a small delay to see if Gerry did turn up and to search for new investors. He would hire a private detective and see what he could come up with but time was running out.

As Dick Cohen left the meeting his mobile phone rang, he moved into the foyer of the building and took the call in private. The soft female voice gave him some good news.

Dick was not a man to take risks but in the coming weeks he changed his views, as a widower and an extremely wealthy man, Cohen decided that a change of lifestyle was needed. The sex with Barbara Lavender had reminded him that there was another part to his life that he was missing and he was going to find some of it.

He turned on his heel and went back into the building; he needed to keep the Spaniard warm on the deal.

'Juan, please wait, I've had a change of mind. I'll still look for Gerry but let's discuss those numbers again.'

'Of course, Mr Cohen, what has changed your mind?'

'Shall we say heavenly intervention?'

Juan smiled. He had no idea what was said in the three-minute phone call taken by Dick a few moments before and Dick was not going to tell him.

'I will see you in your office in Marbella on Monday. Is that OK with you, Juan?'

'Yes, that's fine, Mr Cohen. Please call me next week with your arrival time. If Gerry turns up in the meantime let me know. I'll get someone to collect you from Malaga airport.'

'No thanks, I have my own arrangements and I'll see you about 2.00 pm.'

Chapter seventeen

Here come the Girls!

Sharon Lavender was more than pissed off with Liz Smith. Her early departure from Spain and the condition of the house made her very annoyed with her sloppy tenant. It was not just her own room but the whole of the house, it was like a rubbish tip, the girls had left it very tidy so all this new shit must have accumulated in the last few days.

'Bloody hell, Liz, just have a look at the state of this house, and what about the kitchen, have you never heard of washing up?'

'Sorry, I meant to do it, but I've been busy doing things for my dad and last night I'd some mates round I'd totally forgotten about. Anyway, how did you get on once I left you in Spain?'

'Fine actually, I took a few blokes for a ride but stayed out of trouble. What have you really been up to, apart from not washing up or tidying the place?'

Liz had lived with her father since his marriage broke up but she argued with any woman he brought home, to keep the peace and the close relationship she had with him she decided to leave the Weybridge mansion. Through a friend she met Sharon, who offered a place in her house.

'Have you been screwing my brother again while I was out of sight?'

'No, Sharon, not me this time. You know I was really sorry about that, it all happened quickly and it's over now.'

'So why did you have to get back to England so quick, leaving me with your massive bar bill?'

'Nothing really, just a small job for my dad, but only I could do it as it was a family matter and involved a lot of money.'

'I know you worked in a bank but I didn't know you did money laundering as well, Liz. Be careful, big brother is watching you.'

'Not me, Sharon, but maybe some other people I know could be into that, I keep away from them.'

'How is Mark's girlfriend, Kate? Do you see much of her now, Liz? She used to work in your bank didn't she? I have a feeling from what he says

86

about her that she's losing interest in him. Probably she's looking for a new man and from what I hear he has to be a man with ambition.'

Sharon thought she knew more but she wanted to hear Liz's version of things.

'Yes, funny you should say that, she's been a bit odd lately, she's got a new job in foreign investment and everything is very much behind closed doors. We used to go out for a drink once a week but all that has ended and she rarely speaks to me. Why are you asking about her?'

'Mark picked me up from the airport and he was in a right state, not sure what it was all about but he said Kate had left him. He'd received a couple of text messages from her virtually saying goodbye and nothing else. He said she never sent text messages and it was obvious that he was dumped and she didn't want to talk to him at all. Something else was eating him as well as Kate leaving, but he wasn't saying a word on what it was. I'm worried, I just have a feeling it's serious. I'm going round to see Donna tonight at her house. Do you want to come with me?'

'Yes please, I'd like to see the baby again. I saw him in hospital for two minutes but I want to hold him.'

'Donna's a bit depressed as Vince has lost his job and she's really worried about their financial situation. He's doing some odd jobs and they're lucky that my mother has a few bob to help them.'

'Yes, I'll get ready but I'll clean up this place first. By the way will your big brother be around, I haven't seen him for a year or so?'

'Not sure, Liz, is Vince another one of your many conquests?'

The red face told the story and Sharon did not pursue the question. She wanted to help Liz as somewhere under the rough exterior was a nice girl. She knew her father was a tough man to talk to but he did love his daughter very much.

Her mother didn't want to know her. Liz had to turn somewhere for help and that had to be her father, but Ronnie had a knack of putting her in more trouble than she could handle, almost testing her with his little schemes, but he knew he could trust her and for Ronnie and his women, that was a rarity.

'I promise not to chat Vince up, Sharon, if he's at home, really I promise.'

'You better not, I'll be watching you.'

Liz gave her a big hug and the girls burst out laughing.

'Come on, you get that apron on and I'll find the vacuum cleaner, let's sort this place out properly.'

'By the way, what's that tape on the table?'

'Oh, I forgot about that, Billy Bootle dropped it in to give to Angela. She lives around the corner in the flats and she was out when he went around, and he didn't know which letterbox was hers. I'll put it through the right one with a note.'

Later that afternoon as she got changed to go out with Sharon, Liz got the tape from the table and put it in an old machine she had kept for replaying a silly sex movie she had made with her friends when she was drunk.

She ejected the movie and inserted the tape. The images were crystal clear of both inside the betting shop and outside in the road on the day of the robbery.

The images were of three men, two she knew well. She ejected the tape and put it back in the envelope. It was none of her business; she wanted to get rid of the tape as soon as possible and went to Angela's letterbox.

She hesitated before she dropped it in but then she realised if Angela didn't get it that creep Billy Bootle would be back to the house looking for it, and that was the last thing she wanted.

Her father had probably not seen the tape but that was down to Angela and Billy; it was not her problem and she knew that if she hoped to sleep with a Lavender man again she best forget what she had seen.

Chapter eighteen

The Saga of Billy

Billy Bootle was a man of few friends; in fact he probably had more enemies than friends.

He had failed at almost everything; every job he had tried was lost due to his manner when face to face with the public. Before working for Ronnie in the betting shop he had many temporary jobs, from bus conductor to casual work at horse race meetings. At 45 years old, he now had to find something permanent, and a woman.

One casual job was at the Tote and he learnt the betting trade well, the man's weakness was his own gambling and to supplement his losses he needed a hand in a till somewhere or some petty theft. The Tote did not allow him any opportunities to supplement his earnings, so he did a bit of pickpocketing from drunken punters, selling them tips and then robbing them.

After he arrived at the Cheam shop, it didn't take him long to put together a scam with a couple of customers, one of them being Alan Goody. It all went wrong as Billy didn't give him his full share, as he was always borrowing money from him.

The robbery worked too well for it not to be an inside job. Luke Devine approached him, he knew Luke was not the brain behind the idea but he dealt with him as the front man. Billy told Devine he would tip him off on the exact day that Ronnie would move all the till money from all his various shops to Cheam. He always knew when it would be as Ronnie marked a small cross on the calendar in the back office, Billy had been looking at it for holiday dates when he noticed the mark his boss had made to remind him to make the call to the courier.

The trusted unofficial courier then had the job of moving the money from Cheam to a bank in Spain, usually one of Ronnie Smith's mates pretending to go on holiday. It had worked perfectly for years; the courier and family got a free weekend holiday.

Ronnie was always on-site at the shop to make sure the courier took everything, and to make a few threats if the courier was thinking of double-crossing or cocking up the deposit in Spain. This method had been used many times and the routine collection would happen on the day the boys robbed the shop, but this time the courier would have nothing left to collect.

Billy made three mistakes; firstly, short paying Alan again for his share of the betting scam, then secondly, laughing when Alan threatened to tell Ronnie he had been stealing, and thirdly, trusting a paid-off Angela to keep her mouth shut on what they were up to.

As it turned out, Angela did not want trouble but Alan disliked him immensely. If he was ripping off Ronnie Smith he would get Billy sorted out big time.

The day Billy met Gerry Lavender by chance in the pub changed his life overnight. Once Gerry knew that Billy was working for Ronnie Smith he saw an opportunity to get even with Ronnie on a past deal that had cost Gerry £300,000.

The plan was simple even for Billy. He would call Luke when the money was due to be collected from all the shops and delivered to Cheam. Billy usually only saw the mark on the calendar a few days before but Luke and his mates were ready when the call came through.

The agreement was a three-way split of the money, with Luke taking all the money immediately to Spain. But Luke decided that Billy could not be trusted and en route to Dover they would give him just enough to keep him quiet with a promise that they would invest the rest for him!

After Mark had put his share of the robbery money into the boot of the Mini, he went inside his parents' house. Luke, en route to Dover, removed the stolen money and as he walked away from the car he saw Billy Bootle turn the corner. He waited to see what he was doing. Billy opened the boot with a screwdriver. He left £1,000 and the copy of the betting slip to match a 20–1 win on the bet Mark didn't know he had placed.

The day of the robbery turned out to be a bad one for Billy, the raid went as planned and he met Luke later that night near the M25, but Luke wouldn't give him all of his share. He threatened him so Luke pinned him against his car and stuffed a few grand in his pocket telling him to piss off.

He went back home and made a phone call to his boss, asking him if they could meet up at his house; Ronnie shouted at Billy for being soft with the robbers so Billy put the phone down. He then turned up at his front door 30 minutes later but once over the step, Ronnie just screamed again at Billy and then punched him on the nose covering both of them in blood. He blamed him for the robbery as the prostrate Billy pleaded his innocence.

To make matters worse, Alan Goody had told Billy to meet him that night in the pub, otherwise he would tell Ronnie that he had been stealing from him. This was the second time this had happened to Billy. He had a fight with a punter who was one of Ronnie's best customers a few years before, and the man fell onto the railway track near Sutton.

Billy was wound up as he left his house, spitting blood and needing a drink. He went to his kitchen and found a weapon, a crude double-edge serrated potato knife that would fit up his sleeve in a cigar case. He had sharpened it to cut like a razor and he knew that if he got the opportunity he would use the knife on Goody.

The men met in the pub and sat at a table drinking together, they were soon arguing. After a few pints Billy became more confident of what he would do next but then the landlord lost his patience with the men, shouting at the top of their voices, and he refused to serve them with any more beer and pointed to the door.

Billy was a man who was disliked by everyone as he had the knack of rubbing people up the wrong way, including his own family. His mind was warped from events in his early life when his father beat him up and abused him. He had no other plan as he left the pub other than to deal with Goody.

Alan Goody left first with Billy Bootle running after him. Witnesses confirmed later that the two men had left together. Alan stopped to confront Billy, shouting at him in the street. Alan was a scrapper he came from a tough area of South London and many times he had fought his way out of trouble.

By this time Billy was blazing mad as he had taken enough shit from this nasty little man and he would carry out his plan to finish him for good.

As the insults and threats got worse Billy boiled over, as Alan got more and more personal they moved away from the lights of the pub; Alan's calmness irritated Billy as he could not think of a reply to the abuse other than to swear at him. Alan then made a big mistake, which ultimately resulted in his violent death.

Alan pushed Billy in the chest and described how several years before in the back streets of Brixton he attacked and raped Billy's sister, Doris, the divorced wife of Ronnie Smith. She made a drunken pass at Alan after a party, then mocked him as he tried to make a move on her, swearing at him and finally spitting in his face. This was just too much for Alan and he decided to wait for her as she walked the two blocks to her home and then he attacked her.

Later Ronnie was told she had just been mugged and beaten up, as Doris refused to tell her husband the details of what had actually happened. She was afraid Ronnie would have reacted badly and killed his own brother, Alan Goody (alias John Smith). At that time she regarded a revenge attack by a husband worse than any assault and she didn't want the police involved under any circumstances.

Alan told word for word in full graphic detail what had happened, Billy couldn't contain his anger, Doris was one of his only real friends, and Goody was definitely going to pay for what he had done.

The knife attack caught Alan off guard. Billy was like an animal released from a cage; he grabbed him by the throat and after a fierce struggle he used the knife to mutilate him before smashing his head on the pavement. He cut his hand on the knife in the process, and as he frantically tried to wipe up all the drops of his own blood from the victim's body, some fell onto Goody's sleeve.

Billy ran out of time to finish the attack, he was disturbed by the security lights coming on next to the pub emergency exit; as the staff came to investigate he quickly ran away as his victim gasped his last breath.

He stayed indoors for the whole weekend and when he heard the report of a murder on the radio he felt no remorse. He returned to work in the betting shop on the Monday and apart from a leg wound hidden by his trousers, his scruffy appearance was no different to any other day.

Ronnie turned up just after the shop opened with his daughter Liz in tow, he immediately apologised to Billy for hitting him, and he was yet to learn that his brother was dead.

'Sorry, mate, didn't mean it but this robbery stinks. Do you know anything at all about it?'

'Yes, I got a bloody sore nose.'

To get Ronnie off his back he had to give him a clue and confirm his call to the police after the robbery.

'Look, Ronnie, I'm on your side. I phoned Hampton, the sergeant that came here, because I think the driver was Mark Lavender but I didn't really know that until I checked the CCTV later. I managed to just switch the outside night camera on before that guy fired at the ceiling.'

'Bloody hell, Billy, I knew I'd upset Gerry Lavender big time over that scrap deal but I didn't think Mark would try and pull one on me. Anyway, what did you actually say to the coppers, Billy?'

'Mark had taken the piss out of me several times in the shop about my clothes and the prices I gave on horses, he thought he was being the funny guy but every time he did it I wanted to smash his face in. He was mouthing off in the pub the other night and I told him to stop bullshitting about gambling and get a big bet on for a change. He grabbed me by the throat and told me to put £50 on a horse at Haydock Park on the day of the robbery. With everyone watching he threw five £10 pound notes at me and shouted that he was not paying the tax.

'I got away from him and when I got to the shop the next day I told Angela to keep the money and place the bet on Saturday to teach him a lesson. As the horse was 20–1 odds I was confident that in the November Handicap it had no chance. The horse hadn't run before in a big race, the only thing in its favour was it had a good jockey. I even paid the tax in advance for the cocky bastard. I was amazed when it won and I put the money with the slip in a bag for him.

'When I saw the CCTV picture I saw my chance to get even and just said to the police check Mark Lavender's car, which of course they did that night and found the money I'd put in the boot. I was going to wait until the Sunday and tell him what was in his car but the coppers got to him first.'

'Did you ring me as well, Billy? Someone told me I was being robbed so I legged it here, but as you know, I was too late.'

'No, not me, Ronnie. I think it was Angela. I had an argument with your brother as he tried to leg it after the big race and he wouldn't pay for his bets again. He started to turn nasty and she wanted you to come and sort him out, the call was cut short as the robbers burst in.'

Billy was double-crossing his boss, it was obvious Ronnie thought he was far too thick to organise a robbery. Without Luke Devine's help monitoring a couple of the other betting shops and watching how they moved the money, Billy would have to guess that the marks on the calendar did mean the bulk money was really coming to his shop that day.

'Someone called me and come to think of it, it was a woman, but the voice was muffled. The caller must have had a handkerchief over the mouthpiece of the phone; she sounded desperate that's why I got here so quick. The police will check my mobile phone but it's sure to be from our phone here. I thought someone was winding me up, they just said get here quick and then put the phone down. Let's get back to work. I reckon I lost about £300,000, Billy, so we've some catching up to do. I am so fucking angry. When I find out who all those guys are I'll cut their balls off.'

One thing Billy had learnt since he worked for him was that Ronnie made a lot of threats, but only against people he knew. In this case he had no idea who might have robbed him, but if it was Mark Lavender he was small fry; he might check him out personally, but then he decided to wait. The police might do that; he would sit back and see what they came up with.

The arrival of Liz Smith aroused Billy's suspicion. Ronnie told him that she would be doing a routine audit of the systems in each of the shops before a new computer was installed. Liz would check the books against the receipts and payments going back a couple of months. During her audits she could see if there were any clues relating to her uncle, she had a nose for people lying to her and she knew exactly where to start.

Ronnie left the shop without any goodbyes, leaving Liz to get on with the job. She knew that cooperation from Billy would be limited, but he liked talking so she tried to be nice to him on this one occasion.

'Billy can we go through your computer procedure in overall terms and then Angela can show me how she balances the cash.'

'Bloody simple really, just read the manual.'

Billy casually sat back on the chair and folded his arms across his chest, his trouser legs rolling up as he leaned back. The laid-back movement was one of a man with something to hide and Liz felt it was more than money.

'What happened to your leg, Billy? That's a nasty bruise and cut, do you know you also have a bruise on the back of your neck? You probably can't see, it's as if someone was trying to strangle you.'

Billy immediately went red and sat upright in his chair, almost falling off it.

'Mind your own fucking business, Liz, do you hear me?'

'My, my, you are jumpy, Billy. I was only being polite in enquiring about your health. If my question annoys you I'll just silently carry on with the audit.'

Billy just grunted and sat back again on his chair.

'I've read the manual, these are my five questions.'

The answers to her questions showed that they both knew the system, they had to, but Liz was looking for a weakness, she couldn't find one and the interview was over.

'Hi, Angela, how's life in the shop?'

'Could be worse, Liz, a regular man would be nice.'

'Yes, me to. I met a few in Spain but they all had lots of history, the best ones were foreign and didn't speak much English.'

'What do you want from me, Liz?'

Liz liked the question it opened the door for her so she carefully explained what she was doing.

'So, does it ever happen that you don't give a punter a betting slip copy ticket?'

'No, never, unless of course I mess up and that's very rare. Sometimes they get left behind and that's only a problem if they win with no ticket to show me.'

Liz noted how Angela covered herself; she obviously did frequently mess up. But why, how many times and was it deliberate? She had to get her on her own in the pub as Billy was earholing everything she said.

The meeting ended and the girls agreed to have a drink together after work, fortunately Billy didn't hear the conversation but he was already suspicious.

His leg hurt like hell and he had drunk solidly over the weekend to try and forget what he had done. His hangover did not make him feel any better about Liz's visit and he would be watching out for her.

He went home early and told Ronnie he was sick. His boss had no sympathy, he knew Liz would rattle him and that's what he wanted. Had he known what a dangerous man Billy Bootle was, he would have done the audit himself.

Ronnie, like his daughter, had good instincts and he just wondered about Billy. Was he ripping him off, or sick, or both? He was a thin man but strong, but then he didn't fight back when Ronnie clipped his nose. He must have had a reason not to do that. In a way Ronnie had done it for a reaction, but apart from a bit of abuse he didn't get one. That worried Ronnie even more. He would like to get rid of him but he had to know if he was involved in the robbery and if it had any connection to his brother, Alan Goody.

'What you drinking, Angela?'

'Tonight I'll have a change as I'm walking home. I'll have a double vodka and tonic please, Liz.'

'But that's what you always have.'

'Just checking you remembered.'

'Of course, I also remember that you like Mark Lavender – are you screwing him?'

'Chance would be a fine thing, do you fancy him?'

'No, his married brother is a more interesting date. I've seen him in the swimming baths and he's a very big man.'

'Big? Do you mean big where it matters?'

'Yes, but don't get horny, he's mine first.'

Liz was clever; she was trying to relax Angela without her knowing and she was already on her second V&T. On an empty stomach they had hit home within a few minutes of the meeting. Liz took a long toilet break to phone her dad and when she came back into the lounge Angela had got a third drink on the table.

'How do you take the money but not issue a ticket?'

'OK, but don't get me the sack. Billy takes a bet then I make a note on a pad, the money goes in a box under the counter, only a few punters allow him to do that method. If the horse or dog loses the race or is unplaced, Billy pockets the money, if it wins we put it through the machine and we deduct the tax from money Billy has made from other lost bets. The clock on the machine is easy to fiddle, you just switch it off and type in a time. After it has been rung through you reset the time, easy really. Billy can make £100 a day.'

'Did Alan Goody use the system?'

'Yes, but Sod's law he won a lot and Billy said he didn't have enough money to refund his tax, actually he did but just didn't want to pay him.'

'So he got the winnings but tax deducted sometimes and usually the big ones?'

'They had a big argument on the day of the robbery and in the confusion Billy also gave the robbers his secret kitty of money that he used to pay out his dodgy deals.'

'What did you know about Alan Goody other than he was in the shop every day?'

'Nothing, he was a complete loner and sometimes quite nasty with it, but he was definitely better away from the shop. I bumped into him one day in Sainsbury's and he was quite chatty but the next day he was a miserable bugger again. It was almost as if Billy changed his moods.'

'Do you think Billy or Alan knew the robbers?'

'I doubt if Alan did, he turned to the wall when he saw what was happening and kept his head down watching behind him through the mirror. I'm not sure about Billy, though. He was behind me when the gun went off. I was so frightened that I wet my knickers so I just cried until they left. Billy was locked in the shit hole which was always dirty so he got a bit of his own medicine.'

'Thanks, Angela. I'm not sure what to do next, so for the moment I'll do nothing. Dad will talk to you away from the office soon and in the meantime, watch out for Billy.'

'I will and it's good to get all this off my chest. Can you see any nice boys around the bar?'

'Come on, drink up and I'll take you home.'

The girls were almost friends.

Liz reported back to her father the following day while everything she had learnt was still fresh in her mind. Her disappointment was that Ronnie had moved on and was only mildly interested in what she had to say.

He gave her a wad of £10 notes, which turned out to be a grand and ran to his car. He was late for his football match and she would learn later that the game was now his number one priority.

Chapter nineteen

Eighteen Months Later

The inside of his small room in Langley Open Prison was as good as Mark Lavender could have expected considering the circumstances. He was preparing to leave the prison and he sat on his bed packing the few items of clothing he was taking home, everything else he left behind for other prisoners. He had made some friends but none he ever wanted to meet again on the outside.

Mark had arrived at the prison an angry and bitter young man but he had worked on keeping calm. In the loneliness of his room he had finally come to terms with what had happened to him on the day of the robbery. Yes, he was involved, but so were Vince and Luke and they were free. He was determined to find out who framed him, but then he thought, what would he do about it; he decided to worry about that if and when the time arrived.

His arrest and the subsequent charge of armed robbery were a distant memory. The evidence was conclusive with three separate clues – a fingerprint on the getaway car and from the pen he used in the police station, hairs from his head on the car floor and a CCTV tape which showed his face clearly in the driving seat of the getaway vehicle.

The CCTV film should have been regarded as invalid as it had definitely been altered; apart from Mark in the car it showed no other footage. Billy Bootle had always maintained that he mixed the tapes up and in spite of vain attempts from the defence lawyer, the pictures were permitted as evidence. Mark Lavender did not have a choice about what his plea should be, he had to admit to being the driver in the robbery.

He would not disclose the names of his accomplices to the police and therefore the judge was uncompromising in giving him a four-year sentence, even though it was a first offence. His barrister whispered in his ear that he should be out within 18 months with good behaviour. His guilty plea helped but his loyalty to his brother, Vince, and his friend, Luke, had gone against him in front of the jury, he slumped to the floor as the sentence was read out.

He was a lonely man as he left the court for prison with hardly a friend in sight. Vince was not involved in the court proceedings and after several aggressive interviews with the police, his elder brother was keeping well away from him.

Barbara Lavender was devastated once she knew her son was guilty. He would always be her baby, but now she could not help him and with her husband still missing after almost two years, she was beginning to assume the worst.

She had found a letter in his desk stating that in the case of his death or disappearance of longer than two years, she should take the letter to Dick Cohen and he would deal with the contents of the safe, which in total – cash, gold and bonds – added up to over £2million. In addition, she would have the house and £1million from other savings.

The document was odd, Dick had been worried about the word 'disappearance' when it was drafted but Gerry made a joke of it and said he was thinking of a round-the-world yacht trip.

It was not a will, more an insurance policy for his wife. Dick had made Gerry's request legal through a specific Power of Attorney and the document was very much valid. The timescale to exercise his wishes was a full two years and he had mixed feelings about his old friend showing up before that period had passed.

Dick Cohen had been worried for some time before he left that his friend and client was acting oddly. He had an idea that Gerry was planning something dramatic but now he thought that after two years without any contact at all, he could be dead.

He told Barbara about the document and she burst into tears, fearing the worst.

In addition to helping Barbara with her finances he was also now a close personal friend and a continuous lover. Since the shock of the death of his wife had become a memory rather than a bad dream, he had become much closer to Barbara, which suited both of them.

Initially Dick Cohen also dealt with the police for Barbara. They reported him missing two weeks from the day he disappeared. The resulting search was not as thorough as Barbara would have liked but they had no evidence to suggest he had been kidnapped or worst still, that he had been killed. The police interviewed her at length several times but learnt nothing that could help them find him, she was careful not to mention the contents of the safe.

John Hampton was put on the case initially but then he got promoted to Detective Inspector and he passed Gerry Lavender's disappearance on to the also newly promoted Sergeant Linda Dredge. The police had taken the view that maybe Gerry was somehow behind the betting shop robbery and if he did turn up they would very much like to interview him. They had marked Vince Lavender's card and if he as much as ran a red light they would be after him.

As expected, Linda Dredge suggested to Barbara that Gerry might have another woman, she did not rule this out; the document in Dick Cohen's possession made her think perhaps the policewoman was close to the truth.

Barbara did not want to hear the worst; when some clothes turned up off the Torquay coast with an old football match ticket with her husband's name on it in a pocket, she didn't remember the clothes and the only explanation could have been that Gerry had bought a ticket for someone; it was dated a month before he disappeared.

After several months of doing nothing but sit and think, she had eventually managed to pull herself together and she started to look after her new grandson five days a week. Donna had returned to work full-time and every day she delivered the little boy to his grandmother and collected him in the evening.

Vince could not make contact with Luke Devine; he had not heard from him since the day they shook hands after the robbery and he made off for Spain with the money.

He had not discussed the robbery with anyone and although he met Mark when he was on bail they had nothing to say to each other, which at first Barbara could not understand.

She did later when the police kept interviewing her eldest son.

After the many difficult sessions with the police, Vince decided not to visit Spain for at least another year, when he did he would find his old friend to see what he had done with his money.

Mark did not blame his brother in any way, he just regarded himself as unlucky. He knew Vince would not have grassed him up but he was not sure about Luke Devine; on the other hand, everything was too clean-cut and easy for the police.

Once his sentence was complete he had every intention of finding out who put him in the frame.

Juan Villa had turned up nothing on the missing person but for some reason he didn't appear to be trying very hard. He agreed with Dick Cohen that they would keep in close contact in case Gerry suddenly appeared dead or alive in the UK or Spain.

This was easy for Dick as in his sudden and unexplained change of direction after meeting Juan Villa in London, he decided that he would personally find the £750,000 for the investment in Spain. If his friend Gerry Lavender ever turned up, he could share the properties with him. Juan Villa was pleased and told Dick that he would also take a chunk of euros from his own account and buy in to the investment; for one reason or another, he never did.

The bluff had been to give Dick some comfort and he would waste no time in going to Spain to check out his new investment and sign the papers. Dick had always said to himself he would never invest abroad but circumstances were different; as a shareholder he would have a major investment in the new beach-side complex in Marbella.

The major shareholders in the development company were ADC Developments Inc SPA, from North West Spain. They were a mix of speculators and small-time investors looking for short-term gains. They intended to build cheaply, sell some properties to occupy the site, then offload the remaining properties and leisure facilities without any occupants.

The corporate power in ADC was firmly with the major shareholder, Señor Fernando Lopez; the development was his idea and with his family he owned 40% of the shares in ADC. The other shareholders were fellow Basque friends he had known for many years, people with money who were depending on Lopez to deliver high and quick returns on their investment.

Lopez handled the day-to-day management of the company from his local office in Marbella but he was constantly called back to Irun to keep his other shareholders informed on progress.

The Spaniard had taken a hands-on approach to get the project completed and within budget. He took over after a succession of ineffective project managers had failed and left the company.

His plans involved using cheap labour from Tangiers in Morocco, mostly unskilled; the men not only had to learn how to build but also how to work to a time schedule.

As Dick Cohen had not met Lopez, it had been a big turnaround for a cautious man like him to invest in a foreign country. The way Cohen had quickly changed his mind about investing the money in this building project was bizarre to anyone who knew him. He had always been ultra cautious as even though he was very wealthy, he had wanted to hold on to his money into retirement, which was now only a few years away. He had visited Spain several times to view with the lawyer the slow progress on the site construction. Señor Fernando Lopez had proved to be evasive, this worried Dick Cohen and Juan Villa was given the job of arranging a showdown to get Lopez to finally commit to a completion date on the first phase of building.

The newspapers in Spain had reported a scandal that cast a shadow over the project. The unsolved murder of the Spanish landowner who had originally approached Juan Villa to sell his land was all but forgotten in the police files. Apparently his killer left no clues but a change in personnel in the local Guardia Civil ordered the case to be investigated again after an anonymous message to a local newspaper.

The newspaper had been tipped off that the dead man had some valuable information that could seriously affect the Marbella project. He had to be silenced and when he was murdered it was rumoured the people behind it had paid the police to file the case as unsolved.

The man had no family so the cover-up was easy, nobody asked any questions.

Once the newspaper received the information they immediately told the police and the investigation into the murder had to resume. After just a few days looking into the facts again, completely out of the blue an Algerian immigrant arrested for robbery confessed to the murder. He spoke only

French and he told the local police that he had been paid 10,000 euros to kill the man. The Algerian never appeared in court; he died of a heart attack in his cell but from the information he had given the police during interrogation, it seemed that he must have been the killer.

Unknown to Juan Villa, the murdered man was also a surveyor by trade and he had made an internal report on the land to be used for the new buildings before he sold it. The word on the streets around Marbella was that the site would subside unless deep and expensive piles were put in. No copies of the report were ever found in his possession or at his office.

The newspaper story left many questions unanswered on the whole project.

Fernando Lopez had only a short time to convince all his buyers that everything would be built in a satisfactory manner.

The new date for the completion had been published as early December, which was over 12 months behind the original schedule. The sudden rush to complete was due to an acute lack of new money being invested, as potential buyers now had a lot of choice in an overcrowded and weak property market.

Fernando Lopez was the big man who had organised all the investment and he knew he had trouble on his hands; his financial forecasts were a sorry sight and he had to try to find a way out of the mess he had created. The banks were giving him grief and every day a different investor was phoning his office for news on the completion dates, some were already putting their unfinished properties on the market.

Meetings were arranged with buyers and the building company and the smooth tongue of Lopez calmed the situation. He knew that the new completion date had to be achieved, otherwise he would have to bring forward his own costly exit route from Spain; he had too much to lose.

Chapter twenty

New Employment

The bang of the letterbox never usually bothered Donna Lavender, she would sometimes leave the morning post all day if Vince had gone to work early, but today something told her to go and collect the single white envelope.

The new baby was making noises rather than words, Donna and Barbara encouraging him to speak even if it was rubbish and it would be months before anything recognisable came out of his mouth. As Vince was either working or playing his games most of the time, she often had one-sided conversations with her young son.

'Now, Shane, let's see what that nice postman has brought us today. Maybe we won on the premium bonds but then that's unlikely because I cashed them last month. No, it's probably another catalogue offer, this time just 50% off, surely they'll all go bust soon if nobody is buying from them at all.'

Donna ripped open the flap and started to read a four-page letter from Vince's firm. She had to sit down and Shane started to cry for his mother and for once he had stopped gurgling. How dare she stop, he wanted attention and screamed.

'Shane, belt up!'

She shouted twice, which amazingly worked, stunning the child into silence.

The letter was seriously bad news; the company that employed Vince were going into administration and 40 staff would be made redundant without any payment other than the salary that was paid into their banks the previous week.

Vince Lavender was one of the unlucky ones; the accountants were trying to get the company on its feet as a going concern and they had decided that the best opportunity was to drastically reduce the wage bill. A deal for the unlucky ones would be done if the company continued to operate, if it was wound up, they would be lucky to get 20p in the pound in two years' time.

Before Donna had taken it all in, the house phone rang and Vince described the details of what they had been told at a meeting half an hour before and that he was on the list of departures.

'I know, Vince, a letter arrived telling me what you've just said. Is there any chance that the union can help or that they will reconsider when they see what valuable staff you are?'

'No, not a chance, Donna. The union have been trying to help in their own way for some time but with our salary costs four times that paid in China, we are not competitive any longer. It used to be that their quality was crap but not anymore, they build better, cheaper and quicker. Now they've got a local office we've lost contract after contract, they've taken on two of our salesmen on a commission-only basis to try and take more of our business. That's the nail in the coffin, Donna, we're sunk.'

'What about us, Vince, we only have enough money for a couple of months, can we sell the property in Spain we've never seen or maybe borrow from your mum until you get a job?'

'Lots of questions, Donna, I've a small job to finish here for cash and then I'll be home. We can sit down then and see what we can do. There has to be a job for me somewhere. We are being paid this month as usual and then I can sign on to get jobseekers' allowance until I sort something out.'

'OK, darling, but no pub tonight, we've got some cans here and I'll get Shane off to bed now so we can talk.'

The news of the demise of Atkinson Brothers Engineering Ltd was soon on the streets of Sutton and Cheam. Forty members of staff were leaving immediately, but if the company could not be salvaged, final numbers would be over 200.

Vince signed on and went to see several friends looking for work but most companies were trimming staff numbers; apart from raw, cash-in-hand manual work there was very little employment to be found at the level Vince needed to pay his mortgage and living expenses.

As soon as she felt up to it, Donna would eventually work part-time, with Vince's mum looking after Shane almost every hour that her daughter-in-law could work, it was still peanuts and Barbara Lavender would have to put her hand in her pocket twice in the first month to help the couple out with just the basic essentials.

The marriage between Donna and her husband was strained by the circumstances. She knew from a friend that they could not sell the Spanish property and Vince was surprised she did not ask why. The discussion was for another day, but then she might have to explain how she knew, but probably not if she wanted to stay married.

Barbara had given Vince a few maintenance jobs in her house and paid him cash, he was a good craftsman but painting, decorating and gardening were not his idea of a career.

A week after the letter, he sat on his mother's wall; she had gone shopping with her new grandson in the pram and he was painting the fence. Barbara Lavender's house was the smartest in the road and a reluctant Vince was swamped with offers from neighbours to do work for them.

As he finished the wrought iron gate with a last coat of black paint, a large car pulled up behind him and he looked over his shoulder to see who his mother's visitor was. It was too early for Dick Cohen, he knew he would not be around if Barbara had the baby with her.

'Hello, Vince, that's a good job you're doing. I see you can turn your hand to anything nowadays and that's why I'm here.'

Ronnie Smith was a man who didn't make idle chat and he was at the Lavender house for one reason and one reason only, he had been to Vince's house and had got no reply. He wasn't answering the phone so Ronnie figured he must be working outside.

'Hello, Ronnie, good to see you, mate, how are you?'

Vince would be polite until he knew exactly what Ronnie wanted, he had only dealt with him when he was placing bets and the two had always got on well.

When Vince's father mentioned turning over Ronnie's betting shop he had mixed feelings, but as Luke was keen and Gerry had a score to settle with Ronnie, he went for it. He felt nervous as Ronnie stared at him but he knew that he didn't do small talk and he would get to the point of his visit quickly.

'Yes fine, son. I heard about your predicament and apart from painting have you anything lined up?'

'No, I've been for shitloads of interviews and got fuck all, in other words, I'm struggling badly to find something.'

'In either language it's the same, Vince. Now listen.'

'I need someone to work for me. I have three businesses currently giving me grief plus a project in Spain that I don't have time to sort out. The main business is scrap. Yes, as you know, bloody lovely scrap from cars to old fridges. Loads of profit but the two managers are a waste of space and that's not a pun.'

Vince laughed as Ronnie continued to elaborate on his delightful recycling business; in his own words, 'recycling' was more acceptable when he was talking to some of his new, posh, Weybridge Estate neighbours.

'This is the deal, Vince, I want you to run the scrap business, fuck it, recycling materials, that's what we call scrap and nothing else between you and me. It's a totally hands-on business but you can hire and fire whoever you fancy. I don't want to know what happens other than you've got to make a clear £15,000 a week from the four sites after costs. We already do £9,000 after costs with a bunch of right Charlie's operating it, so I think after a few months you'll be up to the figure I want.'

'No pension or health insurance working for me, Vince, but I'll give you a percentage of what you make so, my boy, you could earn £750 a week times four if you work hard. In the first month, which we'll call a trial, I'll pay you

£2,000 cash, that's my risk and I hope you aren't one. Are you with me, mate?'

Vince dropped his paintbrush and jumped over the wall in excitement.

'Of course I am, Ronnie, it sounds like the sort of thing I want to get into. Yes, I'll definitely give it a go. I'll start Monday.'

'No you fucking well don't, you start tomorrow. Come to Weybridge, the address is on this card. I'll see you about 7.30.'

'Thanks, Ronnie, I promise not to let you down.'

'I'm sure of that, Vince, and one day we'll talk about other things, but that's not urgent, this job is.'

Vince went bright red; Ronnie was either fishing or he had guessed Gerry might be behind the robbery. He thought that he might need to get Vince on his side first and then sort out the whole Lavender family in one go.

'Don't look so bloody worried, Vince, I don't care about the past at the moment, other than I know now I need people I can trust. When I was robbed recently I'd a good guess where the money would eventually finish up and maybe one day, if I'm right, you'll have to help me find it and invest it. Just for your information, Vince, I never talk to the police now about anything unless they nick me. It cost me big time in fees to get off the drink-driving offence. I was just two points over the limit and my brief tore the coppers apart in court, silly bastards.'

Chapter twenty-one

Out

The prison officer opened the large gates at the entrance to the prison and he almost pushed Mark through it like a boy on his first day at school.

'OK, Lavender, off you go and we don't want to see you back here again, do you understand that, son?'

'Yes, no way will you see me again. I've scores to settle and I've every intention of doing them without any violence.'

'Be careful, son, keep your head down for a time. Make sure you visit your parole officer firstly on the days listed on this release form, and don't leave the country for a few months at least, unless you agree it with him first. The Old Bill will be watching you so don't attract attention, that's my advice for what it's worth, just keep a low profile.'

'Thanks, you're a good guy, George, and I'll follow most of your advice. My priority is to sort out a job and catch up with some old friends.'

'Sign this form on the dotted line and you're out of here, there's someone picking you up at the gatehouse car park so go straight out and I'll lock up behind you.'

Mark did not linger. He grabbed his polythene bag of bits and pieces and ran to the car park. Dick Cohen waved to him; he jumped into the car without a word being spoken.

Mark had called Dick as he had a feeling that he was a man he could trust, as his father's accountant and friend he would help him get his life sorted.

After the car had cleared the prison grounds and Mark in his paranoia was convinced they were not being followed, he turned to look at Dick.

'Thanks, Dick, I appreciate this.'

'Don't mention it, Mark. You look in good condition.'

'Yes, I'd a few weeks of feeling sorry for myself then I got in the gym and worked out every day on a training routine. I finished with a class of four blokes, no pay but I got a few treats like phone cards and magazines. It got boring but actually the 18 months went really quickly.'

'How do you feel now?'

'Fucking angry, Dick. Not that I was caught but how it was done. Why me? The others are still free and I can't understand why someone grassed me up. I've no real enemies, have I?'

'You must have at least one, Mark.'

Dick parked the car in the drive to the Lavender house and turned the engine off.

'Wait a minute, Mark, your mum can just hold off seeing you for a bit longer. I want to talk to you. Why didn't you let her come and see you in prison?'

'I was ashamed, Dick, and I did write to her, you know that.'

'She loves you very much, Mark, and I suggest you spend a little more time with her in the next few days. With Gerry still absent she spends her time with little Shane and in some ways the boy arrived just at the right time, otherwise she would have been a very lonely lady. Now, it's not that I want to talk to you about, I've a proposal for you. When the lawyer from Spain showed up I was suspicious of him at first but then I got him checked out and I decided to complete the investment your father was considering. It's a big deal and after improving the specifications of the apartments, I'll not get much change out of £2million. I want to rent the properties and keep one for our use. One day they'll all be finished and I've some people interested in working with me on buying the golf and leisure part of it.'

'What's all that got to do with me, Dick, I'm a personal trainer?'

'I know that, son, as I've bought into the leisure complex as well. The bottom line is that I want people I can trust to look after the sports and fitness activities hands on. I'm offering you a job joining what will be a new team, you'll get involved selling membership, setting up the gym and doing a bit of everything. No favours with this offer, you'll need to work hard but I'm sure you have the ability and I know you learn quickly.'

'Dick, I don't know what to say, the answer of course is yes, but I've the small problem that I'm on parole and if I mess this parole bloke about I'll be back inside.'

'Look, Mark, it's November and I'm talking about starting in April. Most of the complex should be finished next month but more work needs to be done on the roads and apartments before we can operate. I would suggest you give it a couple of months of showing the parole officer you aren't going to mess him about, then tell him your plans with a letter from me and if you're straight with him we'll hope he plays ball. They complete the golf course first and we'll need some professional help, I'm working on that one, we need to be ready by the time the apartments and houses are occupied. Now go and see your mum, she's looking out for you at the window.'

'Thanks, Dick, let's meet up tomorrow. Have you heard anything from Dad?'

'No, nothing at all, it's a big mystery. Some days I think he's dead and then others I expect him to suddenly turn up. I'm off now, see you tomorrow morning at my office.'

Mark jumped out of the car. He thought that Dick Cohen would say more about his dad but he cut him short, he would save his questions for later.

As the car left the drive, Barbara Lavender appeared at the door with her arms wide open for her baby son, but Mark was now no baby, he was a well-toned athlete and from some of the things he had learnt in prison, nobody would mess with him now.

Chapter twenty-two

Death on the Estate

The trip from Sutton to St George's Hill, Weybridge, had become routine over the past year for Vince Lavender. Some days he wondered why Ronnie Smith offered him the job and not one of his South London mates, maybe he wanted to give him a chance, it was just like a fairytale and an opportunity made for him to take.

The decision had been an easy one; he was made redundant from his engineering job; the number of new orders for specialist pumps had reduced dramatically due to the recession and the competitive prices from China. Vince's company had made skilled staff redundant but at first not all of them, he was just one of the unlucky ones.

The quick closure of the business followed and he realised that the offer from Ronnie Smith was a lifesaver and he was determined to pay him back by turning around the profits in his 'recycling' plants.

Ronnie was pissed off with the UK and his frequent brushes with the police. He had money in Spain and he convinced Vince that a foreign business was the thing to have. One day he would sell up in Surrey and maybe leave a few debts behind him.

Vince was sharp and clever; his knowledge of engineering and plant construction was just what Ronnie wanted. The distant memory of the robbery lingered in Vince's mind but as he had lost contact with his so-called mate, Luke Devine, and his brother was now out of jail, he tried to forget it all. Ronnie never mentioned it, he had much bigger things on his mind and he planned to sell or walk away from the betting shops as the leases were running out.

The Monday evening was no different than any other as Vince approached his house in the posh part of Weybridge. The meetings between Ronnie and him were frequently over the snooker table in the basement of his house or sat at the bar next to it.

As he pulled into Ronnie Smith's 200-yard drive, Vince gasped as he saw an ambulance with its doors open and the house surrounded by police. He thought twice about getting the hell out of it but then realised he had been seen. He had to find out what was going on.

'Hello, Vince, that was good timing, I heard you were working for Ronnie.'

Detective Inspector Hampton stood over a stretcher illuminated by the security lights as he spoke to the eldest Lavender boy.

'What's happened here?'

'No idea yet, Vince, but I want to question you so hang around.'

As the two men faced each other, the gates opened on the drive and Ronnie Smith accelerated towards them, braking only feet from his front door.

'What's happened? I got a panic call from my alarm system.'

'Ronnie, come with me, please. Vince, you stay here and don't touch anything.'

The policeman took Ronnie behind the ambulance.

'We were too late, she's dead.'

The girl's body had been badly beaten before she was stabbed to death, the killer had showed no mercy. If he or she had been looking for Ronnie, killing his daughter, Liz, was a brutal second choice.

Ronnie collapsed; Vince picked him up from the bloodstained gravel and helped him into the house. The scene was horrible with blood splattered everywhere; the girl had been on her own in the house and had no chance in the vicious attack.

'Where is your ladyfriend, Ronnie?'

Ronnie ignored the policeman until he composed himself and lifted his head; the shock of the gruesome sight almost made him speechless, the combination of anger and sadness brought him to his feet, leaning on Vince for support.

'She's at her parents' house. Vince, call her and get her back now. Is she a suspect, then?'

'We need to talk to her so we can try to put the picture together and you need someone with you here. Don't touch anything. I suggest you go to your cottage over there and stay put until I join you, the pathologist will be here shortly and then the house will be sealed off until I say it's OK to enter. Can you stay with him, Vince?'

'Sure, I'll ring my wife and stay the night with him here.'

'We received a 999 call from your daughter an hour ago and all she said was, come quick please, and gave the address. The phone call was recorded so we can listen to it again later. The patrol car arrived just five minutes after the call but Liz was already dead when they arrived.'

The pathologist, Oliver Hill, was not a happy man; he was halfway through his evening meal when he got the call to attend the murder scene. It was outside his area but he was covering for a colleague in the Weybridge mortuary.

His junior staff had made it before him. One of his sharp trainees had asked to be on-site to see the girl at the scene. She knew he would be interested.

When Oliver saw the girl it was obvious why.

Murders were infrequent in Surrey so the detectives and pathologists usually remembered most of them over the past two or three years, especially the brutal, sickening ones.

Premeditated death was never a pretty sight but the mutilation of Liz Smith had a pattern.

'Do you remember the other case, Inspector?'

'Yes, as if it was yesterday. It's a similar mess to that you told me about at the scene of the death of that Alan Goody, who turned out to be Ronnie's brother.'

'It looks very much like it, Inspector. Of course, I can't be certain, however, that's your job not mine. I'll just tell you how she was killed and with what. I suppose the knife hasn't been found?'

'No weapon has been found but we'll keep looking.'

The body and the area were marked and photographed after a thorough search for evidence and a weapon. After five hours' intense searching, the body was released and sent to the mortuary, the area where the death took place was roped off and the house sealed overnight. The police searched the grounds of the house, which covered almost an acre, and then repeated it in daylight with dogs, but they found nothing.

Ronnie Smith was a broken man. His daughter Liz was just 24 years old and she had just decided to move back into her father's house. Sharon Lavender had rented a room to her but that week she had moved an old boyfriend into the house, which made Liz feel unwelcome. Sharon had tried to persuade her to stay as there were three double bedrooms in her house, but she didn't like the idea of a strange man in the house and she had gone back to her home only two days before her murder.

The incident room was set up in the police station within hours of the death. Superintendent Ellen Brewster, fresh from the murder squad, addressed the small team who were studying the gruesome set of pictures.

'Sergeant Dredge, you know the Lavender family. What is the connection here? Is Vince working for Ronnie?'

'Yes, ma'am, he is working for Ronnie. He lost his job and now he's working on some of his obscure business interests. We're watching him, as we're certain he must have been involved in robbing Ronnie Smith's betting shop a few years ago.

'Obviously Ronnie doesn't think so, or maybe he does and is going to deal with it one day. Vince did date Liz before he was married, but from what we hear that's all finished.'

'So what else do we know other than the girl had just moved back home to her father's house?'

'She didn't like Ronnie's new ladyfriend, that's well known. Also, one of our admin staff knew her, she worked at one of the high street banks. We can talk to her boss later and see how she was in the last few days.'

'Did you know her, Sergeant?'

'Yes, I pulled her in last month on suspicion of using. We let her go due to lack of evidence. Frankly, I don't think she was involved with drugs but we're still keeping an eye on her mates.'

'Anyone we know?'

'No, she kept to a small group, mostly bank people. I'll talk to them as well.'

'Inspector Hampton, can you tell us more about the pathologist's comments?'

'About two years ago we had a murder of a middle-aged male called Goody in Sutton. The attack had several similarities to this death, the beating and then the stab wounds. The difference, of course, is this time it's a young girl.'

'Did we have any suspects?'

'I haven't finished, ma'am. The dead man turned out to be Ronnie Smith's older brother, so we pulled Ronnie in but we got nothing from him other than abuse. Alan Goody was a fictitious name, a joke name really, he was almost a tramp and lived in a mobile home near the rubbish tip. He spent most of his time in Ronnie's Cheam betting shop, the one that was robbed, and yes, he was in it at the time of the robbery. It was just hours later that he was killed.'

'No motives came to mind then, Inspector? Is it still unsolved?'

'Yes, ma'am. It's unsolved but thinking about it now, I wonder if Goody saw one of the robbers' faces, but the report says that they all had hoods on so it's unlikely that he saw them and then they killed him.'

'Look everyone, you are all guessing. The common denominator here is Ronnie Smith. It's most unlikely he killed his own daughter so my view is that someone could have been sending him a warning or a message, and a pretty dramatic and horrible one at that. I doubt it's a burglary gone wrong. We need to look more into his foreign connections. Pull Vince in and quiz him about Ronnie and Spain, also, Sergeant, check with the Marbella police, they may have something on him. Plenty to do, but maybe we'll solve two crimes. Oh yes, before I forget, get hold of DI Derek Lawson. He was on the original robbery and murder team, probably one of the few major crimes that he didn't solve. Where is he now, Sergeant?'

'He's on drugs, ma'am. I'll call him and tell him about the case, he may have something to help us.'

The superintendent was new to the area and she didn't like mysteries. Double murders had a pattern and she was certain that with some legwork from this team they could get a result. What had the local lads missed before?

Detective Inspector Hampton was physically sick at the murder scene. Normally it didn't bother him but the state of the girl made him even more determined to find the killer. He thought he had been close when Alan Goody died but he never got a conclusion.

Hampton had to be more hopeful on a solution this time, he didn't rule out the robbery motive but he thought it was unlikely. Liz Smith was the only person in Ronnie Smith's house that night so if it was a robbery, she became the unfortunate victim, but the place was very securely guarded, it was more likely she knew the killer and let him or her into the house.

Chapter twenty-three

Mark Catching Up

Mark Lavender had some catching up to do; he escaped from his mother's clutches as his sister-in-law arrived with her young man, Shane.

Donna was pregnant for the second time and with Vince losing his job and going to work for Ronnie Smith, she was edgy and kept asking Mark awkward questions.

Barbara listened intently to Mark's brief view of prison and she noticed how grown-up he had become. Mark soon got bored with the women's conversation and slipped away almost unnoticed as Shane started to wreck the lounge.

He had arranged to meet his sister, Sharon, and her new live-in boyfriend, Claude, in The Plough for a couple of drinks. Sharon had wanted to visit Mark in prison but he would not allow it, he would only see Dick Cohen, who kept his spirits up with all the local gossip.

'Well, hello stranger, you look slim and fit. Maybe we should all go to that hotel.'

Mark grabbed his sister and kissed her, and then he shook the rather damp hand of Claude.

'I would not recommend it, Sharon, too many arse bandits around. In 18 months I saw most things. The gym was great and it kept me in trim and fit for anything. The bad guys left me alone.'

'So you two are together, then?'

Before Sharon could reply her mobile phone rang, it was Barbara Lavender. She had just heard about Liz being murdered on TV. At the same time the police had phoned for Sharon's number and she should expect a call.

Sharon put her head into her hands. Claude squirmed into a corner and left Mark to console his sister.

'Why, Mark? She was a lovely girl, her only problem was her father.'

'I know, Sharon, it doesn't make sense, but we'll know more once we see the police.'

'They want to speak to you as well, Mark.'

'That's OK, I'll help if I can. I'm sure I don't need an alibi but if I do, I was with Dick until 7.30 pm. When did you last see, Liz?'

Sharon wiped her tears from her cheeks.

'Three days ago and she had left the place in the usual bad shape with her clothes, shoes and make-up everywhere. We had another row about it and she said that she was going back to live with her dad. She also made it clear that she didn't like the idea of Claude moving in. I don't think the argument was important in her decision, as she was OK with me later. She said that she was fed up with the bank, she wanted to work with her dad, he had offered her a permanent job and she was upbeat about going home. It seems that Ronnie was pissed off with the current tart he was living with and was going to throw her out, that pleased Liz as she hated the woman.'

'Is her mother still alive?'

'Yes, Doris is very much alive. She has remarried to a social worker, which is ironic as Liz always said her mother needed help. She suffers from depression and paranoia, which disappeared for a few years when Ronnie divorced her and gave her a lump of money. Liz only saw her mother a couple of times a year and the meetings usually ended in arguments. I don't think she would have hurt Liz, she was her first child and from what I saw Liz loved her very much. The problem was that she was like her dad and didn't stand for any of her mother's moans. Mark, I can't understand anyone killing her, it must have been an accident or a robbery gone wrong.'

'We'll find out soon, look behind you.'

Detective Inspector Derek Hampton and his sergeant, Linda Dredge, stood side by side like a married couple. They came up behind Sharon and Hampton touched her on the shoulder.

'Sharon Lavender?'

'Yes, that's me. I just heard about Liz from my mum, I can't believe it.'

'Can we sit down and have a chat? It'll only take a few minutes but tomorrow we'll need to see you at the police station.'

'Yes, OK. Claude, go back home and make some supper and I'll be back soon.'

'Mark, you stay, please.'

He scowled at the detective. He was responsible for putting him in prison and he didn't see why he should help him, but then he remembered his parole officer and as much as he hated the situation, he would have to toe the line.

With just the four of them left around the table, Hampton gave brief details on what had happened to Liz Smith.

'Mark, I hear you only got out yesterday. Where did you go to last night?'

'Just to my mum's house. My dad's accountant picked me up and we just talked.'

'And you, Sharon?'

'I was working from home but I had gone to the post office. I bumped into Liz this afternoon, she said that she was going to her dad's house and would be back tomorrow to pick up more of her things.'

'Did she say if she was meeting anyone?'

'No, but I think she had a boyfriend. I don't know who he is, she was always very secretive about him and she always said it wasn't serious. He's probably married. I was going to suggest to her that Mark took her out before I heard the news.'

'What happened to that pretty young lady Kate Robins, didn't she wait for you, Mark?'

'She's history, mate, let's have another subject.'

Mark regretted his outburst; but he hated people taking about Kate and would tell them nothing.

'I see, nothing to say, then. Funny how she left and has not been seen for over two years.'

'Look listen, she told me via a friend that she didn't want to see me any more and that was just after you nicked me; she's gone.'

'Hopefully not dead history. Stay around, Mark, I still want names from you, your case is not totally closed. I want your associates in crime and I bet you have something to say to them as well.'

The policeman was certain Mark was not directly involved with Liz Smith's death and also the possible disappearance of Kate, his old girlfriend, but he liked winding him up. Mark fell for it; he dug his nails into the palm of his hand and tried to keep calm.

The meeting ended as the inspector's phone rang; they left the pub without saying goodbye.

'What do you make of that, Sharon, why is he putting pressure on us?'

'Come on, Mark, there's a killer out there somewhere and they've got to find him.'

'Do you know, when he was talking I suddenly remembered something. The day we did the robbery a bloke, who I think was in the betting shop, was killed in just the same way as Liz, beaten up then stabbed. They didn't say it, but that's too much of a coincidence for me. There has to be a connection and I reckon it's someone Ronnie has upset who went to see him. Liz was just in the wrong place at the wrong time.'

'Mark, please, you've got to tell me something. Do I know the other people you were with at the robbery? Tell me now.'

'Never, Sharon, and that probably answers your question. I'm cool about it. It's OK now, the others just have to live with it that I got sent down and they are on the streets. The only thing I want to know is who grassed me up. I am 100% sure it wasn't any of my friends, and also in all this, where the hell is our dad? By the way, Dick Cohen offered me a job and I may take it.'

'Yes, he asked me about it and I told him to grab you quick before you started looking around.'

'Thanks, Sharon, at least that's two people on my side that I can trust, plus Mum. By the way, she looked really good earlier today. Is she really missing Dad?'

'You're becoming a little detective, Mark. I know what you mean, she has sort of put Dad into a box on a shelf and got on with her life. I think he's alive but not coming back, she told me that she noticed recently that some personal papers were missing and she has assumed he must have them. None of the papers are joint documents, just share certificates and bonds in his name, anything else they have Mum has got safely stored with Dick Cohen, or was left in the house safe.'

'Sharon, is that Angela Tate at the bar?'

'Yes, but I don't know the girl with her.'

'I do, that's Kate's young sister, Jenny; she's a stunner. I'm going to talk to them, see you later.'

'OK, but behave, we want you back at our house tonight. Remember you are on parole and we don't want your dick getting you into trouble, do we?'

Mark just smiled. They had grown up together and his sister knew better than anyone else that when he wanted a woman he got one and she was powerless to interfere.

Chapter twenty-four

Spain and Problems

'Juan, I have told you many times, don't compete with me. You're the lawyer and I'm the entrepreneur. Get Cohen to pay the rest of the money for the golf and leisure place now and then you can take a few million euros to pay the builders for me.'

'I need everything I can get from you, Lopez, to keep the investors quiet. They are after me big time to get a completion date and you really do have to pay the builders now. The trouble is, Fernando, you don't listen to me, I'm the legal frontman for the other investors as well and a lot of them are losing patience with you. You nearly messed up when you got involved directly with them, it was a silly move offering the properties too soon and then making things worse by propositioning that Englishman, Ronnie Smith. He does not understand how we do things here and more importantly, we have to make sure he has the money to buy. Also, my friend, you went too far with that speculator who was selling his land. Did you kill him? You never admitted it but I know he was a problem and I think you dealt with him.'

Fernando Lopez did not reply he just smiled and touched his nose indicating Villa should keep put of his business.

Juan Villa and Fernando Lopez had known each other for many years and every week they met and argued. This week the main topic was the property, next week it would be energy prices, but they couldn't keep the Marbella property off the agenda; they needed a solution. The two men had mutual respect but it was currently very strained, big money was involved and Juan Villa knew how dangerous his friend could be.

Speculators close to Lopez had invested in the project off-plan from drawings he had shown them. They would never own the properties outright, just for a few weeks, then they would cash out.

As soon as possible, Lopez planned to sell the complex as a package, he had not wanted to sell the golf and leisure facilities early but he was desperate for the cash and he had to pay a lot of interest. The drawback was that the price depended on the completion of the houses and apartments; cash retentions would be made until the finish dates were clear.

What he was planning was perfectly legal, even signing contracts to sell on before they had been built. Ultimately, this irritated Lopez but provided he had some return on the investment he would live with it and when the place started to fall down he would be on the other side of the world.

'My memory is not what it was, Juan, can you please give me a summary of our current position on development as it is today?'

'I have all the details here. Just one thing, did you read the newspapers today, the ones with English news?'

'No, I didn't. Why, should I read them, what's in them?'

'Ronnie Smith's young daughter has been brutally murdered, she was a nice kid I met her once on a plane. Did you do it, Fernando?'

'No, much as I don't like the man I need to do business with him, killing his daughter is definitely not on my agenda. I'm a family man remember, more to the point who did it, Juan? Do you know anything?'

'I doubt if the murder was in any way linked to our dealings with Mr Smith. I spoke with our contact in London and he told me that a similar murder happened the same day as Ronnie Smith's betting shop was robbed. The newspapers said the man killed that day was his brother; but he had changed his name and turned into some type of tramp.'

'It's not our business, Juan, and we have enough issues here to worry about, but call him up later and give him our condolences, show him concern, we need to keep on his right side. That is unless you have any other theories that it could affect us.'

'No, I don't have any, you would be the first to know. So come on, Lopez, it's back to our business. This is the position today, as shown on this financial summary. Our income does not even cover the finance costs, we haven't sold enough of the timeshares and the rental business is really slow, new interest in the properties is virtually zero, the hotel group has gone cold. The conference centre clients you lined up will not commit to any bookings for this year or next, until we give them definite completion dates with penalty clauses, we are not getting in to that one. We need to complete a large part of the development before we can close the deal to sell it as a package to Ronnie, or someone else if he doesn't come up with the money. I estimate about 65% of the timeshares need to be a sold and 25% available for off-plan complete sales. What is your latest timetable? Look at these current figures and cost estimates.'

'Shit, I see what you mean, Juan, we have to get some cash in. It is only slow on timeshares and then rentals because the whole place looks unfinished. I estimate that with the cash we have we can only complete 60% of the timeshare units by March, then that means we still have to sell the rest off-plan at any price we can get.'

'To refresh my memory, don't we still own the freeholds on everything giving us the ongoing income from the ground leases?'

'Of course, actually your company does, but the income isn't massive and we still have to get a valuation on what we can charge.'

'How certain are you that Ronnie Smith will go through with the purchase? We will need those ground rent figures first, but assuming we can complete a large percentage of the buildings and you show him the income projection figures that could be achieved, will he complete?'

'That, of course, is the big question, Lopez, but I hear he's still moving large amounts of cash to Spain and if he's going to continue to do that he certainly must have a plan for the future. Frankly, I think some of it comes from the fact that Mr Smith has a very big ego and wants to be seen as one of the big men in Marbella. The site valuation will be done by his people but I'll speak to the local contacts here to make sure he's told the right things. We have to think now about cashing out, Lopez, and moving to Panama for a year or maybe permanently. We won't be technically doing anything wrong, except if we're honest to ourselves we are selling a complex built by a load of cowboys. We know it won't last ten years, the maintenance men are already patching up the first big cracks in the creek units.'

'I made a big mistake building next to the creek. As the land was almost free, I thought we could build a marina then put the apartments next to it later. I didn't realise that the marina lease will now take longer to sell, it's a bog area and with Puerto Banus a few kilometres away we have big competition. I thought to build the houses first was the right thing to do as the foundations would not need to be as deep, but even with small houses they have turned out to be not deep enough and they are moving all over the place. When do we meet Ronnie Smith again, Juan?'

'We don't have any plans to meet Ronnie at the moment, especially now as he's got the new problem in England. We'll meet with his accountant from London and we can then go through all the details with him and see if Ronnie really has the 20 million euros. I know he has a lot but I'm not certain he can come up with the total amount and we need to know how much he's borrowing. It's the first meeting for me with this accountant man and we need to know more about him, if he's too sharp we may have to pay him off.'

'Yes, OK, whatever it takes. I'm sure you can deal with him, Juan. As soon as the buildings start to crack in a big way the complex will be worth nothing and Ronnie Smith will have a pile of shit, maybe you'll be well away in Panama by then, but is that far enough, do they have cable TV?'

'Yes, but to move I've to make sure I've enough money. Remember, Lopez, I am diabetic so I'll need money for medical bills. I wouldn't be welcome back here for treatment if I've been a part of one of the biggest Marbella stings ever.'

'Juan, I honestly didn't know those builders would make such a mess of the development.'

'It's actually quite obvious Lopez, you paid peanuts and you got monkeys and lazy ones at that; you're the businessman and you need to work your charm on getting those awkward bastards to work harder and finish the place.'

'Fortunately Juan, most of the disappointed occupiers will only blame the owner and that'll be Ronnie Smith. I know it's me they'll remember as I persuaded them to invest but what the hell I won't be here. For certain when they see their properties falling down they aren't going to be very happy, I will be many kilometres away. By the way do you know the Arabs are interested in the whole of Block C around the site for the Marina?'

'Yes I know that Lopez, but we don't own that as the landowner wanted over five million euros for it, remember? When Dick Cohen is here again maybe we can persuade him to pay cash for some of the houses then we could have a look at Block C?'

'I think he will be here soon as he hasn't been in Spain for some time, he'll hopefully come with just Mrs Lavender and not a surveyor as well this time. I expect to hear from him today or tomorrow. Mr Cohen is a careful man you know, and he'll want full details on what's happening on the leisure and golf complex before he pays the first lease rentals.'

'Yes Juan, you will have to have to stall him on questions about the houses, they will see the site when they drive into town past the golf course. I can see him getting nasty, but he's in deep already with the money he's paid so I suggest we just play it cool when we tell him about the further delays.'

'Lopez, just think what happened, Dick Cohen must have been told in the first place by Gerry Lavender that an investment here was a good deal, otherwise he wouldn't have got involved.'

'You did a good selling job on him in London my friend; he said not very much at first if you remember, then he changed his mind within minutes after your meeting. Was it Gerry Lavender suddenly getting involved or someone else, we'll probably never know and I don't care provided I get the money?'

'Yes, Lopez, but I hope he doesn't know Ronnie Smith, we mustn't jeopardise that outright sale. I know we need cash to finish but that's pushing our luck. I think Gerry Lavender must still be alive and keeping his head down for some reason. I'm convinced Dick Cohen is now working on his own and from what I hear, Mrs Barbara Lavender could be his new partner, she's always with him. My past dealings with Gerry were OK. We both made a lot of money but where's he now, Lopez? Nobody knows.'

'No idea either, Juan, why should I, you're the one who knows about everyone. I think if you ask the question "who is he with?" you may find the answer. From the people I met with him I could make a good guess.'

'Keep it to yourself, we have enough issues here, don't get Gerry involved. He vanished when I needed him so he's history, but then maybe by now Mrs Lavender has a clue on his whereabouts so it would be nice to know, wouldn't it?'

Juan Villa smiled at Lopez as the big man brushed his thick greying hair and groomed himself in the mirror; the thought of meeting the middle-aged

English lady again excited the Mediterranean juices of the Spaniard without a woman.

His wife had left him but she still lived in Marbella. Although they hadn't divorced she was very much on her own, like Lopez. The lack of normal female company was now beginning to sadden the tough guy, he could hardly wait for his daughter to finish her exams and come back to Marbella.

Miss Anna Fernandez was heir to his fortunes and his business; in his deranged mind he had to try quickly teaching her the subtle art of shafting more or less everyone she dealt with and getting away with it. His daughter was unlikely to follow the route her father had planned but since she was now the only child she was desperate not to disappoint him.

The death of his son, Fernando Junior, had on occasion made Lopez a very bitter man, he took the blame as the incident occurred when he was waiting in Madrid to meet his son; it was he who should have died. He would never recover from the pain of that day in August 2008.

Chapter twenty-five

Contracts

The two-day trip to Spain was a surprise to Barbara, but once Dick explained that is was to check his investment she was pleased, and looked forward to meeting the Spaniards again.

She had met Lopez once before and the lawyer, Juan Villa, her mystery visitor, several times with Dick Cohen.

The taxi pulled up outside the smart Marbella downtown office and Juan Villa greeted them at the front door.

'Hello again, Mrs Lavender, welcome to Spain. I think you know Fernando Lopez. Welcome back, Mr Cohen.'

'I'm pleased to meet you again, Juan, and please call me Barbara.'

The Spaniard showed the couple into his office, ordered coffee and sandwiches, then wasted no time explaining the current position, which was the reason the pair had made the trip.

'Everything is going to plan we have sold some more developments and the marina build plans are being finalised. We had some wet weather problems which caused cracking in a few buildings but it's all being fixed as we speak.'

Dick looked concerned and focused on Juan Villa.

'We'll have a survey done, Juan. You told me the building would last at least 50 years and now you're telling me that some units are falling down and we are only in the first year.'

Lopez pushed his chest out and stopped Juan from replying, the buildings were his problem.

'No, they aren't falling down. As far as we are concerned the builders have repaired the cracks and replastered the walls, all have been repainted and we've got a survey report to say that it is all OK now.'

'Yes, but if I was to sell my houses and maybe apartments later, a buyer would want to do their own survey. Most of my clients do not have the money to buy outright and would want a mortgage or a local loan, using the buildings as security. The survey must be done properly otherwise I will not be able to sell.'

'On the first point, Mr Cohen, as I told you when you first invested we can influence matters like surveys, this is Spain take my word on it. Also some buildings are OK, it's just the west and south blocks that have been cracking at this time, they have been sorted out.'

'That's right isn't it, Juan?'

'Yes, that's correct. If you have problems with the banks let me know personally, I will talk to them for you. We are quite good at local arm twisting. Please don't worry, Mrs Lavender, it sometimes has to be done this way here.'

Barbara Lavender had not invested personally in the problem-stricken development and at the meeting she remained diplomatically silent. She did, however, think Dick had bitten off more than he could chew with Señor Fernando Lopez and Señor Juan Villa. She very much hoped her friend knew what he was doing.

Juan Villa stood up and produced some papers from a file.

'The outcome, though, will be as we first discussed two months ago. You'll see a good return on your original money eventually, but we have to keep calm and quiet, we must not discuss anything with other people. The word gets around quickly here. These are drafts of the final lease agreements in Spanish with an English translation attached to them, please take them away and call me tomorrow with any questions. We need to get your agreement tomorrow before you leave so we can finalise payments to builders and suppliers, we are ready now to complete your sale.'

Juan saw the worried look on the Englishman's face and tried to divert the conversation.

'When we first met, Dick, you didn't like the investment idea, but then you suddenly changed your mind. Why did you do that? Did you know something we didn't?'

'As they say, Juan, the word was from a friend of a friend but I'm confident that the information on the investment was right. I now insist we make agreements that work, especially when the banks are involved. Completion must be back to back with the sales I've set up. I'm not taking any unnecessary risks with this project. Fortunately my major investment is the golf and leisure complex and that is looking good. Why didn't you use the same contractors for the remainder of the project, Fernando?'

'Simple, those guys were specialists and they did a good job. The ones tidying up now and doing simple jobs are the normal workers but the original ones have moved to La Manga for big money, they're building a new golf course.'

The tone of the meeting changed quickly. Juan Villa agreed to alter the paperwork, the deal had to have bank approval in both directions and he knew Lopez could sort it.

Juan Villa was becoming frightened and he would tell Lopez as soon as he had the opportunity that they might have to accelerate their exit plans. He would talk to his partners the next day regarding selling his interest in the law practice.

Dick Cohen opened the envelope containing the contracts on the office table, pushing the Spanish copy to one side.

'I suggest we go through this document together and then you can alter the Spanish copy tomorrow, and I'll then arrange for it to be checked out before I sign it. The surveys need to be done this week and the reports sent by email to me by Monday. I'll then fly back immediately if everything is satisfactory and arrange for the money to be transferred when we're totally ready. My fellow investors trust me and I have Power of Attorney to complete the deal.'

Lopez nodded at every point as the three men went through the contracts. As the last page was read and the documents put away, he stood up and shook everyone's hand.

The big man knew he had work to do and it would start that evening in his local bar, he would make the phone calls from his car.

As Lopez left the room he smiled and waved at Barbara.

'He fancies you,' whispered Dick Cohen.

He turned to Barbara taking her hand into his palm and gripping it tightly. She could feel the drips of sweat on his hands. The Spaniards had heard his message loud and clear but they tried not to show how desperate they were to complete.

The clients Cohen referred to were all friends at his club with lots of money. The investment was small on an individual basis but for Dick it was his retirement fund completed, he would make a million euros that would never leave Spain and he would still have his beloved golf course.

The couple followed Lopez out of the building and called a taxi to their hotel, the driver would not take any payment mumbling 'Lopez' as Dick and Barbara left the car and checked in to the hotel.

'One night only, Mr Cohen?'

'Yes please, a table for two at 8.00 pm in the restaurant, plus a car to Malaga Airport at 9.00 am tomorrow morning.'

'Certainly, I'll arrange all that. Señor Lopez is paying your account, sir.'

'No, he isn't. I'll pay my own account. Mr Lopez will understand.'

'I doubt it, sir, he owns the hotel and I'll be in serious trouble if I take money from you. I have the same problem with Mr Smith.'

'Interesting. Is he called Ronnie Smith, by any chance?'

'Yes, sir.'

'Look, I know you have to be careful when talking about clients but he's a friend, is he here today?'

'No, sir, he comes only when there is a football match. He's a big friend of Señor Lopez, that is no secret, sir.'

The porter took the couple to their room, a suite large enough for a family of six. The view was over the sea and Dick closed all the shutters and curtains for total privacy.

He failed to notice the car parked in the avenue in front of the beach, the driver was talking to the porter who pointed to the room, they had a brief conversation and the car pulled away.

'Thank goodness that's over, Barbara.'

'Yes. Please tell me what'll happen to us next, Dick?'

'I'll take your clothes off and slowly make love to you.'

'No, no, Dick, I know that and yes of course, but in a minute. First, can you fill me in on the blanks in today's meeting as I'm very confused about who will own what in the future.'

'Yes, sorry, but it's actually now really easy to understand, Barbara. I'm afraid I have to tell you something that perhaps I should've done before. It's Gerry.'

Barbara Lavender went white. 'He's not dead is he?'

'No, well at least he wasn't when I spoke to him on the phone. He called me briefly then hung up. It was just after he disappeared. I could add nothing to what you knew other than this. Gerry was in the process of buying some apartments and houses on the new development here in Spain. Strangely, after my meeting in London with Juan Villa he phoned me and told me to buy on his behalf and told me how to get the deposit funds. He seemed very keen for me to make some money but to be fair I thought if it's such a golden opportunity I'd do it all myself with my money.

'When I came here for the first time and met Juan Villa and Fernando Lopez it was obvious that they were looking for a quick turnaround of their money and I must admit I was suspicious about the site. So after viewing it and considering my options, I was convinced that the best part of it would be the leisure complex and the golf course. It's perfectly situated as it's next to the link to the motorway and also the beach. There are only two similar places on this side of the town but they're too exclusive and their facilities are small. We have a design that will give us a world-class course and room for a golf academy, and believe me, we'll be working with professionals. The concept is to make the course international, not just Spanish, in style, it just happens to be here. I've discussed it with the PGA Tour and European Tour. In principle they have agreed to four completely new competitions annually, as a start. They will be televised and advertised on a worldwide basis, but mainly in Asia and USA.

'I agreed to buy a few apartments and houses on the understanding that I got a very special price as I was buying the leisure complex and the golf course as well. The stumbling block has been making the course and golf centre a freehold concern. This will cost me a lot more money but is essential if we're going to control the running costs. They must be desperate for money as they have agreed today to my offer to buy the lease for a very small sum, provided I pay cash for the leisure complex and golf course.

'The downside is that I've also agreed to buy a total of four apartments and two houses, the idea is to make them for sale like a timeshare, in other words, we'll sell them to several owners for a period of time, usually two months a year each, when they can use the places. We'll keep a house for ourselves and we can talk about other properties for your family.

'Lopez took a large deposit from me over two years ago and we're now ready to complete the deal, if he can finally assure me that he can keep to the new completion date. I've sold two apartments to people at my London club who wanted to move some cash abroad. They aren't really interested in emigrating immediately but will rent them out through me.

'I never heard from Gerry again after that day we spoke on the phone. At first I panicked a bit but then I worked out that it was the push I needed to fully retire and move away from the UK. I'll set up a company here and with your Mark's help, we'll be ready to open a full leisure facility, gym, pool and spa in about nine months' time. I've already discussed the golf course in detail and spent money with two professionals on the course design and layouts. I've both a top resident PGA Tour professional lined up and a first class chef for the restaurant. Already the major golf competitions are looking at it for events in two to three years and that's very quick for a new course.

'A new hotel is being built next door by an international group. They'll sponsor two events and we'll be able to accommodate all the competitors, Marbella will then pick up new hotel business from players, supporters and the media all requiring accommodation near the course.

'Marbella is Benidorm's "classy cousin", it has over 300 days of sunshine a year, some of the world's most chic bars and clubs, golden beaches and it's loved by everyone, including royalty. As you know, it's just under three hours' flying time from the UK and the budget airlines are cashing in on the increasing passenger traffic via Malaga Airport. I'll need to raise extra money to achieve the standard needed for the golf course but once it's fully commissioned and mature enough, it'll be in line to become Spain's number one golf course.'

'Yes, but what about the rest of the complex, Dick?'

'From what I hear, Lopez has possibly a mystery buyer, he's keeping the deal close to his chest. If it's Arabs and building problems occur, which I'm told they will, they have enough money to sort it. Maybe one day they may buy our complex as well but that's a long time in the future. Lopez needs money fast and we have to help him finish the buildings, even though it looks a mess it's no more than a few months' work. Next week when I come back again I'll have lawyers from Madrid with me to make sure Lopez and Villa don't have any new tricks up their sleeves.'

'It sounds great, Dick, but was that the Ronnie Smith mentioned downstairs?'

'Yes, I believe so, the betting shop bloke and the one Vince works for. I can't imagine Ronnie being involved in buying any property unless he's another purpose for it. I'd be surprised if he turned up as a neighbour but then he must be doing something with Lopez. Before I sign on the dotted line I'll have to try and find out what he's up to. From what Gerry told me, usually when his tongue had been loosened after a drink or two, Ronnie and he were acquaintances but not friends. They had a sort of love and hate friendship on deals, always trying to do a good one together then double-crossing each other. It was like some sort of kid's game. It wasn't usually a lot of money but enough for them to frequently fall out with each other. But then once, Ronnie did Gerry for a few hundred thousand quid, at first Gerry went mad, threatening Ronnie that one day he'd pay him back and for more than he'd lost. The funny thing was, it seemed to be only a threat as they went to football matches together after that and it was probably why he first came here to Spain, to watch a La Liga match with him. It was probably then he was introduced to Lopez and Villa.'

'Dick, you should worry about Lopez, he comes over to me as a wise guy and maybe also a crook. You saw the way he looked at me, do you think he's still in touch with Gerry and involved with him somehow?'

'Not sure, Barbara, that's the big question before we sign up and then announce our plans, it'd be nice to know what Gerry's up to and also where the hell he is.'

'You know, Dick, I'd find it difficult to live with you in case he suddenly turned up. We don't need his blessing, just a divorce if he's alive.'

'Barbara, I didn't tell you this before as I wasn't sure how you would react, but when Juan Villa and I met in London after the meeting, as I told you Gerry made that call to me. The number was withheld and he didn't say much about his situation other than he highly recommended the deal as a good investment. He was specific on what to do and when I thought about it later, I thought it was as if he was trying to help me and then indirectly you as well. When I tried to ask him other questions on the phone he would only answer on the business front. I didn't tell you as I thought you may have gone off me.'

'Dick, I guessed you'd had a discussion with him, you were more comfortable with me in bed and I'd a feeling you knew he was a long way away and not coming back to England and me. Before you spoke to him that day, you used to look over your shoulder all the time when we were together expecting him to appear, you don't do that anymore. Later, tell me exactly what he said and if he phones again please let me know.'

'Of course, Barbara, that's the last time I'll keep a secret from you.'

Barbara laughed and pointed her finger at him.

'Good job you said that. Now, what are your plans for Mark? It's been two months since he left prison and you said he's going to do some work for you here. Is that in the leisure place? He mentioned administration, which is definitely not his scene.'

'No, it's not quite administration, Barbara. I've paid for Mark to attend a business course, it lasts for another month and so far he's just learning the modern basics of management.'

'Oh, he didn't tell me that.'

'So far he's doing extremely well and the job I've lined up for him will be perfect for applying his new knowledge. He'll do some debt collecting in the UK for me short-term so he has some spending money'

'It sounds a bit hard for a personal trainer recently out of prison, but I respect your judgement, Dick. Just remember he'll always be my little boy so don't drop him in at the deep end too soon.'

'I have this opportunity for him here in Spain but it's not the full story. I'll tell him at the end of the course. He follows on here straight away with language school in Spanish, which will continue for three months. He'll come here soon to check it all out and then I'll have eyes on what's going on.'

'So the job is in the leisure complex and golf course management?'

'Yes, we'll need a team and Mark will be part of it, we'll hire local people but I need my own man on board to watch over things; it's a great opportunity for him.'

'Wow, yes, that's brilliant. But can he do it, he really is a sportsman?'

'In time I hope the answer will be yes, but we've time. We'll start slowly and choose the employees carefully. Mark will still have to work out how he deals with the parole officer and that could be tricky but we're in no rush, it'll take me some time to wind up in the UK.'

'So what you're saying is that you, Dick Cohen, will move here?'

'Yes, *we* will. But that is, of course, provided you want to, Barbara.'

'I'll come back to you on that, Dick.'

Dick found a nervous smile and changed the subject. Barbara's reaction to his idea was not unexpected but he didn't anticipate it to be as sharp as it came over. It was clear she was still carrying a torch for Gerry Lavender but the flame was getting smaller as the months passed by.

'I'm sure you are aware, Barbara, that Mark is still very bitter. He thinks far too much about his time in prison, he won't rest until he finds and confronts the person or persons who grassed him up. Someone tipped the police off, they knew very quickly it was him in the car, the CCTV evidence was conclusive.'

Barbara had a worried look. Mark was her baby son still and she couldn't go through another prison sentence with him. She wouldn't tell Dick but if Mark was on the warpath for revenge, she needed to talk to him and soon.

'Another subject then, Dick, has this proposed move to Spain been inspired by Juan Villa and or my missing husband?'

'Yes and no. I believe Juan is definitely dodgy but he has a good business. I think from a few things he said that one day he may leave Spain. He's tried to be more than just a lawyer and in doing so he's not selecting business partners, or even his so called friends, wisely. As I already said, my idea is to start a small business here as well, I have few other interests other than working and, of course, you, so I don't intend to retire. I'd hire a lawyer and notary and then I'd have a total legal and accountancy practice here with local, recently qualified staff. I'd need a lot of local help without a doubt, as Spanish law on property and land can be very different to ours. I wouldn't like to get in trouble with the Spanish authorities. With my UK contacts I've quite a few people waiting to buy property and I'll give them advice and if required, arrange the deal for them from here'.

'Are you sure this isn't a front for money laundering, Dick?'

'No, for goodness sake, no. Barbara, please don't say that, I'm a professional man, these are people who just want second homes or investments. I really do want you to come here with me, Barbara. I've a feeling that Vince and Donna may come here as well one day.'

'I thought Vince was happy with Ronnie Smith and what about the kids?'

'I think with the right offer he'd come with us, but we have matters to straighten out first. I'm told by Juan that there is a good English school and they can go back to the UK for university.'

Barbara laughed.

'You have it all worked out Dick but slow down, you're miles ahead of me. Mark is just out of prison and Vince has a well-paid job. Surely you aren't suggesting the whole of my family just up and move here?'

'No, not all the family, but my feeling is that Vince and Donna would welcome coming here to a detached, four-bedroom house with a pool in two acres of land with perfect weather. If needed, we've an airport locally with planes to take us all back to the UK for visits in under three hours. If Mark has problems with management, the experience will still be useful even if he runs his own business one day. Maybe it'll be in personal training or owning a gym.'

'OK you've got me interested, Dick. So what happens next?'

'You say, yes, to my proposal, that's next.'

Barbara turned away; she had no intention of agreeing to his plans at this stage. If he'd asked her to marry him that might have been different, then again that would present its own difficulties. She needed concrete proof that Gerry was either dead or not coming back and in the case of the second scenario, she would file for divorce. Dick would have to wait but then she knew that time was not on their side, both were in their 60s and she wanted to be settled at least for her retirement.

'When we get back to the UK I don't want to keep sneaking around to your house a couple of nights a week, popping in for quickies then leaving in case the kids turn up as we do now.'

'No, it's time I went to your house, Dick, and stayed a night or maybe two or three. As soon as we're back in the UK tomorrow we'll go straight to my house, I'll get my clothes and come back with you, if that's OK.'

'Yes, great, Barbara, I was going to ask you but I was afraid you'd turn me down.'

'Don't be silly we're grown-ups you know. Look, Dick, I'm going to spend some more money on that private detective guy to have another attempt at finding Gerry.'

'I know another company, Barbara, the other one you used will just do the same again and ask the police. They are all ex-policemen and they use just their own network. We need to be more inventive. I've a couple of ideas from papers Gerry left with me, I'm certain he's abroad. The lawyer from Madrid has an investigation service which I suggest you use.'

'Can you arrange it please, Dick?'

She kissed Dick on the cheek as she undressed. The events of the day had made her head spin, and she'd forgotten that 20 minutes before she'd agreed to undress at the suggestion of her lover.

Dick didn't miss his opportunity and within minutes they were entwined in the master bed of the suite. Little was said between them as he caressed her and kissed her body from her lips to her thighs.

Barbara took over and seconds after completion the noise of Barbara's mobile phone terminated any further love making.

'You better answer it, Barbara, it could be important.'

'Sorry, Dick, I'll make it up to you ten times over.'

She grabbed the phone just before it stopped.

'Hi, Mum, can you stay with Donna for a few nights, she isn't well. Ronnie's sending me to Manchester on Friday to help with a deal. I can't leave her on her own with Shaun this time.'

'Yes, of course, but I'm in Spain at the moment with Dick and we'll be back tomorrow afternoon. Is Donna sick then, Vince?'

'Better than that, Mum, she's pregnant again and I think it's morning sickness.'

'Congratulations. I'll be over tomorrow evening about 6.30.'

'Thanks, Mum.'

'Sorry, Dick, I'm needed. It seems Donna is pregnant again and she's suffering. I'll have to help Vince out, he needs to go north and do a job for Ronnie.'

'I'm not sure about Ronnie Smith. Your son needs to be really careful, the police may still have their eye on him.'

'Why? Vince hasn't done anything, has he, Dick?'

'You're answering your own question, Barbara. The police still think he was involved in the betting shop robbery and I've an open mind on it.'

'Don't say that, Dick. I've the same feeling all the time but I try to get it out of my head. It's a long time now and I know that Mark would never grass up his brother if he was involved. Anyway, Vince is now working for Ronnie Smith.'

'Maybe Ronnie suspects him, he's got to as Mark being sentenced makes his brother an obvious suspect, but the police didn't find anything they could use to charge him. In a perverse way, Ronnie probably likes to have him around. I hope Vince watches his back.'

'He needs the job, Dick, even more now Donna is pregnant again. The sooner you can employ him as well the better.'

Barbara grabbed her man and turned him over.

'Dick, I'm in charge. Remove your underpants again and I'll resume where we left off.'

'Yes, very nice, but I'm usually only a once-a-night man, Barbara.'

'Shut up and keep still. We have an hour before dinner.'

'An hour! What's on your mind?

'Just wait and see. We could be late, please do remember Lopez is paying for this room so we need to make good use of it. I hope he's not filming our lovemaking from a hidden camera and will blackmail us later.'

'You've a good imagination, Barbara, now put it to use, we can always have room service if we're late.'

'For breakfast or for dinner, young man, may I ask? Give me your hand and put it just there.'

Barbara Lavender was relaxed. For once in her life she had a plan. After the sudden disappearance of her husband, she was not considering the outcome if he did turn up.

The sex alone with Dick was a revelation; it was like her first few years of marriage when Gerry made love to her every day. He became bored once the kids came along and he started to look around for new partners and used his charm to bed many a willing lady.

Chapter twenty-six

A Big Clue

'Where've you been, Billy? I've been on my own all bloody afternoon.'

'Mind your own fucking business, Angela, and get on with your job.'

'You're a complete clown, Billy. If I could get another job, even for less money, I'd be out of this crap office like a shot.'

'You couldn't even get a job as a hooker, Angela, just get on with it.'

Angela knew there was no point arguing with Billy as he always won the verbal arguments, but she meant what she said and she knew one day something would come along.

As she paid a punter out on the last race at Doncaster she saw a text flash on her phone, she grabbed it before Billy saw it and read the message. Angela smiled, she had a date and it was the one she really wanted.

The betting shop had become run down since the robbery. Ronnie Smith had lost interest in all of his shops and as the premises were all leased, he intended to close them one by one when the terms expired.

Billy had become very awkward. Angela knew that he had his hand in the till but she didn't know how much money he'd taken; as the under-the-counter bets had not gone through her computerised till, it made them almost foolproof. She could only track bets with paperwork and Billy made sure there wasn't a scrap of written evidence for Ronnie to check, it was all in his memory.

In the time since the robbery and the death of Alan Goody, her boss had become very secretive and Angela heard him do betting deals over the phone, but again she never saw the paperwork. Billy was up to his old tricks; he only put his losses through the till, the ones paying out, she complained but he ignored her.

She hated the man with a vengeance; if she could get something on Billy and tell Ronnie maybe he would get rid of him, but she decided the risk was too big and as usual, she kept her head down and ignored him.

Ronnie's visits had become almost non-existent. Since the death of Liz he had done little work. With no help from the police he had gone through in his mind all the possible people who could have carried out the horrific murder.

He kept going back to the way she was brutally mutilated, it made him sick to think about it and the image would not leave his head. The message was loud and clear; it was either someone who copied his brother Alan's death or the same person was sending Ronnie a warning – could he be the next victim?

Ronnie was no fool, he had already guessed that the killer was close to him and he didn't believe it was just a house burglary gone wrong. His ex-wife or him could well be next if the murder was to do with his family.

The police were not interested in the protection of his family and any girlfriends so he moved out of his Weybridge castle to a rented, gated mews house in Chelsea with round-the-clock security.

The police had no real leads on the past murder of Alan Goody or Liz Smith. Detective Inspector Hampton was now depending on the latest forensic evidence to give him direction. He felt sure it was the same killer; the pathologist had said the way the wounds were inflicted were very similar in both deaths, not a fact that would probably stand up in court but one Hampton agreed with.

Superintendent Ellen Brewster was breathing down his neck so he was in turn doing the same to his junior staff through the newly promoted Sergeant Linda Dredge.

'It's well over two years now, John, since Goody was murdered and we haven't a single lead other than confirming he was Ronnie Smith's brother. What do we know? Tell me again, please. Get Sergeant Dredge in here and also ring Ronnie, we'll have another chat with him.'

'Yes, boss, but it's just going over the same ground again. We know Goody was in the shop on the day of the robbery, Angela Tate confirmed that and she also said he was in the shop at least three or four times a week. He didn't get credit, everything was cash and he won occasionally, she confirmed he was no trouble and he told her he was Ronnie's brother. She didn't know if she should believe him or not but if Ronnie turned up he always left the shop as soon as he arrived.'

'Yes, I'm sure, John, that our friend Ronnie didn't socialise with his brother, and in a way he probably wished he didn't exist. Has Ronnie any other family? Check it and call all of the previous women in his life, including his ex-wife. Pay him a visit and get a list. There are probably quite a lot of them. Get Linda Dredge to help you.'

'Boss, I can tell you for certain that he has no other brothers other than Alan Goody. His wives and girlfriends are all the same model, dumb and blonde, we've done them all. They're all most unhelpful apart from Liz's mum. Eventually she gave us an interview and blamed Ronnie for everything, of course, but no new clues.'

'John, still do it again. They can't all be that dumb.'

Sergeant Dredge knocked on the office door.

'Come in, Linda. We're trying to find something that will help us with Liz Smith's murder. I know you've spent a lot of time on this and the Goody murder, you know the characters inside out.'

'I found some new information from the Register of Births, Deaths and Marriages last week when I was looking for someone for another case. As the website was open I also searched for Ronnie Smith's previous and found something that may or may not help us. Liz's mother and Ronnie's ex is Doris Fellows, as she is called now with husband number two, she is also the sister of Billy Bootle, the betting shop manager. I'd a phone call with her two days ago and she didn't stop talking. I'll interview her formally tomorrow. It seems that Ronnie didn't want Bootle in his business but Doris put pressure on to take him into the betting shop. In a bizarre way, a condition in the divorce settlement was that Ronnie had to agree to give him a job for five years, it saved Ronnie paying Doris a chunk more money. The agreement came to an end recently and no doubt if Ronnie remembers the date Bootle will be on his bike leaving the shop.'

'Have you spoken to Billy about this recently, Linda?'

'Yes, I called in the shop yesterday. He was very calm and confirmed that the agreement was true. I felt that he restrained himself when we talked more about Ronnie, he obviously has a big problem with him, but he didn't want to bite the hand that feeds him.'

'Talk English can you please, Linda. Do you mean he didn't want to upset Ronnie?'

'Yes, boss. Sorry I think he has a big chip on his shoulder about his ex-brother-in-law, but he's careful how he deals with him and allows Ronnie to kick him around.'

'Thanks, I understand that one, Linda.'

Superintendent Brewster leaned her large frame back on the desk chair. She was a career policewoman for sure and she was considerably more polite to the women than the men in the police station. In contrast to her predecessor, DI Lawson, she got results and quickly. The two murders were burning a hole in her statistics spreadsheet and she had to have a conclusion so she could tick the box and move on.

'John, you obviously didn't dig deep enough first time around with dear Doris, so get Billy here in the station today. Find out his movements on the day of the robbery after the shop closed and see if we can dig anything out of him.'

John Hampton was pissed off, he knew that he hadn't done the interview with Doris Fellows properly and now he had to backtrack and see what he could extract from her brother.

'Yes, I'm on my way.'

'Sir, before you go, I've some information about a missing person.'

'Who's that, Linda?'

'It's Gerry Lavender. I found him. I even spoke to him on the phone.'

'Good work, you can tell me later how you did it but what did he say?'

'He said he had an email message from an old friend to contact us, he said he wasn't coming back to the UK. Lavender hasn't committed any crime as far as we know so we believe he's clean. He said he would contact his wife soon to discuss personal matters. No more details really and if it's OK with you, I suggest I call her later in the week to make sure he did it. Can we take him off the missing persons' list now?'

'Yes, but not straight away, wait a day or two. I may have a chat with Barbara Lavender first instead. Also ask the Spanish police if they've anything on him, probably it'll be nothing but just explain to them the circumstances.'

'But I don't think he's in Spain, sir.'

'I know but he was, Linda. If he's up to something it'll more than likely have been in Spain not where he is now. Maybe he has a new woman in his life or an old one that he's revived. Yes, that's a more likely scenario, but we need to check in Spain before we close the missing persons' file and, of course, make sure it was him that phoned.'

'Yes, that did occur to me as well, but I did meet Gerry Lavender a few times when he kept having his car vandalised, and I spoke to him later on the phone. He had a very distinctive Liverpool accent and I'm reasonably sure it was him who telephoned, as he knows me and asked for me by name.'

'Not one of your old boyfriends was he, Linda?'

When Hampton made throwaway comments, they were always his way of fishing out information with people off their guard. He knew from the look on the sergeant's face and her discomfort at the question that she knew him well.

'Look, sir, yes I did have a couple of nights out with Gerry, he was a great bloke and really interesting company but old enough to be my dad.'

The colour of her face said it all; she was embarrassed to tell her boss that she'd been taken out by a married man and one that she'd been working with as a crime victim.

'So that's how you knew the call was from him, he told you some intimate details I bet?'

'Yes, OK, I did sleep with him and yes, he has seen the tattoo on my backside, so to check his ID I asked what my tattoo was. He was right first time.'

'Pretty conclusive then, Linda. Is it a butterfly?'

Sergeant Linda Dredge was squirming and her boss was not going to let her off the hook until he'd finished his interrogation.

'No, it's the red rose of Lancashire, sir, and it's a special tattoo I had done at home before I joined the Met.'

'Have you spoken before to Gerry and not told me, Linda?'

'Yes, a few times.'

Hampton was very annoyed; several colleagues had wasted police time on trying to find the missing Gerry Lavender and she was already in contact with him.

'I'm not impressed by any of this, Linda, but my priority at the moment is this murder investigation. We'll have an awayday then go and see Gerry, I assume you know where he is?'

'Not exactly but he's sure to phone again. I'm really sorry, sir, I'd a bit of a thing for him, and if he was still around I would've probably got in more trouble with him.'

'You are in enough trouble already, Linda, but as I said, not for today. I want Billy Bootle here as soon as you can get your pretty backside in a car and find him. Just one last thing before you go, Linda, how do I know you're not telling a story about this red rose?'

Linda Dredge knew what her boss wanted and she was up for it, she put her knee against the door to prevent any visitors and pulled her skirt up to her waist then peeled down her black tights to reveal the briefest pair of pants ever worn by a policewoman.

Detective Inspector Hampton's eager eyes nearly popped out of his head as she pushed her finger inside the elastic and exposed the most perfect red rose tattoo; it was about four inches in diameter and positioned above the neck of her backside.

Before he could comment she made herself respectable, smiling at her boss; then she quickly ran to her car. She had said enough for one day and she thought he had seen enough, a situation that Hampton told himself he had to rectify, but in his own time.

Chapter twenty-seven

Is She a Friend or Foe?

'Hi, Mark, really sorry to keep you waiting but I sure have lots to tell you. Are you going to buy me a drink, then?'

'Yes, Angela. I've finished my studying for today and just been to the gym for a workout. This'll be my first drink for two weeks, I feel like celebrating, any ideas?'

'Let's do that when you pass your exams, Mark. Are you going to carry on working for Dick?'

'Yes, of course, but I want to do my own thing one day like my dad, but then again, I don't want to disappear like he did.'

'Have you heard anything from him?'

'No, Angela, nothing and the way Dick Cohen is behaving with my mum I hope he doesn't turn up here in Sutton. I think he's a long way away and one day I'll find him but anyway, tell me your story. Before you do that, I'm sorry I didn't keep in touch with you or contact you since I got out of the nick, but I didn't want to talk to anyone while I was in that place and I've been really busy since my release.'

'Well then, a summary for you – on the men front, I had a steady boyfriend but unfortunately it was very much me that ended up being had. He lived with me for a year then did a runner taking with him my stereo, TV and CD player, what a bastard. I did eventually catch up with him and he said he took the stuff as I owed him lots of money. He used to pay for me when we went out, what a jerk he turned out to be. Since then I've not bothered with a steady guy just a few dates, and I mean dates, as my days of putting it about are over. You were the best, Mark, in every way but I bet you don't fancy me now as much as you did.'

'Don't put yourself down, Angela, you're an OK girl and I didn't phone you just to say hello. You knew it was me on the CCTV film and I thought you might be able to help me with who else knew and why they told the police. It's been banging in my head now for over two years and I have to sort it so I can get on and live my life again.'

'Yes, I thought that's what you wanted, Mark, and I'll do my best to help you. I'm still at the shop but it'll close soon as the lease runs out. I think then I might try to get on the planes at Gatwick, I've a friend who'll help me and I'm waiting for Ronnie to make me redundant before I apply.'

'Thanks, Angela. Let's go for a curry after a couple more drinks, but listen, who took the film to the police? The prints in the car and my hair didn't help but it was the CCTV that fucked me up. It was all too easy, who had a grudge?'

'I'm surprised at you, Mark, look at the options – your brother is number-one suspect, I know it was him in the shop as he can't look me in the face now.'

'No way, Angela, not Vince.'

'Who else then, Mark? Was it the other guy who fired the gun? I don't know him or his name and I don't want to know. I guess you know him very well so obviously you don't suspect him or you wouldn't be here asking me questions?'

'He's called Luke. You don't know him unless you watch football, he definitely wouldn't grass me up as he's no reason to do it. You don't know him so in case you get in trouble anytime and spill the beans on Vince, it's best I don't tell you any more about him.'

'Yes, Mark, but who else is there to consider?'

Mark put his hands on his chin and just nodded as Angela spoke.

'Fuck me, Mark!'

The invitation, even just as a remark, stirred his lower stomach.

'I should've guessed, why didn't I think of it before? Probably because your Vince locked him in the toilet. I didn't think he could see me but then he must've seen the altered CCTV. It must be Billy Bootle.'

'Of course, Angela. I didn't think anyone would recognise me but he did. When he made a copy of the original he must've carefully left off the other frames with Vince and Luke leaving the shop.'

'Yes, that's possible. I've the original in my flat let's go and play it again.'

Mark swallowed the remainder of his pint in one gulp with Angela doing the same to her vodka and tonic. They got a taxi and arrived back at her place within five minutes.

'Get me another drink, Angela, I think I may need it after seeing the tape.'

Angela handed him a whisky and she poured herself a large vodka and tonic as they waited for the cassette player to warm up.

The tape, when complete, was four hours long and Angela fast-forwarded to the time of the robbery. The pictures were in colour but without sound and they showed only the front exit from the shop.

'So what happened, then? Remember I was outside in the car and I didn't discuss it with the other lads.'

'It's simple, during the robbery Billy tried to switch the camera to the inside so he could later threaten all the boys if he needed money. He probably guessed they must have been local but then that's a bit odd, I wonder if he knew them. Your mate, Luke, saw him move his hand under the counter and he fired the shot from the big gun.'

Angela took his hand and squeezed it she knew what was coming next.

'Yes, that's us, Angela, and the few seconds of me is the section they showed in court but the rest is mostly of Vince and Luke. You can see that it's them as the pictures are much closer and clearer even through the front of their hoods.'

'I kept the tape, Mark, because I thought one day you should see it and you know now that Billy is the man who must have fitted you up. He doesn't know I've still got this tape. What shall we do with it now? I think we should destroy it.'

'Not before I've shown it to Vince, he'll know what to do. Is that bastard Billy Bootle still at the shop?'

'Yes, but he leaves any day now, thank goodness. It seems he had some sort of deal with Ronnie which is running out and he's leaving. He's been working at McDonald's part-time on the till and I think he's a permanent job lined up. I don't think Ronnie will forget that deal and anyway, the shop's closing down. The bloke gives me the bloody creeps. The other day he followed me down Sutton High Street after work, he was walking as if he was drunk but he wasn't, it was only 5.30. I think he's lost his mind, I just couldn't get away from him. He kept shouting after me, calling me Liz.'

'Liz who? Shit, you don't mean Liz Smith who was murdered at her dad's house?'

'Yes, you're right, Mark. I never thought about her. Fucking hell, do you think it was Billy Bootle who killed her?'

'Surely not, but then he's a very odd bloke. He hates me because I wound him up many times, probably too many – that was a big mistake. It's cost me nearly two years of my life. I'll give Vince a ring now and talk to him about the tape and Billy, then we can meet up again and go out for that curry.'

'You aren't leaving just yet. Come here, Mark Lavender, let me unzip your trousers.'

Angela was already partly undressed as she pulled Mark's body towards her. It was nearly two years since he had been with a woman and his balls ached within seconds as she pushed her breasts in his face.

Mark had never been a man for quickies but with Angela it always seemed to be like a race against time; he was inside her for seconds, she screamed uncontrollably as he pounded against her flesh. He had one eye on the clock as she shook to a rapid climax.

'What about you, Mark? Can I touch you or maybe a special blow job?'

Mark kissed her and whispered in her ear.

'Later, Angela. You know what I have to do.'

'Sure, but watch out, Billy carries a thin knife in a cigar case in his pocket or up his sleeve. Be careful, I want you back, Mark Lavender, and soon. Our work isn't finished.'

Chapter twenty-eight

A Message from Lopez

Since his arrival in Spain after the robbery, Luke Devine had kept a low profile in his friend's Valencia apartment. He received a phone call the morning after his arrival and as planned, he arranged to meet a nameless middle-aged Spanish man in the main square.

He knew the password so Luke handed him the parcel of money. They signed the form, each of them keeping a copy; it was a worthless piece of paper but as the money was expected, he had to trust the man.

'You know Gerry Lavender then, do you?'

The man hesitated then nodded, in perfect English he replied.

'I met him just once, he is a customer of Juan Villa, my boss, and they told me a little about you and the money. My job is just to deliver it. Why don't you come to Marbella in a few months and we'll arrange for you to see the site maybe.'

'Why do you say maybe?'

The Spaniard checked himself.

'We are a little delayed with the building but give it until March and it'll be ready.'

'I hope so as my mother and I want to move from here as soon as possible.'

The man shook Luke's hand; he had nothing more to say. As Luke left the town square he wondered if Gerry had double-crossed him, he had no way of checking as he hadn't spoken to Vince since he left England, and he guessed his father Gerry was still a missing man.

That evening his mobile rang again.

'Mr Devine, my name is Juan Villa, I'm phoning to say we have the money. It's £15,000 less than we expected but we understand you have had some unexpected expenses.'

'Mr Villa, good to hear from you. Yes, I needed money to pay off one guy and to help my mother here. Everything I sent you belongs to my two friends, the sons of Gerry Lavender, and myself.'

'Yes, we understand that. As my colleague has told you already, you should arrange to come here. I will call you when we are ready to show you the progress on the development. Just one thing, Mr Devine, I recommend you do not contact Vince Lavender for two reasons. One is the police may be monitoring his phone and two, he has lost his job and is working for a man called Ronnie Smith, who you know. We know him also and he's pretty ruthless. Do you understand me?'

'Yes, no problem at all. That is a dodgy situation and I definitely don't want to bump into Ronnie. I'm not surprised Vince is working for him, he always wanted to be involved in wheeling and dealing. I just hope Ronnie doesn't put too much pressure on him.'

'Not sure about all your English terms, Luke, but when we translate it from Spanish we call it, "knowing the devil".'

'Yes, we've the same phrase, well done.'

'At the right time, Luke, we'll meet up. In the meantime, I would suggest that you scrap your mobile phone but leave the SIM card inside. Who's the provider of the phone?'

'It's British Telecom but I've "pay as you go".'

'Yes, that is the reason you must destroy it in case anyone is trying to find you. Don't bother with the phone company, I'll get one of my men to phone British Telecom anonymously that we found it damaged on a beach. That will be noted on the phone records and stop them sending you texts or trying to find you. Please can you text me your mother's number and if I need to speak to you I'll send you a message with my office number. Use a public phone if you need help. Goodbye and enjoy Spain.'

Luke was taken aback by Juan Villa's precise but abrupt instructions but he was everything Gerry had said about him. He had no choice other than to do everything Juan had told him to do; he didn't want anyone trying to find him and once in Marbella, he'd probably have to take a new name.

'Who was that, Luke?' asked his mother.

'It's just the lawyer guy for the developer in Marbella. He was discussing our property and he wants us to visit it in a couple of months, but I think we need to go sooner. I want to know what's going on. In the meantime, I really do need a job. Can you ask around for me?'

'I have already, Luke, but you need to learn some Spanish and not from Anna or me. We suggest you go to the school two nights a week and they'll be pleased to take you so they can practise English, so no cockney slang, please. Luke, there's something else I wanted to tell you.'

'Yes, Mum, that sounds serious.'

'A man came here a few days before you arrived, he'd got my address from your wife. He said you owe her £155,000, which was the money from the sale of your house, he said you haven't paid it to her, is that right?'

'Yes, it sure is, and to come totally clean with you, Mum, I also owe a loan shark £30,000 and now probably much more with added interest.'

'What are your plans then, Luke?'

'As I said when I arrived, Mum, I can't live with you, it's probably too dangerous for both of us. Mario's place is secure and he's agreed to let me stay for a few weeks provided I do some driving for him, so I'll keep out of the way and won't come to your apartment. You come and see me or we'll meet downtown.'

'How long have you got to hide yourself for?'

'That's the big question, but when we move to Marbella next year, we'd best take new names. Hopefully they'll get bored with trying to find me after a year or so.'

'You were a good footballer, Luke, and people will recognise you, this city is full of English. You'll have to change your appearance, grow a beard and maybe dye your hair. You'll have to be careful, those loan people won't let their money disappear easily.'

'I know, Mum, but I've very few options. The money I came here with is between the Lavender boys and me. I agreed with them that we'd buy property so that has to happen. Their father set it all up but until it happens I've to keep my head down. Vince Lavender will be very concerned that he can't get hold of me. I hope he trusts me but it's too dangerous to make contact with him. At least he'll know I've made the property investment if he checks with the lawyer.'

'I'm very confused, son, and I think you need to make a summary of who and what you owe and then compare it with any assets you've got left. You're possibly right to say that you could be bankrupt and if you ever want to see the UK again you'll somehow have to find money to pay off your creditors. I can't help you, all I have is my small apartment and I'm still years away from receiving my UK pension. See if you can borrow Mario's car next time he's playing out of the country. We can drive to Marbella and meet the lawyer first, then if he doesn't invite us to see the building site, we'll go on our own.'

'Thanks, Mum, you're so sensible. Shame you haven't got a man to share your life with. Got any male friends at all here?'

'Yes, of course, there are several but once I became ill most of them hid from me. In a month or two I'll try to catch up with the ones I like, but only the ones of my age, of which, unfortunately, there are very few. By the way, Anna comes from Marbella and if we drive there we can meet her father. He's called Fernando Lopez and I bet he knows something about the Marbella project. He seems to have his hands in lots of investments.'

'Thanks, that's the type of introduction I need. Please speak to Anna about it and I'll ask Mario tonight when I can borrow the car. Cheers, Mum. I'll call you later.'

The mood of the Englishman suddenly improved, he was glad that he hadn't tried to sleep with Anna, he knew it would have been a one-night stand with no future. She liked his charm and good looks but he was far too old for her.

Mario was already in the apartment when the taxi dropped Luke at the entrance to the underground car park. Since hearing about the call his mother had received from his previous wife, he was consciously looking over his shoulder all the time.

He paid the driver and sat down with Mario, telling him everything that was happening and asking if he could borrow his car.

'Yes, I know Fernando Lopez, he's a big man in Marbella but be very careful when you meet him as people who upset him have suddenly disappeared. I've another car you can borrow, then you'll have time to do what you want on your trip. It's parked downstairs in bay 100 and is a red Seat Ibiza. Don't go mad in it, we have been friends for many years and even though it's old I would like it to find its way back to Valencia.'

'It sounds like one of your women, Mario.'

'Be careful, Luke, you are nearly right. My car has a good memory so treat her well.'

The pointless dialogue from Luke was just aimed at baiting Mario; he had already guessed that his mother had been one of his conquests, but one he was not admitting.

'Who're you playing in the next game, Mario? Could I come and watch?'

'Yes, sure, I'll get you tickets. It's Barcelona next Sunday and we need at least a draw. If you look at the league table we're going down and down, the manager is probably in danger of losing his job and the message is that the owners want to sell the club, so it's not good.'

'How about you, Mario, how long is your contract?'

'I only have a deal to the end of the season and I would like to go to England or Germany, but the main thing is to keep clear of relegation from La Liga, then I get a big end-of-contract bonus. Also, we need a good cup run, the first round we won easily and the TV money gets big from now and we all get a share.'

'I could be your agent, Mario.'

'I've already got one and she's a woman. I'm not introducing you either, Luke, as I know you'll be trying to get into her pants. She likes Englishmen.'

FC Lecont was in more financial trouble than Mario had been told. The players were kept away from the politics of the finance situation. The shareholders wanted out and would take any reasonable offer but there had been very little interest.

Good results on the field were needed and then it followed that good players like Mario would not leave if a new owner took over, provided he was one with money to invest in more quality players.

FC Lecont was a relatively new club; it was only eight years old and had started in the lower division. The owners were from Catalonia; they were a small group of businessmen who were turned away by Barcelona when they tried to buy a large share in the club.

The source of their wealth was believed to be from investments in Chile; they had built large pulp and papermaking factories in a country with lots of natural resources but no money to build manufacturing units. Their sales markets were initially just within South America but as they produced more volume, they set up sales companies in Europe and the USA. The production in Chile had very low labour costs and raw material came from their integrated plants in large forest areas with vast amounts of suitable trees.

Competition had been stunned by the entry of Chile into the traditional European markets and the result was production closures and rationalisation on a scale never seen before in 30 years.

The businessmen from Spain made millions of dollars, which was moved from Chile to Spain. The investment in the new football club was just one of many projects to use the money they had made in a legal and visible way.

The earthquake in Chile in 2009 and the currency uncertainty made the businessmen nervous, the competition was fighting back and the Spaniards decided to make investments in South America rather than continue to fight for new market share in distant countries.

Their plans involved selling all unwanted assets and FC Lecont was top of the list. The accountants didn't like football clubs and the businessmen decided to sell 100% of the club as soon as possible, even at a discounted price.

Maybe one day they would have sufficient money to buy their dream Barcelona FC but not until the Chilean investments were showing good financial returns in their own domestic market and not just in exported goods.

The agent appointed to produce a buyer had difficulty finding any serious interest. Most of the current deals were in the UK with Arabs, Chinese and Malaysians all pouring money into Premier League clubs.

Señor José Valmena, the accountant at FC Lecont, was surprised to receive the enquiry from the foreigner, it came totally out of the blue. It was a ridiculously small amount of money, but it was an offer.

As an agent, he had to check out the financial situation of the potential buyer, he knew that would be difficult but then if Spanish banks were involved, why should he worry? Provided he got his 5% backhand commission he didn't care, he would give no warranties. After all, the sale was just the club and that meant just the players, staff, and TV rights, the ground was leased.

Chapter twenty-nine

A Problem Solved

'Vince, can you join me down The Plough about eight o'clock? I want your help with a small job.'

'Yes sure, little brother. Is it a bank job?'

'No, don't piss about, mate, this is serious. I found something out and I need to deal with it. Just come and I'll tell you the story – it's messy.'

Mark left Angela's apartment in a rush but she knew he would be back as she slipped on her dressing gown and curled up on her couch to watch Coronation Street.

Vince arrived first at the pub and was halfway through his pint before his brother turned up.

'Hi, mate, you look like you've been on the job.'

'Dead right, Vince, but I've got the story we need.'

Mark explained what had happened with the CCTV tape. Vince looked concerned and interrupted Mark before he told him about Billy carrying a knife.

'We've got to get to him quick. Ronnie's chucking him out this week as the deal he agreed with him when he got the divorce has ended. I hear he's a new job but he could just do a bunk.'

'What was the agreement, Vince?'

'It was just Doris, Ronnie's old wife, put a condition in the divorce deal that Ronnie gave the bastard a guaranteed job in his shop for a few years. He had to agree but the time has run out and he's being chucked out now.

'In fact, Ronnie asked me to go and remind him that he was on the way out. I'd a bit of a job explaining to Ronnie that I didn't want to do it. I couldn't tell him that if I was to go and sort Billy out and tell him he was leaving he might grass on me as well. Remember, Mark, we robbed his bloody shop. Ronnie wasn't interested in my excuses, he just smiled in that evil way he does sometimes. He just looked me straight in the face and said, sort it. I'd no choice but to give Billy the news. We couldn't have done the job without Billy's information in the first place but as he's already dropped you in it, my big fear is he'll do the same again. He may tell the police about Luke and me being the others involved in the robbery.'

'Yes, yes, mate, I know all of that and I reckon it's a certainty he'd grass you up as well, probably just because you have the plum job with Ronnie and he's such a jealous geezer. He'd just stir the shit for the hell of it. In all those long nights in the nick, I thought of everyone and he was on my list, but then I never guessed it was him who was responsible for my arrest. But I'll tell you this, Vince, he wouldn't want to be a witness, so anything he did would be by an anonymous call on a payphone like he must have done last time. That wouldn't help you much as no doubt John Hampton would be all over you like a rash and Ronnie would find out somehow. But as far as the police are concerned, the only evidence they would need is in that original CCTV tape and Angela has got it safe at her place. I'll call her in a minute and tell her to lock it away until we can relieve her of it later. So we've got to move quick, Vince, and get to Billy Bootle before he starts blabbing again. We'd better be careful, though, as if he's responsible for the violent death of Liz Smith, he may be carrying a weapon. He's such a fucking coward he'd probably stab us in the back when we weren't looking.'

'Dead right, Mark, he warned me that he'd get me back when I sacked him so we don't have much time.'

'Angela gave me this address for him but she said he's working part-time on the till at McDonald's in the evenings and he should be there tonight.'

Without any plan, the men jumped into Vince's BMW and made for the shop at the south end of the High Street. Parking was not possible in the precinct. Vince did what many customers seemed to do and parked at the back on the double-yellow line.

They were lucky; Billy was at the back of the shop as the boys approached. He was smoking and still in his casual clothes. He didn't start for another ten minutes and he wasn't going to give McDonald's any extra time.

'Hello, Billy. See you've a new job.'

'What the fuck do you two want? Are you going to rob Mac's now? Where's your mate with the 12-bore?'

'That's what we wanted to talk to you about, Billy. Come outside for a minute.'

Vince grabbed his arm and pushed him outside into the street.

'Listen, mate, our message is a simple one – you know it was us who did the robbery, you dropped Mark in it, you phoned the police, probably you didn't know about the forensics but that bloody CCTV was altered by you and that got him nicked.'

Billy broke away from his grip and interrupted.

'So what? Fuck off, Vince. Your brother had it coming to him. I decided to teach Mr Mark Lavender a very big lesson and phoned the police, but at the same time I didn't want to be involved, so I just put the phone down when they started asking questions. Later I gave them the CCTV tape, the one I'd edited. It had just one person on it. You've got a big mouth, Mark, and it needed to be shut.'

'You bastard, Billy. I served 18 months inside because of you and I just can't let that go.'

Billy was shaking. He started to fidget in his pocket and Mark remembered what Angela had said about the knife.

'Vince, he's got a fucking knife!'

Vince grabbed him and pushed him against the wall but Billy already had the knife in his hand and he stabbed it into Vince's chest, but it fell out as Mark pushed him away from his brother.

'Come here, Billy. No knife now, you bloody coward.'

Billy Bootle didn't look behind him, he just turned to run and on his second step he fell into the bus lane in the main road.

The driver of the red double-decker bus didn't see him until the last minute, he had no time to brake as Billy fell under the front wheels, crushing his body and killing him instantly.

'Let's go quick,' shouted Mark.

Vince was already three steps ahead of his brother, holding his chest to prevent any more blood spilling on the pavement. He pressed the remote control and jumped in the passenger seat.

Mark grabbed the keys and started the car. He didn't race the car away just slowly turned it around into the main road traffic. The only people at the scene were the bus driver who had collapsed with shock, the conductor and a badly mutilated Billy Bootle.

The car was at the top of the dual carriageway at Rosehill before the sirens of the ambulance were heard in the distance on the other road; police cars followed behind, they would all be too late.

'How is it, Vince?'

'Don't know, there's quite a lot of blood so I'm going to have to go to hospital so we'll need a good story.'

'I think the best one is to rip your jacket and say that we were mugged outside the pub.'

'OK, but we've got to get this right, Mark. First we'll go to Epsom Hospital A and E Unit, then you phone the police and tell them about it, as the hospital will tell them straight away. Say it happened outside the King's Head. This foreign bloke came up to us as I parked the car, you had already gone to get the drinks ordered. He pulled a knife on me and demanded money, we had a struggle and he stabbed me then ran off.'

'Yes, that should do, Vince, no witnesses and a long way from McDonald's so unless the police talk to each other we should get away with it.'

'Get me to the hospital but slowly, we don't want to be pulled for speeding. If they do bump into you at the hospital and they know you drove the car they are sure to breathalyse you and you are not insured to drive this car. You'll have to say I was driving, just leave the car outside then move it to the Ashley Centre once they've left and walk back here.'

By the time they had done the four-mile journey the bleeding had stopped, the wound looked clean; the knife had only penetrated the skin by a few millimetres. Vince was in shock but nothing that a couple of whiskies wouldn't cure.

The hospital made no comment on Vince Lavender's injury, he told them what had happened and as a matter of procedure on stabbings they called the police. The wound required six stitches but as the blow glanced the ribs it was nowhere near any organs and confined to the flesh on his right side.

Vince gestured from his temporary bed to his brother, an imaginary phone to his ear, and Mark waved as he ran out and put his mobile to his ear.

'Hello, I'm speaking on behalf of my brother, Vince Lavender. He got mugged and stabbed outside the Kings Head and I'm with him in hospital.'

The Duty Officer in Epsom Police Station took the details and said the hospital had already been on the phone to report the admission of Vincent Lavender.

The police took 30 minutes to arrive at the casualty unit, it was not a priority case and the patrol officer was only vaguely interested in what appeared to be a random mugging attack.

When the policeman arrived at the casualty unit he was shown into the first treatment room.

'Are you Mr Lavender?'

'That's me, have you got the guy who stabbed me?'

'No, we don't know what happened yet, miracles take a little longer, so first I need to ask you some questions. I'm PC Butterworth from the local station and you can tell me what happened to you, but first did you drive here?'

'Yes, my car is outside on the double-yellow line.'

'We know that, we just nicked it for being on a double-yellow. Give me the key and I'll get the porter to park it for you, it's blocking the ambulance bay, or can your friend drive it?'

'He's my brother and no he can't drive it, he's not insured.'

'OK, we'll just check it over then someone better collect it tomorrow from the staff car park. Also, I'll need you to take a breath test so we'll do that first.'

Vince was in shock but he managed to blow into the tube and the reading was negligible. The policeman looked pleased, he didn't fancy the paperwork at that time of night.

'Fuck my car and booze, mate, I've been stabbed!'

'OK, calm down, it's just procedure. Now tell us what happened, we need a description of your attacker and some more details. Did your brother see the man?'

'No, he went to order the drinks.'

The policeman started to lose interest in the attempted mugging when an accident came through on his radio; he quickly checked the car as a porter moved it 50 yards to the staff car park.

Mark and Vince left the hospital at midnight, the taxi driver delivered Vince to his home and Mark carried on back to his parents' house, but after paying the driver he dialled a number on his mobile.

'Angela, sorry you still awake?'

'Yes, Mark, what happened? Where are you, are you all right?'

'Don't panic, Angela, I'm OK. What do you mean, what happened?'

'Well, I expected you back after you had seen Vince, then as you were so long I thought you must have gone to see Billy Bootle.'

'I'm really sorry, Angela. Yes, we went to meet him, he pulled that knife you mentioned on Vince and stabbed him with it. He then slipped and fell into the road and got run over by a bus. I think the knife dropped into the gutter but we did a runner and got Vince to hospital.'

'Bloody hell, Mark, is Billy dead?'

'Yes, the bus crushed him and it was horrible, but Vince just needed a few stitches and a good story for Donna.'

'Mark, can you please come and see me tomorrow when you get up? We have some unfinished business.'

'Yes, but open the door first, Angela, can you?'

'What do you mean?'

'I said open the door. I'm outside, I walked here.'

Angela opened her flat door and grabbed him in a bear hug.

'Good job I didn't go to sleep, wasn't it, Mark?'

'Yes, no way I could get to sleep after that. I'd have had to stay up, my mum would have been wondering all night what the matter, so if you don't mind, can I stay here?'

'Have a shower, I'll find you a tee shirt, yours is covered in blood. I'll make us a warm drink then I'll find my best nightdress. Off you go.'

Mark let the hot water just drip over him, he was still shaking at the sight of Billy in the road; he would get over it but never forget it. In a way his death had done them a favour; Mark thought Vince would probably have killed him if the accident hadn't happened.

Vince knew that after hearing Angela's story about the other tape, he guessed that one day Billy would tell the police about Luke and him being involved in the robbery.

Angela picked up the phone as soon as she heard the water running.

'It's me, Angela. I sent you a text message but I decided to phone as well. Sorry it's so late. Mark's here now, he's in the shower. You were spot on, as soon as Mark saw the tape he told Vince. They went to see Billy tonight. He had an accident and is dead. They said it really was an accident, he fell under a bus as they were arguing but fortunately no witnesses, apart from the boys. I know it sounds dodgy but Mark said Billy went for Vince, turned and slipped back into the bus lane behind McDonald's. Vince got stabbed but not seriously. I'm just about to give Mark his reward.'

'Yes, but don't give him my regards. He has the dubious achievement of being the third Lavender man to sleep with you, Angela. I always said you were rather special.'

'Yes, I'm always hoping for a permanent Lavender and Mark is my best bet at the moment, but he keeps saying he wants to go abroad and that wouldn't suit me, I'm a Sutton girl and here I'm staying.'

'Goodnight, Angela, and thanks for calling me.'

The death of Billy Bootle would be recorded as a tragic accident; he had literally fallen off the pavement in front of the double-decker bus.

The bus driver was severely affected by shock and off work. He told the police a few days later that he didn't see anybody else other than the dead man at the scene of the accident and the conductor confirmed his story.

His funeral had one mourner, his sister Doris. The sad man had a sad ending. His brother-in-law, Ronnie Smith, did not turn up and he made no comment on his death until the police visited him with some news on his daughter's murder.

The knife had been found in the gutter and handed in to the police for a forensic check, it was bent and twisted where vehicles had driven over it many times and it was only due to the diligence of a bus inspector that the instrument ever arrived at the police station.

As it was found near the site of a death, the pathologist, Oliver Hill, was called in to see if there was any blood or tissue on the instrument, he noticed in the examination that the blade had sharpened serrated edges. The pathologist was elated, this could be the instrument that he was looking for in the cases of Alan Goody and Liz Smith, but he needed time to have it professionally straightened so it could be compared closely with the wounds on the two victims.

Blood was present on the handle, but other than identifying is as type O, he had only one other observation; the blood didn't belong to the man squashed by the bus.

The inquest on Billy Bootle was delayed. The coroner had read a preliminary report and after discussion with the police he made a new date for six weeks ahead, so the knife and the statements could be investigated further.

Chapter thirty

Instructions for Spain

'That's good news, Mark. So the parole officer has said that he only wants to see you once a month for six months, then it's all over provided you behave. You'll need an EasyJet season ticket.'

'Yes, that's about it, Dick. I said I'd tell him roughly what I'm going to do and how to contact me so I'm free to travel. Look, I've even got my passport.'

'I want you to go to Spain on Monday. Firstly to Marbella and meet up with Juan Villa, then go to the development site. Have a look around and let me know what you think – will they finish stage one in a few months or not? Your opinion, Mark, that's what I want. Ask around a bit but watch your back.'

'Dick, can I come clean with you?'

'Yes, Mark. What's the problem?'

'I know you want to help me but I'm not sure your line of work is for me. I'm into sports and until the leisure part of the complex gets going, I'll be sat on my arse doing nothing.'

'I suggest you keep your options open. We're all uncertain about Spain and since I made the investment things have gone bad on the property side. The pound is weak against the euro, there's been a lot of overbuilding, sometimes of very poor quality, and it's likely many of the places will only last a few years before major repair work will be needed. You need a break and I'll book your flight to Malaga. Take this money – it's 1,000 euros, an advance for anything you do for me. Make the best use of the time and the money and when you're spent up, phone me and I'll get you a flight back. When you are here again we'll talk about which direction we'll go with you in the future.'

'Thanks, Dick, you're a star.'

Mark had no intention of working with Dick unless he was permanent in the golf and leisure plans. It was the message Dick wanted to hear but he was taking it slowly with his new employee. After 18 months in prison he could easily go off the rails and Dick knew it.

In his defence, Dick Cohen was trying hard to help him in the absence of his father. Dick had been a friend of the family for a long time and he hoped one day to become Mark, Vince and Sharon's stepfather, but first they needed to be sure that Gerry was not coming back. The police were saying that from information received, he was still alive; he had committed no crimes and paid his taxes so they would not reveal his location.

Barbara Lavender was relieved at the news from the police, but she was unhappy with the situation concerning Dick. She loved him dearly and wanted a divorce from Gerry.

Her lawyers were on the trail of her missing husband and a private investigator had been employed, she had to find Gerry and speak to him, at least once more, so she could organise her future. The police had said he promised to contact her but she had heard nothing.

The sound of Mark's mobile phone ended the meeting with Dick and he left the office to take the call in the street.

'Hi, Donna, what's up?'

'I don't believe Vince's story about last night, Mark, but I need to see you on another matter. Can you get here now?'

'Yes, sure, on my way. See you in 15 minutes.'

The semi-detached house in South Sutton was basic but perfect for Vince and Donna; it was near the Lavender house and also conveniently near the schools. Shane was coming up to his third birthday and was a handful for the pregnant Donna.

'I managed to get Mum to take Shane to the park and Vince is working at one of Ronnie Smith's scrapyards, sorry, recycling centres, but it pays well so who's complaining. Vince is happy he's earning and so am I.'

'So what's your problem then, Donna?'

'It's a difficult one, Mark, and I think you are the only person I can trust. I need to give you a message, but then it puts me on the spot.'

'Come on, Donna, spit it out?'

'Right here goes. Nearly three years ago, I had a brief fling with Luke Devine. Your brother had no idea and I never told him, he would have seriously sorted Luke out and maybe left me. I don't know why I did it, but it was just circumstances, if you know what I mean. To make matters worse, until recently I wasn't sure who Shane's father was. Since the boy has grown and when I checked the dates again, no way is he Luke's child. He has Vince's nose and his red hair, so no more discussion.'

'For goodness sake, Donna, why did you do it and why involve me? I've had enough grief in the past two years and I don't want to hear what you're telling me.'

'Right, the reason I've told you is that Luke just phoned me. He's frightened of Vince and doesn't know your number. He phoned from a post office in Valencia which has international access and probably he doesn't want anyone tracing the call.'

'Why all the mystery with him, Donna? The bastard's got my money.'

'Yes, you're right, he had all the money but as agreed with Vince, it's now all been invested in a property deal in Spain, which is the easy bit. He wasn't running away from you guys it's just he's bankrupt here and he's got his wife and a loan shark trying to find out his whereabouts in Spain so they can try to recover the money he owes.'

'So what does he want?'

'He wants to meet you, Mark. He said he can't look Vince in the face yet, but if he meets you in Spain he can tell you about the investment and also a way that maybe you could both cash out so he can clear most of his debts.'

'It's all a bit fucking incredible, Donna, but I suppose we all have an interest in Mr Luke Devine as he's the only one who knows where our money went.'

'The odd thing, Mark – or perhaps it isn't odd – is the lawyer, Juan Villa, who turned up at your house looking for your dad, has handled the investment, and Luke has just told me that so he knows that the money is safe.'

'Yes, come to think of it, I do remember now. Vince and Dad met a bloke together, that's obviously who it was. I never realised it was Villa. Are you sure Vince doesn't know were my dad is?'

'No, but I get the impression he knows he's somewhere safe, Mark.'

'Donna, you're very naïve. The money is not safe until I see the investment. From what I hear from Dick Cohen the development is a long way off being built. Your timing is pretty good in some ways because Dick wants me to go to Spain and view the place.'

'Go, Mark. If Luke phones again I'll arrange for you to meet him in Marbella, he said he would wait a couple of days, then he would phone me again during the day when Vince is working. Somehow he's managed to live in Valencia for the past two years. I think he's still living on his football pal's charity, in the bloke's apartment. I reckon he's just about managing to survive away from his creditors.'

'Is he working?'

'Yes, he got a job recently as a caretaker in the local English school. He said his Spanish is now good.'

'I still don't trust him, Donna, but I'll see what he's actually done with the money then I'll discuss it with Vince, not before.'

'And me?'

'You're OK, Donna, but please don't shit on the doorstep again, otherwise Vince will probably find out.'

'He's no saint, Mark, he never has any money and I think he goes up town and meets expensive hookers.'

'Don't put me on the spot. I know nothing, Donna, just what you've told me about yourself, so just forget everything until Luke phones again, then tell me what day in the next two weeks we can meet in Spain.'

'Thanks, Mark. You'd better go before Vince is back otherwise he'll be suspecting that you're giving me one.'

Mark managed a smile.

'I'd love to, Donna, but no and never. Just look after the men you've got, and that doesn't include Luke Devine.'

A few days later Luke Devine telephoned Donna and told her the dates he would be in Marbella and suggested he meet Mark at Juan Villa's office. He did not expect trouble from Mark as all he wanted to know was the destination of the robbery money, but after his prison sentence he knew he would not be sweet about anything if Luke had screwed up.

Chapter thirty-one

Getting the Act Together

Superintendent Ellen Brewster moved her large frame backwards on her chair and it leaned at a precarious angle as she greeted her favourite detective inspector. She put her hands behind her head and smiled at John Hampton, a rare occurrence for the stressed policeman. Since his promotion and the departure of his then boss, DI Lawson, every bit of shit seemed to land in his direction. His clear-up rate on solving recent cases was a lot lower than other forces.

'Good morning, ma'am. You wanted to see me?'

'You bet I do, John. From what I hear you're a magician, are you telling me we've solved two murders and maybe a third, or even a fourth, by a serial killer?'

'No, boss, it's all a bit early yet. I'm just recycling for you the new details Sergeant Linda Dredge gave me yesterday. She's on the way in from the mortuary to see us. I suggest we get the new murder squad involved, after all, they wanted to take the case over so now they can, but they'll need our help in piecing together the bits of the puzzle. There are still a few loose ends, but best we put everything on the table now, before they join us. So I'm getting Linda to put everything on the marker board just to keep it simple for Detective Inspector Wallace.'

The murder squad hadn't given up on the Alan Goody and Liz Smith murders but as no new clues had come to light since the interview with Billy Bootle, they had left the file open; without any evidence they could do very little more.

Ellen Brewster slumped forward on her chair and waved her pencil at John Hampton.

'No, John, it would be nice if we could get everything wrapped up and then we give the file to DI Wallace. We need to score some points here, our success rate is shit and this could be four or maybe even five crimes solved in one day. The thing I like about it is that it looks like we won't be arresting anyone and if that guy Bootle was the killer, his death is the best thing that could've happened.

We must not forget though, we still have a robbery on our desk with some of the culprits at large. Do you have any ideas on who they may be? The Lavender boy is out of jail, have you had another chat with him? It's annoying because he must know who his accomplices are?

In the last interview you told me,John, that you over did it and he told you to fuck off you must have pushed him to hard and he has gone now into his shell. Right, well…we need someone else to talk to him. Send Sergeant Dredge, she may be able to use her charms on him. Do it now, Inspector.'

John Hampton didn't like being told what to do but he saw his superior's point and would do as she asked.

Oliver Hill and his assistant turned up just as the superintendent started to take another partial sleeping position in her chair. She pointed to the meeting room and ordered tea and biscuits.

'We know the background, Mr Hill, so please tell us in a summary what's in your report and basically what will be sent to the coroner regarding the latest death. John, ask Sergeant Dredge to join us now.'

Linda Dredge's promotion had been the result of her ability to remember detail and turn it to her advantage when dealing with all types of police work. She passed her examination with flying colours and was at the start of a career that had no barriers.

If she had a weakness it was too much work and no play. She had many boyfriends but only a few found her bed and she was looking for someone intelligent, handsome, with a good career and wanting children, she would then have found the ideal man.

The four sat around the table as Oliver Hill studied the marker boards on the walls until he came to the one labelled 'Goody'.

The information was scribbled in all directions and since the latest information, morgue photographs of Alan Tinker, Alan Goody, Liz Smith and Billy Bootle had each been placed across the top of the boards.

The superintendent, anxious to get the party moving, tapped on the table and looked at the pathologist.

'Yes, Superintendent, of course, my report. I see you've a lot of detail already so if I can clear up any issues of identity first, it'll then bring me on to my conclusions.'

'Go ahead, Mr Hill, please. It should be simple.'

'The four victims' names are as written on your board. They died in that order. In the cases of the first three, death was caused by a knife wound – to the lower chest in deaths two and three – in case number one, we believe the man was stabbed in the back, he then fell or was pushed over the bridge onto a live electrified railway line. A complication in cases one and two was that extensive beating to the body and head was found prior to the knife being used, it's not in my report but it indicated that they had probably been in a fight with the killer. Blood found at the scene in cases one and two was identified as being from the victims, in addition, a third blood type was found on clothes, the ground behind the pub and the railway bridge. This was all of the same type as the dead man number four on your marker board, Mr Billy Bootle.'

Superintendent Brewster interrupted.

'So it would seem likely that Bootle had a fight with these men before they died but then the knife wound was inflicted to finish them off.'

'Yes, that's correct, Superintendent. The knife found at the scene of Bootle's accident had recently been sharpened; it was an unusual instrument with a double serrated edge, which helped me discover it had been used on the first three victims. It had one recognisable blood smear, which we analysed and I found it didn't relate to any of the victims or Billy Bootle.'

'Are you saying he killed someone else as well?' said John Hampton.

'No, Inspector, I can't confirm that, but he definitely stabbed someone else and not himself.'

'Linda, get one of your PCs to check all hospitals in the area for anyone being admitted in the last few days with a knife wound of any description.'

'Sorry, Mr Hill, please continue.'

'The girl Liz Smith, victim three, was badly beaten. We reported at the time that the killer must have pinned the poor girl to the wall and punched her several times in the face before he pushed the knife into her. She would have died in three or four painful minutes. It would seem that without any doubt the intention was the person had come to kill her.

'So finally, to the death of Billy Bootle which was due to extensive injuries to his head and abdomen caused by the front nearside wheel of the bus. The man died instantly. His stomach contents contained a large quantity of hamburgers and whisky – my estimate nearly half a bottle – both had been consumed in the hour before his death.'

'Could the man have been drunk and just fallen under the bus?'

'Yes, possibly, Inspector. He was expected for work in McDonald's.'

Linda Dredge put up a hand.

'Yes, Sergeant, speak.'

'Superintendent, we found a man who said Billy met two men at the door and left the shop with them. He said he was too far away to see them properly but he reckoned they were both white and about 6ft tall.'

'Does anyone know if McDonald's have a door CCTV, or is there one in the street?'

'Yes and no, ma'am, the shop camera points at the till area and in front of it, not the door. We have studied the road CCTV and there's almost nothing, only one frame of a BMW 5 Series in dark blue, but side view only, parked on the double-yellow line. But when the camera returned to the parking spot a minute later it was gone.'

'Thanks, Linda. Please continue, Mr Hill.'

'The final thing is that as you've been informed of the outcome of the inquests on the first three deceased and from what we've learned in recent weeks, nothing has changed about Alan Goody's death. The original verdict that he was killed by a person or persons unknown still stands. I'll send the information on the knife to the coroner but the verdict can't be changed, just the suspect named for the record. Alan Tinker was an open verdict, the evidence we've got now should put the death in the same category as Goody, so no doubt the coroner will have to give his ruling on any further statements. This was less clear as the beating and the mutilation made the knife wound almost invisible. The verdict on Liz Smith was death by person or persons unknown and the new evidence is included in my report. I can't say it was your suspect Mr Bootle, but it seemed to be his weapon.'

'Thank you very much, Mr Hill, please send us the normal copies as soon as you can.'

'Yes, of course, but privately I'm glad we're rid of that man Bootle. Pathologists should not be judgemental but in cases like these the waste of life of healthy people makes me sick. Thank you, I'll leave now and return to the production line.'

Oliver Hill didn't wait to shake hands with the policemen or say goodbye, he just jumped in his car and left the station; he was sick in the gut. He cut bodies up daily but he never considered the reality of the dead bodies, to hear the account of the waste of life was enough for him to finally take that retirement.

'Our job now, Inspector, is to clean up the pieces. Linda, has anything come through from the hospitals? Why are you smiling?'

'Sorry, ma'am, it's just Epsom Hospital A and E had a knife casualty last night. It was Vince Lavender and he was accompanied by his brother, Mark. The staff nurse fancied Mark and she gave me his full description, definitely him.'

'Interesting. Maybe Billy didn't have an accident after all. Check the camera again, the film must show us more.'

'Yes, we're doing that now, ma'am. By the way, though, Vince has a BMW 5 Series.'

John Hampton smiled at the young sergeant.

'How do you know that?'

'I've been in it, sir?'

'Thought so. Pull him in for a chat, and Mark as well. He hates coming here but we've got to get to the bottom of this. Before you go, let's have a quick word outside.'

Linda Dredge knew what was coming; she left the boss's office and went to the car park.

'Jump in your car, Linda, then we can talk.'

'You said you'd been in Vince Lavender's car. In itself that's not a crime, you have a private life and you can do what you want provided you don't compromise your job. However, you're always a policewoman and if you hadn't noticed, Vince is a married man and even worse, an employee of

Ronnie Smith. I don't want this becoming a case for the internal affairs guys. What have you got to say, Linda?'

'Quite a lot, Inspector.'

'Bloody hell, Linda, give me a break, can you? Call me John in private.'

'I first met Vince Lavender in The Plough pub about six months ago. At first I was attracted to him and I'm a single girl. I know he's married but that didn't mean I couldn't flirt with him. He knew who I was and we had a really long talk in the pub. There was something in his manner that intrigued me, he talked about foreign property, nightclubs, football and women. In fact, he behaved like a single bloke, no mention of family or children or mortgages. I didn't ask too many questions at first, I just let him do the talking. He said he wasn't driving that night and we got a taxi to a club in Croydon. We drank until about 1.00 am and even danced a little when the music got slower and we both became a bit merry.

'The cab dropped him at the end of his street and then took me home. Vince was the perfect gentleman, he just gave me a peck on the cheek and squeezed my hand. His final words were, "see you, I'll be in touch". I smiled and just nodded.'

'So you obviously did see him again as you went in his car?'

'Yes, in a chance meeting, although when I think more about it, he may've been watching me leave the station and followed me to Waitrose. If it was coincidence it was a nice one when our trolleys all but bumped together.'

'A likely story, he was tracking you.'

'You're wrong, sir, as his wife Donna suddenly appeared from nowhere with the little Wayne Rooney at the end of her arm, preventing him from dismantling the shop. He winked at me, then I said a polite hello, followed by the first thing that came into my head – it's good to see a man at work. Donna laughed and the couple disappeared to the check-out. When I unpacked my shopping from the grocery bag there was a business card with his work phone number and a mobile number, on the back was written "hope to see you sometime". I kept looking at the card on my desk for a week and then finally, after a bad day sorting out the drunks at The Albion, I needed a drink myself. Without hesitating I picked up the phone and dialled his mobile. He answered and without too much discussion we agreed to meet in the pub two hours later. Just time for me to get home, have a wash and change my clothes.'

'Yes, Linda, this is all very nice for a Mills and Boon novel, but what the fuck happened next?'

'We had two drinks and then went for a Chinese meal. He said something that worried me, he mentioned a bloke called Luke Devine by accident, and you know when someone tries to change the subject after saying something contentious. I knew then it was pretty obvious what he was doing, and that he wasn't going to tell me any more at all about Mr Devine.'

'Did he take you home then or give you one in the car?'

'John, don't mess about, this suddenly became only police business. I wanted him, that's for sure, and likewise he wanted me. He then said that if he ever got arrested, would I help him? I really got very suspicious. He'd drunk too many beers with his meal to drive and the words were just pouring out of his mouth, he must've been on the piss earlier and what we had was just a top up. I took his car keys and called a car. We dumped him two streets from his house. As he left the taxi he said could we discuss "that" again. "That" probably meaning what he'd done to break the law.'

'Why didn't you come and tell me?'

'I didn't want to tell you half a story and he's called a couple of times. How shall I play it, John, as a friend or as a copper?'

'You probably came to the same opinion about Mr Vince Lavender that I did, Linda. He must've been one of the other men in the betting shop robbery and you bet number three was Luke Devine. Has Devine any form? I know Vince is clean as a whistle.'

'No, he's also clean apart from a couple of driving offences. However, when I went a bit deeper I found a bankruptcy judgement against him, but when I asked about a bit, it seems he's pissed off to Spain.'

'How sweetly put, Linda. You've been digging around without telling me. To answer your question, your interest in Vince Lavender is now official. I suggest we pay Vince and Mark a visit immediately then see what we can get out of them. It's essential they don't talk to each other. I'll collect Vince from his Battersea scrapyard, you find Mark and take him in the back entrance to the station. Buy him a cup of tea as he's sure to be awkward.'

Nothing more was said as Hampton left Sergeant Dredge's car. She pulled out of the station, drove a mile and picked up her private mobile from her handbag.

'Vince, it's me. Look I can't talk but Hampton is coming for you, he's found something at the sight of Bootle's accident, you've got to talk to Mark quickly and get your stories right. I know you didn't kill him but you need to convince Hampton.'

'Shit, did they get the information from the hospital?'

'Yes, Vince. Got to go now, best of luck.'

Linda Dredge had set up the next stage of developing her police career; a CID move would be a certainty if Vince could be linked to the betting shop robbery or even the manslaughter of Billy Bootle.

Her mind was sharp and her memory for detail the best in the station. Her work ambitions came before her private life.

She knew she had to be careful as she had seen Vince privately; a defence lawyer could use that information against her but it was worth the risk. Sure she fancied Vince, but then he was just one of many and at this stage her career was her priority.

Mark Lavender was not surprised when he saw her on his parents' doorstep, it was fortunate that his mother was not at home as she would suspect the worse but Mark was relaxed, he had paid for the crime he committed and he didn't touch Bootle before his death.

The riddle of how he got arrested in the first place nearly three years before was solved, Bootle was the grass and he was dead.

Sometimes he had mixed feelings about his elder brother; they were close and close enough for Mark to cover up for him and as far as the robbery went, his 'no comment' statement would be used again. This cost him dearly before in front of the judge who passed sentence and Hampton was still determined to get the information he wanted. This gave Mark a bad feeling, especially after his brother's desperate phone call.

'Vince, thanks for coming to the station. We've two subjects to discuss, but in some ways they're linked. The first is the death in Sutton yesterday of Billy Bootle, the previous manager of the betting shop your brother robbed.'

'Are you cautioning me? If you are, I'll get a brief.'

'No, at this stage, just a chat, as I'm sure you've a lot to tell us later. Did you see the accident that led to Bootle's death?'

'Look, Inspector, get someone to call this number for me. I need someone down here to sit with me on this.'

Hampton left the room and left Vince Lavender some privacy to phone his solicitor.

His brother Mark was ahead of him and two different legal representatives were on their way down to the police station.

Hampton was intrigued as to how well the legal men had been briefed before they arrived, did the lads know they were going to be picked up by the police? If they did, it could only be from one person. He would make sure he had enough time to talk to her later.

The interviews lasted about an hour each and reached no conclusions other than it was clear to the police that Vince Lavender was the victim of a vicious and cowardly knife attack from Billy Bootle; they had no idea why he hated the Lavender boys so much.

The police were not going to pursue an assault charge against either of them; the evidence clearly indicated that neither Mark nor Vince had pushed the unfortunate Billy under the bus the previous night. Considering his crimes, his end was, in their unofficial opinion, swift and final and in line with the pain he had inflicted on his three victims.

The coroner would hopefully record a verdict of accidental death. He would have information from the police that Bootle would have been charged with murder if he had lived.

In his summary to the jury he would most likely focus on the man's violent death, in his view by his own desire to kill again. The jury would be told that the evidence pointed to him slipping and falling under the vehicle as described by the bus driver, who had since retired, such was the trauma of the incident.

Mark retained his wall of silence on the subject of the robbery in spite of much new abuse from Hampton, who just went over all the previous ground

162

again. Mark's solicitor made it clear to the police that his client had served his sentence, he was now on parole and keen to do nothing that would result in him being sent back to prison.

His pending trip to Spain was not mentioned by Mark or his brief; if he had told any of them he was leaving the country for a trip to Spain the police might have found a reason to prevent him. If they started looking for him again during the next week, they would be disappointed.

Vince attended the police station, complete with a small bandage around his stomach, and when questions got difficult the injury became worse. When Hampton asked about Luke Devine, he admitted he knew him and that he was in Spain, but on the subject of the betting shop robbery, he offered no information.

John Hampton prepared his notes to discuss the Lavender brothers with his Superintendent as he knocked on her office door.

'Come in and sit down, John. Successful interviews I hope.'

'No, ma'am. I hoped to nail those two for Bootle's death but everything I've seen indicates that it was an accident, and a convenient one at that. The involvement of the Lavenders in the robbery is cut and dried but I can't prove it. The third person we believe is an ex-footballer called Luke Devine. He's bankrupt and has done a runner to Spain, but we can't ask for help getting him back to face any charges, other than anything we can dig out from his bankruptcy, and that's not down to us.'

'I assume he's sufficient cash to stay in Spain, the local ex-pats don't like new arrivals without money; he must be hiding out somewhere.'

'We've been told by one of the debt collectors that he's in Valencia staying with his mother, but they've watched the apartment and as yet he hasn't turned up. Probably those guys have frightened him off and he's selling ice creams on the Costa Brava.'

'Through those unofficial channels we use from time to time, get him checked out, and tell immigration about him in case he comes back to watch a football match,' said his superintendent. 'So tell me, John, how do we suddenly know, or think we know, a lot more about the Lavenders, did we have a tip-off?'

'Yes, and I'm checking it all out.'

Hampton swallowed deep when she asked the question; his informant was in the next room but then it was a story for the boss.

'Anyone we know?'

'Maybe, but more information is needed so we may follow the informant for it.'

'OK, John, but don't compromise us, it's been a good day, we've the answer to those horrific murders and a killer who won't need a trial.'

Hampton escaped from her rapidly with one idea in mind – the pub; he would try something just in case she made a mistake.

'Linda, we're going to the pub, your old friend will be tucked up with his wife and Mark isn't your type, that is, unless you can get some more information from him.'

'You're joking with me, aren't you? I think they'll avoid me as if I was a leper.'

'That's all right privately, but one day I think you or someone else will be pulling Vince Lavender back into this police station. If they do keep out of the way, you've helped today but then again also confused matters. The CID job will have to wait, it's about getting convictions, Linda, not just playing with the suspects.'

'Yes, point taken, Inspector, but no drink thanks, I'm going to the gym and meeting a guy I met last week, so maybe another time.'

Hampton, ever alert to changes in behaviour, saw the guilty look in the pretty sergeant's face. Was there someone else she knew in the Lavender clan? She obviously had someone, he thought to himself, but he was running out of possibilities.

He made a mental note to give her a working over the next day, after the debrief on the Bootle death. She would be unprepared and he would try and get the information to see if any of it was the missing piece from the betting shop robbery that was still evading him.

His lonely drink in the pub was interrupted, and by the last person in the world he wanted to see. Ronnie Smith walked into the pub with his latest girlfriend on his arm. No words passed between them, Ronnie just nodded as arrogantly as possible, in total contempt for the policeman.

As he left the pub, John Hampton passed him and couldn't resist a comment in his face.

'Watch your back, Ronnie, a Lavender is about.'

'Fuck off, copper, this is a pub for nice people.'

Ronnie went pink as he gave his expected reply. John Hampton just smirked, he had no reason to make that comment but then Ronnie had employed Vince Lavender and Ronnie didn't do things without a reason.

As he got into his car for the short drive to his empty house, he had a thought; who was it that Ronnie had a close business interests with around the town? And then he remembered.

He said the name quietly to himself as he put the car in the garage. Yes, that's the link to all this, why hadn't he thought about it before. Ronnie would be on the move soon and he would have him watched, a job maybe for Sergeant Dredge. He laughed as he guessed her reaction.

Chapter thirty-two

Marbella

'Luke, that bloke was looking up the street again just now, and I'm sure he's following me around. Don't try to see me, I'll meet you somewhere, but not at Mario's place.'

'OK, Mum, meet me in the bar at the picture gallery. Use the back entrance from the old streets, nobody can follow that route unless they're locals.'

'Yes, fine, see you in 15 minutes.'

Diana Devine was still not 100% fit after her illness but the visit of her only son had certainly got her moving. She had stagnated before and after her terrible ordeal, now she was determined to get to Marbella in a new place with Luke and hopefully see him remarried.

She was not aware of the exact amounts he owed but he had told her that the debt collectors would give up soon. She was uncertain about that and she knew that one day it would probably all need sorting out.

Anna Lopez, her lodger, had almost finished her studies in Valencia and was going home to Marbella to see her father. She had invited Luke and Diana to stay at his house. For reasons of security and cost this was a perfect situation for them and they readily accepted the invitation.

The deal was that Luke would provide the transport, using Mario's Seat Ibiza, and Diana would buy the fuel. The accommodation was agreed after a phone call to her father.

Fernando Lopez would welcome them to his home. He told them he would be away on business when they arrived, but he would join them after a couple of days.

Luke would have the opportunity to meet with Juan Villa and discuss the investment.

The message was that they must stay at least a week and his housekeeper would prepare their rooms and food until he arrived.

The gallery bar in Valencia old town was secluded and away from the public, it was for the staff but friends and relations were allowed in for short periods of time. Anna Lopez had friends in the gallery and she was waiting for both Luke and Diana to arrive.

Diana Devine and her son turned up together in the gallery bar.

'Hi, Luke, where have you been hiding? Not at your mothers, I know that.'

'It's a secret, but a couple of old friends from England are trying to find me, so I've got to be in places where they can't get to me.'

'Why do they want you, Luke?'

Diana interrupted.

'It's a long story but when Luke's marriage failed he had some old debts and people still expect him to pay.'

'Yes, that's right, Mum. The first sum of money I owed was small but every year they add 50% interest so I can never pay it.'

'When we meet my father tell him about it, he has an answer for everything and he likes football so you have a good chance he'll help you if it's possible. No promises from me and I don't want to know anything about it.'

'Thanks, Anna, I'll have that haircut before we go, I look like a hippy.'

'No, tie it behind your head, that's very Spanish.'

'Look you two, this isn't a fashion parade. We have to get to Marbella. We will meet behind Mario's place tomorrow morning at 6.00 am and leave immediately. Hopefully anybody watching us won't be up by then.'

'Yes, OK, but I must meet up with a mate from England, and together we are going to see that solicitor bloke, Juan Villa. He said to ring him when we arrive in Marbella.'

'Who is your friend, Luke?'

'His name is Mark Lavender and he's the brother of a great mate of mine, Vince Lavender, at least I hope he's still a friend as we did some work together and I haven't contacted him since.'

'Why not, Luke?'

'Long story, Mum, but if I can straighten things out through his brother it'll be easier for me to go back to England one day.'

'OK, let's all get ready for tomorrow. Make sure the car has gasoline and we've some water; it's a long drive.'

Anna Lopez was just like her father. She was good at organising people who could not organise themselves. She was a beautiful creature and Luke dreamt about sleeping with her, but now he knew her father's power he decided she would be a dangerous target for any nocturnal plans.

Luke went back to Mario's apartment; the footballer was away again and he had the place to himself so he packed his bags and filled the car up with fuel. When the lights were off he checked the street and he was happy that he could see nobody outside studying the apartment.

Diana was not as fortunate, the same man who had been snooping around for weeks stood on the corner looking at his watch in between taking the odd photo, and smoking his way through a whole packet of cigarettes.

He was nothing more than someone given a job for a few euros. It was the people behind him who were the ones Luke was worried about, and when he saw Anna and Diana leave in the early hours he would report back that the targets were on the move.

Not a lot was said in the car during the first part of the journey, the early start and the reliability of the Seat car was a good excuse for silence. The ice was broken after two hours when they stopped for coffee and Luke made his morning joke.

'Do you know this road is so bad, this car wants a double espresso as well!'

'Not funny, you should sit in the back, Luke, it's like travelling in a horse and cart with wooden wheels.'

Anna looked at them both and laughed.

'You should try the bus it takes three times as long and no toilet. At least we can stop when we need to, even if the toilet is just a matter of going behind a tree. Please remember to keep drinking lots of water, we have six large bottles. The heat is now 35 degrees and it's only eight o'clock, it will get to 40 degrees and more on the open road.'

They drank their coffee and left for the final stretch to Marbella. Luke, in his concentration on the road, did not see the black Mercedes a few hundred metres behind; they had company and at some stage they would have to face up to them.

Anna made a couple of calls on her mobile, one to the housekeeper to prepare lunch, as by the time they arrived at the house they would all be hungry travellers. She also called her father and some shouting was heard, when she had finished she smiled and looked at her English friends.

'My father welcomes you to Marbella and looks forward to meeting you on Friday.'

'Good, he sounds a nice guy.'

'He is, but don't mention your problems, Luke, until I talk to him alone. I've told him we're being followed and he'll deal with it in ten kilometres' time, probably it's best not to look back, please.'

'Shit, I see what you mean, the big Mercedes.'

'Yes, they've been with us for one hour and I guess they'll try to push in front of us near Buena Vista. I don't fancy a confrontation out here as they could push us into the canyon. Keep your speed up, Luke, the road is better here for us as we've many bends, after we see the sign for Buena Vista I want you to drive as fast as possible.'

Diana was clinging to the door and Luke the wheel as he pushed the little car to its limit as they accelerated past the Buena Vista sign.

The Mercedes was caught out for a few seconds and it reached the top of the canyon road at least half a minute behind the Seat.

'What's going to happen to them, Anna, they're after us and this car will blow up if we drive for a long time at this speed?'

'Wait and see, we have less than one minute.'

The Seat started to leave the canyon as the Mercedes climbed the narrow exit, on schedule the aggregate truck pulled out and the car screeched to a halt as the lorry totally blocked the narrow canyon road.

'My father owns the truck company and after a little delay caused by his workmen, like about 20 minutes in total, the truck will recover from stalling in the road and the Mercedes will continue on its journey but with nothing to follow.'

'Well done, Anna. Many thanks to your father.'

'We shouldn't celebrate, the car and driver will soon be back on the road and they want you, Luke, so somehow you have to deal with the situation. My father may help you, as I've said, but don't depend on it.'

The Lopez villa was built on the side of a mountain with one road in and out, which joined the highway after two kilometres. Fernando was very security minded and he had a bodyguard who worked as his driver, in the gardens, or just doing simple DIY if his boss did not need his physical presence.

The Seat waited at the front gates as Anna pressed the door entry and entered a number. The entrance to the villa was carefully guarded with CCTV cameras and surrounded by a large fence covered in razor wire.

'I bet you don't get many visitors, Anna.'

'My father is a very private man and he lives for his business, the problem was that my mother never saw him and eventually she got fed up being the good Spanish wife. She was born in England and that's why my English is good, she taught me as soon as I could talk.'

'So what happened to her, Anna?'

'She's still here in Marbella and occasionally my mother and father still go out together; they're not divorced. She has an apartment near the beach and we'll go and see her while we're here. I'm sure she would like to talk to you, Diana, about England, she hasn't been back home for many years. In fact, she never asks about the UK at all. My mother is called Nancy Lopez and she is a very independent lady. I think she has a lover but she never says anything so we really don't know much about her private life. She is a doctor of medicine and she is always busy dealing with private patients, usually ones with serious illnesses, and mostly from the UK. She has a very expensive apartment in the town, which my father rents for her, she's really very extravagant and it's a good thing she does some work.'

'Have you any brothers or sisters here, Anna?'

'No, none at all and no relations, so it's pretty quiet here. My family in Marbella is quite small. We come originally from Irun in the north west of Spain and the relations we have are all there. It isn't like Marbella and doesn't have the sea or anywhere near as much sun.'

Maria the housekeeper was waiting on the doorstep to greet her visitors and she made a good attempt to welcome them in English. The breathtaking luxury of the villa, its grounds and art collection, left Luke and his mother open-mouthed. Fernando Lopez's wealth was not in any doubt, but how he earned his money still had to be explained and Anna was evasive whenever the subject arose.

Fernando telephoned to check that his guests had arrived; Juan Villa had also informed him of their impending arrival. The name Devine meant nothing to Lopez, but once Juan had explained about a meeting with Mark Lavender he became intrigued as to why Gerry's son was also in Marbella.

Juan Villa was drinking his early evening Martini when Lopez called him.

'Yes, Lopez, I know it's suspicious but he's not in contact with his father and I think he's only come here to check his investment and to make sure we've used the money correctly that was brought here to Spain by that man Devine, who's at your house. Anna tells me he's an OK guy and just down on his luck, he had a bad divorce.'

'Is there ever a good one, Juan? That's why I never divorced my dear Nancy. Anna said that his divorce made him bankrupt. I'll talk to him when I'm back in Marbella. In the meantime, he's being followed by some amateur debt collectors, I held them up today on their journey here after a tip from Anna, but at some stage Mr Devine has to face up to them. I may help a little but really it has nothing to do with us.'

'You missed my point, Lopez. The three men, Mark Lavender, Luke Devine and Vince Lavender have things to do with us. They have all invested money in your unfinished development. Also, please don't forget the very large investment from the accountant, Dick Cohen.'

'I'm up with you, Juan, don't worry. Let me know how the meeting goes and then we can decide what to do. One more question, I hear from Maria that Mrs Devine is a very nice lady indeed. We'll have a dinner party on Saturday, come to my house with your wife.'

'Oh no, Lopez, not another English woman, and you haven't even met the lady yet.'

'I'm joking. You're quite right, Juan, I know nothing about her. Please call me tomorrow.'

Lopez gave no more thought that evening to Devine, his mother or Mark Lavender; he was in Irun trying to raise further investment money to finish the major part of his Marbella development. He knew he had to finish it very soon so he could quickly sell the whole site and make some money, just as he had promised all his anxious shareholders.

The people of Irun had seen many problems in their area since the Spanish Civil War; ETA terrorists still committed the occasional violence. The men with money trusted Lopez to make them a lot of cash, he was doing his very best to oblige but had major, almost insurmountable problems.

In the future, this latest venture was certainly the last building project he would be involved in. His credibility was suffering and his future was probably best away from Spain. He had offshore assets that he could liquidate in a few months and no criminal charges had ever been brought against him. He was a free man to move to a safer haven and in his own mind it would be a long way from Spain.

The likelihood of losing face and his investors' money was very high. The building project was doomed to fail through quality of build, or pure deception on the true lifespan of the badly built properties. His friends would soon become his enemies under those circumstances and a quick exit was his only option.

Chapter thirty-three

We Meet Again

The atmosphere in Juan Villa's office was tense as Mark Lavender arrived to join Juan, his assistant Claude and Luke Devine.

Luke tried to be Mr Nice Guy.

'Hello, stranger, good to see you.'

'It may not be, Luke, until you tell me what you've done with my money, and my brother's. You look like you're having a good life here with that tan. It better not be at my expense. I've been on the inside, mate, remember that?'

Juan interrupted.

'Look, we aren't going to get anywhere unless you two shake hands and try to calm down. Everything here is OK apart from a few small delays.'

'Yes, he's right, Mark, I've nothing to hide. I ended up here in Spain because I'm bankrupt, I've got blokes trying to find me and I'm hiding to keep them off my back. I did get all the money out apart from a few thousand pounds to that creep Bootle and the costs of getting to Valencia. The rest was delivered to Juan Villa. Your old man rang me and told me to do that, I trusted him and Juan has invested it in a property. I had nothing to say to Vince, your father said he'd talk to him but he probably didn't. Am I right?'

'I don't know if he did, but probably, it doesn't matter now. You and the money are here and one day we'll catch up with my father. Have you any idea where he is, Luke, and who he's with?'

'No idea at all, my phone went and I've heard from nobody other than this man, Juan Villa.'

'Yes, OK, Luke. Sorry, mate. I'm still a bit hot about being in prison. Bootle was a creep and he turned out to be a killer as well, Vince and I went to see him and he fell under a bus. He stabbed Vince and in the struggle he just fell into the road, we didn't touch him. He killed Alan Goody and another punter but the worst one was Liz Smith, she let him have his leg over once and he thought he owned her. It's all a bit messy. The police pulled Vince and I in the other day and got nasty. They're still trying to get information on the betting shop robbery. We got a tip-off from that bird

Linda Dredge that we were going to be interviewed, she's now a Sergeant and Vince still gives her one every now and again. It gave us time to rehearse our story and they bought it. They mentioned you, Luke, so they know your name somehow, but they have no evidence as long as Vince and I keep quiet. You owe us, Luke, don't you bloody well forget that, mate. Mr Villa, is all this correct about our money, has it all been paid to the developer?'

'Yes, Mark, it has. When we met in the UK before you were arrested, I needed your father's money to start work on the new development. I met Gerry when he was working here many years ago and I remembered him so we set up a deal. At the last minute he left the UK without any explanation so that's why I came to your house.'

'Yes, I remember your visit.'

'Fortunately, Mr Dick Cohen decided to buy in to our project instead of your father. I don't know what changed his mind but as you boys were investing, maybe he felt you had good information.'

'It sounds very far-fetched, Mr Villa, so what exactly have we bought?'

'The project is a new development on the beach front totalling in area about three kilometres of frontage. It involves the construction of houses, apartments, a leisure centre and a golf course. It did include a hotel but that option has not been taken up, as a major group will build their own hotel. Shops and other services will follow in phase two. You boys have been allocated three houses near the beach, as agreed with your father.'

Luke interrupted Juan Villa's speech.

'Yes, but we paid our money to you over two years ago and probably Mr Cohen gave you a large amount as well. What stage are we at now, when will our place be completed?'

For the first time in the meeting Juan Villa hesitated with his reply and his assistant Claude had his head down, almost touching the table.

'Four to five months, according to the builders, to complete the first phase.'

'Who's the developer of the site, can we talk to him?'

'Of course you can. He'll be here soon and I'll introduce you and Mr Lavender to him. You can then ask him all your questions.'

'Good. What's his name and when exactly can we see him?'

'I will speak to him tonight, he is Señor Fernando Lopez.'

Luke's eyes nearly popped out of his head.

'I'm staying at his house! His daughter lives in Valencia with my mother, she's a student. We all travelled from Valencia together and they are at the Lopez house now.'

Juan Villa stood up.

'Yes, I was hoping to tell you first about the Lopez family before you met him. Anna, his daughter, doesn't know her father is building houses for you. I'll brief him about you both when I speak to him.'

'Look, Mr Villa, we have a car here and I'm sure Luke will agree with me when I say that we want to see the building site now. When we meet Lopez later in the week we need to know the exact position so we can discuss it in detail with him.'

'Right, OK. Claude will go with you both. Here is the plan of the site.'

Juan spoke quickly to his assistant in Spanish and the man nodded but didn't look happy as the three of them left the office and walked to the Seat.

Mark put his arm around Luke's shoulder, he was at least three inches taller and he looked at him straight between the eyes.

'Sorry, mate, I didn't know what had happened to you so that's why I had a go. Sounds like you're having a shitty time here, but at least you were free.'

'It's actually been OK. I've learnt new skills like waiting on tables in a bar and gardening, both for cash. As far as the Spaniards are concerned, I don't exist, I live with an old pal who plays football in La Liga and my mum is near. We meet every few days but away from her apartment as it's being watched by those debt collecting blokes. The problem is that even if I had the robbery money to give them, it still wouldn't be enough.'

'Who do you owe most of the money to?'

'My wife. We are divorced but I still owe her money from a place we owned together that I stayed in. We bought it when I was in football and coining in the money. I must owe her shitloads now if interest is added.'

'I remember now, Vince told me before we did the job, but I didn't think it was into six figures.'

'It wasn't, mate, but I agreed to pay interest at 15% as I was sure that I could buy and sell somewhere quick and make money for both of us. But then the market crashed and I got in all sorts of trouble gambling to try to get back what I was losing in the property market. The bottom line is, I reckon now with interest and the debt collecting charges it's definitely an amount that makes it worth the heavy boys trying to collect from me.'

'We've got to find a way to sort that, Luke. Let me think about it and we'll talk over a few beers once we've seen this building site. What's this guy Lopez's daughter like then, Luke, is she fit?'

'You bet, she's a doll and a Spanish one at that. She's 15 years too young for me.'

'Have you?'

'No, mate, she's probably still a virgin – a 23-year-old virgin at that. At least I think that's her age, she's a private young lady and her old man has probably taught her to keep her trap shut. She's a bit frightened of him and in her excellent English one day she told me that sometimes she worries about him and his so-called business friends. The bloke originally came from the region just over the border from France and he still returns there frequently. They may still have terrorists around Irun, his hometown, and I think some of his friends have invested in his business.'

'Bloody hell, Claude, is that it?'

Luke drove the Seat off the coast road onto a large patch of sand, the area was marked out and some houses partly built; the roads were just sand tracks that finished at the beach. A local company, and not the imported foreign labour that were building on the rest of the site, were building the golf course and leisure centre.

The difference was incredible as all the buildings were complete and the sprinklers were operating on the new fairways, the lights were on at the leisure complex and the outside tennis courts had been marked out and looked almost ready for play.

Claude used his site plan and Luke stopped the Seat about 100 metres from the beautiful, white sandy beach. He pointed to a group of 20 half-built houses. The shell of the buildings were just about complete but no more than 25% built overall, the pipes for water, gas and electricity cables were spread out along the sand tracks.

Luke and Mark walked around the framework of their houses.

'These three at the end are yours, Mr Mark and Mr Luke. They are in a good position as they are nearest the beach and they will also be very near the bars and shops.'

'Hear that, Luke, they're near the bars.'

'Yes, but I hope I can live here without anybody hassling me. The progress on these places is slow so it gives me time to think of a solution, we only paid £90,000 each for these houses so hopefully I can sell them for a lot more and try and do a deal with my wife.'

Claude shook his head.

'You're wrong I'm afraid, Mr Luke, prices have gone down and if you sell it when it's finished you may just about cover the purchase cost. I suggest you both discuss it with Mr Cohen. He has bought two houses and, of course, the leisure complex and the swimming pool. You could rent out two of your properties and, Mr Luke, you could live in the third one, then everyone can benefit. They have four bedrooms so you'll get a good rental price or you can sell fractional shares in all the houses, that's another idea.'

'Look, Claude, I really don't get this fractional ownership business. Can you please explain it in more detail? We've seen enough here, let's go to that café near the road.'

Luke spun the wheels of the old car as he left the soft sand of the beach. The café at the roadside was empty and the three men ordered coffee and sat away from the ears of the owner.

'I don't know every detail on ownership, some you'll have to get from Señor Villa. The idea is that most of the buildings will be owned in parts in a share programme. The owners will be guaranteed several weeks a year for their own use and they'll get income from rentals less local costs, etc. This way you get more money from the place, as more people have a share of it.'

'I see, so we sell the houses in parts and get a premium as each owner pays more.'

'Yes, but you need to find buyers or you keep part for yourself if it's only for a few weeks a year. If you want a permanent home you have to keep your houses as they are. Mr Gerry, your father, has given a Power of Attorney to Señor Villa to sign on his behalf for you, so as he received the money from

174

you three it went into a trust fund in your names to buy the properties. It's all been done correctly, we just have to make sure Señor Lopez keeps up with these builders to finish the houses soon as money is getting low.'

'I think we have the full picture now, Luke, don't you?'

'Yes, I'm a bit disappointed but I can still use my house and maybe you can stay with us, Mark, when you're working here and pay rent if you sell yours.'

'I'm sure we can work something out, mate, but first we have to push Lopez to finish it all.'

'Thanks, Claude, it's clear now. Drop me off at my hotel and then phone me later. If you can get me in the house for dinner, Luke, that would be great. Give me the address and phone number in case you can't contact me, I'm going for a swim.'

Mark was excited, the golf and leisure complex was just as Dick Cohen had described and it was nearly ready to use but he knew that the remainder of the development was still months from completion. They would have a limited number of local members in the first year.

This would give the golf course time to settle down before being played every day under the blazing Spanish sun. It would be a drain on Dick Cohen's cash and Mark hoped he could afford it.

He felt guilty for a second or two when he thought about his stolen money and its investment in the property; he would always know that the place had been bought with the money. Maybe he should sell it as soon as he could or at the worst, rent it.

He also realised that he could do very little with the money; if his bank account in the UK suddenly had a large deposit it would leave him open to investigation if anyone checked it. A monthly rental income paid locally could be hidden much easier but then he would need to use people he could trust and they were few. He knew that his new employer, Dick Cohen, would know what to do.

Chapter thirty-four

Ronnie Does Not Sit On His Hands!

'What did the old bill want then, Vince?'

'It was all about Bootle. Did they tell you what happened?'

'Yes, mate, I heard you just happened to bump into him and he fell under a bus. They said he killed my brother Alan and Liz, do you agree with them?'

'Look, Ronnie, I'm really sorry about Liz, she was a great girl, but Alan I didn't know from Adam, apart from seeing him in your shop. I know Billy killed her, it'll come out that the knife used was the weapon he used in both murders and the one he stabbed me with, the bastard.'

'Vince, I can't tell you how fucking angry I am. My daughter was my life and I cocked up big time deciding to live with that tart. If I hadn't done that Liz might still be alive. She was back home with me and all I can think was that somehow he must've got to her to piss me off.'

'Probably not, Ronnie, it was through the shop he got to know her, when she took things in for you. I know you had to give him a job so he took advantage of you, the bloke had serious problems and he should have been put away a long time before. The police fucked up and missed all the clues when he killed Alan. I know that first hand, a sticky one at that.'

'What the fuck are you talking about, Vince, what's all that crap? You knew Alan was my brother?'

'Yes, I guessed he was. Billy and him argued all the time in the shop like a couple of old women, it was then I noticed that Alan sounded like you sometimes. He was on some sort of fiddle with Billy over the bets and that's probably why they finished up fighting.'

'But it must have been something serious that made Billy kill him, or maybe he was just a fucking nutcase in the first place and even worse after a few drinks.'

'On the clues bit, Ronnie, I've got a small amount of help on some inside information. Sergeant Linda Dredge at the police station is a friend of a sort, we'd been going out a bit over the years and occasionally I give her one, or she gives me one, she's a sex maniac.'

'Stop, Vince. Listen, I've got it now. The coppers never worked out that it was Billy who told you when the large drops of money would be coming to the shop. I should have guessed that Billy was the one, he grassed up your little brother, Mark.'

'Shit, Ronnie, did you know it was us? Why didn't you tell the police at the time?'

'Think about it, boy, I was moving money to Spain and I didn't want them checking how much you'd nicked. Fortunately for you and your other mate, I don't know his name, I guessed that he pissed off to Spain with it. Then in a funny sort of way what goes around comes around. Did I say that right, Vince? I'm not educated like you.'

'What do you mean, Ronnie? Speak English mate.'

'What I mean, Vince, is that your dad, Mr Gerry "the spiv" Lavender, and I, did a deal together about ten years ago and my side went tits up. The bottom line was that your father lost about £300,000. He threatened me but your dad was a pussycat really, but a clever bloke. We met, had a few pints and he said one day he'd get the money back from me. I agreed he'd get it somehow but we didn't discuss it any more. I reckon from that day onwards he was planning to do over the betting shop but he needed information so he must have greased Bootle's palm to get it. Then he would get you boys to do it. It would have been a piece of cake for you, but for fucking Bootle. I used to meet your dad regularly for a pint and once a year in December we had a Christmas lunch in The Plough like a couple of old farts and argued for hours until we were pissed. Great stuff and a top bloke.'

'Do you know were he's now, Ronnie?'

'I've no fucking idea, son, other than from what I hear he's not in the UK.'

'We know that, Linda Dredge had a call from him. He wanted to tell her to speak to my mum and let her know he was OK but not coming back.'

'Just for that, why bother?'

'No, Ronnie, she told the other coppers about the call, but she didn't tell them that Gerry said my mother could have everything in the safe, it was all hers now, including the house and cars. Linda went round to tell Mum personally the bit about the safe and I saw her leave. We finished up in the back seat of the beamer. I'll tell you something, Ronnie, a bird in a police uniform was my fantasy, she was a real horny woman and did she go for it. You know something, Ronnie, us Lavender boys are like rabbits and we all seem to have a go at the same women, but this one is different because Mark hasn't sniffed it yet but my dad did, and I did, so maybe Mark is eyeing her up. To be fair, she's used some of the things we told her to further her career, like an informant works, and some help in both directions on bits and pieces. She's useful, Ronnie, and now we have a bit on her it's someone we can trust if we need help.'

'This is like a bloody television series, Vince. If I hadn't got it direct from your mouth I wouldn't have believed you were knocking off that bird. I get so many stories told to me I'm getting cynical. The shit part for me is the death of my daughter. I'll never get over that. I can't give anyone a kicking other than myself, it was my own bloody fault for employing that bastard Bootle and I'll have to live with that one until I'm in my box. Now listen to this, I've an idea, Vince, and will discuss it only with you, just you mate and nobody else, so sit down, listen carefully and give me your opinion.

'One day, I want to leave this country for good. My son is moving and he's got a new job in Canada and is applying for citizenship, so I've no reason to stay here. I like the sun and my idea is to go and live in Spain. I've moved money over there in large amounts for the past few years and recently property prices have fallen, so it's a good time to buy. It won't be a big place just big enough for me and maybe the occasional friend, if you know what I mean. I've a potential buyer lined up and if he comes across with the money in the next few months, I'll sell my business here, pay my taxes then piss off.'

'That must be only half of it, Ronnie, what are you going to do out there? I've seen your idea of a small house, usually that means a mansion.'

'Forget my house, Vince, that's a minor detail in the scheme of things. I've a serious property plan and this basically is how it's going to happen, if I can get everything sorted with these dodgy Spaniards. When I moved a large amount of money to Spain about three years ago, I got robbed. As it turned out, I think someone was watching me go to the bank and like a sucker I used the same place several times. I couldn't go to the police as they would've checked me out here and then the shit would've hit the fan. I was wondering what to do when I was contacted by a bloke called Lopez, he got my money back less a handling charge, the guy who robbed me must have been working for him but Lopez wouldn't admit that. His interest was in me. He knew I'd a lot of money in the banks in Marbella and I guessed his plan was to relieve me of some of it legally, of course, nobody mugs Ronnie Smith more than once.

'The next day after the robbery, we met and he took me to a site he had bought to build houses, apartments, golf course, everything, even a leisure complex. He had very big ideas and when I had him checked out everyone spoke very highly of him. He originally came from the Basque country around Irun, which is quite near the border with France. When he was younger he worked in investment banking and eventually became a top man in one of them, in fact, a Basque-owned company. Under his leadership it became a very successful company by lending money for property development at a time when Spain was taking off, soon to be the top European destination for holidays and in many cases to buy a property.

'Lopez offered me a chunk of the deal on the site, nearly all of the residential stuff. I'm not into golf and leisure, it's not my scene at all. Anyway, after many boozy meetings, and I mean many, we agreed the basis for a contract that my legal blokes were happy with. We shook hands on it but I've only paid a deposit so far. The price I'll pay isn't your problem but it's a lot of money, even more in a market that has gone down, and went down more in the year following my paying the deposit. The agreement was clear that before I signed the full contract for the development, we had to commit to penalty clauses. If the place is late being completed for any reason other then me delaying it, the purchase price would be adjusted based on the delay period, all straight forward. Lopez then got out of his depth and he's now just trying to rescue his own original investment and at the same time he's going to his Basque mates for more finance to complete the development. He's cut costs and corners to finish it this year, if he doesn't I'd take it over and finish it, that's in the agreement, at a vastly reduced price. At the time of buying, I thought I was being clever, but then I realised that everyone along the line in Spain was trying to get a piece of the action, so I got a London company to put a bloke on the case and he's dealing with the lawyer here today, who I think you know.'

'Not Juan Villa?'

'Correct. He was a guy I met through your father, Vince, but Gerry has no idea about building only buying and selling, he was going to invest shitloads of money in it, but then he got cold feet. That was about the same time he did a runner somewhere. As I've said before, I've no idea where he is, but anyway, he did a double shuffle.'

'In English please, Ronnie. What did my dad do?'

'My lawyer guy from London discovered that Juan Villa had bought the land for Lopez on the basis that they would get money in from Gerry, then he went missing so Villa started to panic as the seller of the land was suddenly found dead. He needed money quick and I couldn't believe his luck when Dick Cohen, your dad's accountant, stepped in and bought a share in the development, probably on Gerry's advice, but nobody knows that for certain.'

'You're right, Ronnie, that's what Mum told me as well. My dad said before the betting shop raid that the money we would steal should be invested in a house or apartments here, but not much detail. The third man in the robbery took all the money to Spain.'

'OK, forget that for a minute, son. Once Dick had contracts in front of him he had power. Lopez needed money quick and he still does, but then as the only major investor, Cohen was calling the tune and Lopez had to go along with him otherwise he would have gone bankrupt. As expected, the Spaniard went mad when he was told the news on what had happened, but due to the delays and the recession hitting him in all directions, he reluctantly gave up his prime share in that part of the development. It was the major single part of the complex and Cohen financed the deal, I think from his own funds. The golf course is almost finished and will be playable later this year and the leisure centre will be ready to use.'

'I think I'm still with you, Ronnie. So what's your final plan?'

'Nothing changes. Lopez is still trying to keep to the agreed completion dates but with difficulty. He's plotting other plans but I've a man looking after that for me, he's called Claude Hernandez. He works some of the time for Villa but I pay him as well so we know what's going on.'

'As you say nothing changes, Ronnie, just like when you paid the lads for playing football for you in the park, you buy success but the difference is that was really small league.'

'Yes, Vince my young friend, this is when Ronnie becomes a tycoon. I've made an offer through Villa to buy all the houses and apartments unfinished apart from a few that have been sold already. I told him to forget hotels, that can be done later if one of the major chains wants the risk.'

'Unfinished, Ronnie? You really are mad.'

'Vince, as I told you earlier, I'm not into property just making money. I've a mate from Abu Dhabi who's found me a company that's buying up sites all around Europe. If I play my cards right and it all works out as it should, I can do a back-to-back buy from Lopez and sell it to the Arabs.'

'The bottom line is I can buy everything from Lopez, he then breathes again with his legs still attached as he can pay back his Basque friends. I've to speak to Dick Cohen as I may need his cooperation with the Arabs. I think you can help me with that, Vince.'

'I thought I wasn't here for the ride, Ronnie, but carry on.'

'Well, actually Dick Cohen is a bright bloke and comes over as a kind guy. From what I hear I think he's in your mother's knickers so if he wants to keep in the rest of the family's good books he should help me when you ask him nicely to cooperate with us. Did you know your bother, Mark, is in Spain? He has also been to see Juan Villa.'

'No, I didn't know it was to see Juan, but I knew he was off to Spain to see the property for Dick Cohen. He was edgy when we got pulled in by the police again, he didn't want them to restrict his travel.'

'You're not as bright as I thought, Vince. I thought you'd be asking me why I'm doing a back-to-back sale.'

'What do you mean, Ronnie? I suppose you just want to make loads of money.'

'Yes, of course, Vince, but you're right, I'll have a considerable fortune once the Arab deal goes through. What do you think I'm going to do with it? I can't bring it back here to the UK, that's for certain.'

'You're probably going to do something daft, Ronnie, or you wouldn't have said that.'

'It's not daft it's my ambition, boy. I'm going to put Ronnie Smith on the international football map.'

'No, Ronnie, surely not. Bloody hell, you're going to buy a club?'

'There you are, Vince, I knew you were a smart guy after all. I'm going to buy for cash the Spanish La Liga club FC Lecont. It's a new club owned by some guys from Catalonia who want out, as they need the cash. They have put a price on it I can afford, as it's just for the team and the club, the land and the buildings are owned by the local authority so it's at a level I can afford.'

'I'm too old to play but do you have a job for me?'

'Oh dear, Vince, wake up. Of course I have. We wind up the business here and move to Spain. If you want to keep the place in Sutton do so, rent it out or something. We'll move to the Valencia area and find a school for your boys and rent a place for you all to see if you like it. If you don't you can come back but there won't be a job with me.'

'That's a big one, Ronnie, but what do you want me to do?'

'Firstly, mate, I hear you speak some Spanish. Is that right?'

'Yes, to A Level but I am very rusty. What's the job?'

'We need a local general manager but I want you to be assistant general manager. We'll hire a financial manager and we'll look at the team coach and see if we can live with him, as their current results aren't good. If we don't like him we replace him with someone, maybe from here, there are plenty of good ones that need a job. So that's it, Vince, timescale about four months. Are you with me then, boy?'

'Yes, definitely, Ronnie. I'll have to get down on my hands and knees to Donna but then if it stops me sniffing lady policewomen and dolly birds, she'll be very pleased.'

'Come on, let's go and have a pint. I'll call Claude on the way and ask how Mark got on. Was he meeting Luke Devine in Marbella?'

'Ronnie, how did you know it was definitely him?'

'Unlike the police, I ask around and your mate Luke had been seen with you on several occasions by one of my drivers so I put two and two together. Because he didn't come from this area, our old friend Detective Inspector John Hampton missed him when he asked at your work and the snooker club. You know who probably did know?'

'No, tell me?'

'Sergeant Linda Dredge, she knew everybody.'

'Why didn't she tell John Hampton then, Ronnie? Oh no, not Luke as well? Bloody hell, no.'

'Yes, I know more about your friendly copper than you do, Vince, I just wanted to hear what you said about her but she's a great girl and very ambitious. She needs a good bloke, how about your brother?'

'It's not a great career move, Ronnie, going out with an ex-convict. Try explaining that to the police review panel.'

'You're probably right. It's your round, Vince, and I need all the money I can get now.'

Ronnie was pleased he had some help in the new business and he felt Vince wouldn't let him down. He knew he was a ladies' man but in Spain he wouldn't have the same opportunities.

When Ronnie caught up with Luke Devine he would have a quiet word with him on both the robbery and his brief liaison with Donna Lavender. Ronnie talked like he knew everything and everyone, or he thought he did.

Chapter thirty-five

Anna

As Luke approached the house he could see his mother and Anna stretched out on sunbeds next to the massive swimming pool. Diana was drinking a beer while Anna soaked up the last of the day's scorching heat.

'Hi, you two look pretty relaxed. At least one of us has been working.'

Diana stood up and faced her son. He was very proud of his mother; she had overcome a serious illness and at the same time kept her body shape. Luke was sad for her as she desperately needed a companion but it was not for him to interfere, he had his own life to sort out and it had been a long time since he'd slept with a woman.

He stared at Anna and was captivated by her incredible beauty, she was not small but then not tall, but lying on the sunbed stretched out she could have been six feet long. Her bikini just about covered her, during her stay in Valencia she had grown quite a lot in all directions; her breasts were just about held inside the taut material.

Her legs were her natural colour; both her parents had dark Mediterranean colouring, even though Nancy Lopez was a girl from Essex. Anna was always careful when she sunbathed as her skin got damaged easily but that didn't stop it staying permanently light brown and slightly greasy looking from the suncream. She always needed to protect herself in the afternoons from burning in the hot Marbella sun.

The bikini bottom was as scant as her top and barely covered her small mound of hair. She had come prepared for sunbathing and showing off, not for Luke, but hopefully one of her friends would come from Marbella with spare men; her posing efforts had been in vain as nobody had arrived that day.

'Hi, Mr Luke, you want a beer?'

'Yes please, Maria, may I also have a swim?'

'Of course, no need to ask me.'

Luke stripped off behind a tree, grabbing his swimming shorts from the clothes line where he had left them after a morning dip. Diana had pegged them out for him anticipating that her son would arrive hot and sweaty.

'Did you have a successful visit to the site?'

'The building programme is a long way behind the schedule and Anna's father needs to apply more pressure to the builders to finish, but the site is right next to the beach and it's very convenient for the shops when they are also eventually built.'

Anna rushed to her father's defence.

'Luke, it will all be OK, my father will sort it. I didn't know it was him who was building for you. Everything in Spain goes slow and the building people are the worst, it gets very hot on the beach sites and they can't work most of the afternoons.'

'Yes, I saw that, Anna, there were no signs of the workers.'

'What are the houses like, Luke?'

'Very small, Mum, but they'll be OK for two or maybe three people, that's probably all we could expect from the size of our investment.'

'Well, Luke, that obviously means we can't all live here together.'

'Yes, possibly not, Mum, but the man that is buying other properties from Anna's father is called Dick Cohen, he's English and a friend of Mark's mother, Barbara Lavender, so we'll have to talk with him and see if we can do anything to get a place just for ourselves.'

'Luke, is Mark coming here tonight for dinner?'

'Anna, he's waiting for my call. I just wanted to check with you that it's OK.'

'Yes, yes, go on Luke, ring him now. I want to meet him.'

Both ladies left Luke to swim on his own. He had many thoughts but no real ideas. Like everyone in the house, they all needed someone to enter their lives, even Maria the housekeeper was lonely since Nancy moved to the town, and Fernando was away from Marbella most of the time.

Luke was despondent; he had no house, only a bit of a job, very little money, no girl and a partly built house in a half-built development. He needed a break; maybe Mark had an idea and after today he would get a message to Vince.

The ring of the house phone broke his daydreaming, and Maria answered it.

In Spanish she told Fernando Lopez who was staying for dinner and she laughed at something he said.

'Anna, your father wants to speak with you.'

'Hi, Daddy, how are you?'

She had forgotten and spoken in English so Lopez replied in the same way.

'OK, Anna, thank you. I hear you have three English guests this evening. Why don't you phone your mother, I'm sure she'll come if I'm not there, especially if men are around.'

'Yes, I will, Daddy, but they are young men.'

'I don't care who they are, my dear, I just need someone to pay her bills instead of me.'

'Don't be horrible, Daddy. At least I love my mother, even if you don't.'

Lopez changed the subject. The visitors could hear his daughter speaking in English and he would talk to her about her mother when they met in two days' time.

The language changed to Spanish and the only person to understand the Basque dialect was Anna; even Maria struggled as Anna spoke very quickly.

Anna put the phone down and invited her mother to dinner. She was thrilled, especially as Lopez was away and she agreed to collect Mark from his hotel and be his chauffeur for the evening.

The failure of the Lopez marriage was mainly due to Fernando being so difficult and inflexible on the way he conducted his life; he only had one direction and it was 99% business.

His wife, Nancy, was a qualified doctor and she had not kept up to date with procedures after she married Lopez, as work opportunities were limited. She met Lopez on the Costa Brava in 1980, he was holidaying with friends and she was with her sister.

Lopez had tossed a coin to decide which girl he took out and his friend Miguel got the sister. It was a whole year before they met again but this time Nancy stayed for a month; she had studied Spanish and she was more confident than her new boyfriend, whose English was only very average with a heavy accent.

She returned to England with him and he worked for her father in Essex while Nancy completed her exams, followed by two years' work in general practice. Her father was a builder and Lopez learnt some tricks of the trade, but more importantly, he'd learnt good English, which would be invaluable on his return to Spain.

The wedding in Surrey was a big affair and the couple moved straight afterwards to Marbella. Briefly Lopez worked in the north with his family in Irun. Nancy hated the north and she certainly didn't like some of her husband's friends. Many carried handguns and she could not come to terms with the politics of the Basque area.

After two years in a small house near the beach, Nancy decided to return to work and she worked in a hospital in the town. She was useful more for her language skills than her medical expertise, but doctors were respected people and she fitted into the social scene well.

In contrast, Lopez spent most of the time in the north doing investment deals on property and land with his own father. He was an only child and when his father died he inherited the family business in investment and real estate. His father was not a builder, just a man who could spot a good deal; Lopez had learnt many of his skills.

Nancy and Lopez moved to a new villa built for them on the outskirts of Marbella and she immediately got pregnant with Anna.

Her husband didn't want her to work after the baby was born and this annoyed Nancy. She decided to defy him and did some work and they employed Maria to run the house and look after Anna.

It was a family affair and Maria's husband, Carlos, and her son, Jesus, both worked for the Lopez clan. Carlos was his driver, gardener and generally a Mr Fix-it, his son helped in the kitchen and eventually became a chef in a large Marbella hotel.

After Anna went away to Valencia to complete her studies, Nancy was lonely; her daughter was gone and her husband was all over the country. The new project in Marbella came as a relief at first that he was doing some work locally, but that had a downside and she noticed his behaviour change.

He became aggressive and visits from local building officials were not to discuss the development but to collect brown envelopes. The building timetable was going wrong and health and safety had ceased to exist on the site. Investors were constantly on his case and he had no time at all for his wife.

Nancy rented a small apartment down in the town and took a part-time job at the hospital. The separation was amicable and apart from many rumours, neither had other partners. Lopez wanted her back. When he had finished the local project he would take some time off and would go on a long holiday with his wife to try to rebuild their marriage. Nancy was unlikely to agree; she knew the minute they returned to their villa he would just be the same man again.

Lopez's plan to get a firm completion date was hampered as the building site had virtually come to a standstill. His imported labour was constantly letting him down so in order to finish he brought workers from his homeland in the Basque country; they cost more but they were starting to make progress on completing the first stage of houses and apartments.

His idea to sell everything in the leisure and golf club to Dick Cohen was a masterstroke and once he had received enough capital from the Englishman to finish the houses and apartments, he would cash out quickly. He had the tame buyer, Ronnie Smith, around his little finger. He would just about break even with the deal and then pay almost everyone who had lent him money, but some would lose out on interest payments and unfortunately they were from his own village in the north.

Lopez only discussed his business with Juan Villa, they both knew that big problems existed with the buildings and they would certainly get compensation claims later. To cut costs the foundations had not been dug deep enough. Large, alarming plaster cracks were already appearing and being patched up before they could be seen and photographed.

Luke knew nothing about building but even he could see that the construction did not look right, the cracks on the inner walls worried him but during his visit, Claude could not be dragged into a discussion, he just answered that cracks were normal.

After he finished his swim, Luke called Mark on the house phone.

'Hi, Mark, we're eating at 9.00 pm, sorry so late but that's Spain for you. The good news is you won't need to drive or get a taxi here, you'll be collected at 8.30 pm by Mrs Lopez. Her first name is Nancy and she has a place in town but as Fernando Lopez is away, she'll eat with us.'

'Thanks, mate, are they separated or something?'

'Yes, he seems to be away most of the time so she's moved to the town and works at the hospital part-time. She's a doctor.'

'I'll be ready and waiting, see you later. Oh, Luke, what did you make of the site?'

'Not a lot, Mark. I know we put in just less than £100,000 each, but from what Juan and Claude said, we won't get much of a place.'

'Yes, that was my view as well. I'll ring Vince before I see you and get his opinion as well.'

'Good idea. I need his number, Mark, I have to square things up with him.'

'I'll help you with that and tell him the basics. He's been checking the position of your bankruptcy with Dick Cohen. I think he's trying to find a way to help you, remember he now works for Ronnie Smith and he has the knack of sorting debts out one way or another.'

'Yes, I heard that, but does Ronnie realise that I'm the third man in the robbery?'

'Pretty sure the answer to that is yes, Luke, but as he had something to settle with my dad, Vince says he doesn't appear bothered about the robbery and is only interested in getting over here.'

'OK, see you then, mate, and tell me more later. Look out for a white Mercedes convertible at the front of your hotel.'

Maria had set the table for the guests, she had arranged for her son, Jesus, to cook a large paella, the dish was both Anna and her mother's favourite and it would be accompanied by local red wine.

Luke and Diana sat by the pool. They were dressed for dinner but Luke had limited options for clothes, his finances did not stretch to expensive shirts or trousers and he felt slightly scruffy in his shorts and tee shirt next to his mother's long, elegant cotton dress.

'I'll buy you some shirts, Luke, but not here in Marbella. We'll get them in Valencia, they'll be half price in the market.'

'Mum, quick, look at Anna.'

Anna Lopez was dressed in a stunning evening outfit, the dress was a lime green colour and just about covered the tips of her breasts, and it clung to her curves as if it had been made specially.

Her hair was gathered up on her head and made into an elegant bun complete with a matching lime green ribbon holding it all together; on her feet she had beautiful lime and gold matching sandals.

'Bloody hell, Mum, I see what you mean, she looks nothing like the Anna we see every day, she looks out of this world.'

'Yes, it's a real pity we haven't got a suitable partner for her, Luke, she's too young for you.'

'I know that but don't forget Mark is coming tonight, he'll be all over her like a rash.'

Anna grabbed an orange juice and sat at the table with the couple.

'I love your outfit, Anna, is it from Marbella?'

'No, Diana, actually it's from Paris, my mum and I went there last summer and spent a fortune. My dad's still going on about it as we spent many thousands of euros on just a few clothes.'

'It certainly looks very elegant, I hope you get your money's worth from it. I used to buy expensive clothes when I was married, but many times I only wore them once as in England, if people see the same dress twice they think you only have one outfit.'

Anna laughed loudly, she had over 50 dresses and her only problem on the day was choice.

The white Mercedes pulled into the entrance and Maria pressed the button to open the automatic electric gates. As she drove up the drive, Nancy Lopez stopped for a couple of seconds then carried on.

'Why did you stop, Mrs Lopez?'

'Call me Nancy please, Mark, not Mrs Lopez, it makes me sound old. Didn't you see those two men in the dark car on the opposite side of the road?'

'Yes, but I thought they lived in this road or something.'

'No, there's something about it, Mark. Nobody, other than people visiting us, ever drive up this road anytime, night or day. I don't like it, they must have been watching the house for some reason. What has my husband been up to now? Those registration plates are not from this area. Write the number down on that pad in the glovebox, Mark. Now forget it, I'll talk to Fernando later.'

Anna ran across the grass to greet her mother with one eye on her passenger.

'Darling, how nice to see you. My goodness you look fantastic, have you been sunbathing?'

'Yes, Mum, but just for a few hours. You don't look bad yourself.'

'Go on, say it, "for an old lady".'

'You aren't, Mum. Come on I'll get you a drink, orange juice I think if you're driving.'

'Anna, don't be rude, introduce yourself to my passenger. This is Mark Lavender from Surrey, England.'

Mark was already blushing before he was face to face with the young lady. Nancy was a very confident lady and he could see that she would be a match for any Spaniard, especially if she didn't get her own way. She was very English and left the couple to introduce themselves as she crossed the garden to meet Luke and Diana.

'Hello, I'm Mark.'

'I know, thanks to my mother's announcement, but I knew who you were anyway. I'm very pleased to meet you. Welcome to the Lopez house, Mark, and what would you like to drink?'

Mark had dried his sweaty hand on the back of his shorts before he held her left hand as she pulled him to the drinks table. Luke waved and Mark did the same, he forgot Diana who had gone to get some ice, the meeting with Anna had stunned him into silence and he needed a drink to calm himself down.

Anna asked again as he hadn't replied to her question.

'What would you like, Mark?'

He wanted to say 'you, and now' but he held his breath and spluttered.

'A beer, please.'

'Sure, is San Miguel OK?'

'Yes please, Anna.'

As he said the words his mouth went dry and due to the heat he could feel the sweat running down his back inside his shirt, it wasn't a sexual feeling, which was fortunate as his shorts were too tight around the important areas. Anna's beauty was like a dream, his head was spinning and he almost drank the beer in one gulp as she disappeared into the house to check on the meal with Maria and Jesus.

'Hello, Mark, I'm Diana Devine, Luke's mother. Pleased to meet you.'

Diana was very formal and there was no warmth in her introduction but she was polite. Mark felt she was angry with him, did she know about the robbery? Probably not, so she would not know he had been in jail.

Shit, Mark thought, this was Spain, nobody would know his secret apart from Luke and Juan Villa, but that was too many. How would he tell someone like Anna? He could take her out for dinner and tell her on the first date, if he got close to her he would find it difficult to hurt her later.

Bloody hell, what a mess. He had never considered his prison sentence in this way, he had served his time in jail but he would still be punished again and again if this girl and others afterwards turned him away.

The hand on his shoulder and the cold beer hitting his stomach brought him to his senses. A problem for later and maybe she wouldn't like him anyway; he turned and pointed a pretend fist at Luke.

'It's good to see you, Mark, the locals are all right but apart from my mum and Mario, they all want to speak their own lingo. Sometimes I order potatoes and get crisps, all a bit silly but I suppose it's better than being in nick or having my wife on my back.'

'It's OK at home apart from prices going up all the time, there's plenty of work but it's the higher-paid stuff you need to be trained for. I'm working for Dick Cohen, his name was mentioned earlier today, he's my dad's accountant. Good news is he's in the process of buying the leisure and golf set up, the bad news is I'm sure he's knocking off my mum. I can hardly blame them both as my dad has really done a Houdini act and nobody knows were he is. Actually, though, he could be here in Spain, or maybe it's Portugal, anyway it's somewhere in the Mediterranean, it's got to be.'

'How do you know that, Mark?'

'Do you remember the randy copper, Linda Dredge? She's better than a talking computer. I've seen her a couple of times since I got out and last week the local police pulled me in over the death of Liz Smith.'

'Yes, sure I know Linda. Bloody hell, they didn't suspect you of it did they, Mark?'

'No, Luke, it's a long and lousy story. I'll tell you all about it tomorrow, but regarding Linda Dredge, who by the way is now a sergeant, she was in the police station when my dad phoned to speak to Hampton, he was just telling them he was OK and to pass a message on to Mum. When I had a beer with her she told me that she heard voices during his call and they sounded Arab or similar, I doubt he would have been in Africa, unless it was a holiday. Then she said the phone cut off. It must have been an untraceable payphone as she couldn't get him back.'

The shout from the dinner table stopped the Gerry Lavender story as Maria told them to get to the table pronto as the paella was due to arrive and it had to be eaten hot.

Nancy did the seating plan.

'Luke, you sit here at the end of the table, you can be my toy boy for tonight.'

'Yes please, Nancy, what an offer.'

Diana Devine screwed her eyes up and gave her son a black look. Nancy was not for her son but then she thought if she did get properly divorced and he got involved with her she would have money, a commodity that was thin on the ground in the Devine family.

'Mrs Devine, please sit next to me. As Señor Lopez is away, I'll join you for the meal tonight and explain how we cooked it and the ingredients.'

'Thanks, Maria. Do we eat all of it, it looks enough for 20 people?'

'We eat what we can now, don't worry, it won't be wasted.'

Nancy smiled at Mark who was looking to find Anna and looking uncomfortable at the same time, nobody had told him where to sit and although all but two seats were taken, he still waited to be officially invited to sit next to Nancy's daughter.

'Oh dear, sorry, Mark, sit in that chair. You're next to Anna but she's just preparing the wine.'

Mark sat down at the table and finished his beer, Anna carefully brought in a tray of glasses and poured the wine for everyone, no questions or rejections allowed; without the Rioja, no paella, and vice versa.

Maria served the food and the diners helped themselves to bread and salad. As the Rioja took hold, the table got noisier. Anna and Mark were locked in their own world of private conversation, she hardly ate anything and they both drank many glasses of wine.

Nancy finally stood up as it was midnight, she was swaying a bit and she threw her car keys to Jesus as she spoke and they landed in the flowerbed.

'Thank you all for coming here tonight. You must stay until Lopez arrives. He will be annoyed, we have had such a good evening. I think I'm drunk, which is unusual, so I must be relaxed in your company. Mark and Diana come and see me in town. Ring tomorrow but not early, my headache will not go before the afternoon. Thank goodness I'm not working.

'Mark, you stay here, the night is young. Get Maria to put some music on, you and Anna can dance or something. So sorry, everyone, I really am pissed. See you all tomorrow, what day is it?'

Nobody replied as she momentarily composed herself to kiss everyone twice except Maria and her driver, Jesus; poor Luke was smothered by her scarlet lips. Diana frowned at her on the second time around; Nancy noticed and tapped his head and said sorry. She then leaned on Jesus to regain her balance before carefully kissing her daughter and Mark like the lady of the house she was, once upon a time.

Jesus helped her into the Mercedes and as they drove away, the car seen earlier reappeared and parked across the road, it didn't follow them and it was obvious that it was not Nancy they were interested in but someone else in the Lopez house.

Maria cleared the table with Diana's help and then they disappeared to watch the TV. Anna and Mark were left alone to finish the wine under the stars on the patio.

'That went well, Mark, I haven't seen my mother talk like that for ten years. When my father is here she doesn't say much or drink much either, tonight she was very relaxed, it must have been your friend, Luke, she liked.'

'Yes, he needs a woman, but as you may know, Anna, he owes a lot of money in the UK so one day he has to go and sort it out. Until then he can't be involved with anybody new here or anywhere.'

'I know, Mark, I live with Diana and she told me everything, and to tell you the truth, my father would not allow her to stay locally and take a lover, he would want to help her and show her he is a big man in Marbella. If a house guest let him down he would lose face, which can never happen, he's very old fashioned. What about you, then? You have been the perfect Englishman all evening. When do I hear about the real Mark Lavender? The plant has a lovely smell, do you smell nice as well?'

Anna was drunk and normally she would not ask such questions on a first meeting but tonight was an exception.

'Anna, I'm a bit shy. What can I tell you?'

'You are not shy you just have a secret and it seems like it's one you don't want to tell me. Look, Mark, come on, get it off your chest now, as I think I'm going a bit soft for you.'

'I love your English, Anna, it's so sweet. Don't drink any more wine, just grab two cups of coffee and I'll tell you my story.'

190

Anna nearly tripped up with the hot coffee, she was anxious Mark would not leave or worse, fall asleep. He had no intention of that, except in her arms, but then he knew he had to tell a good story and he knew that would be difficult.

'OK, here goes. I had a great childhood and I have a brother and a sister, a retired father, at least I think he is, and then there is my mother. Life was OK in England until—'

It took Mark 15 minutes to tell the whole story and throughout Anna sat with her hands resting under her chin without showing any emotion.

Her upbringing was coming out as she had been taught to listen; she had seen a lot of action in her family with her older brother being killed by ETA terrorists in Madrid, her father constantly bringing home his business problems and her mother being ignored and held under a type of house arrest.

'That's it, Anna, I'm here now working with Dick Cohen, he's bought the leisure and golf side of your father's development and he's some interest in a few houses. The reason I'm here is to report on the builders' progress and from what I've seen today, I'm worried about the houses which Luke, my brother Vince and myself have a small investment in.'

'It's a big story, Mark, a big story indeed!'

Mark touched her hand. She was shaking slightly, probably from the booze but also maybe from what he had told her in detail about the robbery and jail. She pushed her little fingers inside his in a first gesture of friendship; he turned and kissed her gently on the lips.

She then got to her feet and looked straight at Mark, holding his hands as she spoke.

'I'm off to bed with a lot to think about. I know you're meeting Luke tomorrow, why don't you call me when you've finished and I'll come to town. We can have a coffee and talk.'

'Yes sure, Anna. I've missed nothing out of the story and I hope it didn't shock you too much.'

'No, Mark, when my brother died and my mother left, that was shock. Your story is intriguing but I need to sleep on it, as you English say.'

Mark laughed.

'Yes, that's what we say, Anna. All right, can you get me a taxi, please, to my hotel?'

'No, Jesus is over there, he'll take you. What's he doing hiding behind the car?'

The couple walked to the Mercedes, which was still warm from the journey to Nancy's apartment and back.

'Are you OK, Jesus, why are you hiding?'

'It's OK now, señorita. Some men were watching this house, I've seen them two times tonight and so did Señora Lopez. I've to phone your father and tell him after taking Mr Lavender back to his hotel.'

'They seem to have left now, Jesus, and by the way it's "twice" not "two times" in correct English.'

'OK, señorita, twice or two, they were still here and they didn't look good.'

'Take Mr Lavender now. Have you got your mobile telephone with you?'

'Yes, it's here.'

'If you see anybody, just take the number plate and put it in your phone, we'll get it checked tomorrow. My mother also has a number from earlier today.'

Jesus didn't hang about; he drove quickly to Mark's hotel and didn't wait for goodbyes as Mark jumped out. As he turned into the drive to the Lopez villa he saw a car pulling away from the kerb, he took the number and put it in his phone, it was the same car that Nancy saw earlier and he would get it checked.

The driver of the car had not expected to see the Mercedes again and accelerated quickly down to the main road as if his plans had been changed at the last minute.

The automatic gates closed after he parked the car in the garage. Anna and Maria were waiting for him on the terrace; he took his phone out of his pocket then wrote the number down on a piece of paper and handed it to Anna.

She stood up and pressed a pre-set key in the phone.

'Hi, it's me. They came again tonight and it's frightening. Can you do anything about it, Papa? Maria and I are very worried. Shall I call the police or one of your men from town?'

'I'll deal with it, keep the gates locked until I arrive at 11.00 am. My plane gets in at 10.30 am so ask Jesus to collect me and not in your mother's racing car but in my Mercedes. Don't go out, Anna, tell Luke and his mother I want to meet them.'

'Yes, Papa, but I want to go to town later to meet Mark.'

'You in love already, my daughter? Take it easy, I want to meet Mark Lavender as well, I know his father and also his history. Has he told you about his life?'

'Yes and I'm thinking about it all.'

'You ought to, but remember it's what he does now and in the future that matters. He has paid the penalty and everyone deserves another chance, maybe even with me.'

'No, Papa, definitely he's not working with you, please. Anyway, I'm not sure about him at the moment.'

'Remember, keep the gates closed, don't open them to anyone. Go to bed now.'

Maria and Anna were more than frightened; the visit of several unwelcome male visitors was the start of a series of events that resulted in some men being found dead in Marbella a few months before. This time the car had been seen twice in full view and that meant to Lopez that the occupants were amateurs or they just wanted to be seen.

The previous events resulted in two men getting into the house but Jesus was on his own. They climbed over gates, which were lower than now and flimsy, Jesus had a gun and fired at them so they left without taking anything; two days later two men were found drowned on the beach, one had the Lopez address on him.

They had not come to steal but to get money. Lopez knew why and he used his contacts to have them dealt with but he knew more would follow. It was his number one problem and if it was issue number one, it would not go away until he paid all the men in full who had worked for him on the building project. If it was issue number two, he knew they would not stop until he was dead.

The call from Anna had worried him; his daughter was the most important thing to him since his wife left. He was concerned about Mark Lavender but then that was minor; if more unwelcome visitors had turned up at the villa, that was a big problem. This time he had to catch them and find out exactly who they worked for, then he would know what to do.

If it was one or both of the Tunisian groups that he had sacked and not paid, he knew that he had to come up with money as these men had nothing to lose, but they would need Lopez to stay alive until he had paid them the money they were owed.

The night was already short and Anna did not wake until 10.00 am the following morning with the expected headache cracking her skull. The house was noisy, everyone was up apart from her. Maria had made breakfast for the guests and Jesus had left to collect Fernando Lopez from the airport.

The shriek of the house phone made her headache worse and she covered her ears.

'Miss Anna, the phone is for you, it's Señor Mark.'

'Hi, Mark, how's your head?'

'It's OK, Anna, I drank a litre of water and I'm just about stable now after cornflakes and milk. How are you?'

'Like shit, but it'll get better. I'll meet you in the coffee shop in your hotel about two o'clock for your brief tour of Marbella, then we'll call in and see my mother, she's sure to have a headache as well.'

'Yes, OK. What are Luke and Diana doing?'

'No idea. Other than Maria, I haven't seen anybody else in the house but their rooms are empty. I'll find out where they've gone, see you later.'

The abrupt end to the call was due to Anna being sick, she just got to the toilet in time. She only had about half an hour before her father arrived and she had to look better than she felt.

'Maria, I've been sick so I'm going to have a shower before Señor Lopez arrives. By the way, where are Diana and Luke?'

'They used the Seat car and have gone to see the building site. They said they'll be back here by midday.'

'That's good, I have to talk to my father before they arrive.'

Anna's warm shower was completed in double-quick time with a short blast of cold water over her body at the end. She looked at herself in her long bedroom mirror. She was proud of her figure apart from her breasts; they were a good shape but quite small. She knew that would be temporary until she started to have children and the meeting with Mark had already made her broody. She finished dressing and was beginning to feel normal again when she heard the noise of a car pull up outside the house.

'Anna, come here for a very big hug, it's over five months since I saw you, how's life in Valencia?'

The girl loved her father deeply but she worried about his business contacts, his early life had always included violence and she knew that he had many enemies. Her mother never succeeded in getting the truth from him, the family had lived in fear permanently since her brother was killed by an ETA terrorist bomb attack in Madrid.

The circumstances of his death were unclear and the inquest conclusion was death by terrorist action. The Guardia Civil interviewed Fernando Lopez but in his grief he was less than helpful, the boy's death would put a cloud over his family for ever.

Nancy Lopez blamed her husband for his death, the reason he was in Madrid that day was family business and Fernando was not specific as to what that was, to both his wife or the police.

Anna was in England staying with her mother's family when the death occurred; she rushed back to Madrid to be at her parents' side as the boy was buried.

Demonstrators marred the funeral service and the ceremony was cut short; questions were then asked as to whether the son of Fernando Lopez was an innocent victim of terrorists, or did the boy work with ETA, was he maybe one of them?

'OK, my dear, I've been updated by Jesus about our visitors in the car. I've arranged for someone to watch for them and then find out who they are. The odd thing is that the car number Jesus wrote down we checked out, it's a Hertz rental car. Local men don't use hire cars.'

'Have any of your guests from Valencia still got a problem? Maybe it's your friend Luke they are following. We slowed down that car you said was following you so what I want to know is who do they want, your guests, you, or possibly, but unlikely, just me? The car following you was a Mercedes so my guess is they are private investigators from Valencia. My enemies are usually more subtle and don't confront me near my house but maybe this is a change of tactics from those Tunisian guys.'

'Luke Devine has financial troubles in England due to his divorce and if the car is hired it could be someone from London chasing him for money.'

'Well, I don't want them here, Anna. Ask Mrs Devine and her son to leave tomorrow, no better still, today. I'll talk to them. When are they back?'

'You can do it now, Papa, they're here.'

Fernando disappeared to get a clean shirt as Anna waited to greet her visitors.

Luke drove the Seat to the front of the house in the shade and left the windows open, the air conditioning had broken down and the vehicle was like a greenhouse inside.

'Good job I found our way back so quickly, I'm roasting. What did you think about the site, Mum?'

'It will be a great site when it's finished but I didn't like the look of those cracks in the walls. It's also no good for us unless you can manage to get a house without other people involved. We need something permanent, Luke, not a holiday home.'

Luke nodded in agreement as he left the car and climbed the steps to the front doors of the villa. They had been seen already and Maria opened the door from the inside and Anna shouted for her father to join her on the terrace.

The big man greeted them like long-lost friends to his house, giving the middle-aged Diana Devine a second look. It was a long time since Nancy left and he had a partiality for English ladies.

'Hello, it's my pleasure to officially welcome both of you to my house. I'm sorry that I wasn't here last night, I was working in Northern Spain but I hear that you had a bit of a party?'

'Thank you, Señor Lopez, we're grateful to you for letting us stay here and also for the meal last night, tomorrow we'll return to Valencia.'

Fernando's embarrassment had been saved, he wanted to talk more with them both but he was pleased he hadn't been forced to tell them to go.

'Why such a short visit?'

'We had hoped the investment Luke made here would give us a home to live in permanently, but it seems that won't be the case and I don't have enough savings to pay more or even rent one of the houses.'

'Sit down, let's have some lunch. Anna, a beer for Luke and me. What would you like to drink, Diana, is it OK to call you that? Call me Lopez, everyone else does?'

'Yes please, call me Diana and I'll have a beer as well, thank you.'

Lopez liked Diana Devine and he was already thinking of a way he could help her but he needed to know about Luke's problems first.

'Luke, I'm a very direct man so I know you have some difficulties. I may be able to help you a little, as we did when Jesus slowed the car down that was following you. Please tell me exactly the problem you have with these people who have been following you from Valencia.'

'My wife divorced me and we agreed to divide the value of the house and any money we had between us 50/50. We split the money half each immediately but the house was in my name and it took a long time to sell. In the meantime I spent more than my share of the house. In fact, I was stupid and spent nearly all of it gambling. My job had finished and I wasn't earning anything. The only real money I had left was from a deal I did with two friends and I decided to take it and get out of the UK, then stay with my mother in Valencia until things calmed down. But it got worse and my wife has made me bankrupt, so maybe it's the debt collecting guys trying to recover what little money I've left. I live with Mario, an old mate from my football playing days, and apart from my mother and Anna, nobody knows where I'm staying. I only see men watching me when I'm near my mother's place.'

'Yes, I understand. We've had some visitors watching the house, which is bad. It can't happen here, Luke, if they're after you, but then it may be for other reasons they're here.'

'Sorry, Fernando, I fully understand and that's why we'll be leaving tomorrow.'

The explanation from Luke had given Lopez time to appraise the situation, or at least to carefully study the lady. He had already made his mind up that he wanted to get to know Diana much more and not from Valencia.

'Diana, apart from your apartment in Valencia, is there any reason why you should live there? Anna returns here soon to live in Marbella permanently, so then from what you tell me you'll need someone else to stay with you, a lodger I think they call it in England. Why not rent one of my houses? I'll look at the figures on a place here. Maybe we can rent one for you and Luke. I don't have a specific job for you but if you're flexible I'm sure something is possible on the building site, painting or digging.'

'That sounds great, Lopez, but I have to sort out these debt collectors.'

'Yes, I know that and I have to talk to a friend or two, there could be a way to do it. Drink your beer. How is your Spanish, Luke?'

Lopez didn't wait for an answer as he moved his seat next to Diana; she already guessed that he might be interested in her. She found him attractive; it was a long time since she had been with a man, and she was already thinking what a catch the elegant Spaniard would be for her.

'Papa, I'm off to meet Mark, I'll meet you for dinner. I suggest we eat in town tonight.'

'All these English visitors, Anna. I hope you're safe with Mr Mark, but don't worry, I've already checked him out with Juan Villa and he said he is OK – he'd better be right.'

Anna could not leave the house quickly enough; she called a taxi and went straight to Mark's hotel and to the coffee shop.

Mark had just put the phone down after giving his report to Dick Cohen, he was planning to visit the leisure and golf course sites that afternoon and he hoped his new ladyfriend would join him.

He felt his shorts suddenly tighten as Anna swept into the shop; she pushed her long hair off her face and gave him a kiss on the cheek. Mark squeezed her tightly and she momentarily put her head on his chest then quickly pulled away, but still softly holding his hand as they sat down.

'My father's home already, he's trying to help Luke work out how to get rid of his debts and also he thinks those guys outside our house were following him. He seems to have his eye on Luke's mother as well.'

'Quick worker your father, just like you then, Anna.'

Silence was the answer. She was desperate to kiss him but she would make him wait, she had only known him for two days but already the Lavender charm was working on her, she could not wait very long.

'Anna, have you a car we can use? I need to go to the building site to see the leisure and golf places which Mr Cohen, my boss, already owns. I think the place is nearly finished but I need to see what stage they're at.'

'Yes, I think the leisure centre is nearly ready to use after the fire brigade and safety people have given it a certificate. The course looks good but you have to see when it'll be ready from the workmen, if we can find anybody to talk to. The sprinklers on the course can be seen from the auto route, which is a good advert for the place once they get the signs up. My father said the leisure centre security fence should also be finished, so hopefully we can find someone with a key. I'll call my mother, she lives only three streets away and I'm sure she'll let me use the Mercedes coupé.'

'Sounds great, Anna. My boss, Mr Cohen, has given me the number of the security firm. Can you call them for me so they can let us in for a look around? We can have some lunch first and then you can tell me about Marbella. Can we also go to Puerto Banus afterwards?'

'Yes, it's not far. I'll call my mother up. Go and get yourself a tee shirt, your skin is so white and the sun will burn you quickly in her car. I'll be here when you come back ready to go to my mother's and we can have lunch with her.'

Mark was beginning to enjoy his working holiday; he knew he was already falling in love with Anna but he had to keep focused on the job that Dick had given him. He needed Anna's help, she was neutral and would explain things for him; Juan Villa told everybody there were no problems with the site when he could see many and in all directions.

He had almost forgotten about Luke, he knew that he intended to look at the house the three of them were supposed to own one day. His brother, Vince, had taken over all the work on the deal, originally set up by his father, who was less than vague about how it would all work.

Vince was naïve, he thought they would buy a house to share between the three of them and rent out, what they had bought was just a share with other investors. The thought in Vince's mind was it would be just a holiday home, Luke hoped he could live there all the time and Mark wasn't interested, other than making sure his money from the robbery was invested.

Gerry Lavender must have realised he had made a big mistake when Mark was found guilty and sent to jail. Gerry had planned the robbery just to get even with Ronnie Smith and he had never thought that someone would frame his son for the robbery, and then only Mark.

Mark pulled on his best tee shirt and shorts, he didn't bother with underwear the Marbella heat was getting to him and the less clothes he wore the better. He was just about to leave his room when his mobile phone rang.

'Mark, it's me, Linda Dredge. Look, Hampton is after you again, the top guys have put a lot of pressure on him and he's going to give you a working over about the other guys who were with you on the robbery. He'll use the fact you're in Spain as his reason to suspect you're out there checking on the money. I suggest you get back pretty quick. If you stay cool you should be OK, but just don't argue with him. Got to go now as I'm on my own phone. Text me if you need to talk. I'll see you when you're back.'

'Yes cheers, Linda, you're a darling. I'll get a plane tomorrow and ring Dick tonight with a story about my parole officer. I don't want him to know Hampton wants to see me again.'

Linda Dredge put the phone down and leaned across to Hampton at his desk.

'He's coming back, John, we'll see him by the end of the week. Do you think he'll agree to my suggestion?'

'I hope so, Linda, if he wants to keep in my good books, or I'll pull in his brother for the robbery.'

Mark was surprised at Linda's call but he had nothing to fear, he had done time and that was the book closed as far as he was concerned.

'Sorry I was so long, Anna, it was a call from my mother. Let's go. Wow, is that the car? You better drive, I'd probably pile it up.'

'Yes sure, press the lever and the hood comes down.'

The warm air hit their faces as Anna blasted the Mercedes down the autoroute. They quickly arrived at the golf and leisure area and Anna parked outside the security fence. A man wearing a hard hat and fluorescent jacket shouted to them in Spanish and Anna replied, slightly raising her voice.

'He's the site manager and at first he didn't want to let us in as he's just leaving for the day, the workers start early and finish about now as it's too hot to work outside for very long. He's gone to get the keys and we have to drop them back at his office later today.'

'He's very trusting, Anna.'

'Yes, but he knows who I am. My photograph was in the local newspaper recently with my father and everyone knows it's Fernando Lopez's project. The manager would not want to upset my father, but we've to wear hard hats for health and safety reasons. Come on, he's leaving and he's waving the keys.'

The couple locked the gates behind them as the man left the site. The first area was the golf clubhouse, it was almost finished and it looked very smart with oak-panelled changing rooms and a small indoor swimming pool for cooling down after a game.

The walkway lead to the leisure centre and the first section was a larger pool yet to be filled with water, more changing rooms and some elaborate treatment rooms.

Mark saw the gym area and without equipment it looked massive, next door was a sauna and steam bath area. The large counters on the veranda overlooking the sea and 18th hole of the golf course was the buffet area for the main restaurant and bar.

'Seen enough, Mark?'

'Yes, I'm really impressed, it's fantastic. I'll call Mr Cohen later and tell him.'

'Come on we'll go back to our private pool.'

Anna laughed as she took Mark's hand and led him back to the golf club house. He thought, surely they weren't going to swim, he had no trunks and she had no costume.

'Here we are, Mark, I hope you're not shy?'

'Only a little, I'm so white, my skin has no tan.'

'I like that you are English and pure. Turn around while I'll undress. When you hear the splash you follow me, I won't watch you.'

She grabbed his hard hat and her own and put them on the ground, he turned around and he could hear her taking her clothes off and putting them into the hat to keep them dry and clean. He heard the splash and shyly removed his shorts and tee shirt placing them in the hat with the keys.

'Hurry up, Mark, it's cold in here.'

All he could see was Anna's head but she was watching him and giggling. He was bigger than average and his well-toned body took away the self-consciousness of his white skin.

He dived into the pool and made a large splash, he didn't quite get the correct angle, and he was worried about hurting his testicles as he hit the water.

'Hi, big boy, come here.'

Mark was shy but in his own heaven. He grabbed the girl around her waist and she wrapped her legs around him, squeezing him tight.

'That's one hell of a grip for a little girl?'

'Yes, I did quite a lot of classes on self defence, but not with people your size. I really love your body, Mark. Please touch my head and put your fingers in my hair.'

Mark obliged and held her out of the water, as he touched her she closed her eyes then put her head on his shoulder. He pulled her up and planted a big kiss on her lips, she made no attempt to break away from him as she moved her lips to his neck and her hands to the back of his head.

The couple were lost to the world and not prepared for the massive noise from the car park outside the complex gates.

'What the hell was that, Anna?'

'It sounded like an explosion. We need to get out of here quick.'

They climbed out of the water and shared an unused towel conveniently left by one of the builders. They dressed before going to the front entrance.

The flames and smoke were already 50 feet into the sky and as they walked up the path they could see Nancy's Mercedes was no longer a car –

the explosion was the petrol tank and the vehicle had turned into a total wreck as the upholstery melted, leaving just springs and twisted red-hot metal panels.

'Stop, Anna, don't go near it, we don't know what happened. Cars don't blow up on their own, someone must have done it.'

'I'm frightened, Mark, do you think somebody was trying to kill me or both of us?'

'I don't think so, the car was empty and there was no sign of us. I think someone was just sending a message, but to who, Anna? Listen, what is that noise coming from the autoroute?'

'It's the police and fire trucks.'

Anna unlocked the gate as the firemen soaked the car in foam then water, leaving just a lump of metal with smouldering rubber.

The two policemen took all the details; they knew Anna Lopez and the family so most of the formalities were completed without questions until they asked Mark for his identification.

All he had was his slightly damp photo driving licence; his passport was in the hotel safe with his flight tickets and euros that Dick Cohen had given him.

'They're interested in you, Mark, why do you think that is?'

'I need a beer, Anna, then we can talk. Can you get us a lift or is that being cheeky?'

She turned to the senior policeman and asked him in Spanish if he had any more questions, she explained that they had been swimming and they had lost everything in the car, which wasn't strictly true, but good enough to get them a lift to Marbella.

The second policeman then surprised Mark by speaking to him in perfect English.

'Yes, someone from England is asking us questions, Mr Lavender. As far as we can see you haven't committed any crimes here so you're welcome in Marbella. Our information is that when you get back to the UK you go and see your usual contact, he's been checking that you're here for some reason. As I've explained to Señorita Lopez, someone put a crude bomb in your car. Sorry, señorita, your mother's car. It was probably just a lighted cloth dropped into the fuel tank. Someone didn't like you or maybe didn't like your mother. In any case, we'll be checking some possible suspects. How long are you in Marbella for, señorita?'

'Just a few more days. I'm studying in Valencia and need to return to the college.'

'And you, Mr Lavender?'

'On the first flight to England would be a good idea, but I've still to check some building information for my boss but I'll leave as soon as I can.'

'We'll take you to Señora Lopez's apartment now and I think Señor Lopez will join us as well. Please get in the car.'

Anna grabbed Mark's hand as they were shown to the back seat of the police car. The fire truck had finished and a pick-up lorry decided the car was too hot to take to the police inspection area.

The English-speaking policeman turned to the couple.

'We will not have the wreck of your mother's car until later today, señorita, but I suggest you tell her to get the insurance people here. Although there is very little to see, they need to be told. Did anybody know you were coming here?'

'No, definitely not, the only person we saw was the site manager. His first name is Pepe and I don't know his family name, he let us in and I've to return the key to his apartment.'

'We'll do that for you, señorita, please give me the key, we can talk to him.'

The journey back to Marbella was quiet, nobody spoke. Mark and Anna were in shock, the policemen kept looking at their watches as they were near the end of their shift.

Nancy Lopez was on the front step of her apartment and Fernando Lopez was just arriving. He rushed to his daughter, ignoring everybody else.

'Anna, my darling, are you OK? Come here.'

She hugged her father then went back and stood next to Mark.

'We heard what happened, did you see anyone at all?'

'No, Papa, we were swimming in the new pool when we heard the explosion but we didn't see anybody other than Pepe.'

'Nancy, have you upset anybody recently.'

'Don't talk rubbish, Fernando, you know this'll be down to one of your *nice* friends. Remember that's why I live here and you are somewhere else.'

'Shut up, Nancy, the kids could have been killed, don't you understand that?'

The policeman interrupted.

'Please, everyone, we have a serious crime to solve and we need everyone to help us. We'll get a report on the car tomorrow so please can we all meet at the police station at 3.00 pm. In the meantime, we'll follow our own ideas. Can we have a word with you on your own outside please, Señor Lopez?'

The policemen said their goodbyes and Fernando followed them outside.

The senior policeman took Fernando Lopez to his car and closed the door.

'Do you know who it was, señor?'

'Not who it was but I've a good idea who sent the arsonist.'

'It's not a professional job and our opinion already, señor, is that it was someone sending you or Señora Lopez a warning. Can you find out who it was and deal with them, or do you want us to deal with it for you?'

Lopez was well known and had many police friends in Marbella. They knew his connections in Northern Spain but they warned him that they would not tolerate terrorism in Marbella.

'Yes, as usual it's a question of money, I'll sort it. These guys can't get to me so they use my family to send me messages. I'll kill them.'

'We would prefer you not to do that, señor, but if you do, please not here in Marbella. Just one other thing, do you know your daughter's boyfriend has been to prison for armed robbery?'

'Like hell I did. Are you sure?'

'Yes, the English police want to see him about something but they say it isn't serious enough to put him on a plane immediately. He's been to prison for two years and they say it's the other people in the robbery that they're still looking for.'

'Thanks for that, I'll speak with him.'

The atmosphere in Nancy Lopez's apartment was very tense. Anna and her mother sat on the large settee and Mark sipped a beer as Lopez made several phone calls then returned to the room.

'I'm sorry, Nancy, I've a good idea who this was, it's small time and probably the same people who watched the villa. At first I thought the men outside were after Luke Devine but when Jesus checked the hire car, it was rented to one of the guys who worked for me on the new houses. They messed up on the building site and were all sacked. They think I should pay them – I will, but not what they want.'

'So they aren't terrorists like the ones who killed our son?'

'No way, Nancy, I would be dead by now. They just saw your car and followed it to the golf course.'

'This is going to cost you, Fernando, that Mercedes was a dream car. I want a new one.'

'Sure, Nancy, anything you want.'

'Even a divorce then, Fernando? I've waited over three years.'

Anna started to cry and her mother hugged her. The comment was not for her daughter's ears and she was sorry she said it.

'Another day for that. I want to talk to Anna and Mark on my own. Go to the Hertz place and get a car for a month. Go now, please.'

Nancy knew the sign in her husband's manner, he was concerned about something and it wasn't her wrecked car. She grabbed her handbag and left the apartment.

'Mark, the police told me about you. Does Anna know?'

Mark went red and bowed his head.

'No, señor. I'm sorry this is our first meeting, please let me tell you what happened.'

'I was really short of money over two years ago and with some friends we robbed the local betting shop. My father gave us the plan and it worked except we didn't know that the CCTV recorded outside as well as inside the shop. I was just the driver. The police couldn't get any evidence on my mates and I wasn't going to tell them anything. I got sent to prison and I came out a few months ago. The worst thing was that I was grassed up, which means someone told the police it was me. With the CCTV evidence, I'd no chance of getting away with it. When I got out of jail, Dick Cohen, who I think you know, gave me a job and that's why I'm here. I'm angry with myself, I found out who grassed me up and he had an accident and is dead.'

'Was it an accident?'

'Yes, definitely. This bloke stabbed my brother with a knife then turned to run away, slipped, and was run over by a bus.'

Lopez laughed and Anna scowled at her father.

'Look, Mark, I've met your father a few times and he's a good guy. I'd like to meet him again but he seems to have gone missing.'

'Yes, we think he's OK as a friend had a message that he's all right but not coming back to England.'

'You said your father gave you the plan to rob the betting shop, that doesn't sound like him, unless there was something else connected to the robbery.'

'Yes, Fernando, the shop was owned by a bloke who cheated him out of some money. No, not cheated really, just a slight misunderstanding. All the money we got is here in your property.'

'Don't tell me you robbed Ronnie Smith? What a joke.'

'How do you know that, Fernando?'

'He's been here and we may do some business and he did mention about the robbery but then laughed, he must've known your father was behind it.'

'So, young man, do I trust you as a potential son-in-law, or not?'

'Papa, we have only just met and we are just friends.'

'Yes, yes, I know that, Anna. Why don't you marry the boy one day? He'll look after you, just look at the size of his chest and arms, he'll make a good husband and a father for your many children. Now call up Maria and tell her we'll all eat at my house again tonight, but this time with me as well. We can have a good talk about things. Even invite your mother, Anna. Probably a good idea to ask her not to go on about cars all evening. Check out of that hotel, Mark, and stay with us and I suggest you get a flight back to England the day after tomorrow. Dick Cohen will be pleased to hear about his lovely golf and leisure complex. I'm going to make a few enquiries about the accident with the Mercedes so I'll see you later.'

Chapter thirty-six

Plans

A stressed Jesus and his mother, Maria, produced another delicious meal of roast lamb for the guests. Fernando was the perfect host; Mark and Anna were inseparable and were looking into each other's eyes all evening.

'Mark and Luke, come with me, please. We'll go and drink some good Spanish brandy in my study.'

The instruction was obeyed; the three men went into his private room and he closed the door behind them, he reached for the brandy bottle then filled three glasses half full and passed two of them to his guests.

'I assume, Luke, you're number two in the robbery, who's number three?'

'Pretty good, you guessed right, Fernando. As you seem to know everything, it won't surprise you to learn that my brother, Vince, was number three.'

'It does surprise me. You must be joking! Isn't he now working for Ronnie Smith?'

'Yes, we all know that but Ronnie doesn't care and Vince was out of a job, they seem happy enough together. Are you involved with Ronnie Smith in a big way, Fernando?'

'He's a very important part of my future plans. Ronnie wants to buy everything he can from me but I need to finish as much of the housing quickly, then get the roads in, before he finally buys or I'll have to reduce the price dramatically.'

'So, Fernando, please tell us, who owns what today?'

'OK, but this is only for your ears and I want to talk more about an idea for Luke in a minute. My company owns everything apart from the golf and leisure complex, which Mark's boss Dick Cohen owns. He paid me outright for that and the place is nearly finished, he got a very good deal as I needed the cash. The remainder of the site consists of houses, apartments and later someone can build a marina with bars and restaurants, but not me. Nearly half the properties are going to be sold as timeshares or fractional shares, the owners will either rent the places or use them as holiday homes. They weren't really meant to be for permanent residents but the market has changed. The problem I have is that in some of the early houses and apartments the walls are cracking, the foundations are too shallow and the builders have been sacked. I'm sure the people who watched our house from the hire car and also set fire to Nancy's car are Tunisians. I'll pay them off soon, after receiving the next payments. The bottom line, you will be pleased to know, is that Ronnie Smith wants to buy everything, excluding, of course, the golf and leisure and any properties already sold. That includes properties which are unfinished. He will get lease and service charge income as he will own all the land and even the marina site, which I can't afford to build.

'So that's the simple story. I don't know why Ronnie Smith wants to buy, it's costing him a load of money but he's keen to close the deal soon. I won't make much on it, if anything. It's been a big expensive lesson for me. I owe a lot of my friends money from the development and they won't get as much profit as I promised, if any at all. I may sell up and get out of Spain. Any questions?'

'Can the houses with cracks be repaired?'

'Yes, of course, and we've put money into that but people get nervous when they see cracks you can get your hand in. We will put them right or sell them off cheap.'

Luke coughed.

'Why do you want to leave Spain and retire, Fernando?'

'My son was murdered in Madrid in 2008. It caused me many problems with my wife as his death was due to the actions of a terrorist group you may have heard about. My wife thinks that my son was a member of ETA because I once was. She's wrong, he wasn't a member but she will not accept it. He had gone to a rally in the city as a spectator and ETA exploded a bomb.

'I come from Irun in the north and my family were once all involved, but now I'm finished with all that. I do financial business in the area but it's time now to sell up and retire. I have a heart problem but don't tell Anna, she doesn't know about it.'

'So you mentioned you want to help me, but you hardly know me?'

'Your mother has been good to my daughter, Luke, she deserves some good fortune. I will speak with Juan Villa tomorrow and suggest that the money you three boys have paid in is put into one house, a much bigger one than originally planned for you and then you have room for Mark and his brother when they visit or even stay.

'Diana can live there with two extra bedrooms that can be used for holidays as you originally planned, so a five bedroom house is the ideal, near the shops. I'll get Ronnie to exclude it from his deal. You'll have to pay some ground rent and service charges to him, but I won't charge you any more for the property. How does that sound? Luke, I hear there's probably a job football coaching at the leisure complex but you'll have to talk more to Mark about that. You guys don't have enough money to have separate properties so you have to work it all out between yourselves.'

'That's brilliant, Fernando, but first I have to get those guys off my back regarding my bankruptcy in the UK.'

'I suggest you ask Dick Cohen about that, I'm sure those debt collectors are looking for a deal. You need to check what's going on. I discovered the people watching my house and setting fire to the car are almost certainly not after you. Can I now talk with Mark alone? Arrange to go back to Valencia as soon as you can so Diana can put her apartment up for sale. Keep your nose out of trouble and then talk to Juan, he'll tell you what to do about the house. You'll both have to speak with Vince Lavender as you'll need his agreement as well.'

Luke was beaming as he left the study, he would ring Dick Cohen from Mark's phone and tell him the story. Things were looking up for him and he was also convinced Fernando was after his mother.

'Mark, you know the most precious thing in my life is my daughter. Whatever happens between you two is OK provided she doesn't get hurt. If you can work something out with her, good luck to you both. She doesn't seem too concerned about your history, she must have seen something else about you she likes. I think you're planning to move to Spain maybe, and work here for Dick Cohen. Just make sure you clear everything with the UK police otherwise they'll never leave you alone. Off you go and join the others. I have to ring Ronnie Smith and ask him when he's coming to finalise matters.'

'Thanks, Fernando.'

Mark almost ran from the study. He wanted to get away from Fernando before he got asked more awkward questions; he was burning for his daughter and just hoped he hadn't screwed it up telling everyone his history.

He knew that he had no choice but to come clean and tell the truth, at least now she knew he'd been to jail and if she wanted him she knew what he'd done.

As on the previous evening they again fell into an alcoholic haze. Nancy disgraced herself and fell in the pool and had to be rescued by Jesus. Fernando changed his seat several times until he got next to Diana and he was there to stay, Mark and Anna were now openly lovers holding hands and whispering to each other.

Luke had drunk many large glasses of brandy and he staggered to his room, falling onto his bed fully clothed, and immediately went to sleep.

'OK everyone, it's bedtime. See you all tomorrow. I think we're all going to be working on our travel arrangements so I suggest we meet here for a final supper at eight o'clock.'

The table cleared and Fernando went to his room. Within minutes he had taken the back entrance to Diana's room. She didn't protest as she knew he was coming. What could she do? It was his house and she had not had sex for a long time. Fernando had a lady in every port, but usually the kind that needed paying. Diana would not be paid but he would still try his best to please her.

Anna had hardly drunk all evening as she was worried about Mark and his history but she had succeeded in putting negative thoughts to the back of her mind.

He had explained clearly what had happened and although it was wrong, he deserved another chance. In her father's world he was almost a hero.

The couple sat on a bench outside Mark's room, he had checked out of the hotel and Anna had arranged for him to have the best suite, one reserved for special guests only and in a separate wing away from the main house.

'You know we never have a dull moment here, Anna, it was a shame about your mother's car but at least nobody was hurt in the fire.'

'From what my father said I don't think they would have set the car on fire if we'd been in it, they are not killers just simple people wanting paying. It's sad, really, but they simply didn't have the skills for the jobs they were given. My father tried to do the job cheaply but he got it all wrong and now he's paying for it. Do you trust Mr Cohen? Is he your father's friend?'

'Yes, he's his accountant. His wife died from cancer two years ago and since my father disappeared he's been seeing a lot of my mother, but yes, I do trust him. Why do you ask that question?'

'The golf and leisure complex is a big project and it'll take a big and qualified team of staff to make it work. I just hope he sticks with it and doesn't sell to that man Smith.'

'No, I'm sure he would never do that and Ronnie Smith wants the rest of the development for something. I've a hunch that it's not just to earn from renting and the ground leases, we may find out via Vince. I'll tell him about all this, but then he may know about it already.'

'Mark, I've just made a big decision.'

She held both his hands and looked him in the eyes and gave him a deep kiss.

'What is it?'

Mark was concerned that she had decided he was too much of a risk.

'I'm going to my room to pack my small overnight bag.'

'Where are you going at this time of night?' said a concerned Mark.

'Only to your room, my friend. I'm going to sleep with you and you are going to make love to me until we're exhausted. Go and have a shower, I'll follow you in ten minutes. Don't worry, everyone is asleep. I'll leave at eight o'clock in the morning before anybody gets up.'

Mark was stunned, she had just taken over the romance and pushed it into top gear. His erection was almost visible as she left for her room and his testicles were aching for relief.

Was this really happening, he thought, or was he dreaming? If she turned up he would know it was no dream. She turned up in exactly ten minutes and she didn't leave until the next morning.

Fernando had similar success but fell asleep after ten minutes' lovemaking. Diana was relieved that he fell asleep, she was pleased to have him but the overweight Spaniard was puffing and blowing like a steam engine; she was concerned that he might have a heart attack.

If this arrangement was going to continue when she arrived in Marbella, he would have to get fit and that would be the condition of any liaison. This would be new ground for Lopez but she didn't know then that better fitness might later save his life.

Chapter thirty-seven

Police

Detective Inspector John Hampton paced up and down his office.

'Yes, I think he's back in the country now, John, but I'll call him later to check.'

'We need to talk to him, Linda, so we can sort out the plans.'

'Why don't we arrange to meet him in The Plough tomorrow lunchtime? He'll be over his jet lag by then.'

'Don't be silly, Spain is only two hours ahead, Linda, it's not bloody Australia.'

'I know, I was just teasing you, sir. But really, regarding the robbery, we only have the loose ends of who his partners in crime were, the superintendent doesn't seem too bothered about it, so why should we worry?'

'Yes, I see what you mean. We've got all the reports now from Oliver Hill, our happy local pathologist. He's confirmed that after further examinations, Billy Bootle's knife was definitely the murder weapon in the case of Liz Smith. That case is now finally closed.'

'What a bastard that bloke was. I reckon, John, that he probably screwed her once and then thought he owned her and she couldn't get away from him.'

'Yes, you might be right. I doubt he'd many girlfriends and he probably wouldn't leave her alone. It's a good job Ronnie Smith never got his hands on Bootle, or we could have had another murder to investigate.'

The meeting broke up at the sound of Sergeant Linda Dredge's mobile phone.

'Yes, of course. I'll be there in 30 minutes, but it'll be official and I'll bring some cakes.'

'Who the hell was that, Linda?'

'It was Barbara Lavender. She is very concerned about something and wants to talk privately to me and nobody else.'

'OK, but is it about her missing husband, the mystery man Gerry Lavender?'

'Doubt it, he's tucked away somewhere and out of sight. My guess is she has had her hand in Dick Cohen's trousers again. But why does she want me?'

'Charming tone of phrase, Linda, but that's what I like about you. In fact, I love it when you talk dirty.'

Linda smiled and left for her appointment.

The Lavender family had been continuously high on police priorities since the robbery and Gerry's disappearance. Gerry's whereabouts, the part Vince played in the robbery, if any, and Mark's sudden interest in Spain, were all in the police files.

Detective Inspector John Hampton was now happy for things to stay in the files and a meeting with Barbara could possibly mean new trouble he didn't want.

Linda could only guess why Barbara Lavender had asked for the meeting. She drove straight to the Lavender house and parked in the drive.

'Come in, Linda, I'm expecting Mark later so we need to have a good talk and you must get away before he arrives.'

'Why, Barbara, what's he done now?'

'No, no, Linda, it's not Mark, it's Vince.'

'Tell me, but you know it's official and I'll have to report anything you say.'

'I know that but I want you to use your discretion as Vince is my son and he's in trouble. I clean for Vince and Donna as well as looking after Shane and yesterday I found a notepad in their bedroom, I was being a bit nosey as it was half hidden.'

She stopped talking and put her head in her hands.

'It's OK, please go on. Barbara. What did it say on the pad about Vince, then?'

'Oh, nothing much about Vince, it was just notes she had written and pushed in her make-up drawer about an affair she was having. It was pretty easy to understand as she'd noted every time she'd been with him in a sort of diary.'

'Stop it, Barbara, I'm not interested in affairs unless they involve crime.'

'It's worse than her just having an affair as it was with a bloke called Luke Devine, a mate of Vince, and this is what was written down: "Call me tomorrow, the robbery money has been used to buy a pile of shit, we need to work on Vince".'

'I see, so this bloke Devine was knocking her off and he took part in the robbery, so I expect the third bloke was your eldest son, Vince. We more or less knew what you're saying but had no proof. Why are you telling me this now?'

'Linda, it's all about my son. That cow can rot in hell. I'm off to Spain for good in the next couple of years. I don't want never to see my grandchildren again, I look after them five days a week and I even still bottle feed the baby as well.'

'I didn't know she had two. Is that right?'

'Yes, Alex is number two. I hope Shane was Vince's and not Devine's baby.'

'I'm not a marriage guidance counsellor, Barbara, but listen to this carefully.

'I say again, we have no evidence to charge your son, Vince, or Mr Luke Devine. I suggest you destroy the notepad. Donna won't ask you for it as she'll then know you've read it. I'll see what I can find out about Devine. My suggestion is to burn the notepad and I won't mention any of this to my colleagues. John Hampton will ask what you wanted, so I'll say an invitation to a dress party, he won't believe me but he'll soon forget about it. I suggest you also tell Donna what you know. It sounds like it was a brief affair and she just needs to tell Devine if he contacts her. Try to carry on as normal and don't discuss this with Mark or Vince. If Devine is in Spain we could get him back, but only if we had some evidence that he was involved in the robbery. If he returned here on his own account we'd have to talk to him.'

Linda Dredge left, her head was full of ambition regarding her job and personal life, she had opened a can of worms again on the robbery that this time she knew could screw up her plans. She knew she had to be really careful when she saw Hampton as she had no intention of letting him know what Barbara had said to her.

She did not know Devine in person, although Vince had mentioned him a couple of times when he took her out. Why did she go out with him? she screamed to herself in annoyance. It was not worth it for just a quickie in the park. She was as guilty as Devine and even Donna.

The lounge bar in The Plough was almost empty, they only had a few customers at lunchtime and Mark had ordered a pint and was waiting at the bar for the policewoman to arrive.

'Hi, sexy, how are you? Blimey, you look slim and fit, where's the uniform?'

'Yes, Romeo, I'm fine and in love, and I'm supposed to be off duty.'

'Don't tell me that I'm in second place again. Does that mean I can't even give you a kiss or two or three.'

'Yes, it bloody well does, but then I need your help, Mark, that may be worth one kiss so come here.'

Linda kissed him once on the cheek and backed away.

'On 6th June I'm getting married. I know it's unusual for the bride to ask you this question but we agreed I'd do it because I know you very well. That is, of course, better than my man would ever know. We want you to be our best man, the wedding is in Cheam at the Parish Church near my parents' home.'

'Bloody hell, Linda, that's a shock, I thought the best man was usually the groom's best friend, do I know him?'

'You sure do, it's John Hampton.'

'I don't believe it! Linda, are you sure? Not John, he nicked me remember?'

'Yes, very sure. We don't want a copper to be best man. John didn't prosecute you, in fact, if you remember, when he gave evidence he put in a good word for you, which got him a roasting from the chief. He was also your friend at school and he talks about you a lot. We know it's very unusual but you were mates and he respects you in the way that you've sorted yourself out. The police are off your back now, you've done your time and it's good to see you working and that all the parole reports are complimentary. If you agree, he'll meet you this week, and you can sort the rest out with him. Mark, this is a really big favour I know, but please do it for us. You know us both well and very few people do.'

'Yes, OK, but two conditions. The first is please don't invite any senior coppers and give me a big kiss before you leave. No way will I screw up again, Linda. I've a new doll in Spain called Anna and I could be doing the same as you in a year or so. This is a surprise but I'm really pleased for you. Bloody hell this is a big one, Linda, come here.'

The kiss he gave her nearly lasted a minute but they broke apart eventually.

'Thanks, Mark, that was lovely. Now I'm off, John will ring you soon.'

Linda left, smiling, she loved John Hampton and she was desperate to have his children. Mark would be a great best man and he would be the talking point for all the guests at the wedding; they all knew he had done time but then everyone had a bit of history, so what the hell.

The comments made by the Marbella police made sense now; they would not have been told about the wedding, just to pass the message on that John Hampton wanted to speak with him and his ace card was to send Linda, he knew he could not refuse the job of best man.

Mark had another pint and read the newspaper, he didn't see the person come up behind him but he smelt the perfume. Two small hands covered his eyes and for the second time within a few minutes he got another kiss, this time on his neck.

The barmaid banged the glass she was polishing down on the counter.

'Mark, for goodness sake, how many women have you got? How about me next, I'm available.'

'No sorry, Alice, I'm fully booked up so can I have a vodka and tonic for my friend, nothing for me, I'm driving.'

Without turning around he waved and laughed at the barmaid.

'You remembered, clever boy.'

'Yes, of course, Angela, I know your smell anywhere. What is it, by the way?'

'It's Chanel Coco Mademoiselle and my boyfriend bought it for me?'

'Wow, Angela, a real boyfriend.'

'Yes, Mark, a real boyfriend. He's not old, young, a footballer or even a film star. He's called Brian and he's a librarian.'

'You are kidding, Angela, not a librarian?'

'Yes, and why not? We've been going out now off and on since you got out of jail but over the last few months we've seen more of each other. He could be the one, he's wealthy or should I say, his family are very wealthy. So you've been in Spain, are you going to live there, Mark?'

'Probably. It's complicated but then it's not. I'm just in shock, Angela.'

'Why, what's happened?'

Mark told her the details of the meeting with Linda Dredge and she just sat at the table with her mouth open.

'That's amazing, it's got to be one for OK! Magazine. Has John Hampton been divorced a long time?'

'Yes, about five years. I think the marriage was a very short one.'

'Why do you ask, Angela?'

'It's nothing, Mark, nothing.'

Mark grabbed her wrist.

'Tell me or I'll put you over my knee.'

Angela went very red and squirmed on her seat.

'Awkward really, but a few weeks ago I was in here and I saw John Hampton talking to your sister, Sharon. She saw me and they did a very quick runner. No idea what they were up to but I caught the end of her conversation and she finished up by saying, "I'll tell my mother".'

'I don't see much of her nowadays but I doubt she is seeing Hampton, she still hates him for getting me put in prison for the robbery. I suppose there is one way to find out and that is for me to ask her. But I'm not worried, Linda is very smart and she'll be watching Hampton closely, it may have been something official between them. I'm off Angela, do you want a lift?'

'Yes, I only came in for some fags, then I saw you.'

Mark knew she was lying. He could smell girls that smoked, the odour got in to their clothes and was the ultimate turn off; Angela did not smoke anymore.

They jumped into the Mini and stopped at Angela's apartment.

'Can't stop, Angela, I'm off to see my boss, Dick Cohen, he's waiting for me.'

'I've something for you, I found it in my desk when I was cleaning it out.'

'I can guess what it is.'

Angela unlocked her apartment and went straight to her desk.

'Here take it, Mark, I don't want it, it's like a hot potato.'

'I'll take great pleasure in taking it to the incinerator at Morden and personally seeing it melt.'

As Mark studied the box she went to her bedroom but rushed back to the lounge before he could leave.

Angela had very quickly taken off her dress, she sat in a wooden chair back to front Christine Keeler style; she had slimmed down, the number of vodka and tonics she consumed had reduced and she was now a really sexy girl.

Red garters held up her stockings and her two-piece underwear had been designed for a stripper, a style to remove in an instant.

As she passed the pub earlier she had seen Mark's car and she saw him through the window. She took a chance and went home to change. When she returned, Linda Dredge was just leaving. At first she thought he was in trouble but she was relieved when he told her the wedding story.

'Oh dear, am I making you late, Mark?'

Mark picked the girl up in his arms and took her to the bedroom. Although comparison was at the back of his mind, Mark fully appreciated what a serious lover Angela Tate was, he was uncertain if she would ever change but then children could do that.

He was not gentle or rough just at a level where she still knew hours later they had been together.

'I really have got to go. Regards to your librarian or perhaps not. Why are you laughing, Angela, am I funny?'

'You are a lovely man and will make a girl really happy if she lets you. Don't make a mistake, choose carefully. I'm working on Brian, he's improving and we don't have any accidents now. The main thing is he'll look after me, as I know you would've done.'

'You're a darling, give me a big kiss.'

They had a short clinch then Angela pushed him out.

'Bye, Mark. Keep in touch but at arm's length.'

He waved as he left and thought the tape was in his coat, he would destroy it later but when he came to look for it in his coat pocket it had gone.

Under his breath he cursed, he had to find what he had done with it, but then events moved on and he forgot all about it.

'Hello, at last, I thought you'd found a woman and eloped with her.'

Mark laughed at the perceptive Mr Cohen. The sparkle in Mark's eyes was a giveaway to the professional man why his employee's arrival had been delayed.

'Right, to work. I suggest we pick up from your phone call, then later I'll tell you what I've found out from Luke Devine.'

Dick listened and commented on Mark's report even down to the arson attack on the Mercedes.

'It's all pretty much as I expected, the sooner you get out there the better. I'll need a local manager, for the time being you won't have a specific job title until we're ready to see where we need expertise. I expect you to be on call 24/7.'

'That's a tall order, Dick. We'll need to clear everything first with my parole officer.'

'I already had an unofficial word on that and he'll probably say that you should fly back and meet him monthly as he originally suggested. Please keep out of trouble, Mark, I can't deal with any nonsense. That plan will also fit in with us, he'll want your address and phone number in Spain and no doubt he'll alert the local police.'

'No problem, Dick, they know me already after the car fire I told you about.'

'Hire a small car from the airport. Try to do a deal with them, tell them about the complex and what we're doing. Ask for the manager and I'm sure he'll give you a special price. Maybe you'll have to offer him some free golf or gym membership but don't do that at first, just say we'll recommend his company. I'll pay you from here so open a bank account, you will get 3,000 euros a month net to start with and I will pay your tax and NI. You'll have to get a temporary one-bedroom apartment until the one on the complex is sorted out, that could cost you up to 800 euros a month. So can you leave tomorrow?'

'Yes, sure, but just one thing, Dick, I'm to be the best man at a wedding on 6th June, is that OK?'

'That's fine, who's getting married?'

'Detective Inspector John Hampton and Sergeant Linda Dredge.'

'What, you a best man at a coppers' wedding, are you bloody mad?'

'No, if you think about it I'm a safe bet, been to prison, need to keep my nose clean so I won't say anything dodgy about them and, of course, I know both of them well. It will be a bit of fun really.'

'Yes, I suppose so. By the way I saw your sister Sharon talking to Hampton the other day.'

'Not another one, Angela Tate just told me the same story. I'll go and see her now or at least before I leave for Spain.'

'Yes, do it now and call me from Marbella tomorrow night. I'll book your flight and send you the booking reference. See Juan Villa and get him to introduce you to that recruitment firm, we need people and the right ones.'

'Thanks, Dick, but quickly, what's the score on Luke?'

'He's bankrupt and must come back here to the UK and face the music. I have no details other than the amounts are not massive, his wife has remarried and she's living in Thailand. Don't give him a job and tell him to call me, he has my number. Off you go, Mark, and don't call in again at Angela's, I think you may have someone new to tell us about soon.'

'How did you know about Angela?'

'You mentioned her a minute ago and your zip is undone so I put two and two together. I'd probably make a good copper.'

'No way, you're too honest. See you soon, Dick, and thanks, I won't let you down.'

Mark pulled up outside Sharon's house just as she was leaving.

'Well, hello, it's my jet-set brother. I was just about to ring you, come in and we'll have a drink.'

'Thanks, Sharon, is everything OK with you?'

'Yes, really good, I got rid of the bloke that moved in here before Liz left. I'm now going out with a doctor, he recently qualified and has been thrown into the deep end at Epsom General, he's learning fast. Why are you concerned about me, brother?'

'Only that I've met a few people today and two of them have told me you've been seen talking to John Hampton. Are you in trouble?'

'No, of course not. Did he talk to you?'

'He didn't but Linda did. Did you know what they were going to ask me, Sharon?'

'Yes, but only the other day. Did you accept?'

'Well, yes, I suppose I did, without really thinking about it properly, but then I know them both and it should be a good bash as it's being held in Cheam.'

'That's good, but John also had a message for us, he asked me to pass it on to you and Mum. Don't look so worried, it's good news, or at least I think it is.'

'Spit it out, Sharon, you're making me nervous.'

'Our dear missing father has decided at last to put his head up over the fence. He rang John and said he wants to meet us all. The word "all" means anyone who can spare the time and is interested in seeing him again. Hampton must have his phone number but he's not telling us what it is, or perhaps Dad just phones him from a public box. Fortunately the invitation does not include the police, so it's just you, Mum, Vince, Donna and, I suppose, Dick Cohen, and, of course, me. It seems Dad specifically asked Hampton to make sure Dick was with us.'

'That's not unusual, Sharon, because Dick is Dad's accountant.'

'The odd bit is that we have to buy a ticket to Malaga without knowing where we're going. I'm told Juan Villa knows where he is as well and he'll tell us where to meet him. Dad specifically said that nobody was welcome to stay with him but he hopes we all go to the meeting, that's the message.'

'It's just like Dad, Sharon, the man of mystery as always. If you remember, none of us, including Mum, ever knew what he was doing or who he was with and this sounds like it's no different. I don't think he's in Spain. I met Fernando Lopez last week, the bloke who is building the development site, he said he was sure he wasn't in Spain and he knows everybody.'

'I hope we aren't going on one of those small planes to Africa or somewhere like that. It would be just like him.'

'Please can you call John Hampton for me and ask him to contact Dad. We'll be there on Saturday. Next, tell Mum, Dick, Vince and Donna that we'll book the tickets, no better still, tell Dick and he'll pay for them, he still has some of Dad's money.'

'Yes, sir. I think, Mark, you are appointed as our official tour guide, sunglasses and insect spray are already in my bag. You're getting very bossy, you know!'

'Sharon, at last we'll have an end to this mystery. I just hope we don't walk into a load of new problems just when everything is settling down.'

'Mark, he's still our father, we have to know what he's doing then I'm sure we can all rest a bit easier, and, of course, that includes Mum.'

Chapter thirty-eight

A Deal and maybe a Divorce

'Yes, I think it's time now to sort ourselves out, Nancy.'

'What do you mean, Fernando?'

'I think we end our marriage. I may leave Spain and you already have your own life here in Marbella without me.'

Nancy Lopez burst into tears and put her head on her husband's broad shoulder. The marriage had been good for the first 15 years then his time away on business got to her. She finally moved out of the villa, the love had gone between them and he was now suggesting a simple exit to the marriage.

'Who have you got your eye on, Fernando?'

She was baiting her husband but in the final analysis it would only be about how much money she would get. He would be generous but the majority of his wealth was invested in the development and he needed completion of the sale before he could cash out.

'I hate it when you call me that instead of Lopez and I know that's why you say it. The lawyers will get the paperwork moving this week and they'll make a preliminary evaluation of my estate with the help of Juan and his colleagues.'

'Wealth or debt, from what I hear you are being pulled in all directions?'

'That's enough, Nancy, we can't afford to go to court. I suggest we meet in four weeks' time and see if we can make a deal.'

'Yes, all right, but don't try and cheat me. I'll smell it if you do and make things awkward. Do you think Anna could marry Mark Lavender? She's said nothing to me but I suppose it's early days. It would be nice to get the wedding out of the way before we officially divorce.'

'You're sharp, Nancy, even where your own daughter is concerned. Of course, I agree, but Anna must make her own mind up. They shouldn't rush as we don't want another Spanish/English marriage failure.'

'I'll talk to her, Fernando, in time for our next meeting. I did love you once you know, and all this makes me feel very sad.'

'Yes, my dear, but you knew what I was like, it was the way I was brought up by my father. You would not live in Irun and that was the big problem. I needed to be there a lot of the time, it's family, you know that.'

'How will you ever get away from them?'

'I don't know, but one day I'll have to risk it, then I must live far away from Spain.'

Fernando Lopez left his wife's apartment. He was thoughtful, meeting Diana Devine had brightened up his life, she had everything he wanted and she was a basic person with very little money or assets, he was sure that they would live together one day.

As he drove back to the villa he was startled by his car phone; he did very little business by phone and wondered who was calling, as there was no number shown on the screen.

'Hello, Ronnie. Yes, I'm fine. Come to my villa tomorrow, Jesus will collect you from the airport.'

'I'm already here in Marbella. I want a meeting tonight with Juan Villa, my bankers and yourself at your place. We'll have dinner afterwards. See you at 7.00 pm.'

The phone went silent, he had no time to protest. He rang Juan Villa, who knew about the meeting already and told him to book a restaurant near his home. He hated meetings over dinner and especially this one with millions of euros at stake.

In the Hilton Hotel, Ronnie sipped a glass of iced Evian water as did the banker. He was excited and the adrenalin was almost bursting out of his veins, he would only drink alcohol once everything was signed. The banker just saw profit and risk in reverse order, it was a black and white situation and Ronnie so far had come up with every one of the bank's requirements but now he needed a little more from Lopez.

'I know the amount has gone up, Mr Smith, but so has the risk. Let's be absolutely clear and transparent before we meet Lopez, we believe he's desperate but if we push him into a corner he's a very dangerous man, my colleagues know him well. You have the schedule I gave you, both in Spanish and English. First is the purchase, you buy everything in the development excluding the golf club, the leisure centre and its surrounding land as marked on the plan. All the houses and apartments built, half built and the land for the next phase is on the plans. There are a few houses not included, they are in the small block of five-bedroom versions which back on to the new marina site. You buy the land for the marina in a separate contract. The houses on the west side, outlined in blue, are already sold leasehold. All the properties, excluding the golf club and leisure centre complex, will incur ground rent and service charges to be paid to you by the owners. The places you are going to rent, timeshare or fractional share, you should include ground rent and service charges in your calculations, and recharge them accordingly.

'As I said to you earlier today, Mr Smith, you have to allow for some rebuild and major repairs, we found some buildings with cracks during the survey and the professional view is you need to make a provision of five million euros for all this work.'

'I know all this, Señor Garcia, as far as I can see it's simple. I pay 20 million euros to Lopez for everything and you provide a loan to me of 15 million. My income will more than pay your ridiculous interest charges and you have the properties under a legal charge in case I default.'

'That is correct, so the debt via the bridging loan to the bank is 15 million. If we can get any more off Lopez, we can reduce the figures pro-rata. You have been up front with all your plans and that's good because we knew anyway before you came to us what you were doing.'

'I bet you did, but you probably thought it was Real or Athletico Madrid I was after.'

'No, we guessed it was possibly FC Lecont. We knew the Catalonians wanted cash so after you met with them the word passed back to us, that's how things are done here in Spain.

'So what's the final deal with them, have they given you more help on the final price?'

'Yes, they didn't want to help but this is how it works now. The local authorities own the stadium and it has no security, just a 40-year lease with the club and with five years left at a fixed rent. In future, it has an inflation-linked fixed-rental increase every five years for the remainder of the period. The lease is full repairing and the club will need to make provision for that. The owners will sell the club to me 100% – see my schedule, everything is listed, players, values, contracts, training ground, etc. I will pay them 20 million using your loan of 15 million and 5 million of my cash.'

'So overall, I'm standing in the middle of a Spanish road investing 20 million and you are providing a 15 million bridging loan. The part of it I think is bollocks is that you want a legal charge for a day against assets of 15 million on the club, this is a back-to-back deal you know.'

'It might be bullocks, Mr Smith, but it has to be. This is 2011 and we can't risk unsecured debts, even for a short term.'

'It's bollocks not bullocks, they are cows, I'll explain later.'

'Thank you, my English, is not good.'

'It's fucking brilliant when it comes to charges and guarantees. My guys in London fly over on Monday and they'll go through all this again, so in my mind the only issue I have is whether Lopez will drop his price anymore.'

'I think you understand where I'm coming from now, señor. It's simple isn't it?' Ronnie Smith was secretly pleased, the valuation on the club was 20% more than he was paying for it; the club was doing well in the cup and attendances were nearly always a full house. They finished third in La Liga the previous season so the income was much more than forecast from this year's Champions League fixtures.

This was Ronnie's big deal, nobody would ever look down on him again as a scrap metal dealer, and the money he had put in the local banks in Spain over many years would now be used as planned.

He decided he would now move to Spain permanently and sell up in the UK.

The work done by Vince Lavender had got him a really good price for the business and Vince would be well rewarded with a £400,000 one-off tax-free bonus, but then he would deduct £300,000 to cover the robbery, no way were the Lavenders stitching him up. Vince complained but knew he had no argument, he had already robbed Ronnie and he laughed at his boss's logic.

He would make sure Gerry knew that he was the loser again.

He had changed his mind about employing Vince in the football club, he saw problems with Vince and women and didn't trust him enough to give him a job in Spain. The bonus was a sweetener and Vince had no choice but to accept Ronnie's decision. £100,000 would keep Donna quiet until they had reviewed their future plans.

Ronnie would now be a top dog in South East London and his old mates would be green with envy. His football team would play Chelsea in the next round of the Champions League; he would be a proud man as he sat near Abramovich.

The Arabs were on board, he had brokered the deal. All he ever had in mind had been to buy a football club, not real estate. His lawyers had set it up that he would pay Lopez, then sell to the Arabs immediately back to back, with some money left in the bank for a house, pension and working capital for the club, he had no debt.

The bank and lawyers had signed confidentiality agreements with penalties if they divulged information on the two deals.

Everyone was a winner, except probably a desperate Lopez. The banks would make a quick profit, the football club owners would get out of the game for good, and the Arabs would have a prime site at a knock-down price, which they would throw cash at to repair and finish, then follow on with their own marina.

Ronnie would get his special dream and the problems that came with it. All he needed now to go with the club was a Spanish whore and his fantasies would all materialise at the same time. He would never learn, but since the death of his daughter he didn't care and his new home would definitely be Spain.

Chapter thirty-nine

Revelations

The British Airways flight from London touched down on schedule at Malaga Airport.

Juan Villa was in the arrivals area with a driver and a minibus outside to take the visitors to their unknown destination. Gerry liked a bit of drama and although some good guesses had been made, nobody knew for certain where they were going.

'That's good, at least we aren't getting on a small bus or plane to some mountain retreat and we can't drive to Africa by car. Does Gerry know I'm coming, as I heard he said family only, plus Dick? Does that include you as well, Juan?' asked Luke.

'I'm not sure if he wants me at the meeting, he's paying me to take you to him. But knowing him, my answer would be possibly yes, it's possible. I'll be a referee, if one is needed.'

The minibus had just about enough room for the Lavender party and luggage. They all grabbed bottles of water from a cool box in the vehicle; the temperature on the tarmac on the short walk to the car park was over 30 degrees and double the UK temperature.

Juan Villa's instructions were clear, that he should not talk too much with the Lavenders about anything, they should get everything from Gerry's own mouth.

'At least we know he's alive, Mum, but can you cope with that?'

'I hope so, Vince, let's wait and see what his story is before we pass judgement, I'm still married to him remember.'

'Juan, is this autoroute the one that goes past the development?'

'Yes, Mark, we'll stop on our way back if there's time. You're booked in tonight at a hotel halfway on the route to our destination. For everyone's information, from this road we can see the golf course in about 30 minutes' time. It's designed so that the properties, and later a marina, are hidden. They mostly face the seafront, as do the last three holes of the golf course. We are planting trees and shrubs, it'll be very beautiful.'

Sharon tapped Juan on the shoulder.

'It's a nice area, that entrance to Marbella is very impressive. I suppose Puerto Banus is pretty good as well.'

'If you have money to burn, Puerto Banus is the place to be seen. But don't worry, Sharon, your father isn't there, once the development here in Marbella is complete with the new marina, they will have some serious competition.'

'When will that be, Señor Villa?'

'The marina site is not really started, other than the sea wall, it needs a lot of work, Sharon, including deep foundations. In today's financial climate nothing much is happening but one day it will, either by the Arabs or Russians, or someone similar. Watch this space, as you say in England.'

'Juan, you will sell the development as well, is everything still going to plan with sales?'

'Of course, everything is well.'

The few words spoken by the careful lawyer indicated to Mark that whatever the deals were, they were almost complete. The leisure centre and golf course would be directly affected by membership as soon as the properties were occupied. The purchase price of the properties would include golf membership with a free first year and the plan was to build a second course within five years.

The minibus drove south until the hotel appeared on the horizon.

'It's got dark really quickly, Dick, I hope we're safe here it's the middle of nowhere.'

Juan Villa's family owned the small hotel; his hometown was behind, towards the seafront. The party were tired and after dinner they all went to bed early.

Mark sat outside in the moonlight and phoned his Spanish girlfriend.

'Hi, Anna, I'm safely in the hotel after a sweaty journey from London. The plane was late and it was dark before we got here. Are you back in Valencia?'

'Yes, everyone's back here OK and it's study time again. I'm worried about Luke he got the message from Dick Cohen about his bankruptcy and he really doesn't know what to do.'

'I'll talk to him tomorrow.'

'Mark, I think I love you. I have thought about your life, your crime and prison. Now provided you remain honest and do not see other women, we can be together. I want you in my life and as soon as possible.'

'Yes, Anna, I feel the same about you, but once we've spoken with my father I'll be happier. I'm not sure why he's been away from us but we'll find out tomorrow, and we can meet up as soon as I'm back in Spain. I'll drive to Valencia for a weekend then we can talk more about our future.'

'Yes, that will be fantastic. Go to sleep now and call me on Monday.'

Mark sat on the terrace of his room drinking coffee and didn't hear the footsteps behind him. His thoughts were in Valencia and the rhythmic noise from the waves had put him almost to sleep.

He nearly jumped out of his skin when a pair of soft hands touched the back of his neck and the smell of perfume was slightly familiar. He knew there was no danger from the intruder. Mark turned to face his visitor.

'Shit, you frightened me to death. How did you get in? What are you doing here?'

'I stay here a lot and they know me, but anyway, all the door locks have the same mechanism. I guessed you must have stopped the night so I found your room number, gambling you were on your own. There's very little decent accommodation in the place we're all going to.'

'You said we, this is beginning to make some sense, so what've you been doing for the last three years?'

'I've brought some brandy. Get two glasses, Mark.'

All he could find on the sparse minibar shelf was two tumblers; he took the brandy and poured an inch in each glass.

She pulled up a chair and touched his glass.

'Here goes, to old times.'

'Yes, cheers. What's your story then, Kate?'

'When we broke up, which was down to me, Mark, I never liked goodbyes so when you were arrested I felt less guilty about putting my plans into action. I got offered a job with an investment company based in Spain and it involved financing property and business for British ex-pats with money to spend, or should I say, money to lose. The deals are straightforward and we invest in funds yielding over 10% gross but medium to high risk. A couple of times I've been threatened as things have gone badly wrong. Fortunately, in the majority of transactions I've done good business and my company has earned a lot of money. So I've earned well and also seen lots of sunshine. That's it really. I've an apartment in the Barbican and I travel here every other week to keep up with my customers.'

'So why have you suddenly turned up here today? How did you know we were all coming? I get it, my old man has helped you.'

'Drink up, Mark, we're going to sleep together. I miss you like hell and I want you tonight.'

Mark could not refuse, Kate was red hot. She was dressed in a short skirt and blouse and he suspected that she wanted nothing that night but sex, he had to find out.

'Agreed, but then, Kate, very early tomorrow you must give me some more answers before we leave this hotel. Now come here.'

He kissed her like she had never been away from him and he picked her up and threw her onto his bed.

'I always did like you when you were rough with me. Don't mess about now, I'm tired and you look desperate.'

Nothing else was said; they made love and then fell asleep together.

When the light broke through the flimsy lace curtains Mark woke up and turned over to see if he'd just been dreaming. The bed was empty Kate had gone and a note was on the bedside table; he unfolded it and scribbled inside in pencil were just three words, 'See you later x'.

He joined the others for breakfast with no sign of Kate, she had already left and there was no one else other than his party in the dining room.

By the door stood Juan Villa and the bus driver.

'Hurry up everyone, please. We have a journey of a couple of hours then a return journey maybe, so can you all be ready soon?'

Vince was the spokesman.

'We'll be ready in five minutes, Juan, but now is the time to tell us our destination so we can prepare for trains, boats or planes, or whatever is taking us to see my father.'

'OK, none of those will be needed. We are going to the Rock of Gibraltar, you will soon by back in the UK.'

Barbara smiled at the news.

'We should have guessed that Gerry wouldn't have left English territory without a good reason and the place has lots of England in its culture. I went there with your dad about ten years ago, even the policeman look like ours at home with the same uniform.'

'Yes, Mrs Lavender, this is his home now. Please get all your passports ready for immigration, they do still check everyone.'

The journey from the hotel was much quicker as the driver was eager to complete his journey and soon the imposing rock appeared on the horizon. The party drove over the airfield, documents were checked as they left Spain and also by the UK border control.

The charm of the island was clear as the bus parked in the old town area; the visitors were shown to an apartment block overlooking the sea. They entered the small lift and went up to the penthouse suite; it took them right into the centre of the apartment's reception area, totally private and self-contained.

As the lift doors opened someone they all knew, even Dick Cohen, greeted them.

Vince took the stage.

'Kate, what the hell are you doing here?'

'Vince, that's a nice greeting from an old friend. Is your ego still as big as that thing between your legs?'

'Just the sort of comment I would expect from you, Kate. Answer the bloody question, why are you here in Gibraltar?'

'I'm not hiding from anyone if that's what you think, but you should be hiding as I hear from a reliable person that you, or one of your mates, terminated the life of the one and only Billy Bootle, the top employee of Ronnie Smith.'

'You should talk to the UK police, Kate, because that's total rubbish. If he hadn't fallen under that bus we would've had a fight. All we wanted was to talk to him but then he pulled a knife and before I knew it he stabbed me, he fell off the kerb in the struggle. It really was an accident, Billy slipped, case closed.'

Kate dropped the inquest as the lounge door suddenly opened.

'Hello everyone, welcome to Gibraltar,' bellowed Gerry Lavender.

Gerry was the same height as Vince and Mark and well over six feet tall but he had put a lot of weight on around his waist since he left England. He had a grey beard and a deep Mediterranean tan; he sat down and put his hands behind his head and smiled at his visitors.

'Dad, what the hell are you doing here in Gibraltar? What happened, why did you leave us? This is crazy, we get this invitation to come here and find you with my brother's ex-girlfriend.'

'Yes, Vince, I think you also knew Kate pretty well once, after all, you are a Lavender.'

'I did know Kate, Dad, but that was before Donna and, of course, Mark.'

'Should I give you Lavenders all marks out of ten, Gerry?' Kate smiled as she said it and moved to the back of the room. She did not want to be in the middle of some difficult questions.

Gerry moved to kiss Barbara on the cheek but she moved away and stood next to Dick Cohen with tears streaming down her face.

Gerry then waved to a lady standing near the door and spoke to her in fluent Spanish, pointing to the large circular table.

'Please, all of you sit down. I know I've some explaining to do, let's all have a drink.'

Vince ignored him.

'Are you two an item, Dad, or are you available for all of us to share again then, Kate?'

Gerry put his arm on his son Vince's shoulder and gripped him tight; he raised his voice and looked at them both.

'That really is enough, both of you. If you want to hear my story you'd better get a drink and then we can all say our piece.'

Barbara changed her mind and went up to her husband and without any emotion kissed him once on the cheek and then immediately turned her back and sat down next to Dick.

The middle-aged lady brought into the room a selection of beer, wine and soft drinks on a tray, which she offered to everyone.

Mark shook his dad's hand and scowled at Kate. Sharon looked at her father as if he had not been away.

Vince took the stage.

'Dad, this is all very bizarre, we didn't know what to think about you. Yes, we'll drink your booze but tell us the story quickly, you can see the suspense is getting too much for Mum.'

Dick Cohen and Juan Villa took glasses of wine but moved well away from Gerry.

Vince looked at his brother, Mark.

'You look a bit pale, mate. He's not a ghost, it is him you know.'

Barbara started to cry and made no attempt to look at her husband as she spoke.

'I thought you were dead at first. Why did you do this to me, Gerry?'

'Not just you, Mum, but all of us,' shouted Mark. 'Kate, you bitch, so you are Dad's lover?'

Vince put his hand up.

'Please, all of you sit down. Let my father speak and tell us his story.'

They obeyed Vince's command and all looked at Gerry.

'Right then, Dad, give it to us,' said Vince, arms crossed and frowning.

'Firstly, I had a brief fling with Kate four years ago. It was brief. We met at my 60th birthday party and we slept together several times in the following months, details are not important. It was good but not meant to last, or at least we thought that until we discussed business. The next time we met was nine months later by accident in Sainsbury's. We had a coffee and Kate was looking to place some foreign investment but she had few options on the table. I agreed to try and help so from a business point of view we then started to work together. Believe me, Barbara, I've not slept with Kate for four years and we don't live together. I live here in Gibraltar and she lives in London. She works for an investment company linked to a UK bank, her job is an Export Business Financial Advisor and her area is the Balearics.

'I put a scheme to her to finance part of a major building project, which was recommended to me by Juan Villa here, who you know. The main man behind the project is called Fernandez Lopez, a big name in the Marbella region. I believe also that Dick Cohen has an investment in the project and before someone asks me the question, yes, it was me that told Dick to contact Juan and suggest he invest personally. I looked at the figures then and the return on investment and it all made sense to Kate's employers. The big problem now for the bank is that Lopez has just done a deal and owes them millions of euros on which he has paid only an initial small set-up fee and a small amount of interest. Very little is complete on the site for the bank to take if they decided to. Lopez has sold his shares in the project to a third party, his so-called friends in Irun in the Basque country. As the original guarantees here were with Lopez, he has nothing other than his house and even that's in his wife's name. The bank is stuffed, they didn't set up the security for the loans properly and they'll lose a lot of money, plus Kate will probably lose her job.'

Kate stood up and pointed at Vince.

'My turn now. What Gerry has told you is correct but, Barbara, you need to hear some more details. Yes, I had met Gerry at the party but it really all started one day in Sutton on the way home from the office when I saw him parking his car. We went for a drink and he told me that his marriage was well and truly over. He had been on the verge of asking you for a divorce many times. He had fallen out of love and he was pretty sure you felt the same way. The matter was decided for him a few days before our last meeting at my apartment. Gerry arrived home one afternoon to hear his best friend Dick Cohen in his house and noisily making love to you upstairs in the family bed.'

Dick went bright red and took Barbara's sweaty hand.

'He probably reacted wrongly doing what he did, but once he got away he knew for certain that he was doing the right thing by just disappearing from the UK, an opinion not shared by some of his old business friends. Gerry hates confrontations so he decided to move here and I helped find him this penthouse apartment to rent. Events moved quickly and once Mark went to prison for the betting shop robbery he decided to stay away from the UK permanently. He bought this place from the landlord for cash. He's not going back to the UK.

'By chance he had a call from his old sparing partner, Ronnie Smith, who decided to get on the next plane to Gibraltar with a few mates to put a proposal to Gerry. The first idea was a simple one, just to launder money. Much of it would finish up with Ronnie but then Ronnie would take most of the risk. Gerry set up a deal buying very dodgy fake antiques from Thailand and Burma and shipping them legitimately to the UK for vast sums of money, sometimes ten times more than their true value, with Ronnie or one of his cronies sending the money here. The UK customs eventually got wind of it all but couldn't prove it, until one day they got hold of a consignment which didn't have any documents. When they requested them, nothing could be found, someone had destroyed them all. The shipping line was fined a lot of money and the antiques scrapped. So the scam with cheap antiques came to an end but the two of them had enough money here for Gerry to be more than comfortable and for Ronnie to buy his dream.

'In Ronnie's case he had it all worked out, you know some of this I think, Vince, so stop smirking. I suggest in your position that you don't try to be too bloody clever, otherwise a tax man may turn up on your doorstep one day.'

'Don't talk bullshit, Kate, I was legally employed by Ronnie and I pay tax.'

'I'll continue but not much more, thankfully, then I'll go for a stiff drink and consider my next move. Ronnie's original plan was in some ways a mad dream but he wanted to make it happen. Since the violent death of his daughter he had become a recluse. Vince will tell you that Ronnie ditched the live-in girlfriend and is selling up in the UK. His new home will probably be near Valencia. No doubt he will have a nice place but not on the scale of the Weybridge castle. The word is, this month he's buying a Spanish La Liga football team based near Valencia, called FC Lecont. Ronnie has always wanted to own his own football team; his only previous experience was with lads in the park who were paid cash in hand in the pub. He knew he could never do a deal in the UK as too many questions would be asked on where the money came from, so he decided to buy in Spain. The current owners wanted to sell and the word is that La Liga will approve the deal. His deal with Fernando Lopez is using a lot of his cash to buy as much of the new development in Marbella as he can, although it's still today far from complete. The idea, I understand, is to buy everything he can, the apartments, houses, timeshares and golf course. But he has discovered that he can't do that as Dick Cohen owns the golf course and leisure complex, so instead Ronnie is going to buy the land for the marina as part of the deal. Have I got this correct, Juan?'

'Yes nearly, Kate. As we speak, Ronnie Smith and Lopez are meeting in Marbella, my employee Claude is with them and we hope the deal is done today.'

'None of this helps me if Lopez and his cronies default on the loans,' Gerry interrupted.

'Ronnie will immediately sell to the people from Abu Dhabi, it will be set up back to back, then he will use the capital to buy the football club. Yes, Gerry, you missed out on that one.'

'Come on then, it's my turn, Kate. Back to my story and the reason why you are all here. Apart from my old friend Dick, whose face I should punch into his brain, you are all mentioned in my will. I have no intention of returning to the UK but, of course, technically I'm still in our country here in Gibraltar. For now, I'll help each of you with some cash. Barbara, all the contents of the safe at home are yours plus the house and savings in your name, of course. If I die before you, it's clear you get nothing else. Barbara, I want a divorce. Mark, you have a job I believe with Dick, good luck to you. Vince, you now have no job and you have to keep away from the UK as the police will one day catch up with you for the robbery. I told you when we first did the job to move to Spain and I suggest you do it now, hopefully Ronnie gave you some money as well.'

Vince forced his lips to move.

'He gave me £100,000 and I moved all the robbery money to Spain. Luke made sure Mr Villa got it as you told me to do. Ronnie just gave me a bloody great box of notes and shook my hand, unbelievable.'

'Yes, you were lucky, Vince, there will certainly be no ongoing favours from Ronnie Smith. You did well to get a handout.'

'Sharon, you are OK. I have put some money in your account to pay off the mortgage on your house. Make sure you don't give half away to a boyfriend as you'll only get the money once.'

'Thanks, Dad, I'm just pleased to see you but you put us through hell. Why couldn't you face up to us? Mark needed you when he was nicked. He kept Vince and the other bloke out of jail but nobody helped him.'

'Yes, that was unfortunate. I got it wrong with Billy Bootle but there was no point coming back to sort him. I couldn't help Mark, it was too late. I've done the same financially for you, Mark, as I'm doing for Sharon. You have money here in Gibraltar in an account I've set up. I'll give you the details before you leave.'

Barbara composed herself and drank her sherry down in one gulp.

'I'm sure your revelations are going to continue but when you've finished we have to talk alone, without Dick and the children. I have something to say to Vince, he is very much like his father in his behaviour. The same can be said, of course, for our daughter-in-law. Your dear wife, Vince, had regular meetings with Luke Devine. I found a notepad when cleaning your house. She cheated on you and if your kids didn't look so much like you, I would have suggested you have a paternity test. You need to sort this out, Vince, before you move to Spain.'

'Thanks, Mum, but that's old news. Don't worry, I know all about it. Donna was just getting her own back as I'd been putting it about a bit. The note you saw was left from when she phoned Luke to get him out of her life and I know everything. One day I'll square it with him and it may cost him a few beers.'

Mark shook his father's hand.

'I think I'm the only one here, Dad, without a problem. Yes, it's shitty what you did, but what could you have done about Dick? I suppose by leaving that was your way of making them both suffer.'

'Yes, son, you're dead right.'

'Dad, one question, did Angela Tate know what you were doing? Did she phone when I was there with her?'

For once Gerry was lost for words but he quickly recovered his composure and looked directly at his youngest son.

'She was my nose on what was going on, Mark, and I met her originally in the betting shop. Angela thought of me as a father figure, the original Mr Tate is no longer around. Before you ask me the question, yes, she had my advice several times.'

'That's one way of putting it, Dad, you definitely were her father figure.'

Gerry wanted to finish his speech and get away from awkward questions; his voice got louder and speeded up.

'OK, right, it's time for you all to leave. Follow me into my office Barbara and Dick, the rest of you have another drink then we'll all say our goodbyes downstairs.'

Dick wanted to speak but discretion got the better of him. He had plenty of his own money and also the contents of the home safe were all intended for Barbara. They worked out how to conclude matters in a civilised way; the tears from Barbara would come later.

Gerry did not produce another woman and it was clear that Kate, at over 30 years younger, was nothing to him and likewise. She didn't wait to say goodbye. Gerry had given her a lump of money and she was off to seek her fortune away from Spain and Gibraltar and maybe also well away from the UK.

Gerry and Barbara left the party and sat in a small bedroom. Gerry closed the door.

'Do you know, Gerry, I've almost no tears left. You ripped my heart out doing what you did. It was one thing leaving me but then why just one phone call, what was the real reason? Please tell me if it was just my affair with Dick.'

'How do you think I look, Barbara?'

'Bigger, older, but you look OK. You aren't ill are you?'

'We're all dying from the day we are born but I knew I was seriously ill. My bowels were not functioning properly and I needed urgent treatment, this happened before I left England. My plan was to get it all sorted in Spain, as I knew a top surgeon. I would then appear again at our own front door like the "genie of the lamp" as if I hadn't been away. In between, I would do business in Spain here that I could eventually pass on to the boys. It didn't turn out like it should've done. I had many operations over the years and I became very weak. For nearly a year I was kept in hospital and my body virtually came to a standstill. When I finally left hospital I had to learn to walk again, that took six months. I thought you would have noticed my movements today. I'll never be the same again.

'I suppose I owe you a big apology and I really am sorry I didn't contact you, Barbara, but then I thought about Dick. I knew his wife had died and I guessed you would definitely be seeing him. I hired a private detective to check you out and his pictures told the story enough for me to write off our marriage. You are better of without me.'

'Are you OK now, Gerry?'

'No, I've only 50% of my guts and I'll need a colostomy bag for the rest of my life but by all accounts that could be less than a year. I take loads of pills and I can't leave this place easily. I may look fine but that's probably down to the drugs. I don't want to risk another operation as I could finish up permanently in hospital on a machine so my time is limited. That's it, my dear, over and out from Gerry. Please try to understand why I didn't return. Make your own life now, Barbara.'

She found her tears again and hugged her husband dripping all over his shirt. She had got the message loud and clear, they had no future. She kissed him once then pulled away and opened the bedroom door. She grabbed Dick's hand and they took the lift together, she would never see her husband again.

Chapter forty

Retribution

The cut-glass champagne flutes were filled, Ronnie and Lopez clinked their glasses in the hotel lounge; the deal was complete.

Lopez was left to square the money he had borrowed, the local banks all had their cut and he was free of the disaster development. He regretted ever getting involved with it in the first place; he had told both his friends in the north of Spain and Kate Robins' investment company that he would struggle to pay them back. He was waiting to see what action they would take.

The new owners were sending architects to Marbella to design the marina and the same people would evaluate the site further to consider an Atlantis-type property, as had been done in Dubai. Money was no object and they had not demanded any warranties, just support from the local authorities that they could develop the site in the way they wanted.

Money talked and Lopez had introduced them to the right people.

'I'm leaving tonight for Valencia, we can have a drink and dinner next time we meet. I will invite you to see my football team as soon as I get my feet under the table and that won't be long.'

'Yes, Ronnie, we have come a long way since I helped you get your money back that night when you were robbed.'

'Did your people rob me then, Lopez? It doesn't matter now.'

'No, actually it was nothing to do with me, but we knew who the likely culprit was and when we broke his finger he confessed.'

Ronnie put his arm around his new friend.

'Good job, Lopez, although from what I hear a few of your enemies have disappeared or been found with their throats cut.'

'Sometimes I may have gone too far, I admit that, but most of the time I was just looking after my family. My background was very straightforward and I was only protecting them, especially when I had to deal with bad people.'

Lopez shook his hand and left the hotel in a hurry.

As Ronnie packed his bags after dinner, he heard the noise of fire engines and police cars, from his window he could see smoke on the horizon. His phone rang to tell him that his driver had arrived. He ordered a porter to take his cases to the car and he walked down to reception.

The reception clerk printed Ronnie's invoice.

'Mr Smith, thank you for staying with us, this is your invoice. Señor Lopez told us you pay this time.'

'Did he indeed? Yes, of course I'll pay, but when did he tell you that? He didn't mention it in the car as we agreed that all the costs of our deal would be paid by him.'

'He phoned about an hour ago, he said he was leaving Marbella as well and he said that we probably wouldn't see him again. That's not like him, he's always here, he's a very good customer.'

'Yes, I agree that's strange. He was very quiet when we drove here from the airport this afternoon.'

'Anyway, Mr Smith, your car is waiting outside and ready to take you to Valencia. It's about a seven-hour drive. I've made a reservation for an overnight stop in Murcia and these are the details. Your driver knows the route, he'll stay with you overnight and complete the journey. Have a good trip.'

Ronnie nodded to the driver. He opened the back door of the large Mercedes and put his bag in the boot. Ronnie smiled, the car looked like Lopez's private vehicle but it was not the normal driver; was this the last free gift he would get from Lopez?

'Will we see you again soon?' enquired the desk clerk.

'No, probably not if my plans all work out, and I'd only come here to see Señor Lopez one day maybe.'

The clerk bowed his head and spoke in a low voice.

'Sorry, sir, you may not see him again. This car is just one he hired from my employers. My office phoned to say that there was an explosion at his house an hour ago. The police have just put a message on the local radio to say that the road next to the villa is closed until further notice without any explanation. One of my colleagues has just sent me a text to say that the police think it was a bomb and it was at Señor Lopez's villa.'

'Shit, that's terrible. I was with him just two hours ago. I wonder what happened.'

'I'm sure we'll get more news later on the TV. Look, you can see the smoke, we don't normally have fires like that, it must be a big explosion.'

Ronnie arrived at his overnight hotel and he switched on the TV. He couldn't understand what was being said but the pictures told the story.

The police were giving little information, all he could understand in Spanish was the fireman had confirmed that three people had been killed and another person was missing.

Ronnie found it difficult to sleep. Had he made the right decision moving to Spain? But then bombs also went off in the UK. He had a feeling that Lopez knew that something was going to happen; if he had been killed it would certainly be murder. He would phone Juan Villa the next day and try to get some information.

In the safety of Diana's apartment in Valencia, a distressed Anna Lopez was in the arms of Diana Devine, with her son Luke staring out of the window, gripping in his hand a very large brandy, as if it was the last drink he would ever take.

'He was killed instantly, Anna, your mother has just left the hospital and she's now with the police. She promised to call you early in the morning. Maria and Jesus also died in the blast. It seems a man who was supposed to be servicing the swimming pool planted the bomb and the police have roadblocks in place. Juan Villa was also at the house according to his office and he's missing, the firemen can't get inside the burnt-out building for at least a few hours. If he's inside, he must now be dead.'

Anna fell to the couch and buried her face in her hands, her tears dripping down her nightdress.

'I knew it would happen one day and so did my mother, my father had done one deal too many and he'd people waiting for him to repay money he'd borrowed. I know he'd repaid some debts but somebody must have decided that they had waited too long. In some ways it's strange because now he's dead, nobody else will get paid. The police will never find the culprits as they never found who killed my brother in Madrid, this is an organised crime against my father and my family. We now have new pain and it won't be over until they make my mother pay, then me if she can't, I know she doesn't have any assets.'

'Go to bed, Anna. Have some of Luke's brandy, it may help. I won't be able to sleep but you must. Luke, stay here tonight, we need you.'

'Yes, sure, but unless it's a coincidence there is a guy watching this apartment. Look under the olive tree, do you see him?'

'No, darling, I can't see anybody.'

'Mum, he's just moved, he's been watching us since we had dinner.'

Anna started to cry and shout.

'This is the end! They are here for me now, they want revenge!'

Luke took hold of Anna's hands.

'Listen, this doesn't make sense. Dead men and women do not pay debts.'

The loud bang on the door prevented any answer.

The shout that followed in Spanish was very clear.

'Open the door! This is the Guardia Civil!'

Diana opened the door slightly and a badge was shown. She opened the door to two plain-clothed policemen. They stared closely at the Englishman at the back of the room.

'Mr Luke Devine. Is that you, señor?'

Luke knew he had no chance of escape and nodded.

'Yes, it's me.'

The older of the two policemen resumed speaking in perfect English.

'I have an instruction for your extradition to the UK to face charges of armed robbery. You may call a solicitor to act on your behalf. We can give you a phone number at the station. My advice is not to do that in Spain, they will charge many euros and nothing will change the situation. Come with us now, first we need to put these handcuffs on.'

Luke did as he was told; he had no option. He had waited nearly three years for the knock on the door and now it had arrived. What intrigued him was whether the police had new evidence. What did they know now that they didn't when Mark was sentenced?

Someone must have given them new information and he wondered if that included Vince Lavender also. He would not have long to wait to get answers.

Chapter forty-one

Aftermath

'That's mucked the plans up for my best man, Linda, but then it was probably a silly idea anyway. I doubt if he would have gone through with it.'

Sergeant Linda Dredge was looking glum at a charge sheet with pictures of Luke Devine and Vince Lavender staring from it.

'Where did you find the tape, John? It's a complete story not just the part that convicted Mark Lavender.'

'It was an absolute bit of luck, Linda, if you can call it luck. I went for a quick drink in The George and bumped into Angela Tate. She was very drunk in a chair at the back of the lounge and she was really abusive to everyone around her. I had intended to just give her a warning and send her home. She then started shouting at me and got very nasty so I had to grab her wrist and restrain her. She screamed at me and tried to punch me. She then poked me in the gut and said she had a tape on people that would do me in, a threat you could have believed in the way she said it. She was very pissed. I calmed her down and took her home and then she gave me a tape in a box, mumbling at the same time that she had given it to Mark Lavender but he dropped it as he got in his car and she found it lying on the path to her apartment. I asked her to come to the station yesterday, she did, spot on nine o'clock and sober. She was crying that I must give the tape back. I didn't, of course. I gave her a warning and got shot of her, still crying her eyes out.'

Linda played a copy she made of the tape.

'It's a pretty clear scene, John, Mark's in the car on the bit of the tape we took to court. There's a full frontal of Vince Lavender and both sides of Luke Devine's head, totally clear pictures of all of them, even the time and date on the bottom.'

'I think we'll need a new best man, John. Pity because Mark would have been good and we could have put two fingers up to coppers who said we didn't have a dialogue with our customers. So I better call him and tell him the news, I think he's in Spain.'

'You don't need to tell him, he'll know by now, look outside.'

The doors swung open on the police van in the yard and Luke Devine and Vince Lavender were led to the interview rooms separately but their stories already matched. Once they knew about the police evidence, they would be advised by their solicitor to enter a plea of guilty.

Mark Lavender would not be required to give evidence. As well as information on the tape, the police somehow had intercepted e-mail from Vince Lavender to Juan Villa in Spain concerning Luke and his own share of the money from the robbery and the property they were buying.

Vince admitted he had sent it, the e-mail was found by accident, another police unit investigating the dealings of his boss Ronnie Smith had tipped off Hampton. The unit were close to putting together sufficient evidence to charge Ronnie with money laundering and the name Vince Lavender was thrown up and a check revealed his brother Mark's conviction, leading them back to Hampton.

'The problem this now gives us, John, is what do we do about the money? Mark obviously invested a third or maybe more of it with this bloke Villa. We know he didn't personally take it to Spain but it should now be recovered at least.'

'Linda, we aren't going to charge Mark with anything new. Maybe you can talk to him on his mobile, I think you have the number, and tell him all that's happening. Can you manage that without falling in love with him again?'

'Yes, don't be silly that's all over, you know that. I'll talk to him tonight. Did you speak with that lawyer, Juan Villa?'

'No, his office was closed and I got an answering machine. The Spanish police say he has either done a runner or worse, he was killed in a bomb explosion in Marbella, which incidentally also killed one of his clients, a bloke called Lopez, who owed a lot of money to his friends, and two of his staff.'

'Bloody hell, what a mess. Is Mark really working there?'

'Yes, for Dick Cohen, the accountant. You know that, John, don't mess about.'

'Of course I do, but just checking you, Linda.'

'I've had enough of you today, John. Being my boss doesn't work, we have to talk about this, my promotion can't come quick enough and I'm not sure I want to marry you.'

'Your problem, Linda, is you can't get the Lavenders out of your mind and I'm not playing second fiddle to a bunch of crooks.'

Linda left the office. In a few days' time she was getting married with an ex-convict for the best man; now all she wanted was to see him again. She had leave due and would book it immediately; she had to see Mark in person.

Hampton had realised that the police marriage was not going to work and he had already been looking for a way out of it. The split would be amicable. Fortunately, they had both kept their own houses. He would apply for an immediate transfer as far away from Surrey as possible.

Epilogue

A Year Later

'Anna, I know what you are saying and I do like you a lot. Your father is dead, Juan Villa is missing presumed dead and people are threatening you and your mother again. I've been to prison and I want a clean new life. I'm sorry, but we shouldn't meet again.'

Tears had dried up months before for Anna Lopez. Out of respect, Mark went to the funeral of Señor Fernando Lopez, but he feared for his life if he continued to be involved with the family. The chief of Marbella police had interviewed him and he had left with some firm advice, if he wanted to stay in town, the Lopez family should be history.

'Yes, I do understand, Mark. Thankfully we only had a short time together. I'm not sure if English and Spanish cultures mix in marriage, it didn't work for my mother and father and it's unlikely that it would work for us. I have passed my examinations now and I'm going to live in Chile and work for the Spanish Embassy. If you ever go to Santiago look me up, but then not many English go to Chile, in any case, you would be welcome.'

'Is there another man in your life, Anna?'

'No, but I have many friends in South America. My father also had some business interests. Please don't mention that to anyone, Mark, you know why.'

'Yes, I guessed he had moved money from here. Pity he didn't get out in time. Is Juan Villa dead or in South America?'

Anna smiled as she drove away, that was her answer.

The holiday market changed with high fuel costs negatively influencing holiday destinations beyond the still relatively cheap Europe. The property markets in Spain in particular were recovering with many new visitors, especially from Scandinavia, Russia and China.

The men from Abu Dhabi built their marina on the new complex. The apartments and houses built by Lopez had been made safe at a cost only an Arab could ever afford. Berths in the marina were being sold for enormous sums of money and Puerto Banus was now becoming, the number two marina in Spain.

The bonus was the build quality of the places was now first class. The Arabs had bought the golf and leisure complex from Dick Cohen. The shrewd accountant negotiated a five-year contract for Mark to operate the leisure part and he was making good profits for the new owners.

The divorce between Barbara and Gerry Lavender was completed but she decided that Spain with Dick was not her future, it was too close to Gerry in Gibraltar and she would worry about him visiting her. She still felt that his disappearance had not been properly explained and although she intended to marry Dick Cohen, she kept delaying, with just a hope in her mind she would one day get back again with Gerry.

As he did when he first left the UK years before, Gerry continued the habit of doing the unusual. At 65 he now had a 25-year-old Latvian girlfriend. She did everything for him and without any complaints; he knew it would not last but then he would have to think of another plan, maybe Australia, but he was kidding himself, he knew his health would not last.

Ronnie Smith lasted two seasons in La Liga. He lost everything (or nearly), the club went into administration, FC Lecont were evicted from football and the local council took over the ground they owned and turned it into an athletics track.

It would have been easy for Ronnie to go back to England. He had been cleared on money laundering charges, which he had bravely faced in a UK court and he could have stayed and bought a small property. Instead he moved to Benidorm and went into a gambling business, which kept him in food and beer, plus the occasional lady.

Vince Lavender and Luke Devine received no mercy and both were jailed for seven years by a judge who hated violent crimes, even though the only person to physically suffer in the crime was Angela Tate and her wet knickers.

Linda Dredge left the police and went to Spain. She quickly mastered the local language and got a job as a security advisor, renewing her interest in Mark Lavender at the same time.

Mark felt he had come a complete circle. He was still less than 30 but he had lived a lifetime already. His bitterness on leaving prison had disappeared and he realised how lucky he had been.

The shadow of shame over him as he stood in the dock that day as his sentence was read out was something he could never face again. His crime was a painful lesson and without ever admitting it, for Mark Lavender it was life changing.

The End